DADDY
DARKEST

ISBN: 978-0-692-88096-8

Book Developmental Editing/Manuscript Evaluation & Line Editing/Copyediting/ Proofing:
AnnCastro Studio with Ann Castro and Emily Dings
Cover Designer:
Giovanni Auriemma
Interior Formatting:
Mallory Rock and The Illustrated Author Design

Disclaimer: This book is a work of fiction. Places, events, and situations in this book are purely fictional, and any resemblance to actual persons, living or dead, events, or locales is entirely
coincidental. Daddy Darkest contains adult themes, including descriptions of sexual abuse, and is recommended for a mature audience.

For Gar

My partner in crime

"Murder is not about lust and it's not about violence. It's about possession."

—Ted Bundy

CHAPTER ONE

BLACK SOCK, BLUE SOCK

I wish my first plane ride had ended in a crash. An unforeseen plunge to Earth. A few minutes of white-hot terror, followed by a rising ball of fire. And no survivors. Sure, I'd be gone at eighteen. *She was so young,* they'd say, but at least I would die believing my life was my own. Not a lie somebody else concocted. Then, it was simple. I was still small-town girl, Samantha Bronwyn.

"Sam, easy with the death grip." Ginny freed her arm from under mine and jiggled it. I watched the color return to the white fingertip marks I'd left behind.

I shrugged. "Sorry. But that noise ... "

"So you can sink a free throw to win state, no problem, but the safest form of travel inspires a full-on meltdown?" Ginny—and Google—had assured me I had one-in-eleven-million odds of death up here. At the time, two feet planted on the ground, it seemed reasonable.

"As far as I know, that sound means we're plummeting to our deaths right now."

"Uh, it's the landing gear, dork." Ginny exaggerated an eye roll—not for my benefit—then leaned in and whispered. "And you're blowing the cool college girl thing we've got going."

I offered a polite smile to 4A. Thanks to Ginny and her relentless flirting, I knew his name—Levi Beckett. "We're not in college," I reminded her.

"*Yet.* A minor technicality." She shook her head at me, then returned to the task at hand. Being cool, obviously. "So, Levi, do you have any recommendations for our first night in the big city? We wanna hit all the hot spots."

I swallowed a sigh as Ginny tossed her hair from her shoulder. *Why did I let her talk me into this trip?*

"Hot spots?" He'd told Ginny he was twenty-one, but his tone was my mother's—a thought that came with a wave of guilt, which I promptly ignored. "You're eighteen, right?"

Oblivious, Ginny nodded.

"You girls should be careful."

Ginny leaned around me, pursing her pink-glossed lips at him. "Oooh, sounds dangerous."

I felt my cheeks warm, but I kept my eyes fixed on the seat back in front of me, watching sidelong as Levi tapped his fingers against his blue jeans, a black backpack he hadn't opened stanchioned between his leather boots. Since Levi had claimed his spot, I'd avoided his face. Except that once when I bumped his arm from the miniscule rest in between us, my *excuse me* met with a flash of his green eyes. It seemed strange to sit so close to a total stranger. And the way Ginny acted, I could tell he was freakishly handsome, and therefore hers.

"Seriously," he said. That word implied he was talking to me. "San Francisco has its share of unsavory characters." He unfolded the newspaper tucked next to him, turned it toward me, and tapped the familiar headline and picture below it. *Notorious San Quentin inmate pulls off unprecedented second escape, manhunt enters 10th day.*

The smirk beneath the slate-gray eyes of Clive Evan Cullen leveled me like a double-edged blade. Part menace, part seduction.

Ginny giggled. "Is it wrong to find a murderer attractive?" I elbowed her, and she winced. "Because if it is, I don't wanna be right."

"See what I mean?" Levi said. "She's practically begging to be Cutthroat Cullen's next girlfriend—I mean, victim." He pointed to a smaller headline: *Female body found floating in the Bay believed to be prison employee who aided Cullen.*

"Ha. Ha. Ha." Ginny narrowed her eyes at him. "As if I would ever work in a prison."

"Your sister is nuts," he teased.

"Friend." It was the typical assumption, with our matching blonde hair and cornflower-blue eyes. But beyond that, Ginny was my complete flipside. "We're best friends."

"Well, then, you should watch out for your friend. She's going to get herself in trouble one day." My nod felt like a betrayal, but I couldn't help myself.

"Hmph." Ginny pulled my letterman jacket closer around her shoulders and turned away from us toward the aisle. She'd warned me the cabin might get cold, but she wore a tank top anyway, pilfering my royal blue Bellwether Bulldogs memento halfway through the flight.

"Gin, c'mon." I touched her shoulder, but she squirmed away, and I bristled. Annoyed. By him. Levi Beckett. Condescending jerk. *Unsavory characters*—who talks like that anyway? If his hand wasn't close enough to hold, his knee a mere fingertip from mine, I would've glared at him.

"Ladies and gentlemen, we've started our descent into San Francisco. In preparation for landing, please make sure your seat backs and ..." I plucked my ticket out of the pocket in front of me, staring at it, committing the details of my first plane ride to memory. Flight: Virgin America 221. Destination: AUS to SFO. Passenger: Bronwyn, Samantha.

"Look. It's the San Francisco Bay." Levi lifted the shade, revealing an expanse of blue water. I caught my breath. Almost two thousand miles from Bellwether and my mother, it looked like freedom.

****

Ginny sulked as we lugged our carry-ons up the jet bridge. "How long are you planning to be mad at me?" I teased, holding my watch up to my face. "Ballpark figure, so I can set my stopwatch."

"Shouldn't you be getting your boyfriend's digits anyway? Don't let me keep you, Mrs. Beckett."

I groaned. "You were the one who started chatting him up in the first place. He wasn't even that cute." It was a blatant lie. When I'd finally freed myself from the seat belt, I snuck a well-deserved glance at Levi as he secured his backpack. Curly chestnut hair, wiry muscles, a shadow of a beard. And those green eyes.

"Ahem."

Oh God. "Is that ... ?" I hissed at Ginny through clenched teeth. She only smiled.

Levi split the middle, fast walking between us. "You were saying?" He didn't wait for an answer, but I could hear him laughing, even after I lost him in the sea of passengers mingling by the gate.

"Smooth, Sam. Really smooth."

"Whatever." I parked my suitcase at the edge of the crowd and turned on my cell phone. The guilt I'd managed to shove down for the duration of a three-and-a-half-hour flight came back with a vengeance. Ten text messages. Three missed calls. All from my mom. "I told you she'd freak out." When Ginny didn't answer me, I looked up from the screen and called her name.

"Going to get beautified," she announced, playfully skirting around a yellow WET FLOOR sign that blocked the bathroom doorway, bag in tow. I watched her ponytail swing the way it always did, brushing across my letterman jacket. My ponytail never did that. Sometimes I wondered if she practiced. Her back—**BRONWYN, STATE CHAMPIONSHIP BASKETBALL 2016**—disappeared inside.

I dropped my phone into the cavern of my purse. *Don't look*, I told myself. *You can call her later. Explain everything.* I leaned back against the row of seats and took in the crowd rushing past me. I'd never seen so many people—practically the entire population of Bellwether, Texas—packed into one cramped space. Small-town girl meets big city. That's what Ginny proclaimed this trip when she'd surprised me with the ticket weeks ago, just after we watched our graduation caps land side by side on the football field.

Small-town girl—me, of course—watched the bathroom exit, already aggravated. Big-city was probably blotting, brushing, and lip glossing her way to perfection. A little girl toddled by, dragging a stuffed bear alongside her. Her white booties picked up speed, her tiny arms barely keeping pace. She let out a high-pitched shriek just before she tumbled to the ground, wailing. Her red-faced panic was contagious.

With urgency, I headed for the bathroom door—the wheels of my suitcase clicking behind me—and navigated around the same yellow sign Ginny ignored, hoping no one saw me.

It was the fanciest public restroom I'd ever seen: marble counters, soft lighting, electric hand dryers. But it smelled exactly like our high school bathroom, post-janitorial visit—its floors slick with a chemical sheen. I measured my steps just in case Ginny hid nearby, messing with me.

A quick glance to my left and right turned up nothing. The stalls stood empty, most of their doors partway open, inviting me inside. *The first stall is the cleanest.* That's what Ginny always said, so I pushed my way in, half-expecting to find her there laughing at me. But there was no one. The only sign of life, a curse word etched into the metal. On the freshly scrubbed counter was a tube of uncapped lip gloss. I picked it up gingerly, like it might explode in my hand, and examined it. *Cotton Candy.* Ginny's color.

"Hello? Ginny? Are you in here?" My words sank like stones in the silence.

"Excuse me, young lady." I jumped. Then stumbled backward, steadying myself against the wall. My heart fluttered like an insect in a jar. I let out a long, rattled breath. Something—*a roach?*—scuttled beneath my foot and across the tile, and I shuddered. A man's pockmarked face appeared in the mirror.

"You … scared me." He raised his gloved hands in surrender. They were large, paw-like.

"I'm just finishing up in here," he said. "But I think ya dropped … " My eyes followed his. It was the black cap from Ginny's gloss. Not a roach after all. I picked it up.

"I'm looking for my friend. She came in here maybe ten minutes ago. This is hers." I showed him the cap, holding it with care as if it was as precious as a rare jewel. He shrugged, barely looking, while he strangled the end of a brimming garbage bag. I screwed the cap back on and slipped the tube into my pocket, feeling silly.

"Haven't seen anybody. Usually, the sign keeps 'em out. I can radio my partner for ya, if you'd like." The man gestured over his shoulder. "He just left with a load of trash."

"That's okay. I must've missed her or something." Even though I knew missing Ginny was as impossible as overlooking the sun. He folded up the yellow sign and waved to me.

"Why don't ya give your friend a call? She probably wandered into the bookstore."

I waited for him to leave me inside the cool, white tomb of the bathroom. Then I fished my phone from the bottom of my purse and pressed Gin Rummy, the name Ginny typed in herself when we met playing basketball our freshman year. That was before Bellwether's point guard, Kelly, took an elbow that fractured her jaw, and Ginny deemed herself too pretty for sports. I waited for the ring, Ginny's typical—*Hey Sam, I found a Starbucks. Hot guy behind the counter.*

I thought I might be dreaming when I heard it. *I'm still on the plane. I've fallen asleep. My head is inching toward 4A's shoulder. I better open my eyes now.* There was that unsettled feeling, the one when disconnected things, mismatched things—a black sock, a blue sock—come together somehow. But after a kind stranger exhumed Ginny's phone from its resting place, the little sanitary disposal box in the stall furthest from the door, I knew I was wide awake.

The surface of Ginny's screen saver, a shirtless Channing Tatum, looked at me with expectation. I clicked a button, and the phone came to life. The notes application was open. With a shot of game-time adrenaline swooshing through my veins, I read the words that seemed meant for me. It was my mother's name after all.

Clare, come find me.

CHAPTER TWO
ROULETTE WHEEL

TEETH. Bone. Blood. I jogged through the airport, hightailing it to baggage claim, where I suspected Ginny waited for me—just a misunderstanding after all. But I couldn't shake that fractured jaw from four years ago. When I'd caught a glimpse of a tooth hatching from beneath our point guard's eggshell-white skin, I headed straight for the bench, vomit burning my throat. But not Ginny. She'd sprinted across the court to comfort her, their hands clasped together in a sticky mixture of blood and sweat. *That was absolutely disgusting,* she'd told me later as we sat together on the bus ride home. That's when I knew Ginny was braver than me and tougher than she looked. Somehow, the message on her phone reminded me of that tooth. Horrifying in its strangeness. Impossible to unsee.

Clare, come find me.

I slowed my pace as I stepped onto the escalator—hopeful—and watched the bag carousels spinning round and round and round beneath me. "She's fine." I didn't sound convincing, so I gave it a second try. "She's *fine.*" Baggage claim was swarming with blondes. Surely,

Ginny was one of them. She was punishing me for taking 4A's side. *You win, Ginny. You win.*

I fixed my eyes on the board at the edge of the crowd until I found it. Flight 221. Carousel 3. Ginny would be there retrieving the extra bag I'd teased her for packing. Tugging my own suitcase behind me, I made a straight line through the other passengers. They were busy—heads down—calling, texting, reuniting, lugging bags like bodies. It was so normal, too normal, and the seed of my unease started to grow.

Though I was too young to remember him, my mom always said the hardest part of losing my father was the way life trudged on without him. Like he was a misplaced key or a broken pair of glasses. Nonessential. Easily replaced. Not a shrink whose plane took a terminal nosedive into the side of a mountain. Now I could see what she meant. But Ginny wasn't dead. She wasn't even lost. She was here. Somewhere. I knew it.

"Did she ditch you already?"

I turned around, nearly colliding with a grinning Levi. "What is that supposed to mean?" The fierceness in my words registered as his eyes widened and his smiled deflated. "Why did you say all that stuff on the plane?"

"What are you talking about?"

"About Ginny being careful? Remember?" I knew I sounded a little unhinged, and after a few heads turned to look at me, I realized I was practically yelling.

Levi started walking past me, pretending he didn't know me. "You agreed with me," he mumbled. "And I thought *she* was the crazy one." Backpack slung over one shoulder, he kept moving until he was on the opposite end of the carousel—as far away as he could manage. The red light flashed, the horn blaring like it was announcing the end of the world. The sheets of metal came to life, and the bags dropped like marbles on a spinning roulette wheel.

When I saw Ginny's bag—the bright pink ribbon she'd tied around the handle giving her away—I waited. It fell in line with the others and began its slow procession. It passed Levi and all the other expectant eyes until it was right back where it began. With each revolution, the suitcases dwindled, plucked off and wheeled out to their awaiting adventures, and the tightening in my stomach became impossible to ignore. I sat down on the edge of the cold metal and watched the pink ribbon go by. Again. It was the last bag. The only bag. I buried my head in my hands.

"Um … " I didn't look up. I didn't have to. After staring at those boots for the three-hour plane ride, they were unmistakable. "Don't bite my head off, but are you okay?"

I didn't want to say it out loud. It felt irrevocable, like casting a spell, but it demanded saying. "I can't find my friend. She's gone."

CHAPTER THREE

OCCAM'S RAZOR

ARE you sure she didn't leave without you?" Levi joined me on the carousel's edge as it ground to a stop.

"No!" I smacked the top of Ginny's unclaimed suitcase with my palm, and he jumped. "Sorry," I murmured, waiting for him to do something—walk, run, or excuse himself away from me, crazy airport girl. "She wouldn't do that." I flipped her phone between my palms, that message still gnawing at my brain. "She never came out of the bathroom." I was sure of it now.

"It's Samantha, right?" I nodded half-heartedly, wishing I was someone else. "Well, Samantha, that doesn't make any sense."

He was doing it again. That adult voice. "I know it sounds crazy, but that's what happened." I produced the only evidence I had. "This is her phone. I found it in one of the stalls." Levi read the message to himself. Frowning, he rubbed the stubble on his chin. "Clare," he said aloud. Then he got quiet. *Good*, I thought. *Keep your judgments to yourself, hot airplane boy.* But then, "There's got to be a logical explanation. A simple one. You know, Occam's razor and all."

"Funny you'd say that, creepy stranger who made a subtle threat to my missing friend." I stood up with no idea where to go.

"Touché." His laugh was a warm blanket I wanted to nestle into—Ginny would be back any minute to steal my spotlight like she always did—but instead I shrugged it off. "Am I really that creepy?" he teased.

To my horror, I actually giggled. Ginny was missing. Gone. And I was making eyes at hot airplane boy. *What a complete bitch!* That's what Ginny would've said. "This isn't funny. In case you haven't noticed, I'm kinda freaking out here." Tugging both bags awkwardly, one in each hand, I turned my back to him and started fast walking.

"Oh, I noticed." He was right behind me. "There are police at the security counter up on the ticketing level if you're interested."

"Police?" That word landed like a sucker punch, and I spun around to face him.

He shrugged. "You said she wouldn't leave. She's not here. And you seem to think I had something to do with that. So ... "

"Do you think something *bad* happened to her?" I whispered that word the way a child would. As if saying it would make it so.

He shook his head. "I don't think she's hooked up with Cutthroat yet, if that's what you're asking."

"Fine." I produced my yearbook smile. "Thanks for your help. I'm sure you have somewhere to be."

He backed away from me and gave a lukewarm wave. "Suit yourself."

****

"Virginia Dalton, please report to the Terminal Two Security Desk." Ginny was going to skin me alive for telling them her full name. When our freshman English teacher had called roll that first day, her face had turned crimson. *It sounds like the name of a pilgrim. An unattractive pilgrim,* she'd lamented. I'd thought it sounded lovely. Mature and distinguished. Two qualities Ginny lacked.

"What happens now?" I asked. I'd been standing there staring at Officer Guthrey since he first paged Ginny ten minutes ago.

In between bites of a thick sandwich, he'd already echoed Levi's skepticism.

"We wait for her to turn up." *Chew. Chew. Chew.*

"And if she doesn't?"

He took a swig of coffee from his mug. "She will. They usually do."

"They?"

"Missing teenagers."

I sighed. "But what about the note? Ginny would never leave her phone."

"Listen. I know you're worried about your friend, but more than likely she's playing games with you. You said yourself the two of you had a little tiff on the plane—"

"It wasn't a—"

" … about a boy. She's probably gone to the hotel—"

"She wouldn't—"

" … ahead of you. It's getting late. I betcha she'll be there waiting." I opened my mouth to launch another protest, but he held up his hand. "Here. Take my card. If you haven't heard from her in forty-eight hours, we can file a missing person's report. In the meantime, I'll take a walk up to the bathroom and see what I see. Okay?"

"Forty-eight hours?" Our flight home left in less.

He answered my question with one of his own. "Is there someone you can call? Your mother? Her mother? A friend? To let them know what's happened."

I nodded, hoping my face didn't give it away. No chance in hell I planned on telling my mom about any of this. Not yet anyway. She'd already responded to my I'm-fine-and-will-call-when-I-get-to-the-hotel text with three unanswered calls. I pocketed Officer Guthrey's card and left the security desk. Still Ginny-less.

****

The glass doors parted for me, and I wheeled the bags into a cold fog, unthinking, like a zombie unearthed in the world of the living. I laid my suitcase onto the sidewalk, rifling through its outer pocket for my sweater. An unwelcome reminder that Ginny had my jacket. I pulled my arms through the sleeves and sat on my bag, trying to ward off the sudden nausea with a long inhale, exhale. At least Ginny paid for the hotel in advance with her mother's credit card. The graduation money in my wallet—a grand total of $500—wouldn't get me far.

"What now?" I said aloud to no one.

"Want to share a taxi?" Levi leaned up against the wall, headphones in his ears, hands in his pockets. I had to admit, as pathetic as it sounded, I was relieved to see him, grateful for the momentary shushing of the panicked voice in my head. I didn't even care he caught me talking to myself. Because I'd never taken a taxi anywhere. Bellwether had two stoplights, more tractors than people, and zero taxis. And, if I'm being honest, because he was ridiculously good-looking.

"Okay. Now you're officially creepy."

He half-smiled, but the lights from inside cast tiny half-moons under his eyes, making him seem serious, pensive. "I figured you'd say that. You can tell me no if you'd like, but I thought you might want some company, given the circumstances."

"And what circumstances are those?"

He ticked them off on his fingers. "You being in a new city alone. Your friend being missing. That cryptic note. The police not believing you and telling you to come back in forty-eight hours … I'm just guessing here."

"All true," I admitted. "I'll share a cab if we drop you off first. I don't want any creepers to know where I'm staying."

"Fair enough."

A few minutes later, Levi and I sat in the back of a taxi, his closeness already familiar to me. I leaned toward him just a little, inhaling the scent of his leather jacket. It barely drowned the stench of stale cigarette smoke. I felt giddy. I felt guilty. I wasn't sure how to feel, so I pretended to be Ginny. Within a three-mile radius of a cute boy, she always knew what to do.

"Do you really think she could be at the hotel?" I asked as he settled in, winding the cord of his headphones into a tight coil.

20

"It wouldn't surprise me. She's probably researching the hottest hot spots right now." His words were a comfort, a momentary paperweight for the chaos inside me, even if I didn't believe them. "In fact, I'll bet she's typing that exact phrase into Google."

I grinned, then redirected. *Get him talking about himself—a boy's favorite subject.* That tidbit was somewhere in Ginny's playbook. "You never told us why you came to San Francisco." Despite her best efforts, Ginny had only coaxed the vital stats. Name: Levi Beckett. Age: Twenty-one, almost twenty-two. Favorite basketball team: San Antonio Spurs. Relationship status: Single.

"Long story. Short cab ride."

"So that's how it's going to be. Man of mystery, huh?"

"For now."

I pushed my lower lip out into an exaggerated pout, hoping I didn't look as silly as I felt. "If I guess right, will you tell me?"

"If you guess right, then we're going to Vegas, because you, Samantha, are a mind reader." Maybe I wasn't as hopeless as I thought. The way he said my name sounded a lot like flirting.

"Well, Mr. Beckett, you don't strike me as a tourist. You're not visiting your girlfriend. Um … job interview? It's that or a super-secret spy mission."

Levi threw his head back, laughing. At me. Not with me. And I squashed the sudden urge to karate chop his Adam's apple. Headphones in hand, still chuckling, he reached down to open his backpack. His backpack. His *backpack*. His only luggage. I scoured my memory hoping I was wrong.

"You travel light." When he nodded, I pushed harder. "So why were you waiting at baggage claim?"

He didn't answer right away. His crocodile-green eyes were such a compelling distraction, I almost missed it, deep in the gullet of his backpack. Like most of Bellwether's residents, my mother owned one just like it, hidden in a safe under her bed. *Just in case,* she'd told me when I turned sixteen. Right before she'd sent me to a weapons safety class and revealed the eight-digit password—my birth date—to open Pandora's box. I'd never asked in case of what.

Before Levi caught me looking, I turned my face to the window and listened for the sound of the zipper. When all its teeth were gnashed together, the quiet palpable between us, I realized I was holding my breath. Still, I didn't move until he spoke.

"I was headed out of the airport to my, uh, ... *job interview* ... " He paused for my obligatory eye roll. " ... when I ran into you. It seemed like you needed help. And what can I say? I'm a sucker for a damsel in distress."

My throat closed around unspoken words, snuffing them out like a flame pressed between cold fingers. My insides were alive, crawling with the inexplicability of my new reality. Ginny, missing. Me, in a taxi with Levi Beckett. And his gun.

CHAPTER FOUR

NAÏVE

I found a hole in the taxi's seat just beneath my hand, a small wound in the Naugahyde. I prodded the foam flesh with my finger as we drove, desperate for a diversion. Levi's backpack had taken on life. It was squatting like a toad—mouth closed—barely visible in the darkness. He hadn't reached for it again. Thankfully. Still, the metallic taste of fear lingered on my tongue, no matter how many swigs of bottled water I downed. Ahead of us, a procession of brake lights snaked toward the city. Stop and go. Stop and go. Levi rolled down his window, letting in a gust of air that felt more December than June. It shocked me into speaking.

"Short cab ride, huh?"

Levi shrugged. "Typical Bay Area gridlock. Should've figured. I guess you don't see a lot of traffic jams in Bellwether, Texas."

"We don't see much of anything in Bellwether—unless hayfields and farm animals count."

"So you're a cowgirl?"

"I'm a guard. Basketball. No cows involved." I wasn't about to tell Levi about my mom's herd of cattle. Or the chickens she kept in a coop behind our house.

"That's too bad," he said. "I lived on a farm for a little while."

"You did?"

"Why so surprised? Can't picture me in Wranglers, boots, and a cowboy hat?"

"Not really. You seem like a textbook city slicker."

Laughing, he pointed to my cell phone, propped precariously on my thigh. "I think your leg is buzzing." I flipped it over, face down, hoping he hadn't seen it. "You can answer it. I don't mind."

I shook my head. "Trust me, you don't want to hear that conversation. My mom didn't exactly give this trip her blessing."

He narrowed his eyes at me like he was seeing me for the first time. "Really? I wouldn't have figured you for a rebel."

The old me would've left it alone, laughed it off. Ginny had the big mouth. But without her here, I felt different, altered in some inexplicable way. "What would you have figured me for then?"

"Hmm. That's a tough one. You didn't say much on the plane. Hardly looked at me. But then again … to hear you tell it, I'm not much to look at."

My cheeks flamed, so I took refuge in the darkness, turning my face from him. "Ginny talks enough for the both of us."

"Maybe you like it that way," he offered. "Then you can be just as mysterious as me."

I caught my own eyes in the window, wide with surprise. "I'm about as far from mysterious as it gets."

"I know." A part of me wished he hadn't agreed, that he'd entertained the idea at least.

"You think I'm naïve, don't you?"

"No. Ginny is naïve. You're just inexperienced."

"There's a difference?"

His nod was stern, like a teacher. "Absolutely."

Before I could get clarification on that essential distinction, the cab slowed to a complete stop. It was a trick of the flashing lights—blue, then red, blue, then red—the way Levi's backpack pulsed like a beating heart. His hands left his knees and searched it out, tucking it closer to the seat while I pretended not to see him. "What's going on?" I asked him, pointing out the window. A line of orange traffic cones dictated our path. A few cars ahead, a stop sign loomed.

"Looks like some kind of police checkpoint."

The driver cursed under his breath and laid on the horn in protest. "Damn criminals, always screwing things up for the rest of us. I tell you, they ought to just take 'em out back and *pop-pop-pop*. A bullet to the head. Save us the trouble."

"Criminals?" I directed my question to the back of his head, where a thin wisp of jet-black hair covered an otherwise bare surface.

"Yeah. I'm sure you've heard of him. What's his name? Calvert? Culligan? Cull—"

"Cullen." The name left Levi's mouth fast, like it'd been poised on the tip of his tongue all along. "Cutthroat Cullen. What's he got to do with this traffic?"

"Dispatch said somebody reported him walking on the freeway. Trying to hitch a ride, I guess." We inched forward, and an officer waved us ahead. "Or jack one."

Levi scoffed. "Bullshit. No way he's stupid enough to take that kind of risk."

The driver shrugged. "The way I figure it, he's not that smart. Got caught once before, didn't he? Anyway, I hope you two don't have nothin' to hide." His chuckle made me shiver like I'd packed that gun myself.

"Evening, folks." The officer leaned in through the open window. Behind the sweeping beam of his flashlight, his face was all angles and shadows. "We're looking for this man. Have you seen him?" He held up a laminated poster. Cullen's mug shot. The words **ARMED AND DANGEROUS** in bold red type.

I gulped, murmured *no*, and waited for Levi to do the same.

"You really think he's out here with his thumb up? With all due respect, Officer, that seems unlikely. You're wasting your time and ours." Levi's fingers drummed on his lap—ready—and I saw it all unfolding. The way he would reach toward the black cave of the floorboard, the mouth of his bag gaping, and exhume the thing he buried there. He would point it. Fire it. The bullet an extension of his obvious contempt. The policeman would never see it coming until he did. His knees would fold. His body would crumple. His blood would rain, showering the driver's bald head. And I'd be next. Collateral damage.

"Just doing our job, sir. Sorry for any inconvenience." The officer ushered us past the stop sign and back into moving traffic. I snuck a glance back just to be sure. Still alive. My pulse pounded in my ears, unconvinced, the drum of my heart echoing like a ball bouncing on hardwood. Surely, Levi could hear it. But when I finally mustered the courage to look at him, he did the unthinkable. He winked.

****

It would be a lie to say I was glad to be rid of Levi. We dropped him off at the Dragon Gate entrance to Chinatown, where he disappeared into the lively crowd. But I was relieved to see that black backpack get farther and farther away from me. Far enough so I could pretend I'd imagined it. I found the gate in the guidebook Ginny had given me, a heart drawn next to it. One of her big-city tour stops, no doubt.

Despite my protests, Levi paid the cab fare for both of us and sent me on my way. "Good luck with Ginny." That was all he said. I felt his warm hand on my forearm for a heartbeat. Then, he was gone. I sank back against the seat and closed my eyes, immediately exhausted. Levi reminded me of Ginny. He was like a lightning rod, taking the current with him and leaving me dull and empty. *This is how it's going to be.* I began the inner monologue I'd been practicing all spring since I accepted a basketball scholarship to Baylor. Me. Lonely. Next year. All the time. Ginny at UT—and me in Waco (or Wacko, as Ginny called it). *Better get used to it, Sam.*

"Westin St. Francis," the cab driver announced. He might've been saying bread or rock or carpet. The words sounded just as lifeless as I felt. He opened the door—left it that way—and walked to the trunk, producing the suitcases. "Have a good one." In Bellwether, most goodbyes were longer than you preferred, even perfunctory ones. But the driver was head down and pedal to the metal before I could even get my bearings.

I wheeled the bags inside, ignoring the doorman's offer to help, and found myself at the entrance to another world. A chandeliered, marbled, polished, something-out-of-a-magazine world. One where girls didn't go missing. Ginny would definitely be here, probably lounging in a chair nearby, watching me. She'd remind me to ask about room 1219, the haunted one, where that jazz musician died. Another heart in her guidebook. And then we'd stay up late, whispering about Levi. I might even embellish a little as payback. I didn't look for her. I wanted her to see me checking in, nonchalant, like I could do this without her.

****

"Are you sure? Could you just double-check?"

"Ma'am, I'm sorry, but there are no messages for you."

"And no one else checked in? You're positive?"

"Positive."

I'd walked the length of the lobby too many times to count. Watched the rotating picture screen behind the front desk show the same picturesque views of the Golden Gate over and over again until it seemed I'd been there myself. I avoided the bathroom for obvious reasons, but sat for twenty minutes staring at the oversized clock hanging at the entrance. I catalogued its movements. 9:10 p.m. 9:11 p.m. 9:12 p.m. When the minute hand reached the VI, I went back to the desk, now certain Ginny had checked in before me. She was up in the room, showered, bundled in a comfy robe, and watching a pay-per-view movie. Probably one with Channing. Or Ryan Gosling. Maybe even Jake Gyllenhaal, if she was in the mood for something serious.

"Are you okay?" The hotel clerk could've been in a movie herself. A thriller, judging by her wild eyes and breathy voice. "Do you need help?"

I didn't know the answer, but I knew what I had to do. There was no other option. And my phone was staring at me, judging me, chastising me, even from the bottom of my purse. *Call her already.* It was nearly midnight in Texas. My mom should be fast asleep—except I knew she wasn't sleeping. She'd be up waiting for my call. And once I told her, everything that happened tonight would be real. It always was. I felt sick with the first ring. The answer came before the second.

"Samantha." That was it. She wasn't screaming. It was worse than I expected.

"Mom, I know you're angry. But please don't hate me."

And there it was, the dreaded sigh. "I don't hate you, honey. More than anything I'm just so disappointed. It's not like you to disobey me, much less gallivant off to San Francisco."

"But you said I could go."

"That was before."

"Before what?"

"You know what."

"You seriously expect me to believe you canceled a cruise with Ginny's mom—*a cruise!*—and changed your mind about my trip at the last minute all because one of the stupid cows was about to have a calf? C'mon, Mom."

"I'm allowed to change my mind, Samantha. As much as you hate to admit it, those cattle are part of our livelihood. And I didn't think it was safe for the two of you to go alone. You know how reckless Ginny can be." My mom still blamed Ginny for pilfering the bottle of Grey Goose from the locked cabinet last summer, and I never set her straight. Besides, it had been Ginny's bright idea to sneak into the city pool with those two senior boys—and that's how we got caught. "I'm sure Ginny's parents are enjoying themselves just fine."

"Mom?" Now seemed as bad a time as any to tell her. "I can't find Ginny."

"You what?"

"We got off the plane, and she went to the restroom. It sounds insane, but she never came out. I told the police, and they didn't—"

"Where are you?" She was rummaging. I could see her in my mind. She was in a full-on panic, combing through the kitchen junk drawer for a pen. "Specifically."

"At the hotel. The Westin St. Francis at Union Square. Room 403."

"Listen to me. Stay put. Do not leave the hotel until I get there. I'll be on the first flight tomorrow. Do you understand me?" Her tone allowed only one answer.

"Yes." In the silence—the line dead now—I trembled. My mother's near hysteria bit at my bones. I had to coach myself to walk, not run, to the elevator. *Up*. The only direction this trip could go.

CHAPTER FIVE

RED!

I fished my pajamas—a Duke basketball T-shirt and a pair of sweats—from my bag and sat down on the bed, Ginny's suitcase at my feet. Opening it felt like an admission. *Ginny is not coming back.* So I left it there.

I showered, barely glancing at myself in the mirror, and climbed beneath the softest sheets I'd ever felt. That, of all things, finally did me in. I let my tears dead-end into the pillowcase until it was wet against my nose. I was too tired to flip it. With the heaviness of sleep pressing down on me, I remembered something important. Ginny's phone. The message. *Clare, come find me.* Tomorrow. I'd tell my mom then.

****

It was one of those scorching summer days that goes on forever, as far as the hayfield behind Bellwether High. And that's where I was, knee-deep in kleingrass. Beads of sweat took a long, lazy roll down my back as I walked. *Why am I here? Where am I going?* To find Ginny. She would be hiding here like before. Our freshman summer. "Who bleeds all over the first boy they kiss?" she'd asked me when I found her, eyes brimming with excitement. She flipped up the edge of her T-shirt to show me the evidence, the bright-red stain along the hem where she wiped her lips, nicked by his braces.

My jealousy, I kept to myself. "Life isn't a race," my mom reminded me. But sometimes it felt like one, and Ginny always got there first. And now, she was back here laughing at me. I could hear her. I plodded toward the sound, ignoring the grass stinging my bare legs. She lay sleeping in the sun, wearing her favorite powder-blue dress. "It's vintage," she'd told me when she bought it. "Like Rachel McAdams in *The Notebook*."

A soft breeze blew waves in the thin fabric. Her skin paler than I remembered, her eyelids a muted shade of lilac. I moved closer, intent on waking her, telling her how angry I was. But the buzzing stopped me. The desperate flutter of translucent wings. A fly—black as ash—crawled from Ginny's mouth, pausing on her lower lip before scurrying down her chin. Then another. And another. And another. So many I could barely make out her face. I screamed, but no sound came. I ran, but my legs anchored themselves to the earth like gravestones. Captive in the swarm, I fell to my knees. And that's when I saw it. The slit in Ginny's neck. Razor thin. Bone deep. And red, red, red. Red!

I woke with a howl rising in my throat, and the blinking red eye of the telephone. I had a message.

There was a whir, a hiss, like wind slicing through trees. No one spoke at first. And I almost hung up thinking it was a mistake. Then, a voice. Too young and unsteady to be Ginny—that's what I thought—but it was. The more I listened, I heard the bare bones of her, the familiar lilt, the way she spoke my name. A wave of relief overwhelmed me, and my eyes were watering again.

"Sam, it's Ginny. I need you to come get me at Pier 39. I'll explain when I see you. I'm really sorry."

I played the message again and again. So many times I recited her words along with her. And I recognized that whir, that hiss. It was Ginny's rattled breathing. *Was she running?* On the map in the guidebook, I traced an arrow shot to Pier 39 via Stockton Street. If I left now, I'd be there in thirty minutes, less if I jogged. I pulled on my sneakers and stashed my phone, wallet, and room key inside the deep pocket of my sweatpants, right next to the broken promise I'd made to my mother. Surely, she would understand. Getting Ginny back was a reasonable exception.

****

The only faces left in the lobby belonged to the clocks. The hanging one and the Great Magneta—the iconic grandfather clock where everybody used to meet, apparently. I discovered that fact myself in the display case at the Westin's entrance. Ginny was never keen on history.

In Bellwether, 2 a.m. is black as coal. The kind of black that allows the stars their shine. Summers, Ginny and I would lie down on the hood of her jeep and try to see how many we could count. One night we'd made it to 951 before the coyote howls drove us inside. My first kiss—Tobey, junior running back—had happened there too, but boys don't have patience for stargazing. They don't know yet that waiting makes the good things even better.

In San Francisco, 2 a.m. was lonely and dark. The kind of lonely that makes people do desperate things. The kind of dark that lets them get away with it. The only comfort was the building-sized Burberry model, making smoldering eyes at me. In Ginny's honor, I took a moment to appreciate the lines of demarcation across his shirtless abdomen.

I made a right on Post and set a brisk pace, holding my phone in my hand in case I got lost. A mass of a man—I think it was a man—huddled in the corner in front of Tiffany's, just a mangy shock of hair under a stained blanket. One arm protruded, the nails long and thick as calluses. A left turn on Stockton, and I was jogging now. Ahead of me, a woman stumbled, holding a half-empty bottle in her hand. She braced herself against a storefront as I crossed the street, already feeling breathless and cold.

"Hey there, girlie!" A voice from the shadows scratched at me as I passed. "Where ya goin' in such a hurry? Want to have a little fun?" I didn't look. Couldn't look. Just kept running. My own footsteps were heavy, my breath ragged in my ears. By the time I reached the Stockton Street Tunnel, I was convinced there was someone behind me. Someone fast and wild tracking the scent of my fear like a wolf. That faceless voice had taken form. This small-town girl, his idea of a little fun. Stunned by the headlights of an oncoming car—blind as a Bellwether deer—I still ran. If this was a game, it was a fast break, a steal, and I plowed down the court with a steely-eyed defender at my heels.

I forced myself to turn around when I found Washington Square Park—a little patch of grass and a row of trees. There was no one. No one I could see. But it was all I couldn't see that unnerved me. I consulted my phone. I was close, about a half mile from the Pier. And I had a text from a number I didn't recognize.

Sam, please hurry. I'll be waiting by the sea lions.

I dialed it back. First ring, I expected Ginny to answer. The second came and went. By the third, I knew it was pointless. *What's up? You've reached Marco's voicemail. You know what to do.* Marco? He sounded like a frat boy. A frat boy with an accent like Enrique Iglesias. Maybe Levi was right. Ginny flirted her way into the city. I hit redial.

Most changes happen at a glacial pace. Puberty, for instance. A virtual Ice Age passed between gawkiness and adulthood—measured in pimples and awkward formal dances. But really, it only takes a snap of a finger, a wrong turn, a knife blade to the throat, to take who you are and turn you into somebody completely different. *This,* for instance.

"Gimme your phone, bitch." The mouth—angry for no reason—opened wide and spewed at me. The world closed in and that mouth was all I could see, spittle collecting in the corners of chapped brown lips. A tongue like a cow's, thick and rough. Corn-kernel teeth. "Now."

I offered my phone to the mouth, but I knew it wanted more. "Money," it said. "You got any money?" I reached into my pocket, uncertain. *Did I bring my wallet?* Everything before the mouth seemed fuzzy, a dream upon waking.

"C'mon, baby, I know you do." It talked sweet and low now, which was worse than the other. The lips smacked softly. "Or maybe you got something else to offer."

I gave everything I owned—a handful of neatly folded bills. Unsatisfied, the mouth came closer. Closer still. Until I felt its hot breath on my cheek and sucked in its sourness. I stepped back, but the mouth knew how to hold me in place—"Don't move, you little slut. Don't tease me." And it knew how to keep me quiet—"Scream, and I'll slit you open." The mouth recited its vile threats like poetry. Then, the lips parted, setting free a moan, and left a trail of acid down my neck. "Be good to me, and I'll be good to you," the mouth whispered.

No. I silent-screamed the word before I said it. "No!" I heard my voice as an outsider, an observer, a neutral party. It sounded contrived, nearly hysterical. Like a bad actress in a horror flick.

The mouth was still, but not surprised. It expected a fight. Wanted it even. "No?" Slowly the corners turned up, pleased with itself. "I don't remember asking." The mouth pushed itself against mine hard and insistent. It tasted of bitter rot, too putrid to stomach. I smashed my fist into the mouth, my wallet curled in my palm like a brick.

"Fuck." The mouth angered again, and I liked that better. The lips turned the color of OPI's Girls Just Want to Play, the one Ginny insisted we both wear to prom because she liked the name. "You want to do this the hard way, huh?" A hand with clawed fingers swiped the blood from the mouth, smearing it across the chin. *A knife!* There was a knife in that hand. The mouth grinned at my realization. "Look what you did. I'm gonna have to hurt you now."

"Do that, and you'll have a bullet in your head." A voice—calm and vaguely familiar—came from behind me, and with it, the spell broke. I hurled myself away from the mouth, the hands, the arms, the legs, the feet, the face—the entire man to whom it belonged. He looked scrawnier than his voice let on. Gaunt even. Made of bones and dirt. But his eyes, now that I could see them, had an unexpected power. Darting from Levi to me and back again, they possessed the boldness of a cornered animal.

"And who the fuck are you?" The man danced toward Levi with his fists raised, slaying invisible air dragons as he approached.

"A man who's brought a gun to a knife fight, evidently."

"Levi?" The gun tucked close to his chest answered me back. It glinted in the glow of the lone streetlight. I backed up, smacking myself against a tree trunk.

"What are you doing out here alone?" he shouted.

"What am I doing? What are *you* doing? You followed me."

"You let yourself be followed." Levi trained the black-eyed barrel on the man, then waved it down the length of his body as he squirmed. *"Clearly."*

"What's that supposed to mean?"

"It means you're in way over your head, Samantha Bronwyn." *Did I tell him my last name?* Definitely not. But Ginny shared hers, of course. Along with her Facebook page, Twitter handle, and every other thing you shouldn't share with strangers. *Unless that stranger looks like a Calvin Klein model,* she'd whispered when I cautioned her with Levi out of earshot in the airplane bathroom.

While I contemplated my options—Potential Murderer #1 or Potential Murderer #2—the man scurried toward the shadows like a rat. "Where do you think you're going?" Levi demanded. With two broad steps, he grabbed the man's shoulder and spun him around. "Give her the money back."

"And my phone."

"And her phone." Levi repeated. His fingers tightened on the man's arm, reddening with the effort. I waited for the snap, the break of his bird-like bones. The knife dropped from his hand, and Levi kicked it into the gutter.

"Alright, alright, alright. It's in my pocket, dude. I wasn't gonna do nothin' to her. I was just messin' around." Levi pulled one pocket inside out. Then, the other, and my things tumbled to the sidewalk, along with a small baggie and a hypodermic needle that explained a lot.

"Now get out of here."

"Uh, okay." The man side-eyed Levi's death grip. "But I can't move ... I—*oof.*" Leveled by Levi's punch, the man went down hard. And stayed down. One of his jaundiced teeth skittered from his mouth and mixed with the gravel until I couldn't tell it from all the other pebbles. I flinched, then flinched again when Levi turned his attention to me, his raised eyebrows issuing a challenge.

"I'm fine," I insisted. "I mean—thank you, but I'm fine ... now." I gathered my phone and my wad of money so fast, I scraped my knuckles against the sidewalk. Flesh seemed a small price to pay for a hasty exit. "I have to go."

He shook his head. "You're not going anywhere." I hoped he couldn't hear me gulp. Levi slipped his gun into his waistband and centered his knee in the back of the fallen man, stretching one of his limp, skeleton arms awkwardly behind his back. He'd obviously done this before. Then he looked up at me. "You're coming with me."

"Like hell I am."

He sighed, exasperated. "Are you country girls all this stubborn?"

"It's a Texas thing," I said, wondering if I could outrun him. *Doubtful.* Not with those legs. He had at least six inches on my 5'6" frame. "Didn't anybody ever warn you about Texas girls?"

He didn't laugh, his eyes calculated and focused. "Do me a favor. Open my backpack. Hand me one of those zip ties." I hadn't noticed his bag until now. He'd dropped it in the darkness, a few feet away.

"Guess you were right about those unsavory characters." Still nothing—not even a smile or a nod of acknowledgment. "Is he dead?" I asked. Levi prodded the man's ribs with his knuckles, inducing a low groan.

"Zip tie, please." Reluctant, I shuffled toward the bag and spread it open wide.

"What else do you have in here? Duct tape? Bleach? A shovel?"

"Funny. You should be thanking me, you know. If I hadn't shown up, Skinny here would be practicing his knife skills on you."

"I already said thank you." I plucked a plastic zip tie from the top of the bag. Underneath, I felt something soft. Maybe a T-shirt. "You gonna use these on me too?"

"Nah. I'm not into that kind of thing."

"But you're into following a complete stranger? Bringing a gun on an airplane? How did you even … ?"

"Zip tie." I shoved the tie into Levi's extended palm, and he started to secure Skinny. With his hands busy, I grabbed the gun from the holster on his waistband and pointed it at him. *That was too easy.* I couldn't believe my luck. It was the same size as the one in Pandora's box. Finally, my mother's *just in case* came in handy.

He studied me with surprised amusement. "Seriously?"

"I'm not going anywhere with you until you tell me who you are and why you followed me."

"Fine." I hadn't expected him to agree. Not that easily. The urgent stiffness in my shoulders loosened. "Just put the gun—" Levi lunged toward me, strong hands on my forearm, and wrestled the gun from my grasp, but not before I landed two strong kicks to his shin that he barely noticed. "—down."

"What are you—a ninja?"

"Actually, it's pretty basic self-defense. You lost your focus—I saw an opening." He grinned. "But you were pretty tricky, grabbing my gun like that. Let me guess, it's a Texas thing?"

I shrugged, annoyed with myself. "Please. I heard from Ginny. I think she's with some guy named Marco. Just let me leave. I won't tell anybody about you."

He walked to his backpack and rummaged inside, producing his cell phone. "At least read this before you make your last stand at the Alamo."

I got no further than the breaking news headline before I felt my knees buckle.

Body of SFO employee discovered at Candlestick demolition site, police suspect foul play, fear escaped prisoner Cullen involved.

CHAPTER

SIX
THE WRONG CLARE

I let Levi help me to the curb, then watched as he dragged Skinny deeper into the park. I listened to the sound of his limp body swishing the dewy blades like a grass snake. For the second time that night, I had the feeling of witnessing myself. *Who is this girl? What is she doing?*

When Levi joined me, I felt grateful for the two feet of space he left between us. "Just breathe," he said. I was trying.

"I thought you said Ginny would be fine. That she'd turn up." I spoke through a tunnel of panic—my words echoing strangely in my head.

"That was before."

"Before what?"

Levi paused, and I knew. Whatever he was about to say was bad. Life-altering bad. "Before I knew who you were."

Who *I* was? Who *was* I? An eighteen-year-old girl from the sticks. A star basketball player, sure, but nothing else. Nothing special. "What do you mean?"

"Your mom ... her past."

I felt like I was back in fourth-period Calculus, Mr. Willett writing gibberish on the board. *C'mon, Ms. Bronwyn, you know this one. Derivatives, remember?* "My mom? You know her?"

Another mile of silence stretched between us before Levi shook his head. "No. I'm sorry," Levi murmured. "I thought she would've told you."

"So you don't know her?"

"I know of her."

"I think you've got the wrong person. My mom owns a clothing boutique in Bellwether. She has chickens and cows. Lots of them. Her name is Clare—"

"Keely," Levi finished for me, but it was wrong. All wrong.

"Bronwyn. Same as me," I corrected.

"And it's always been Bronwyn?"

I glared at him. "Yes, always. She kept her maiden name when she married my dad and passed it along to me. He's dead, by the way. Or did you already know that too?" Pity wrote large all over Levi's face, and it rankled me. He was the one confused. "You've got the wrong Clare."

"Right," he said. "The wrong Clare." He stood up, fidgeting with his hands. "We, uh, you should probably get out of here. Skinny's going to wake up soon. At least let me come with you, wherever you're going."

I knew I should stand and start walking. *Ginny.* I had to go to her. But I felt cemented to the ground. My limbs pinned by four words. *Clare, come find me.* "So who is Clare Keely?" I asked.

LOOKS like we're both new around here," he said. Half of his mouth was smiling at her, and she smiled back. Pleasantries. Not exactly what Clare Keely—Doctor Clare Keely—expected from her first session with Clive Cullen. But then again, nothing about her inaugural week at San Quentin State Prison had gone the way she'd imagined it.

That morning, as she slipped her tweed jacket over a red blouse, she practiced. She'd already broken her supervisor's first rule—*don't look too nice*—so she wanted her introduction to roll off her tongue, effortless. Not like the ink was barely dry on her diploma.

Hello. I'm Dr. Clare Keely. It sounded rehearsed.

Hi, I'm Dr. Keely. Too casual.

I'm Dr. Keely, but you can call me Clare. Bad idea. Very bad. This doctor thing would take some getting used to, but damned if she wasn't going to use that title. She'd earned it.

Cullen watched, amused. Magnetized, her eyes went straight to his hands. They were clasped on the bare table. Strong and capable. Capable of crushing her windpipe. Splintering her bones. Snapping her neck like the pencil in her hand. Clare tapped its eraser against the thick file on her lap, knowing the only thing between them was the rudimentary push-button alarm she'd checked every morning. It would take at least ten seconds for the officer to make it up the stairs from his post. She'd timed it herself.

"You transferred?" She already knew the answer. It was right there in that file. Everything she needed to know about Clive Cullen. *Cutthroat.* She had to be careful not to call him that by accident.

"I started down south. Wasco in Kern County. It's a level four." *Level Four?* Clare was certain she should know exactly what that meant—they'd reviewed all this during the orientation—but she couldn't remember. Neal had been right. The prison was another world with its own language, and its own set of rules. She felt like a newbie, but she nodded anyway. "Then they sent me to Corcoran. Real nice place. Manson's digs. And now, lucky me, here I am. The prison by the Bay."

"Why did they transfer you here?"

He cocked his head at her, grinning, and a flush crept up her neck. "You already know why. Are you testing me?"

Clare cursed herself silently. She felt outmatched. Incompetent. And they'd barely begun. "Um, I was just trying to ... " She tested the options in her mind. *Build rapport? Hear you tell it in your own words?* What would her clinical psych professor say? Her supervisor, Dr. Fitzpatrick?

Cullen laughed. A real laugh. Soft and deep. It was the nicest sound she'd heard all day. "I'm just kidding," he said. "I'm sure you want to hear it from the horse's mouth." He pointed to himself. "Me. Horse."

She giggled before she could stop herself, then busied her own delicate hands, opening Cullen's file. *Overfamiliarity.* It was the first word on the first page of the disciplinary infraction that sent him to San Quentin two months ago. A prison word. Clare had to ask Fitzpatrick what it meant.

"I'll admit I got too close to her."

"Who?"

"Gina. She worked in the library where I was a clerk. I know it must sound crazy—no pun intended—to you, Doc, but I thought I was in love." Cullen ran his fingers through his dark hair, then looked up at her. His stare felt intense. Like he was casting a spell with those eyes as gray-blue and mercurial as the sea. *This is what happened to Gina*, she thought.

"Have there been others in here?"

"A few. I can't help it. Prison is lonely, you know? That's why I got depressed in the first place."

Clare fingered the diagnosis in Cullen's file—adjustment disorder with depressed mood. As if anybody could make a seamless adjustment to this place. She made a noise of agreement before the irony hit her like a brick to the face. Or more appropriately, a knife to the throat. "But ... you've always had ... " She stepped around the land mines selecting her words. "Problems in relationships ... with women?" It had the sound, the lilt of a question, but they both knew it wasn't.

There was that sheepish grin again. "Dr. Keely, that might be the understatement of the century."

Before Clare knew it, she laughed again. A real laugh.

****

Clare printed five sentences in Cullen's chart. She selected her words with care, using the example note Fitzpatrick had given her, the morning of their first supervisory meeting.

Inmate attended appointment. He was oriented to person, place, and time. Mood was neutral. Inmate was introduced to the undersigned clinician and reminded of limitations of confidentiality. Inmate discussed criminal and relationship history.

According to Fitzpatrick, "Don't use their names. It makes things easier." *What things?* she wondered. And brevity was key. "Less there for them to hang you with," he'd said. Whatever that meant, whoever *them* was, Clare planned to play it safe. Before she closed the file, she turned to one of the pages she'd marked. The autopsy report for Cullen's last victim. She couldn't stop reading it. It was as appalling as it was fascinating, the way it reduced human brutality to weights and measurements. Unfeeling science. *This is my life now*, she thought. *These kinds of men.*

DADDY DARKEST

Office of the Alameda County Coroner	
DATE and HOUR AUTOPSY PERFORMED: 3/7/90; 8:30 a.m. by David Keller, M.D. 2000 Broadway Avenue Oakland, CA 94607	**Assistant:** Frederick Gaines, M.D. **Full Autopsy Performed**

Office of the Alameda County Coroner	
Name: Pierce, Emily B	**Coroner's Case #:** 189
Date of Birth: 8/9/68	**Age:** 22
Race: White	**Sex:** Female
Date of Death: 3/5/90	**Body Identified by:** Susan Pierce, mother of deceased
Case #: 000-A6-980-11B-1990	**Investigative Agency:** Alameda County Sheriff's Department

EVIDENCE OF TREATMENT: N/A

CRIME SCENE EXAMINATION:
Apartment was small and situated near a college campus, having 3 rooms sized 15 feet x 10 feet each. There were no signs of forced entry. The room in which the body was found had 1 door. Body was seated upright in bed. There was pooling of blood in the front and along the sides of the body. There was spurting of blood on the floor and bedding at a distance of 1 to 2 feet away from the site where the body was lying. Furnishings were properly arranged in the room, and there were no signs of struggle. An empty wine bottle and one half-empty wine glass were intact on the bedside table.

EXTERNAL EXAMINATION:
The autopsy is begun at 8:30 a.m. on March 7, 1990. The body is presented in a black body bag. The victim is wearing a white cotton nightgown and light-blue underwear. The front portion of the gown is completely blood soaked. Jewelry included one heart-shaped, cubic-zirconia pierced earring, worn in the right ear. The left ear also was pierced with no earring present.

The body is that of a normally developed white female, measuring 65 inches and weighing 125 pounds, and appearing generally consistent with the stated age of 22 years old. The body is cold and unembalmed. Lividity is fixed in the distal portions of the limbs. The eyes are open. The irises are brown and corneas are cloudy. The hair is light blonde with tight curls and approximately 9 inches in length at the longest point.

On the neck, there is a cut-throat injury in the form of a deep, gaping incised wound present over the front aspect of the neck, cutting through the skin, superficial fascia, platysma, sternocleidomastoid muscle on the left side, left jugular vein, left common carotid artery, and anterior and lateral wall of the trachea. The wound is 6 inches in length with a maximal depth of 3 inches.

On the left wrist, there is a fully healed, raised, linear scar—two inches in length consistent with a prior cut injury. The mother of the victim reported the wound occurred in 1988 as the result of a failed suicide attempt by razor blade.

The genitalia are that of an adult female; there is no evidence of injury. Vaginal and perineal swabs were preserved for analysis. Limbs are equal and symmetrically developed. Both hands were partially clenched. There were no defense markings present on the arms or hands. The fingernails are short and painted red. There are no other scars, markings or tattoos.

Drug Screen Results:
Urine screen was NEGATIVE.
Ethanol: .10 mg/dl, blood

Valerie Skaggen, Ph.D.
Chief Toxicologist

OPINION

Time of Death: Body temperature, rigor and livor mortis, and stomach contents approximate the time of death between 9:30 p.m. and 11:30 p.m. on 3/5/90.

Immediate Cause of Death: Shock and hemorrhage as a result of cut-throat injury caused by a hard, sharp-edged object

Manner of Death: Homicide

Remarks: None

//Hui Chen, M.D.
Alameda County Coroner's Office
3/7/90

It was a minor detail—the one missing earring—that intrigued her most. Emily Pierce didn't seem like the kind of girl who lost an earring, even if it was cubic zirconia. Though she had no reason to be, Clare felt certain of that. She would ask Cullen. Not right away, of course. She imagined his gloved hands as skillful as a surgeon's, removing the earring, slipping it in his pocket. A sick memento. Without thinking, Clare touched her own gold hoops.

"Clare?" Fitzpatrick barged in without knocking. He wore a standard, sad uniform—a white, coffee-stained button-down, pleated khakis, and scuffed penny loafers. *This is where supervisors go to die*, she thought, trying to avert her eyes from the gray bags under his. She closed Cullen's file and arranged it with the others on her desk. "How'd it go with Cullen?" he asked.

"Okay, I guess."

"Did he hit on you? Say anything inappropriate? Get too personal? He does that. It's his thing." She wanted to laugh. *He should know.* A month ago, after her callback interview, Fitzpatrick had asked her out for a drink, giving her that hand-in-the-cookie-jar face when she'd rebuffed him.

Clare knew she sparkled. It was her curse. She'd known it since that seventh-grade slumber party when Lisa Taylor's stepfather slipped his hand onto her knee under the vinyl birthday-balloon tablecloth. She was dangerous. Like a siren. The kind of pretty that turns men's heads, leads them out into deep water. And men are willing to drown themselves for shiny things. Even supervisors.

"I don't think so," she said. "He was actually ... " Clare shuffled through a deck of words, considering. *Funny. Nice. Insightful.* " ... polite."

Fitzpatrick shook his head. "Oh boy. You're in more trouble than I thought." Then he winked at her.

SEPTEMBER 16, 1996

CLARE fiddled with the ruby ring on her finger. Probably not even a real ruby, mind you, but she couldn't bring herself to part with it. Even though she and Neal—Dr. Neal Barrington by now—had broken up months ago, it was a touchstone. A touchstone of rage.

"You're seriously breaking up with me because I took a job at a prison? How sexist are you?" Clare sat on the edge of Neal's bed, fuming, watching him run a hand through his chestnut hair until nothing remained of its gelled perfection.

"It's not that, Clare, and you know it. I can't be with someone who won't acknowledge her own issues. You're in denial. Complete and total denial."

"Thank you, Freud. Remind me to never date another shrink. It's exhausting."

"Yeah? Well, remind me to never date a shrink who hates therapy."

It was true. Clare had gritted her teeth through every one of her fifty-two required sessions. Only because she couldn't graduate without checking that box. Her therapist had reminded her of Neal. Always acting like he knew her better than herself. They both seemed to think Clare's chosen profession—criminal psychology—had to do with her past. That birthday party and everything that came after. *What did they know?*

"I'm taking the job, Neal, whether you like it or not. I have to prove to myself I can do it."

"Prove away. I'm not coming along for the ride."

She stormed out the door without telling Neal the truth because it sounded ludicrous. *Mental*, even. But the truth was, she got them. Criminals, the dredges of society, the castoffs, the undesirables. She understood their darkness, as if she'd been born from it herself.

"Is that from someone special?" Cullen asked her, noticing the ring as he took the seat opposite her desk.

"Uh, no," she blurted before she could stop herself. *Dammit, Clare. Boundaries.* "What I mean is, we should really stay focused on you."

"Of course, Doc. I shouldn't have asked." He leaned back in his chair, wide-eyed. "The spotlight is on me. What do you want to know?"

Clare put a tight lid on the hundreds of questions she had for him. Too soon. "What would you like to talk about today?"

His breathing was audible in her small office. It marked time. "I've never done this before," he offered.

"Therapy?" Clare knew that wasn't true. There were stacks of notes from his five years in prison—mostly carbon copies of Fitzpatrick's exemplar. Miles of data, saying nothing.

He shook his head. "I want to talk about something … someone … I've never talked about before." She waited for him to continue. "Emily."

Her heart hitched in her chest—she didn't expect Cullen to open up so soon—and she turned the ring on her finger. *This is why, Neal.* This, she lived for.

SEPTEMBER 24; 1996

ARE you sure you don't need an escort?" Clare shook her head. Shoulders drooped, Sergeant Briggs—aka Robocop—seemed disappointed, but Clare couldn't be sure. His eyes were walled off behind black-mirrored frames. Hence her secret nickname for him. "Just keep walking up past the lower yard and West Block is on your left."

Clare stared straight ahead, walking along the cement path at the perimeter of the yard. She'd only walked it a few times. And just twice on her own. But Fitzpatrick was right. It got easier, now that she knew where to look. She focused on the sky, blue as a robin's egg. Past these walls, invisible to her now, was the postcard view she marveled at every morning. Yesterday, third session, Cullen had told her that view was his least favorite part of San Quentin. "It's a tease," he'd said. "Beautiful, sure. But completely unavailable. So close, it hurts." There was an ache in his voice that chilled her. *Was he still talking about the view?*

On her right were two picnic tables. Inmates lounged there like construction workers on a lunch break. She passed them and their chorus of *good afternoons* without a word. To Clare, their pleasantries were no more than catcalls. And those who didn't speak, stared. She'd never been so aware of her own body. Her tan runner's legs hidden in boring slacks. The cream sweater that hugged her chest. Her bright blonde hair pulled into a messy bun at the nape of her neck. Not since the second day of that fateful slumber party—when Mr. Taylor had *accidentally* brushed against her budding breasts in the Taylor's swimming pool—had she felt so conscious of every part of herself.

"Doctor Keely!" The voice belonged to Cullen. He waved to her from the basketball court. He took a shot, swished it, and let the ball bounce, bounce, bounce, and roll. *Great,* Clare muttered. *He's coming this way.* It wasn't so much she didn't want him to come over—he was her favorite patient, after all—more she didn't want him to know she wanted him to come over. And she certainly didn't need anyone else to see them talking. It was part of her curse. Talking equaled flirting, especially if you were talking with Cutthroat Cullen. Especially if Cutthroat Cullen was shirtless and sweaty.

"I'm in a bit of a hurry," Clare said, hoping that would stop him.

He laughed, and the thick muscles across his stomach tightened. It was hard not to look with his body flushed and radiating heat. *There's nothing wrong with looking.* Unless you get caught looking. Cullen folded his arms across himself, and her cheeks warmed. "This is a prison, remember, Doc? Nobody's in a hurry around here."

Clare shrugged, then half-smiled, outwitted. She realized too late they were not alone. Lurking in earshot, one of the men from the picnic tables. His arms were all brawn and ink. Clare recognized one of the tattoos—an *M* on his bicep—from the prison-gang training last week. La Eme (EME), the Mexican Mafia. This was *their* bench. Well, at least the ones who hadn't been validated as gang members and shipped off to solitary at Pelican Bay.

"Sí, I've got all day for you, mamacita. Si la belleza era un crimen, tendría una sentencia de cadena perpetua."

Like poured concrete, Cullen's face hardened in an instant. "Get out of here, Ramirez!"

"Or what, Guero? She ain't your novia."

"Yeah, well she ain't your novia either. Show some respect."

Ramirez stepped in front of Cullen, chest to chest. When he spoke again, he spit each word like a poison dart. "Respeto, ese? Were you respecting those broads when you sliced and diced them up like Freddy Krueger?"

Everyone looked now. Even Robocop. Clare felt featherlight. All the blood drained from her, and she wished she could float away. Over the wall and the barbed wire, out into the ocean.

"I think both of you are getting a little heated. Maybe we could all take a time out." Clare practically laughed at the ridiculousness of her own words.

"That sounds nice," Ramirez oozed. "As long as you promise to keep your mouth closed … " He directed a pointed glance at Cullen. " … and your legs open."

Fists clenched, Cullen stared at Ramirez. Clare's mouth turned to cotton. It wasn't possible, but Cullen's heart seemed to move like an animal under his taut chest. She held up her hand to stop him. A *please* was all she could manage.

Cullen turned toward her, his eyes softening, and he started to walk away. Relieved, Clare closed her eyes and took a breath. Mid-exhale, something wet splattered against her cheek. Her hand went there as her eyes opened wide. Cullen's blood on her fingers, running in teardrops from his nose. He smeared it away with the back of his hand. Ramirez was waiting, fists still raised. And just like that, the yard erupted. Like the air had changed frequency. The alarm blared, and the inmates followed protocol, dropping to the ground on instinct.

Clare stumbled back. Her knees weakened, and she thought she might fall. But a large hand encircled her forearm, steadying her. "Are you okay?" Robocop asked.

"I'm sorry."

"For what? Don't apologize for those goons." He pulled her away, and she let him. But she glanced over her shoulder to see Cullen, chest to the pavement, still watching her.

****

For the next hour, Clare was elbow deep in paperwork, documenting the incident on the yard. *Mouth closed, legs open.* She wrote Ramirez's words until her hand hurt—form after form—until they sounded like a campaign slogan. Trite. Annoying. But impossible to forget.

50

Robocop didn't leave her side. Clare couldn't decide if his coddling was endearing or pathetic.

"What happens now?" she asked him, letting her hand rest.

"Don't worry." Robocop's assumption, true as it was, irritated her. "Ramirez is in Ad Seg. He'll get a 115. Probably be transferred. You won't have to see him again."

Clare nodded to mask her surprise. She never considered he'd be sent away. He, *Cullen*. She couldn't care less about Ramirez. "And Cullen?"

"Cutthroat?" Robocop's laugh sounded exactly as she imagined it. Methodical. A little maniacal. "He'll be living that one down for a while. Poor guy. I almost feel sorry for him."

"What do you mean?"

"He got called out. And by the EME, no less. When you turn your back on that kind of thing in prison, it makes you a punk."

"So him not fighting back was a bad thing?" She lowered her head, shuffling through the papers in front of her. Anything to avoid his condescending smirk.

"I guess that depends who you ask. But I'd say Cullen got exactly what he wanted." He was baiting her, and she knew it. Capping her pen, she stood up and headed for the door. *Take that, Robocop. I'm not biting.* "Be careful out there, Dr. Keely. You're not in Kansas anymore."

****

"James?" Clare kept her distance from the bars as she'd been instructed. She didn't need any more problems today. "Mr. Dumas?"

An unsteady voice answered her. "That's me." A tall, gangly man unfolded himself from the bottom bunk and waved. The gesture didn't say hello. It was more of an acknowledgment, a reluctant *I'm still here.*

"Hi, I'm Dr. Keely." Finally, she'd gotten the hang of it. "I'm here to check on you. To see how you're doing." Dumas gave a small, pained shrug of his shoulders, as if the weight of them hung too heavy for him to bear. Even from here, she could see the yellowing bruises on his neck where a paper-thin, prison-issued bedsheet had almost squeezed the life from him. "So how are you doing?"

51

"Better." He tried to smile, the effort of it obvious. "All things considered."

"Are you ... " Clare's training—all six years—failed her. She'd never been face-to-face with someone back from the brink. " ... still thinking of ... "

"Suicide?" he offered. Just another word to him. "No. There's something about being that close to six feet under that makes you rethink things. I guess I've got somebody—a few somebodies—to live for. I'd forgotten that." He reached behind him, pulled a picture from the wall, and held it up to the bars for her to see.

She wanted to ask more. The smiling woman with a chubby-cheeked toddler on her hip demanded it. But a cell-front visit meant listening ears. So instead, she nodded and refocused.

Stick to the script, Clare. Fitzpatrick reviewed the standard procedure that morning when he assigned her the case. *Got a new guy for you. Bank robber. Just got released from the crisis bed. Tried to do the dutch,* he'd said. She had to ask Dr. Lauer, another recent hire, what he meant.

"How would you describe your mood?" That question bored Clare. It sounded like something a shrink would ask.

"I ain't happy, if that's what you're getting at. But I'm not sad either. I suppose I'm just here." *Flat, indifferent,* Clare scrawled on her notepad.

"How have you been sleeping?"

"Decent. At least three, four hours a night." He gave a rusty chuckle at Clare's raised eyebrows. "This ain't the Ritz. Plus, you've gotta keep one eye open around this place." *Poor sleep, anxiety,* she wrote.

"And your appetite?"

"Prison food still tastes like crap. Just like it always has. I'd kill—I mean I'd give anything for a Big Mac and fries right now."

Two boxes left to check. The C.Y.A. boxes. That's what Fitzpatrick called them. *Cover your you-know-what,* he'd said, glancing a little too long at her you-know-what as she shuffled out the door. "Are you intending to hurt yourself today, Mr. Dumas?"

"Nope."

"And what will you do if you start to have those feelings again?"

He managed his best smile yet. "Steer clear of the bedsheets for starters."

"I see you haven't lost your sense of humor."

Dumas' green eyes brimmed, and he flopped back on his bunk to hide his face from her. "Dr. Keely, was it?"

"Yes, that's right." She jotted *tearful but not hopeless*.

"Well, Dr. Keely, it's just about the only thing I've got left."

SEPTEMBER 30, 1996

CLARE-BEAR, I'm worried about you." It'd become a familiar refrain. Her therapist. Neal. And now her best friend, Lizzie. "These creeps you're working with—"

"You mean, my *clients.*"

"Yeah, your clients—whatever—they're predators. This guy, Ramirez, you said he's in a gang. They could find out where you live." Lizzie pursed her lips and blew onto her steaming coffee.

"Ramirez is not my client." Clare regretted telling Lizzie about the dream she'd had last night. And the night before. And the night before that. The one with Ramirez breaking her body against that picnic table, choking her until she was too limp to fight back. Then he took what he really wanted. What all men wanted from her. "And the whole thing was my fault anyway. I shouldn't have—"

Lizzie raised her hand in front of Clare like a stop sign. "Now you sound like your prick supervisor. I can't believe he blamed you." *Don't fraternize with your clients, Dr. Keely, and this kind of thing won't happen.* His exact words. "And don't even get me started on what's his name."

"Clive Cullen." Clare knew she wasn't supposed to talk about her cases, but she couldn't help it. Cullen was famous—or infamous, as it were. His story had been in all the papers. Besides, Lizzie didn't count. She worked as a travel agent in San Francisco, as far from San Quentin as anybody could get. And she was Clare's oldest friend. The only one who knew everything. Well, almost. "He's really not that bad."

"Seriously? Even his name sounds evil." Lizzie lowered her voice. "Doesn't it scare you? Knowing what he's done?"

Clare rolled her eyes. "I can take care of myself. I'm twenty-seven years old, remember? Not a little girl anymore."

"I know, Dr. Hottie." Lizzie chuckled. "That's what worries me."

"Speaking of hotties … " Clare held the words in her mouth. She knew once she said them, there was no going back. She was admitting something to herself. "Cullen is actually sort of good-looking."

Lizzie nearly spit out a bite of blueberry scone. "Oh, Jesus. You are hopeless, girl. Don't you shrinks have a name for that?"

"Countertransference." Clare owned at least three books on the subject. "But it's not like anything is going to happen."

"Well, you've always had a thing for the unavailable ones," Lizzie teased. "But this is taking it to a whole new level." *Except for Neal,* Clare thought. He was too available. Boring her with every little detail of his semi-charmed life, expecting her to do the same. *No, Neal, I don't want to talk about how your pretentious mommy didn't hug you enough. I'm not your therapist, thank God.* She'd never said that aloud, of course. She felt vile just for thinking it.

Clare glanced at her watch. Her fourth session with Cullen started in thirty minutes. "I'm just saying, I can see why those girls fell for him. You know I'd never … "

"I know you wouldn't. Just remember who you're dealing with, Clare. You're the mouse. He's the cat."

****

It was 9:37 a.m. The cat was seven minutes late. Not that Clare was counting. In fact, she dreaded this session. She knew they'd have to talk about the incident on the yard. The sucker punch from Ramirez and the sick things he'd said to her. *Mouth closed, legs open.* Ramirez didn't know a thing about her, and yet he knew the most important thing, like she'd been marked somehow.

At 9:40 a.m., Fitzpatrick urged her to call Cullen's unit to tell them he hadn't responded to his ducat, the slip of paper allowing him entry into the building. *He's testing the limits, Dr. Keely. Show him who's boss.* Clare held off. After he stood up for her, she didn't want to get him in trouble. Maybe he wouldn't come at all. But when he finally appeared in the doorway, wearing a Cheshire cat grin, Clare felt a relief she couldn't explain.

His face flushed, like he'd been running. "I'm so sorry. I got held up at the gate."

"If it happens again, I'll have to call and report you," she said. "It's important you get here on time."

"Believe me, Doc, this is the only appointment I look forward to. I won't be late again." She opened her notebook, signaling she was ready to begin. Before she could prompt him, Cullen spoke. "About what happened last week with that asshole, Ramirez—it was my bad. I shouldn't have called you over. For a minute, I think I forgot where I was."

"Me too," she admitted, grateful he brought it up first. The seriousness of Cullen's face surprised her, his mouth a thin dash.

"I may be out of line for saying this, but you have to be careful around here."

"What do you mean?" she asked, knowing perfectly well what he meant.

"You're a beautiful woman." He made the pronouncement so matter-of-factly, Clare almost agreed.

"Mr. Cullen—" She'd never called him that before, and it sounded strange. Overly formal. In her head, he was Clive or Cullen. Never a mister.

"But not only that. Some people like to step on flowers just because they can." Cullen avoided her eyes. "I know because I used to be one of them."

Somehow, he saw the invisible mark, just like Ramirez. Clare hid her shame behind a question. "With Emily?"

He nodded. "With all of them." Clare caught her breath. It was the first time Cullen had spoken about the others. He'd been charged with three murders. Convicted of only one. Enough to land him in prison for life. "But Emily especially. God, I loved her. I loved her too much. See, that's the problem. I could never love anyone just a little."

56

Clare scribbled furiously in her notebook, the one where she wrote the real stuff. Not the sanitized Fitzpatrick version. "And Emily was vulnerable?" *Like me.* Clare already knew. She had read the detective's interview with Susan Pierce, Emily's mother, and committed it to memory.

"Yes. I told you last time how we met." Emily stripping her way through UC Berkeley. Cullen visiting the club with a business colleague. That was the lie he'd told her. "And she trusted me so easily. I didn't have to work for it. She told me what her stepfather did to her. I used it, Dr. Keely. I used it against her without even trying to."

"How did you use it?"

"I turned into the monster she feared the most. No, I take that back—it wasn't me. It was like my love grew so big, it became a separate person. A needful person."

Clare stopped writing. The world stood still. "What did that person need?" *What did you need, Clive?*

"Control." As if on cue, the alarm blared, and she jumped. Her pen fell to the ground and rolled beneath her desk.

"Dammit," she muttered. "It gets me every time." Head down, searching for her pen, she heard Cullen sigh.

"Emily was like that too. Jumpy." He'd already sprung to his feet, heading for the door. Protocol required him to stand outside anytime that alarm bell sounded. Proof he was out there, harmless. Not in here, doing God knows what to her. "I promised I'd protect her, but … " Before he closed the door behind him, Cullen snuck a look back at her, his eyes more gray than blue today. "I couldn't."

****

"So, how's it going, Clare?" The worst hour of the week began. Supervision with Fitzpatrick. He crossed his leg, revealing the pale, hairy skin between his sock and his pant leg. Clare smiled to disguise her disgust.

"Fine."

"I know it's been a rough couple of weeks." She watched in horror as he extended his small hand to pat her forearm. "You can talk to me. That's what I'm here for."

"I think I'm finally starting to get the hang of it," she offered. "I've never worked in this kind of place before."

"Prison is not for everyone. You've got to have solid boundaries. Rock solid."

She nodded, knowing her boundaries were more like Swiss cheese. Mr. Taylor guaranteed that the moment he told her thirteen-year-old self she made him hard. "I'm working on it."

"Are you?" His lips curled up over stained teeth. "I'm aware it's been a problem for you in the past. During your postdoctoral fellowship."

Clare swallowed, then removed the burgundy scarf she'd laced around her neck that morning. Suddenly, she felt way too hot. "That was *not* the issue. As I explained to HR, I was sexually harassed by one of my clients. I don't think it's fair to criticize my boundaries when somebody else clearly violated them."

"Of course not, Clare. But sometimes we give people permission—unintentionally, I'm sure—to cross the line. Ted Bundy said that, you know. That he could spot his victims a mile away. They invited him."

Clare wished she had a gun to put a bullet in Fitzpatrick's skull. Or maybe just in the soft, doughy flesh of his stomach. She pushed the thought away, recoiled from it—*where did that come from?* "Actually, I believe Bundy's exact words were, 'I have known people who radiate vulnerability.' But we're not taking advice from a serial killer, are we?"

A deflated Fitzpatrick fiddled with his tie. "Shall we talk about your clients?"

CHAPTER SEVEN

LIARS

LEVI still hadn't answered my question. "Clare Keely?" I reminded him as we walked side by side down Stockton toward the Embarcadero. But he told me one thing that made all the difference. *If it means you'll trust me, you can carry the gun, Texas.* It was jammed uncomfortably in the elastic of my sweatpants.

Another exasperated sigh. "She was a shrink at San Quentin back when Cullen first got there."

"And?"

"And that's all I know."

"I call BS, but I'll let it slide. For now. How much further?"

Levi stopped to look at the map on his phone. "Less than half a—" A siren cut him short. Then the blur of a police car, followed by two more just like it. "Sam?"

"Yeah?"

"I think we should pick up the pace a little. Looks like they're heading to the same place we are." He tugged at the straps of his backpack, cinching them tighter.

I didn't answer, just started jogging, and Levi matched my pace. *Fast.* I couldn't shake the feeling I was running from something. My mother. Skinny. Ginny's lifeless face in my dream. "Damn. You *are* an athlete," Levi huffed, in between breaths.

We both slammed the brakes when we saw it. At least five police cars, arranged helter-skelter on the Embarcadero.

"Give me the gun," Levi whispered. There wasn't time to protest. Besides, the way my day was going, I'd end up in a jail cell, booked on a weapons charge. "And let me do the talking." I rolled my eyes hard at him. Typical boy. He didn't realize the talking meant nothing. I zeroed in on the first car. It was the listening that mattered.

"208, do you copy?"

"This is 208."

"Additional reports of a 415-2 in progress at Pier 39 Embarcadero."

"10-4. We're on scene now."

I started typing *415 police code* into Google, when Levi interrupted. "It's a disturbance call."

"How do you know?" Levi raised his eyebrows at me, as if the answer was obvious.

"I just do, okay?"

"That's a lot of police cars for a disturbance."

"Exactly what I was thinking."

A few officers milled near the entrance to the Hard Rock Cafe, talking. I walked in their direction, pretending to study the statue of a crab at the center of the sidewalk. But Levi yanked me back, pulling me onto a bench facing the doors.

"Hey," I said, a little too loudly.

"Don't make a scene." His voice was low but insistent. A growl.

"I wasn't planning on it."

"Then stop acting so suspicious," he said through clenched teeth.

"It's after 3 in the morning. We're suspicious by default."

"Fine, but you're making it—"

"Shh." I hushed Levi and put my head against his shoulder. *Unbelievable.* Even after roughing up Skinny and running half a mile, he still smelled good. Like leather and soap. "Just pretend we're taking a moonlit stroll." He groaned but didn't move away. The rise and fall of his chest soothed me like the push and pull of the beach tide.

None of the officers noticed us. Yet. But I could only make out a few words.

" … anything?"

"Nothing … where did … him?"

The officer pointed down the pier, toward the storefronts concealed in darkness. "You really think … Cullen … ?"

I stabbed Levi with my elbow. "Did you hear that? They said Cullen—*Cullen!* As in Cut—"

Levi's mouth felt warm and wet. And it was on mine. *Why is Levi kissing me?* For a heartbeat, that was all I could think. Like there was a short circuit in my brain. Then I noticed the way his stubble tickled my lips. How he tasted like butterscotch. Even when I realized the why, I didn't want him to stop. But he did.

"Excuse me, sir. Miss?" A flashlight spotlighted the space between our faces. The officer at the other end nodded. "Evening—or should I say, morning? I'm Officer Whitlock, SFPD."

"Can we help you with something?" I didn't sound as believable as I hoped. Luckily, Levi saved me.

"Is it morning already? I guess time flies when you're uh … " He cocked his head toward me, exchanging a conspiratorial grin with Officer Whitlock.

"Fooling around?" Whitlock offered.

"Something like that." Levi chuckled, but the officer didn't laugh. That boys' club smirk had morphed into a hard line.

"Well, son, did you happen to notice you were in the middle of an active police investigation?"

"No?"

"Is that a question?"

I stood up, dragging Levi by the arm. "I think what he means is we were just leaving."

"Not so fast." Officer Whitlock whipped out a small notebook, gesturing for us to sit. "I've got a few questions for you lovebirds.

You don't mind, do you?" As if we could answer honestly. "Could I get your names?"

Levi remained mute, leaving me no choice. "Samantha Bronwyn. B-R-O-N-W-Y-N."

"And what about you, Romeo?"

I nudged Levi. "Flynn. Flynn Ryder. R-Y-D-E-R." Thank God Officer Whitlock glared at me. That glare held me together, my laughter trapped safely inside. I knew Flynn Ryder. *Tangled* was the last Disney movie I'd seen before I declared myself too old to crush on a cartoon hero. Lying made Levi stupid or brave. I couldn't decide which.

"What brings you to Pier 39?"

"We were looking for my—" Levi squeezed my hand, and I stopped talking.

"For the sea lions," he finished for me.

"Hmm. I see." Officer Whitlock may as well have extended his finger and screamed, *Liars!* "And where are you staying?"

Levi and I spoke simultaneously. "The Westin St. Francis."

"A youth hostel downtown."

"Well, which is it?" *Liars!*

"We're staying separately," Levi said. "We just met last night. Did something happen out here?"

Officer Whitlock closed his notebook, apparently satisfied with our fabrications. "A passerby reported a girl screaming. Hear anything like that?" We both shook our heads. "Have you two seen this man?" He unfolded a piece of paper and held it up for us. For the second time that night, I was face-to-face with the two-dimensional likeness of Clive "Cutthroat" Cullen.

Levi took the paper in his hand, and for a moment, I wasn't certain what he would say. "I wish we had, Officer. I wish we had."

CHAPTER EIGHT

FOUND

WELL, that was interesting," I said, following Levi toward K-Dock, home of the sea lions. Some small part of me—miniscule as it was— still expected Ginny to be there, leaning against the wooden rail, the wind blowing her hair back.

"About that kiss," he mumbled. "That cop heard you. He was coming over, and I just—"

"Couldn't resist a Texas girl?" I laughed at my own joke and watched his cheeks pink just a little. Let him think that kiss—my sixth in total, eight if you counted truth or dare—was something to apologize for. Now I knew why Ginny had told me to stop at five. *Save the next one for college, for a real man,* she'd said. "Seriously, though. You're such a guy. I can't even believe that is what's on your mind right now."

Levi smirked. "As opposed to?"

"For starters, I didn't realize you were a Disney fan, Flynn. What were you, like eighteen, when that movie came out?"

"I was sixteen. But my sister was younger. She watched it every day for a month. That and *Aladdin.* I guess she had a thing for thieves with a heart of gold."

"Is that why you're here? To visit your sister? And why did you lie about your name?"

Levi didn't like those questions. His expression stayed flat, but his jaw clenched. "My sister is in jail."

"Oh." *Why?* The obvious question, but I picked my spots. "That sucks."

"And my name is on a need-to-know basis."

"So Ginny needed to know? Is Levi Beckett even your actual name?"

Without answering, Levi pointed out toward the water. It was so dark I couldn't see where the sky ended and the ocean began. "Sea lions."

I nodded. Their fat, slippery bodies formed a huddled mass, barely visible on the floating dock, but the barking gave them away. "Did you know they can live up to twenty-five years in the wild? It was in Ginny's guidebook."

"I'm sorry she's not here." He sounded sincere, but unsurprised.

"Do you think that was her screaming?"

He shook his head no. "Most people are unreliable witnesses. It was probably some drunk idiot running amok."

"The passerby or the screamer?"

He chuckled. "Both, most likely. I have an idea. Can I see your phone?" I fished it out of my pocket and handed it to him. He opened my texts and dialed the unfamiliar number. Frat-boy Marco. Whoever he was. "Let's just see if we hear it ringing."

I thought of Ginny's phone buzzing in the bathroom stall, those flies buzzing in my dream, and I shivered. "You really need a jacket, Sam."

"I'm not cold." Marco didn't answer. And the phone didn't ring. Only the water whispered, telling me something I didn't want to hear.

"What's that?" Levi walked toward the bench at the far end of the dock. It faced out toward Alcatraz. Another spot Ginny marked with a double heart. A must-see. "Isn't this yours?"

And just like that, my letterman jacket—**BRONWYN, STATE CHAMPIONSHIP BASKETBALL 2016**—was found.

64

****

I sat on the bench—numb—staring out at Alcatraz's flashing beacon with my jacket folded next to me, just the way we discovered it. "Do you think anyone has actually escaped from there?"

"Doubtful," Levi answered from behind me. He was pacing. "But the Anglin brothers and Frank Morris … their bodies were never found, so I guess we can't say for sure."

"You know a lot about San Francisco."

"I used to live here. When I was a kid."

"Before the farm?"

He nodded. "A lifetime before."

"We have to tell the police," I said, for at least the third time in the last five minutes. "Something bad happened to Ginny."

When the silence stretched between us, long as the night itself, I reached for the jacket. "I'm going to find Officer Whitlock. To tell him everything." I'd never heard such a scornful laugh. "I'm glad this is so funny to you, Levi. Or whatever the heck your name is."

"It's not funny. It's the complete opposite of funny. But that guy Whitlock is a complete buffoon. He has no idea who he's dealing with. He can't help you."

My shock-frozen heart cracked, and I felt the thaw coming again. "Then who can?" Inside my pocket, my phone beeped. I knew better than to hope. All I felt was dread. Brushing a tear from my cheek, I forced myself to look. "It's Marco again." I read the text aloud.

There are worse things than murder. Do you believe me now, Clare?

"Clare?" Levi repeated. "It says *Clare* again?"

Jacket in hand, I walked away from Levi. "This sicko has Ginny. And I … I can't just do nothing."

"Sam, wait." I heard him running to catch up to me. "I'm a cop."

CHAPTER

NINE
VOLUME B

I stood under the shower, letting the water—as hot as I could stand it—pound my head until I felt clean. Skinny, Levi, Officer Whitlock, Cullen, Marco, all of them circled the drain and went under. Then I slowly adjusted the temperature. Cool. Cold. Icy. My favorite post-game ritual. The best way to soothe sore muscles. But tonight, it just made me feel human again.

There are worse things than murder. On the taxi ride back to the hotel, I'd wondered aloud what it meant. What could be worse than ending a life? "You'll have to ask Clare," Levi quipped, when I'd asked him. My frustrated sigh had forced a second answer. "It's easy to say there are worse things when you're the one doing the ending."

I wrapped myself in a plush Westin St. Francis bath towel and faced the steamed mirror. A swipe of my hand, and there I was. Samantha Bronwyn. This time, I studied my face. Catalogued my parts. Long, honey-colored hair. Wet. I ran my comb through it, letting the drops waterfall down my chest. Eyes so blue my mother said the sky lived inside of me. Freckles on either side of my nose that darkened in the summer like cinnamon sprinkles. Yep, me alright. I felt so changed, I expected a stranger. Maybe it was the gun on the counter—another peace offering from Levi. For a cop, he'd been quick to surrender his service weapon.

I slipped on jeans and a tank top and sat on the edge of the tub. All I could think of was my mother. By my calculations, she'd be arriving in about four hours on the first plane from AUS to SFO. But I was stuck on something else. How annoyed I'd get every time she sent me searching through her ancient set of encyclopedias, when we had the whole world at our fingertips. *Why do cows have so many stomachs? Where do rainbows come from? How do fireflies glow?* Now I understood the reason she'd made me dig through those relics. When the information you needed could change everything, uproot the entire life you carefully planted, you didn't want it to come with the push of a button. You wanted to have to work for it.

I typed *Clare Keely, psychologist* into the search bar. There wasn't much, just a letter dated January 17, 1997, and addressed to the California Board of Psychology.

> *Dear Members of the Board:*
>
> *Please be advised I have decided to permanently surrender my license to practice psychology in the state of California. This decision has been prompted by the investigation of my license by the Board. By virtue of this letter, I understand that I may not render psychological services to any individual in any capacity in California. I agree that I may not rescind this letter, and the effect of this letter is permanent ...*

So Levi told the truth. Clare Keely was a psychologist—but obviously not my mother. My mom never even cracked a self-help book. And she'd scoff with unbridled enthusiasm any time Dr. Phil came on.

There was one more name that demanded searching. I wish I could've opened volume B for Beckett and leafed through the pristine pages until I found what needed finding. Instead, I typed.

****

As quiet as a mouse, I opened the door and padded out into the bedroom. The television chattered at a low volume. Levi lay on the bed, on top of the covers, remote in hand, fast asleep. He'd changed clothes since I'd been in the bathroom. His jeans were folded over the top of the desk chair, his boots side by side beneath it. Something about his hair mussed to one side and his feet in white ankle socks made him seem a lot less mysterious. Boyish, even. On his right shin, two bruises. My handiwork. A little further up, a sliver of olive skin between his T-shirt and his shorts. *Pathetic, Sam. You're turning into Ginny.*

"Levi?" Last chance to stop me. His lack of response indicated tacit agreement.

In the light of the early morning, his backpack looked different too. Ordinary. Just like the ones slung over the shoulders of most of Bellwether High. I opened it.

Zip ties.

Four T-shirts, size XL. Two with the APD logo. Austin Police Department, just like he told me.

Five pairs of boxer jocks. Brand: Under Armour.

The silver-and-gold police badge he'd shown me to prove himself. Apparently, he'd earned it just a few months ago after completing the academy.

Toothbrush, toothpaste, deodorant, a razor, shaving cream. *Where was it?* And by *it*, I meant anything incriminating. Anything to explain what I'd read.

Okay, now we're getting somewhere. A pocket stun gun. Ginny's mom had given her one just like it to carry in her purse.

A bottle of Xanax. Prescribed to Kate Beckett. My mother had the same white bottle in her sock drawer for years. I'd discovered it once by accident. And every time I'd snoop, it was still there. Still full. Just like this one.

A book. A journal? A logbook? Thick with notes and newspaper clippings. When I opened it, a photograph—yellow with age—fluttered to the ground like a dead leaf. I picked it up and examined it.

68

Three people. A mom. A dad. And a little boy, who looked a lot like a toddler version of the one in my hotel bed.

"Find what you were looking for?" Levi snapped, snatching the picture, then the book, from my hand before I could explain myself.

"You must think I'm really naïve. Oh wait—*inexperienced*. That was your word, right? A real inexperienced, small-town hick."

"So that gives you permission to rifle through my stuff?" Levi slipped the photo back between the pages, shut the book with authority, and returned it to his backpack. He sat on the bed, head in his hands, brooding.

"Why didn't you tell me the truth?" I demanded.

"What are you talking about?"

"Really, Levi? You want me to say it? Fine. I googled you. You're on administrative leave. For bribery. You're not even supposed to have a badge anymore, are you?"

"So Google knows everything now?"

"Are you denying it?"

"No. It's true. But it doesn't really tell you anything, does it? What if I said I googled you? I looked at your Facebook page. Your Insta-whatever."

"Gram." A half-smiled slipped through. Still, I felt irked with myself for hoping he'd been that curious about me. "Dork."

"I learned a lot about Samantha Bronwyn. Superstar athlete. Smart, but not too smart. Basketball scholarship to Baylor in the fall. Part-time job at Clare's Couture—small-town nepotism at its finest. Single. Slutty best friend." I kept quiet, denying him his reaction. "Arrested for minor in possession of alcohol at age sixteen. Charges dismissed." *How did he know that?*

"That's not on Facebook." I narrowed my eyes at him until I vaguely remembered Ginny's drunken post about our lucky jailbreak. Which was really my mom's doing—the sheriff had a little thing for her. Like a lot of men in Bellwether. Not that she ever expressed interest. *Your father was the only man for me*, she'd said once when I pried. "Never mind. Don't change the subject. We're talking about you here."

"My point is—"

"I get your point, Officer Beckett. But you have some serious explaining to do."

He raised his hands in surrender. "Alright. Can we order breakfast first? My lips get a lot looser with a short stack of pancakes in me. I'm guessing you already know that though, since you googled me."

****

Levi and pancakes. Pancakes and Levi. I tried to stay mad, but the sight of him stuffing one mountainous bite after the other—whipped cream, syrup, strawberries, the works—it made for a losing battle. I nibbled on a slice of toast, but everything tasted wrong. Like the sour stench of Skinny's mouth had seeped into my tongue.

"Ready to talk now," he announced, wiping the final smear of whipped cream from his lips. "And for the record, I didn't lie. I just omitted unnecessary information."

"I'll be sure to enter that into the record, Officer. Off the record, it's the same as lying. And I'll be the judge of what's unnecessary."

"Duly noted." He muted the television, propped a pillow behind his back, and fluffed the other one for me, patting the spot next to him. "Let's start over. My name is Levi Beckett. I'm twenty-one years old, and I'm a rookie police officer in Austin, Texas. I was recently placed on administrative leave for offering another officer a bribe—my first month's salary to be exact—to keep my sister out of jail. I'm supposed to turn in my badge and service weapon on Monday. What else would you like to know?"

"Better," I said, sitting at the foot of the bed opposite him. I pulled the pillow onto my lap. "Nice to meet you, Levi. I have a few questions."

"Hit me."

"Why is your sister in jail?"

"Short answer: burglary and drug possession." I frowned at him.

"Okay, long answer it is. We bounced around a lot as kids and got into trouble. I went to the Junior Police Academy. She went to juvie, and she's been in and out ever since."

I laughed. "Junior officer, huh?" In front of his wide grin, he raised his middle finger.

"Alright. Why are you here? And why did you follow me?"

"I told you. I can't resist a damsel—"

"There's a stun gun in your backpack, so you can spare me the Prince Charming routine, Flynn." I held up my cell phone. Austin Police Department, my newly entered contact, on the screen. "You have five seconds to tell me the truth—the whole truth—or I'm calling your bosses. I'm pretty sure they'd want to know about your little zip-tie arrest last night. It wasn't exactly by the book."

Levi's smile dampened. He ran his hand through his hair. "Don't freak out, okay?" I nodded, but that meant nothing. Inside, my freaking out was well underway. "I think Ginny is in big trouble. Really big. But so are you. I—" Levi's mouth hung open, as if I'd pressed pause. Then, he grabbed the remote and turned up the volume. I spun around just in time to see the image that stonewalled him. The mustached face of a middle-aged man. Not a frat boy. Not even close. Under him, a caption: Murdered SFO employee identified as 41-year-old Marco Guzman.

Police have identified the body discovered yesterday at the Candlestick demolition site as that of SFO employee Marco Guzman. Guzman was employed by SFO since 2014, as a member of the custodial staff. He was last seen by airport staff early yesterday evening but did not complete his shift. Police have not disclosed the manner in which Guzman was killed, but have indicated escaped-prisoner Clive Cullen is a person of interest. Cullen may be driving Guzman's black Chevrolet Silverado, which has been reported stolen. Investigators suspect Cullen replaced or removed the license plate to avoid detection. SFPD are asking anyone with information about Guzman's death to contact police headquarters immediately.

"Holy shit, I was right." I heard Levi, but his voice sounded strange, far away. Like we were playing telephone with tin cans.

Ginny and I tried that once when we were bored … and a little tipsy. Levi pulled off his gym shorts—Under Armour, I muttered—and tugged on his jeans and boots. "Sam? Sam? Samantha!"

"What?"

"Did you hear me?"

"Um, I think so. You said you were right."

His hand squeezed my shoulder. It was the only thing I could feel. "I said a few other sentences too."

"A few other sentences? Oh. Sorry."

"Whoever took Ginny made a mistake."

"A mistake?" I kept repeating things, but I couldn't stop.

Levi's head nodded fast—so fast it seemed disconnected, unattached—and I almost laughed. "I think he meant to take you."

"He?" *You're doing it again, Sam.*

"Cullen."

OCTOBER 10, 1996

SINCE her run-in with Ramirez, Clare avoided the yard whenever she could. Leave it to Fitzpatrick to assign her an errand that sent her directly through it. Messing with her probably. Pushing her to the limit just because he could. Watching her squirm. But Clare, clever girl, had a trick. She fixed her eyes on her destination—the hunk of concrete that was West Block—and silently sang the song she'd heard on the radio that morning. *Hey, Macarena.* It was one of those awful-but-catchy tunes that stuck like a burr. When she was thirteen, Mr. Taylor's hand between her thighs, Olivia Newton John or Rick Springfield had always gotten her through it.

"All want me ... can't have me ... come ... dance beside me." Clare hummed a little, sang a little, chuckling at the irony of the lyrics. It was a private joke, a private *screw you.* Sort of like the times she'd channeled Olivia Newton John's "Let's Get Physical." Mr. Taylor's voice, dripping with lust, faded to background noise. Instead, Olivia's husky crooning. Clare's therapist called it disassociation. Fine, if you wanted to be technical about it. Clare preferred to think of it as an essential distraction. Survival. If her mind went somewhere else, refused to participate, it didn't really count, did it?

Halfway to West Block and almost to the chorus, Robocop flagged her down. With his signature glasses perched atop his head, he was barely recognizable. Chestnut brown and flecked with green, his eyes softened him, smudged his edges a little. Clare considered commenting, but thought better of it. *Don't encourage him.*

"How are you, Dr. Keely? It's been a while."

She nodded. "A few weeks. I'm steering clear of the yard for a while."

"That's what I wanted to talk to you about. Did you hear about Ramirez?" He barely paused for a response, like he couldn't wait to tell her. "His transfer didn't go through. He's getting out of Ad Seg next week. I figured you'd want to know."

Clare's rage hovered close to the surface. It only took a flick—the strike of a match—to ignite. But she couldn't let Robocop see it. It would scare him, or worse, he'd draw in like a moth to her flame. "Is there someone I can talk to about this?"

****

Clare knocked and knocked again. But Lieutenant Bonner didn't look up from his Grisham novel, so she let herself into the half-opened door. She offered the most genuine fake smile she could muster—then, a flip of her hair. Clare wasn't above using her powers for her own benefit. Sometimes her curse could be a blessing.

"Can I help you?" He kept one pudgy hand inside the book to hold his page. The other fondled the ends of his mustache.

"I'm Clare—uh, Doctor—"

"I know who you are. You testified at Arturo Ramirez's disciplinary hearing last week." He sounded utterly unimpressed.

"Right. That's me. I actually just heard he might not be transferred, and I wondered if you could tell me why." The lieutenant smirked at her the way some men did, like a cute, harmless, little thing—a toy poodle, barking at the passing cars from the window.

"We had some concerns about your credibility, Ms. Keely." *Doctor, you prick.* "After all, Clive Cullen is your therapy patient, is he not?"

"I'm not sure what that has to do with my credibility."

"You portrayed him in quite a positive light. I, for one, just don't buy he wasn't the instigator. Need I remind you, his nickname is Cutthroat."

74

"There were other witnesses. I'm sure their statements matched mine."

"Glad you brought that up. There were two inmates sitting at the picnic table, and they didn't hear Ramirez say anything to you, much less anything of a sexually explicit nature. Perhaps you misheard him." The lieutenant opened his book, a not-so-subtle hint. "Besides, I've been told Cullen's got a way with the ladies. You wouldn't be the first to take his side."

Beneath Clare's surface, that flame was licking higher and higher, coloring her neck a vibrant red. "I know what I heard."

"Ms. Keely, if I may offer a piece of advice." She felt his eyes laser focused on her chest, sights on the low point of her V-neck sweater. "Young women do best in this environment when they tone down their appearance. A little less makeup. A little higher neckline. Draw a bit less attention to yourself if you want to be taken seriously."

"It's *Doctor* Keely." It was the only thing she had left to cling to, her last shred of dignity.

"Now, if you don't mind, Doctor. I've got a runaway jury to attend to."

OCTOBER 15, 1996

CLARE arrived early that morning, her head still spinning from Cullen's sixth session the day before, Manic Monday. That's what she called it now. She'd hardly slept—three hours at most—but she wasn't tired. Her whole body awake, nerves buzzing like she'd downed a shot of espresso. Usually she slogged through a three-mile run before breakfast. Today, she'd done five at an all-out sprint.

She ignored the red eye of the answering machine, blinking since last night. Lizzie probably wanted to meet up for coffee, but she couldn't fake it with Lizzie. *Is Lisa's stepdad into you? What a perv!* Lizzie had whispered to Clare post-slumber party when they'd woken first, surrounded by a tangle of girls in sleeping bags. Lizzie wasn't like most people—Clare's mother, for starters—trudging through life, eyes closed. Lizzie paid attention. And when she'd ask about Cullen, which was a given, Clare wouldn't say the words *business as usual.* Because Lizzie would counter *bullshit.*

Clare couldn't explain it but chapter five in her Humanistic Psychology textbook—*Maslow*, circa 1960—came close, describing the peak experience as rare, deeply moving, exhilarating, and oceanic, generating an advanced perception of reality. *Oceanic.* She'd written that down. That's how it felt when a client had a breakthrough. But not just any client. *Him.* And she didn't know why.

There had been others. The heroin addict who shot up so many times he'd nearly lost his arm. The rebel-without-a-cause teen who took out an entire family with one drunken ride. And now, Cutthroat. Serial murderer. Serial seducer. Incubus. Whatever he was, Clare held her breath and dove down deep, not coming up until she reached the bottom. *Oceanic.* But she knew what Lizzie would say. What Neal would say. Her therapist. Her mother, if she cared enough to ask, which she didn't. Not then. Not now. Not even a *Why is Mr. Taylor picking you up on a school night again?*

Breathe, Clare. Breathe. Focus. She sprinted up the concrete staircase to her office, hoping the effort would still her mind. It had come unlooped, unloosed like a spool of thread. She had to reel it in before her session with Dumas at 9 a.m. Cullen wasn't the only one making breakthroughs. Dumas was off suicide watch and had endured their last session—a whole fifty minutes—without getting glassy-eyed. Definite progress.

Clare's mind paused. Suddenly. Finally. Her door was slightly ajar. She felt certain she'd closed it, locked it. But Manic Monday had a way of leaving things undone. *Her,* for instance. Especially yesterday, the way Cullen saved his best for last. One foot out this very door, but doling insights like breadcrumbs she wanted to follow and gobble.

"I'm beginning to understand why," he'd told her, while putting on his jacket and preparing to leave. It was still wet from the rain, and she'd watched the drops puddle on the floor.

"Why what?" she'd asked, barely able to contain her excitement.

"Why I killed her." Pointing to the clock hanging above her head, he'd added, "Guess I'll save it for next time." Clare had nodded against everything in her being.

But she couldn't get it out of her mind. Cullen's *why* seemed like the un-gettable get.

She sighed—maybe she had left the door open after all. Fitzpatrick wouldn't be happy with her if anything came up missing. *You're responsible for your belongings*, he'd ranted on her first day. *Whatever you bring in here, lock it up, or be sure to bring it out with you. Pens, umbrellas, glasses. Hell, even your goddamn lipstick. MacGyver's got nothing on these guys. They can make a shank from a paper clip.*

A quick scan of the room, and everything seemed intact. Relieved, she tossed her purse on her desk, and that's when she saw it. A note. Typed and addressed to her. Before she picked it up, she wrestled with the thought—*hope?*—that it came from Cullen. And with that, a thousand questions, but only one that mattered. What would she do with it? She whispered the first line aloud. Then she went silent and still, like she always did. Hiding like a bunny in the tall grass, Mr. Taylor's voice in her head, though she'd called him Rodney by then. *Just relax and let it happen, Clarie. You want this. You like this.*

Dear Dr. Keely,
 Consider this a warning. Mind your own business or we'll mind it for you. We wouldn't want to have to carve up your pretty face. Your boyfriend wouldn't like that. Tell him we promise not to be greedy. We'll leave your neck for him.
 Sincerely,
 Your friends

Clare glanced over her shoulder, half-expecting Fitzpatrick to be there. Or Ramirez. *Gotcha*, he would say with a jack-o-lantern grin, locking the door behind him. But there was no one. She balled up the note in her fist and stuffed it deep in the pocket of her khaki trench. She wanted to burn it. *Boyfriend.* That word stuck to her. Worse than all the other words, as ugly as they were. She knew what it meant— *who*—it wasn't even a question. This was the kind of thing that happened when you were cursed. *I haven't done anything wrong.* She'd said that before. At her postdoc. After her divorced, father-of-two client had sent her roses. *I didn't treat him any differently. No, I didn't encourage him.* Nobody bought it. And they certainly wouldn't buy it here. From the mouth of Lieutenant Bonner, she was too pretty to be believed.

And she had no one to blame but herself. Clare ran through the list—all the shouldn't haves. I shouldn't have talked to Cullen that day on the yard. I shouldn't have written a report on Ramirez. I shouldn't have complained to the lieutenant. And worst of all, I shouldn't have told anybody what happened, much less Cullen.

78

Clare had known it was wrong, even as she'd said it. But she'd ruminated about it all weekend, how she could tell him first thing, before they started their session. *You know, they decided not to transfer Mr. Ramirez.* Robocop warned her Cullen might be in danger from the EME with Ramirez returning to the main line. It seemed only fair he know. But if she was honest with herself, she wanted an ally, a partner in outrage. It was an offering, and he'd given something in return. Something big. That hint of a why.

She zipped her coat pocket, making sure the note stayed safely buried inside. *You asked for this, Clare.* That was Mr. Taylor's go-to line, and the rightness of it, the trueness, burned. He always followed it up with another classic, *Does your mother know what a bad girl you are?*

"You're here early this morning, Dr. Keely." Clare jumped at the sound of Fitzpatrick's voice as he passed her doorway.

"Early bird catches the worm," she called out, hoping to sound cheerful.

"Indeed. But that begs the question. Are you the bird or the worm?"

****

Clare was back where she wasn't supposed to be. Where she promised herself she wouldn't go again. But that note had her off-kilter, spinning like a crooked top. And she needed to right herself. As sick as it was, as much as it hurt, this place grounded her. Like pushing on a bruise to feel the ache, the pain anchored her.

She didn't plan to end up here. It just happened, like so many times before. After work, she hurried back to her car, desperate to be alone. She waited until she passed through the gate—flashing her ID and a perfunctory smile at the guard—before she slipped the crumpled note from her pocket and placed it on the seat beside her, a watchful companion. Together, they drove.

Clare's mind traveled to the usual places, a well-worn route. Stop number one, the backseat of Mr. Taylor's BMW. Not the first time, not the last. *This is what you do to me, Clare.* He picked up her hand by the wrist, where she wore a coil of friendship bracelets, and placed it on his crotch. His need for her was so real, so urgent, so literal, Clare felt sorry for him. A man could never hide his desire. It was a separate thing—alive—with demands of its own. *This is what you wanted.*

Stop number two, Neal's bedroom. The first time. *Are you okay? Did I hurt you?* He cupped her face so tenderly, Clare forced herself to look at him. No one had ever asked her before, not that way. Like he cared about the answer. *I shouldn't have told him,* Clare thought, his pity obvious in the frown lines on his forehead. It disgusted her. She had to make it go away, and she knew how. God, did she know. She slipped her hand under the covers and found his desire.

Stop number three, a new detour. *You know, they decided not to transfer Mr. Ramirez.* There, she said it. No turning back now. Cullen didn't react the way she expected. He didn't react at all. She considered repeating herself. Clearly, he didn't hear her. She pretended to straighten the pencils, lining them side by side. *Can I trust you, Dr. Keely?* The kind of question—simple, but momentous—that felt like it asked something else entirely. Something more. But there wasn't time to answer. *Fuck Ramirez. I'm so sorry he dragged you into this. It's me they're after. I won't be their little puppet, and they don't like that.* A stark contrast to his words, his voice was low and soothing, practically a lullaby. She saw his hand reach out and graze her sleeve. But her arm played dead on her desk, and she said nothing. She didn't want him to stop talking. *I'll watch out for you. I'll never let them hurt you, Dr. Keely Clare*

Just like that, she missed her exit. So she kept driving. 580 West, 101 South, CA-1 South, Panoramic Highway, past the stone wall with the sign, Muir Woods National Monument. By then, she knew exactly where she was going, even if she wouldn't admit it to herself. She pulled off the road into the narrow ditch and listened to her heart beat as fierce and frenetic as it had at sixteen when she marked this place forever. It was nearly dark and darker here, where the trees grew taller than any she'd ever seen. Ancient and wise, they were the only witnesses. She walked three hundred paces into the forest—she'd counted many times—to the spot where the redwood's roots tangled themselves like lovers. Nestled there among the ferns was a single stone she'd carried herself. She knelt down and laid her hand to rest on it. It felt cold to the touch.

OCTOBER 21, 1996

CLARE acted all business, waving Cullen into her office. *Get your shit together, Keely.* And that's exactly what she planned to do. That morning, she selected the most matronly outfit in her closet. A black turtleneck and loose black trousers. Flats. No makeup and a tight ponytail. Whatever Cullen thought, he better unthink it. Now.

"Good morning, Mr. Cullen." Not a hint of emotion, exactly as she intended. Her practice in the mirror paid off. "Have a seat."

He responded with an aw-shucks grin. "Morning, Doc."

"I need to talk to you about something important. It's called transference." She paused to let the word settle. Inexplicably, Cullen seemed ready for this. "Our relationship is like a mirror. The way you relate to me as your therapist might be similar to the ways you relate to other people, other women in your life. It's totally normal for clients to develop feelings—"

"Erotic transference, right?"

"That's right."

Cullen buried his head between his hands, then peeked through his fingers at her. "Man, I feel like a jackass. You must think I'm a total nutcase."

"No, of course not. This happens all the time."

An ironic laugh escaped his mouth. "I'll bet. So I'm just one of the many loons to fall for you."

"It's not like that. I'm hoping we can talk about what you're experiencing. The feelings you're having. Last week, you said you wanted to watch out for me. Maybe our relationship, me, reminds you of something … or someone."

He nodded. "Emily. You remind me of her." A shiver—part excitement, part fear—tickled the fine blonde hair on the back of Clare's neck.

"How so?"

Cullen licked his lips. It seemed more nervous than seductive. But Clare felt seduced. *Sexualizing him again*, she wrote in her note-book. "May I speak frankly?" he asked.

"Please."

"I find you extremely attractive. I'm sure you already know you're stunning. Outwardly, that is. But, you get me. You understand me like no one ever has. And that makes me want you."

Clare blushed. Her body revolted her, the way it responded to him. To men. The way it betrayed her. "Did Emily understand you?"

"Yes and no."

Clare was on the verge of the *why*, and she knew it. She treaded carefully, lightly, so not to spook him. "Tell me more."

"I thought Emily loved me. She understood certain things about me. She knew every button and how to push them—but she used that against me. That's not love. And she thought I would let her get away with it. That's what she didn't understand. I couldn't."

"Couldn't or wouldn't?"

"Is there a difference?"

"So you killed her?" She said it perfectly, without a hint of judgment.

Cullen's gaze met hers, and he didn't look away. "There are worse things than murder, Dr. Keely." The blueness of his normally slate-gray eyes unnerved her. They seemed unreal, painted like marbles. All seeing. All knowing. Though there was no way he could know. Not *that*. No one did. Not her mother—*as if*. Not Lizzie. Not Neal. Or her therapist. Not even the priest her mother made her confess to every single Easter Sunday.

"Worse?" she wondered aloud. "What could be worse than that?"

Cullen spoke without pause. "Betrayal. Humiliation. Dishonesty. Degradation."

"Hmm ... " She pretended to mull it over, but there was no uncertainty. He was right. Worse things? Absolutely. She could think of one, and she did. All the time. Mr. Taylor rubbing his hand against her pink panties, finding his way inside. *You like this, don't you? Don't you, Clarie?* Her answer: *I guess so.* Because she didn't, but she did. And that was worse, far worse, than murder.

CLARE paged through Dumas' file again. Searching for something. Anything that would explain how he'd ended up here. No prior criminal history, serving twenty-five to life. She prodded. She coaxed. She channeled Sigmund Freud—*tell me about your dreams*. Then Carl Rogers—*what would you like to talk about today?* Dumas was like a brick wall. Whatever secrets he kept were as closely guarded as her own. As much as she could respect that, she was determined to tear down that wall, brick by stubborn brick. And she would start today.

On 11/23/95, Officer Machado responded to Bellingham Jewels in the 900 block of Raven Avenue in San Francisco at 2 p.m., after receiving a 911 call with a report of shots fired inside. Distal Security Company also contacted police, after the store's silent alarm system was triggered. Upon arrival at the scene, Officer Machado made contact with suspect James Dumas. He stood outside the store with his hands raised. A Glock 9mm handgun was located on the sidewalk in front of him.

Store personnel reported Mr. Dumas and an unidentified accomplice entered the establishment shortly before 2 p.m. Both were armed and wore masks. Mr. Dumas, later identified on the store's surveillance cameras, ordered the two customers present to lie down on the floor. He then approached the cashier, Jennifer Stewart, and demanded she place all their cash inside several large envelopes he provided. As Ms. Stewart retrieved the cash, store patron Thomas Aikens entered the front door. The unidentified accomplice fired a shot striking Mr. Aikens in his chest. The accomplice fled the scene on foot and has not been apprehended as of this report.

Mr. Aikens was transported to the hospital, where he was pronounced dead later that evening. Mr. Dumas invoked his fifth-amendment rights and was placed under arrest and transported to the Alameda County Jail, where he was charged with first-degree robbery and murder.

Dumas' accomplice was never caught, and he refused to talk to police about his motives. But one of the witnesses described the accomplice's voice as high-pitched and feminine, when a cry of surprise escaped from beneath the mask after the gun discharged. Clare had a theory—the woman in the photo, his wife, fired an accidental shot. Unconfirmed, of course, and Dumas seemed dead set on keeping it that way.

He knocked on the door. The privacy glass warped his face, but she knew him by his tall, thin silhouette.

"Come in."

He ducked his head under the frame and arranged himself in the chair opposite Clare. Electric green eyes brightened his dreary face, but he couldn't hide those dark circles. It seemed he hadn't been sleeping again. "Hiya, Doc."

"How have you been?" she asked. "You look a little tired."

"My cellie keeps me up with his snoring. If it wasn't for him, I'd sleep like a baby." His sarcasm was evident in the twist of his mouth.

"I'll bet. So what's on your mind today?" The non-directive approach usually got her nowhere, but nowhere was as far as she'd gotten with anything else. Like last week, when she'd asked him to pretend his father sat in an empty chair in front of him.

What would he say to you? He laughed at her. *Would he be sitting in it playing poker?* Yes. *Sitting in it talking to me like you're doing?* Never.

"There is something I'd like to share since you're such a kind audience." Clare felt hopeful. Maybe she had finally cracked her hard-boiled egg.

"My wife came up for a family visit this weekend. First one in a couple months. She told me she's pregnant." Clare raised her eyebrows. "Before you start thinking anything squirrely, it's mine. Guess it happened last time she visited."

"How do you feel about that?"

He shrugged. "Good. And not so good. Kinda like most things in here, it's bittersweet."

"You told me you already have a son, right?"

"Yep. He's two. I suppose he'll be the man of the house now, what with me gone and all."

"What does your wife think about your being in prison? About your crime?" It was the closest she'd come to revealing her theory.

"We don't talk about it. *I* don't talk about it." He folded his arms across his chest, and they sat in stony silence. Clare refused to speak first. *Be comfortable with silence*, Fitzpatrick had told her. One of his few useful pointers. She was relieved when Dumas' face softened. "But she's excited for the baby. She thinks it's a girl."

Suddenly, Neal's voice was in her head, co-opting Lizzie's nickname—*Clare-Bear, you'd be a great mom. You want to have kids, right? Two or three at least?* She had to keep talking to force him out. "How can she tell the gender already?"

Dumas' wide grin made it painfully obvious. It was the first time he'd smiled since he walked in the office. "Cravings for ice cream, apparently."

"What else makes you smile, Mr. Dumas?"

"That's a funny question."

"Well, I'm a funny gal."

"Alright. I'll bite. Do you have a quarter?"

Clare dug inside her pocket and produced a coin. "As long as I get it back." Money was contraband here. Like a lot of other ordinary things. Blue jeans, aerosol cans, cameras. Fitzpatrick had given her a list.

Dumas nodded, accepting the coin. "I'm going to use my magical powers of telekinesis to move your quarter from one hand to the other." He deposited it in his closed right fist and waved his hands in the air. Clare laughed. "Now, where is the coin, Dr. Keely?" She pointed to his right. Nothing. He uncurled his left fist, where the quarter rested on his palm. "It's magic."

"Impressive. So magic makes you smile?"

"It used to. Growing up, the other boys worshipped Willie Mays, Muhammad Ali. You know who I idolized? Harry Houdini." He chuckled to himself. "But then I learned a little sleight of hand, and I realized something. Once you know the trick, it's not magic anymore. It becomes mundane, ordinary. Life is like that too. The more you know, the more you see—and then there's a lot less magic to hold on to." Clare felt his words like a lit match to her chest. "I don't reckon you've been around the block enough to know what I mean."

She shrugged. "Is that why you won't open up? You don't think I'm old enough to understand what you're going through?"

"It's not a matter of old enough. I just can't imagine you've walked through the kind of fire most of us screw-ups have."

If you only knew. I'm a world-class screw-up, Clare thought. "Well, you can't judge a book by its cover. Or a therapist."

He spun the quarter on the table and watched it turn until it lay flat in front of her. "I'll keep that in mind."

****

After Dumas left, Clare ate an early lunch at her desk. A tuna-salad sandwich she'd packed from home. It was easier than avoiding Fitzpatrick at the snack shop, just inside the gates. He always sat at her table. Between bird bites of a chef salad, he'd attempt small talk while the other new hires watched with obvious contempt. It was more than she could bear. Besides, she was better at being alone. That's the line she gave Neal when he proposed to her last summer, slipping that ruby ring on her finger—the one she was fairly certain

88

was a real ruby despite the lie she'd told to make herself feel better. The band was engraved with their initials. Neal down on one knee, with those puppy-dog eyes, she'd almost said yes. But he wanted the white-picket fence. The happily ever after. And Clare had no doubt that part of herself, if it ever existed at all, lay buried under a rock in Muir Woods. *Let's just see what happens. Maybe you'll change your mind.* Neal, ever the optimist.

She penned Dumas' notes—the usual mumbo jumbo—and paged through the files for her afternoon clients, when the telephone rang. *Fitzpatrick.* Clare knew without answering it. He was the only one who ever called, and the shrill sound made her nerves hum.

"Hello, this is Dr. Keely."

"Could I see you in my office, please? Right away."

She couldn't disguise her dread. "Coming."

Fitzpatrick sat at his desk, piles of paperwork on either side. The piles were a permanent fixture. Never smaller nor larger than the last time she'd sat across from him. Clare wondered if he arranged them there to make himself seem busy. He gestured to the chair without smiling. Clare knew something bad was coming.

"Dr. Keely, we have a situation." It sounded as if he'd been waiting his whole life to say that. *He probably practices too*, Clare thought, disgusted they might have something in common. "Lieutenant Bonner advised me of some graffiti bearing your name." As Clare tried to steady her breathing, he pushed a photograph toward her. "This was discovered yesterday evening in Mr. Cullen's cell after he returned from the yard. The Lieutenant suspects the EME is responsible. We thought you should know."

Clare didn't want to look, but she had to. Like the first time Mr. Taylor unzipped his pants. *I'll show you what a man looks like, baby. I'll teach you what a man needs.* It was three days after her fourteenth birthday. He'd been working up to it—the big reveal—for a while. Mostly touching her, kissing her sometimes, bringing her silly little presents. Grooming, that's what her therapist called it. Her shame was all-consuming, the fire she walked through. The inferno. Mr. Dumas had no clue.

She held the photograph up to her face to show Fitzpatrick she wasn't afraid. A rudimentary drawing scratched into the wall with something sharp. Two stick figures, labeled. One with round circles for breasts. That was her, apparently. *Dr. Clare Whore.* Next to her, Cullen. *Punk Bitch Clive.* Above them, in large capital letters, DIE.

"I'm sorry," he said. "I know it's hard to look at."

"Why do they think it was the EME?"

Fitzpatrick seemed surprised at her question. "Cullen hasn't told you … in your sessions?" Clare remembered Cullen's hand on her forearm, his reassurances. But she didn't answer. She already felt supremely stupid. "He's had a beef with the EME for some time. They tried to pressure him to join the AB."

"AB?"

"Aryan Brotherhood. The white supremacist gang that has an alliance with the EME. They should've covered that in your training."

"I remember now. But what does that have to do with me?" Her bewilderment, a deliberate fabrication. The vile note from last week had met its end in her garbage disposal.

Fitzpatrick smiled without showing his teeth, the way he always did before he planned to say something inappropriate. "Good question. I was going to ask you that. It seems they believe Mr. Cullen is fond of you. Perhaps in a romantic way, a sexual way."

"A sexual way? What is that supposed to mean?"

"Dr. Keely, you can't deny this drawing is overtly sexual." He tapped his finger on the crudely drawn breasts. "Now, I'm not saying you've done anything wrong, but perhaps we should reassign Mr. Cullen to another clinician. A male."

"I shouldn't be penalized for the way an inmate depicts me in a drawing. And neither should Mr. Cullen. He's making real progress. You're welcome to take a look at my session notes if you'd like."

"I already have." Clare had the thought again. *If only I could blow your brains out.* It hit her like a wave, disoriented her. She wondered if Neal had been right that this kind of work would change her. *They're sick men,* he'd said. *Monsters.* And now she was thinking like one of them. "I found nothing of concern," Fitzpatrick admitted.

"Then … " *Screw off.* That's what she wanted to say. "I'm not sure what else I can do. But I'll address this with Cullen in our next session."

"Very well." Clare was partway out the door when Fitzpatrick called her back. "I know these incidents can be overwhelming, especially for a young therapist. If you ever want to grab dinner to talk off the record, my offer still stands. It's my treat."

"I'll let you know," Clare called out, glad Fitzpatrick couldn't see her face. Inside the safety of her office, she locked the door behind her and opened her notebook. She flipped to yesterday's date, where she'd written:

Sexualizing him again. Maybe he reminds me of R. T.??? But I feel safe with him, pulled to tell him things about me, to show him I understand him.

She scrounged through her desk until she found a fat black marker, then obliterated the lines. It felt necessary to make them disappear even though she'd already decided. From now on, Fitzpatrick's sanitized session notes would be the only record Clare kept.

CHAPTER TEN
LA HIJA DE PUTA

CULLEN?" There I went again, parroting Levi. "Why would Cutthroat Cullen be after me?" The sheer ridiculousness of his suggestion brought me back to my senses. I walked over to the dresser, where I'd left my wallet, and plucked out Officer Guthrey's card.

"I already told you," Levi said, haphazardly stuffing his things inside his backpack. "But you don't believe me."

"Don't say this is about my mother. That lady, Clare Keely, I looked her up. She is *not* my mom. No way. And where are you going? We have to call the police and tell them about Marco and Ginny." He raised his eyebrows at me. "The not-on-administrative-leave police."

"If you want to see Ginny alive again—that is, if Cullen hasn't killed her already—I wouldn't recommend that."

Levi, as handsome as he was, was obviously delusional. Ginny always said the hot ones had issues. *Nature's way of evening things out,* she'd teased. "Then what would you recommend, Officer?"

"Let me handle it." I felt his eyes on me as I typed the phone number, 4-1-5. "Nobody knows Cullen like I do."

"What the heck is that supposed to mean? You sound crazy, you know?" 7-9-3. A hollow knocking on the door stopped my fingers and my heart. "What time is it?" I demanded. "8:30? Crap! She's early!" I tossed the phone on the bed and grabbed Levi by the arm. "Go in the bathroom."

"And *I* sound crazy?"

"It's my mom, okay? She'll have a coronary if she sees you in here. Just give me a second to get rid of her and then you can sneak out the front." Ignoring my instructions, Levi walked toward the door and peered through the peephole. He cursed under his breath.

"Told you," I chided. "Now seriously, get in—"

He held up his hand to silence me. "It's not your mom." Joking, pancake-gobbling Levi disappeared. This Levi turned full-on police-man. "Get my gun. Now." Somehow, my legs wobbled to the bath-room, where I'd left the gun on the counter with my makeup, and back again. More knocking. Insistent, this time. Then a voice. A snarl. More animal than human.

"Room service." I stood next to Levi, squinting my eyes to watch the action flick unfolding outside my hotel room. Five men stared back at me. The one nearest had oil-slick hair pulled into a tight po-nytail. A large tattoo looped around the front of his neck, the letters EME. Beneath my palm, the door felt paper thin, and I felt certain he could hear my heart beating.

"What the fuck, Garcia?" He bludgeoned the door with his fist, and I stumbled back. "I thought you said she was in here."

"She's in there," another man replied. "Aren't you, niñita. La hija de puta. Probably right on the other side listening. El lobo feroz está aquí." Two years of Spanish taught me enough to be horrified. El lobo feroz. *The big bad wolf.*

"Sam, help me move the dresser." Levi set the TV on the floor and positioned himself on the other end of the drawers, giving them a shove toward me.

"Who are those guys?" I whispered as we pushed the dresser flush against the door. My hands shaking, his steady. "Do you know them?"

"I'm pretty sure they're here for you." Levi secured his backpack and tugged me toward the privacy door for the adjoining room. "La hija de puta. Do you know what that means?"

"Uh … daughter … something?"

"Whore's daughter," he said. "And they look like Mexican Mafia. EME. It's a gang."

Levi was completely insane. Certifiable. The Mexican Mafia—any Mafia for that matter—did not belong in the same sentence with Samantha Bronwyn. Not the same paragraph, not the same chapter, not even the same book. And he was talking about my mother again. Like she had something to do with this. *Bonkers*, as Ginny would say. I opened my mouth to tell him but—a scream and a gunshot!—no words came out. Then the sound of heavy black boots—that's how I imagined them—beating against the front door like oversized paws.

"They're coming in," Levi told me. "We need to go through there, okay?" I tried to nod my head as he pointed in the direction of the adjacent room. "Okay? Sam? Are you with me?"

"Okay." Levi took my hands in his and placed them over my ears like beach shells. I pretended I was listening to the ocean, not the *pop-pop-pop* of his gun striking the deadbolt. He pulled me through the open door into Room 404. There was no one inside. I ran my hand over the smooth bedspread, the perfectly tucked sheets, wishing I was sleeping beneath them. And this was all a bad dream. "Now what?" I asked.

"We wait."

"For the police? I mean, for more of you?"

Levi shook his head. "If we wait for the police, we'll both be dead before they get here. These guys aren't afraid to die for what they want." He walked toward the outer door and watched from the peephole.

"And they want … me?"

Two more forceful kicks rattled the walls. "It looks that way. As soon as they get into our room, we're going to make a run for it. The stairwell is straight ahead and to the left. When I tell you to go, go like hell. I'll be right behind you. Got it?" My head felt like a wind-up toy, agreeing without my permission. Levi kept one eye zeroed on the peephole and one hand on the door. I measured the seconds with shallow breaths. Another kick and Levi shouted, "Okay, go! Go, Sam!"

Go, Sam! I heard Coach Crowley shouting from the sidelines. Fourth quarter in the state semifinals, ten seconds remaining. We were down by two to the Dixon Devils, when I poked the ball from their point guard's hands. It rolled down the court, both of us in hot pursuit. She wanted it. But I wanted it more. Sometimes that's the difference between living and dying. Between the *and-one* to win the game and a long bus ride home. I wanted to live. More than the EME wanted me dead.

Just like that hardwood court, the hallway seemed to extend forever. Legs churning under me. The feeling of someone just behind. In the blur of it all, a man lay on the ground. His once white button-down—Westin St. Francis Security—spotted with a vibrant shade of red. In a last gasp of effort, his hand extended toward me, begging for something I couldn't give. His fingers grazed my leg. His mouth released a sigh of surrender. It was the worst thing I'd ever seen, the kind of thing that should turn you to stone. Frozen, right there, forever. But I kept moving.

A bullet zipped past me, piercing the wall. "Keep running!" Levi urged, returning fire. And I did. Through the door and into the stairwell, where the air was as cool as the marble beneath my feet. I made quick work of the first flight before my chest started to burn. "Faster!" Levi's prodding was muted by the boots stamping above us. They were close. Too close. I concentrated on every step. *Do not fall. Do not fall. Do not fall.*

Another flight down, a gunshot sliced the air, pinging off the ornate rail next to me. "Keep your head down!" At the sound of Levi's voice, I turned back for a split second. And I went down hard, bones juddering on impact. My wrist bent beneath me, but there was no time to assess the damage. Levi pulled me up by the arm and steadied me.

"Almost there." His calm tone obliterated by another gunshot. Then the horrified yelp of a businessman, mid-sip on his morning coffee, outside one of the meeting rooms. "Get down!" Levi yelled. The man dropped to the floor and covered his head, whimpering. Still, I kept moving. Two more flights of stairs, and we were smack-dab in the middle of the lobby.

I expected chaos. I expected panicked faces. I expected the police. But the lobby had the look of a meeting interrupted. A few suited men lingered near the staircase, looking upward with confusion. Early morning tourists raised their heads from their cell phones, perplexed. All their questions answered by a spray of bullets. Then came the screaming, the stampeding for the exit. *This* was what I expected.

I followed Levi's finger straight ahead to the hotel's side entrance. "We've got to get out of here. We'll lose them on the street." As we busted out into the San Francisco morning, sirens wailing past, I heard the EME find me.

"There she is!" It was the voice from behind the door. *La hija de puta*. And he pointed at me.

****

Huddled behind a rack of folding fans, I stared at Levi's back for ten minutes. There were worse things to look at. Finally, he turned to me. "All clear."

"Are you sure?" The last we saw the EME, they walked right past us, after we'd ducked inside the China Bazaar. Still, I kept looking out the oversized windows, expecting them to be there—hiding, waiting, stalking—in the crowd. Inside, I prickled with pins and needles, but truthfully, I felt kind of exhilarated. So close to being dead, I'd never felt more alive.

"I'm sure. C'mon." Levi reached for my hand, and I winced. My wrist had already swelled. Probably sprained. "Sorry," he said.

I shrugged, half-smiling. "It's okay. It's not my shooting hand."

Levi chuckled. "Thank goodness for that, because if those guys come back, I'll need you to pull your weight around here." He gestured to his side, where his gun was concealed under his T-shirt.

"Not *that* kind of shooting."

"I know, I know. Your career as the next Sheryl Swoopes is intact. Now let's get out of here."

My stomach flip-flopped with the thought of walking out those doors, returning to the Westin. I'd traveled so far from the girl who checked in last night, there was no going back to her. "To the hotel?" In my mind, I saw my mother's face. Clare Bronwyn. Clare Keely. *Who was she really?* I wasn't ready to find out.

"Not yet. There's someone I want you to meet here in Chinatown." My face betrayed my utter confusion. "He knew Clare."

CHAPTER ELEVEN

SNIP, SNIP

SNIP Bailey's studio apartment smelled like Chinese dumplings. Which made complete sense. It was a short stair climb above Mr. Chow's Palace, where the all-you-can-eat buffet is only seven dollars. "Worth every penny," Levi joked, producing a small white slip of paper from his pocket, apparently a remnant of dinner the night before. *You have been poisoned.* "They do funny fortunes."

Snip himself smelled of car grease and chocolate cake. Not entirely unpleasant. He stood smack-dab in the middle of the doorway. His arms were thin, his skin like crepe paper, but when he extended them wide to block our entry, I took a step back. Just over his shoulder, inside, a uniform—labeled *Edward Bailey, automotive technician*—draped over an ironing board.

"Back so soon?" Snip asked Levi, an unspoken *I told you so* in his voice. Levi shrugged, but said nothing of our near-death experience with the EME. "I suppose you want to come in." Stalemate. Absolute silence. I shifted from one foot to the other, wondering who would break first. Mercifully, the relentless beeping of a timer interrupted their staring contest.

"I'm baking," Snip said, directing his explanation to me and only me. He extended his hand, calloused and weathered from the sun. Then gave me a once-over like he'd been expecting me—recognized me, even—but didn't trust me.

"Snip, this is Samantha."

"Well, well, well. Samantha Keely?"

I groaned. Levi shook his head vigorously. "Bronwyn," he corrected. "She doesn't know any Keelys."

"I see." Snip didn't seem convinced either, but he lowered his arms, allowing us entry. That single concession seemed to diffuse the tension. "Well, you look a lot like her anyway. Real pretty, ain't she, Levi?" Avoiding Levi's eyes was a losing battle. He gave an exaggerated shrug, noncommittal, then smiled at me.

"I assume you're talking about Clare Keely. Levi said you knew her."

"That's right. Dr. Keely." He gestured to his kitchen table, where a cake was cooling on a wire rack. "It's time to ice this beauty. How do ya feel about cream cheese?"

"I feel really good about it." Levi answered for me.

"I'll bet you do. This boy has his father's appetite." He winked at me, and I grinned back, trying to keep up. Until I saw Levi—stone-faced—strike a whipping glare in Snip's direction. "And you, young lady? Ms. Bronwyn?" I nodded. "Pull up a chair."

"Do you bake often?" Of all the questions sprouting like weeds, it seemed the safest one to pluck.

With the care and precision of a surgeon, Snip transferred the cake to a serving plate. "A fair bit, I'd say. Being down as long as I was, it's the simple pleasures that mean the most."

"Down?"

Levi cleared his throat, shifted in his seat. "It means being in prison. Incarcerated."

"Oh. How long were you … ? I'm sorry, I probably shouldn't ask." I busied myself, inspecting the bluish bruise on my wrist. It ached with dull persistence.

"Nonsense." Snip laughed, plunging a spatula into a can of cream cheese frosting. "Of course you should ask. I was in prison for thirty years. March 15, 2014. That was my release date. I like to think of it as my second birthday."

"Wow. That's a really long time." *You must've done something really bad.* I kept that to myself, but Snip seemed to guess my thoughts.

"Murder." He didn't flinch, and neither did Levi. I stayed quiet, but my eyes gave me away. "Don't worry," he said, spreading a dollop of icing across the surface of the cake. "I'm guilty." He smoothed the frosted edges until they were perfect swirls. "It's the innocent ones you have to watch out for. They're either bold-faced liars or the most desperate men you'll ever meet."

Levi rolled his eyes. "Since when did you get to be such a philosopher?"

"I still got a few marbles rollin' around up here." He tapped his head, shaved as smooth as an acorn. "Dr. Keely would've given this old noggin her seal of approval."

"Was she your therapist?" I asked.

"No." Snip side-eyed Levi. "But my cellie was awfully fond of her." Taking a sudden interest in my arm, Levi reached over to me and examined it. It throbbed with each prod of his fingertips, but I didn't complain. "It looks bad. You should probably put some ice on it."

Snip chuckled. "Is that any way to comfort a beautiful lady? Especially since that bruised wrist has *misadventure with Levi* written all over it?"

"It's okay. I just fell." Snip offered a sympathetic smile, then turned his attention to Levi, giving a deliberate jerk of his head toward the freezer where he'd pinned a business card underneath a 49ers magnet. I couldn't read the name, but the logo read *California Department of Corrections and Rehabilitation, Parole Office*. Taking his not-so-subtle cue, Levi stood up from the table.

"Attaboy," Snip ribbed, prompting a grumble from Levi.

"So how do you know Levi's dad?" At the freezer door, Levi stiffened, as if the cold air iced him solid. "Was he a cop too?" Tight-lipped, he tossed a bag of frozen peas in my direction.

"A cop!" Snip guffawed.

"I'm guessing that's a no."

"Well, that's a story for Levi to tell." Snip placed a strong hand on Levi's shoulder. "You know, his appetite ain't all he got from his daddy. Stubborn as an ox. Both of them. And real quiet."

"They say still waters run deep," I teased, hoping Levi wouldn't be too upset with me for prying.

Solemn, Snip nodded. "Deep enough to drown in."

****

Five minutes and one giant piece of chocolate cake later, I'd been exiled to the sofa. My own fault for asking too many questions. And now, not even the scrumptious cream-cheese icing could smooth the uneasiness between Snip and Levi. They'd excused themselves to the only other room in the place—Snip's bedroom—partitioned by a makeshift bedsheet curtain. Lucky for me, voices carried right through it. I clicked the remote and settled on a soap opera, adjusting the volume to prime eavesdropping level.

"I told you not to come back here. Not if you're going through with it."

"I don't have a choice. Of all people, I thought you'd understand. Besides, I've got a lead."

"And you brought a gun here. You know I'm on parole."

"What was I supposed to do with it?"

"Dammit, Levi. Didn't you learn anything from your daddy? From me? You always have a choice. And I'm making mine. I don't want to be involved."

"Then why did you tell me?"

"Closure. Resolution. Peace of mind. Believe me, I regret it. Besides, it was just a hunch, a possibility … "

"I thought you said everybody—"

"There had been some talk on the yard, and he hadn't ever denied it. Not that I know of anyway. I told you before, I wasn't even there when it happened. I wished I'd kept my big mouth shut. First, Katie, and now, you've got *her* in the middle of it. Think about what you're doing. You're an officer of the law. Supposed to be anyway. Your father would be ashamed of you."

I thought that would end it. Surely, Levi would storm out, taking the flimsy curtain along with him. But he didn't. For a few minutes, the only sound I heard was the rehearsed voice of Dr. Drake Abbott, pondering the fate of his comatose wife.

"At least tell me why the Mexican Mafia is after her."

"The EME? Jesus Christ, Levi. Is that how she got hurt? You're in way over your head here."

"Are you gonna tell me or not?"

Dr. Abbott started crying, head down on his wife's limp shoulder, until a buxom nurse consoled him. I strained to hear Snip's voice over the doctor's sobbing.

"If she is who you say she is, they're probably trying to settle a score. Cullen wasn't short on enemies. There were rumors they greenlighted him." *Greenlighted?*

"But after all this time? It must've been some beef."

"Yeah, well, Cullen was some SOB."

Dr. Abbott locked lips with the nurse, moaning with pleasure, as his wife suddenly opened her eyes.

"You need to tell her. Now. All of it. Or I will."

Levi might've replied. But I don't know, because I stopped hearing everything when my mother's panicked face appeared on the TV screen, replacing Dr. Abbott's perfectly chiseled jaw. Beneath her, the ticker rolled across the screen:

BREAKING NEWS … TEENAGE GIRL KIDNAPPED FROM HOTEL. DISGRACED POLICE OFFICER IDENTIFIED AS PERSON OF INTEREST.

I found my voice balled in a tight fist at the base of my throat. It croaked on the way out. "Levi?"

"Yeah?"

"I think you should come in here." The answer came with footsteps and a swishing curtain. "It's my mom." She stood behind a podium flanked by two police officers. I watched her twist the ruby ring on her finger—the one my father gave her—the way she always did when she was upset.

"Earlier this morning, my daughter, Samantha, was taken—kidnapped—from the Westin St. Francis Hotel in San Francisco, after a gang of armed men broke into her room. I am asking, pleading, for anyone with information on her whereabouts to contact the San Francisco Police Department or FBI tip line immediately. Even the smallest piece of information could help lead to her safe return. To the person or people who have her, please let her go. I'm begging you. She hasn't done anything to deserve this. It's all my—" The sentenced dissolved, along with the rest of her, her shoulders shaking under the weight of it all.

"I'll be damned," Snip muttered. "It's her. In the flesh." I stared down the front of a steam engine barreling straight for me. A long time coming and too late to get out of the way now. "Dr. Keely."

CHAPTER TWELVE
BUTTERFLIES

I sat on the edge of Snip's bed. There was a permanent dip in the mattress where he slept, and the walls were painted a sickly green. Still, I could see why he liked it here. Across the hardwood floors, a large window offered a perfect view of Dragon's Gate. The telephone stared at me from his nightstand. Its position next to a well-worn Bible seemed fitting. I held the receiver in my lap, hand poised above the dial. But my fingers resisted until a persistent *beep-beep-beep* mocked me.

"Do you want me to talk to her?" Levi asked from the doorway.

I shook my head. "I don't think that's a good idea." I wiped my eyes again on my shirtsleeve, glad Snip's only mirror was cloudy, damaged by age. "I just … I can't believe she lied to me about who she is. *Was.* And you've been lying to me too. Again. I overheard you with Snip."

Levi didn't seem surprised by my accusation. "I guess that bed-sheet wasn't as soundproof as I thought." His smile dimmed when he saw I didn't laugh. "People lie for lots of reasons, Sam. I'm sure your mom was trying to protect you."

"And you? Why are you lying?"

He sat next to me, palms on his knees, his long legs dwarfing the twin-sized bed. "To protect myself." His sigh made me want to be close to him. But I barely knew him. I felt all mixed-up inside. *Butterflies.* Ginny's go-to diagnosis. I'd felt those before. Never like this. Levi reached across me and hung up the receiver, the authoritative click momentarily settling my nerves. He took my hand in his and looked up at me with such tenderness, I thought he might kiss me. For real this time. "My dad was in prison for murder. Snip was his cellmate. That's how I know about Cullen."

"And Cullen was a greenlight?"

Levi chuckled to himself. "He was greenlighted. It means the EME put him on a hit list."

"I guess I'm greenlighted too then."

"Recent events would certainly seem to suggest that."

"But why? Because my mom was his therapist?" The idea of Dr. Clare Keely still seemed ludicrous to me. When I told her Ginny's parents were in couples counseling, my mother guffawed. *They should just throw their money on a pile and burn it.* "It doesn't make any sense."

Levi's mouth twisted, like it held something in, and he went silent until I squeezed his hand. "I don't know for sure. But she kept all this from you for a reason."

"Does your dad know Cullen too?"

Levi released my hand, making me regret the question. "He did. But he's been gone a long time." Rising to his feet, he backpedaled toward the curtain and pointed at the phone. "Now call your mom."

****

As soon as the ringing stopped, I started talking. "Mom." I didn't get any further than that. After that word, the only one I could be sure of, I didn't know what to say.

"Is this Samantha?" The voice was a woman's, but not my mother's. "Samantha, this is Special Agent Gretchen McKinnon with the FBI. Are you okay?" Those letters—FBI—dropped like boulders in the pit of my stomach.

"Yes, I'm fine."

"Where are you? Is Officer Beckett with you?"

"Can I talk to my mother, please?"

"Hold on. Let me get her. Don't hang up, Samantha." Levi told me they would trace our location. He didn't seem worried that the Internet had branded him a kidnapper.

"Is it really you? Samantha?" My mother sounded breathless, like she'd just returned from one of her long runs.

"Yes, it's me, Mom." She made a noise, part gasp, part sob, and my eyes welled. "Stop crying. I'm okay. Levi—uh, Officer Beckett— didn't do anything wrong. He was just helping me find Ginny. Then these guys starting banging on our door. They were yelling things … " *La hija de puta.* " … and shooting at us." My mother whimpered, and I lost my nerve. "You can call off the troops, okay? We'll meet you wherever you want."

"What if those men are still looking? Let us come to you."

"Right. And your showing up here with the cavalry won't tip them off."

She groaned in frustration, sounding like herself again. "Okay. The Tenderloin Police Station in twenty minutes. If you're not here by then—"

"We'll be there."

"Samantha," I heard her gathering strength, a storm of anger brewing. "Why didn't you just stay in the room like I asked? They have you on video leaving at some ungodly hour. What were you thinking?"

"Ginny. I was thinking about Ginny."

"Me too, honey. We're looking for her too. Her parents can't get here until their cruise ship docks at the next port. They're worried sick." After a pause so long I thought the line disconnected, she added, "The police found her phone in your hotel room. We really need to talk."

Levi told me it would be best to wait, to save Clare Keely for a face-to-face, but I blurted it out anyway. "Mom … I know. I know about your big secret." I hung up the phone before she could reply.

106

OCTOBER 28, 1996

NEAL called again last night. Just to talk. That's what he said. But Clare knew better. He'd always finesse his way back with persistence and polish. *Remember that day we drove to Muir Beach?* Of course she did. Neal's idea, she'd spent half the morning trying to change his mind. The rest of the day, she held her breath waiting for it to be over. It wasn't logical, not at all, but she kept thinking he would drive to the spot, the secret one. Tell her the jig was up. That he'd figured out what she really was. A monster with a hole where her heart should be. *That was one of my favorite days ever, Clare.* Mine too, she'd answered, hoping the quiver in her voice didn't give her away.

She pinched her leg, another trick she'd learned to bring herself back to the present. The now. Because now was 9:29 a.m. and Cullen would be here any minute. After their last session, the discussion about erotic transference, Clare had to be on her toes.

Cullen arrived right on time, an eager grin on his face. She liked the way he smiled at her, like she was in on the joke.

"I hope we can pick up where we left off last time," she said. "Worse things than murder … "

"Not taking notes today?" She silently cursed him for being more observant than she'd given him credit for.

"I want to focus on you."

He gave a quick up-down, up-down of eyebrows. "Really?"

"You know what I mean. Don't make me have the transference conversation again." She realized mid-sentence her scolding tone came out more flirtatious than she intended, and she suddenly wished she had her notebook to hide behind.

"Not the dreaded transference conversation," he joked, holding up his hands in mock surrender. "Anything but that."

She forced a straight face. "Okay. Last week, you said that betrayal and humiliation were worse than taking a life. What did you mean by that?"

"To answer your question, Doc, I have to tell you about the first woman who destroyed me. My mother." Clare practically squealed with excitement. Cullen had quashed all prior attempts to discuss his parents, and the file was—per the usual—vague. "Truth is, I can't even call her that with a straight face. Half the time, she was a spineless jellyfish. A worm. The other half, she was a heartless bitch. I only wish I would've killed her instead." A shot of cold water down her back, Clare was awake.

"Go on." That was all she could manage.

"She slept with anything that moved. Drunk, married, pedophile. Hell, she didn't care. The more messed up, the better. And most of those losers beat her like a rag doll."

"Is that something you witnessed?"

"Witnessed? Who do you think was there to clean up the blood, put her in bed, doctor her bruises? And that wasn't the worst of it. When they started using me as a punching bag, she let it happen. Like I deserved it."

"How did that make you feel?" Typical therapist lingo. But it had to be asked, not assumed.

"I hate her," he hissed through clenched teeth. "This is what she did to me." He raised his chambray, prison-issued shirt and pointed to his stomach before she could spit out the words to stop him. His bare skin looked different, more vulnerable than that day in the prison yard when he was slick with sweat. She sickened at her urge to touch the raised scars across his abdomen. "I was her boyfriend's personal ashtray."

108

"Put your shirt down," she told him, careful to be firm, but not admonishing.

"Sorry." He tucked the shirt inside his pants as if nothing had happened, and she willed away the memory of Mr. Taylor doing the same. "I got carried away."

"You wanted me to see the way your mother hurt you," she said. "Why?"

"The same reason I showed Emily on our first date. I thought she was different, polar opposite of my mother. I wanted her to understand me, how I got to be me."

"And?"

"Betrayal. She was exactly like that bitch. I knew it the second I caught her screwing that loser in her sociology class. That's what I meant. Seeing that sweaty pig grunting on top of her was worse than anything I did to her."

Clare nodded, but she was spinning, trying to keep her composure. Cullen never talked like this. So vulgar. She wondered if he wanted to rattle her. "It sounds like your view of women is fairly black and white. The virgin or the whore. There is a middle ground, you know."

He tilted his head in contemplation. "No one's ever put it to me like that before. You're right. I guess I do idealize women … until I don't."

"Do you idealize me?" Clare felt a little thrill being so direct.

A smile curled half of his mouth, and the steely hardness in his eyes softened to a forget-me-not blue. "What do you think?"

****

"This is wrong, isn't it?" Clare knew she was dreaming because Mr. Taylor had no face. Just a blur like a finger-smeared Polaroid. He cupped her breast in his hand, kissed her neck. Of course it was wrong. She knew that. But she liked feeling special. Was that wrong too?

He laughed at her, and she felt her face get hot. "It's natural, Clarie. These are the things that happen between a man and a woman."

"I'm not a woman though."

"You're fourteen years old. You get your period, right?" Her shame weighed so heavy she could barely nod her head. "That makes you a woman." He kissed her mouth, shoving his tongue inside until she pushed him away.

"But I don't want anybody to think I'm a slut." Lizzie said there were worse things to be, but Clare wasn't so sure. Besides, Lizzie didn't have a clue about the things that happened in Mr. Taylor's backseat. Not that she didn't suspect. But Clare met all her questions with furious denial. And she planned to keep it that way.

Mr. Taylor sighed like he didn't want to be bothered with her silly questions. After all, she was usually quiet. "Nobody knows, baby, but if it'll make you feel better, I'll make you a promise."

"What kind of promise?"

"I won't have sex with you. Believe me, there's nothing I want more. That's your fault, you know." He rubbed his hand down the front of her. "It's not wrong if we don't go all the way. You're still a virgin. My hot little virgin." He ran his hand through her hair and twisted it in a knot around his fingers, pulling her lips to his. She let him do it. She owed him. This *was* her fault. When he released her, his face had changed. Taken form. A form she recognized.

She tugged him back toward her, moaning his name against his mouth. "Clive."

Clare opened her eyes to the pitch black of her room and sheets that were soaked through with her own sweat. That dream seemed to last all night, but the clock read 11:13 p.m. Only seven more hours to go until morning. "Just another Manic Monday," she whispered.

OCTOBER 29, 1996

CLARE marched back on the yard determined to show Ramirez she wasn't afraid. She had no choice. Dumas refused to leave his cell that morning, and she was worried. *He's been skipping meals too*, Fitzpatrick told her after his briefing with unit officers. Dumas needed her and she wasn't going to let some too-big-for-his-britches gangbanger stand in her way. Ramirez had no idea what she was capable of, the dark things she could be pushed to do. All a part of the speech she used to psych herself up, standing at the opposite end of West Block with a long walk ahead of her. Robocop offered an escort, of course, but she politely declined. She had something to prove.

The fall air crisp, she felt tempted to pull her jacket tight around her, stuff her hands inside her pockets. But she didn't. She wanted Ramirez to see her strength. She saw him squatting like a vulture atop the picnic table, surveying the yard as his cronies flocked around him. He locked eyes with Clare. She didn't look away. Her Thursday, 3-o'clock client taught her a word for that. Mad-dogging. As in, "That guy at the bar was mad-dogging me, so I shot him." *Mad-dogging?* she'd asked. "You know, staring me down all angry like one of them pit bulls."

Clare thought of every hateful thing she could conjure. From the beginning with her father's funeral. Seven years old and tugging at her dress, the hem unraveling, one button already discarded just underneath the church pew. Her mother, too busy chasing the next

Mr. Right to be bothered. Rodney Fucking Taylor. The man who changed who she was or revealed her—she wasn't sure which. The night he made that twisted promise. The night he broke it. And that's where she settled, in the cold place where she could be as vicious as anyone. Even Ramirez.

"Good morning, Mr. Ramirez." Later, she would curse herself for speaking at all. But right now, she celebrated the way the words rolled off of her tongue. She didn't flinch. Didn't stutter.

"Buenos días, Doctor Keely." His lips peeled back in a perverse smile, revealing his pointy canines. "Dónde está tu novio?"

"I'm sorry, I don't speak Spanish." A partial lie. Clare had taken a semester in college. She knew enough. But it was only fair she gave him a chance to reconsider. To be smarter than that.

"Where's your boyfriend?" he repeated. His friends laughed and waited for her to cower, to turn tail. When she looked at him and his disgusting grin, she saw Rodney. He thought he knew her, how she would react. Like a scared little girl. He counted on it. A pit bull would've lunged for his throat. Torn it out. Clare was no pit bull, but she knew how to bite.

"Why are you so interested in Cullen? Got a little crush? Sorry, Ramirez, he's taken." A chorus of *ooh*s, impressed by her insult, was the music in her ears the rest of the way. She let it drown the voice inside her. The one screaming, *You're losing it, Clare.*

****

You're losing it, Clare. By the time she reached Dumas' cell, her own voice was all she could hear. Neal told her that once, when she caught him ogling a picture of Tiffani-Amber Thiessen from her *Saved by the Bell* days. "Really, Neal? She can't be more than sixteen. Are you into teenagers now?"

"I'm not him, Clare. You're losing it. I'm not him." And she knew he wasn't. But sometimes, in the dark, she couldn't tell the difference. Every man she'd ever been with became Rodney Taylor. It would always be that way.

Clare came as close as she could to Dumas' cell. He was sitting on his bunk, still wearing his sleeping clothes, though she doubted he'd had much of it. His eyes were gray and sunken. "I can't do it, Doc. I just can't." His voice sounded all one note. Flat.

"That's why I came to you," she said, forcing more cheeriness than even she could stomach.

It seemed it took all his energy to shake his head. "That's not what I meant. I can't live anymore. Don't want to."

Clare had never heard anyone say it out loud like that, so matter-of-factly. She wasn't up for this. Not today. "What do you mean? What happened?"

He set a piece of paper aflight in her direction. It made a soft landing on the cell floor, a few feet in front of the bars. The headline told her all she needed to know: **California Department of Corrections expected to initiate severe restrictions on family visits**.

"I'm so sorry, James."

He shrugged. "Not your fault."

"It's not yours either. Or your family's. Do you really think taking your life is the best solution to this problem?"

"You got a better one?"

She ignored his impossible question for now. "Tell me about them," she said, pointing to the picture he'd showed her when they first met.

"Don't really feel like talking." He laid down with his back to her, hiding his face. "And before you ask, no I don't have a plan. Not yet. And even if I did, I wouldn't tell you." Dumas was an expert by now. Thoughts, intent, plans, access to means—he knew all the bases she needed to cover.

"Fine." She felt helpless. Like she'd wasted it all on Ramirez and had nothing left. "Have you and your wife picked out a name yet? For your baby girl?" His body tensed, but he said nothing. "What about this little boy with the green eyes? He looks a lot like you." She watched the seconds, the minutes tick by on her watch.

"Mr. Dumas, I'll have to put you on suicide watch again. Officer Franklin will escort you to the Crisis Bed. But I'll be back to see you tomorrow." Her stomach turned at the thought of crossing the yard again. *You lost it, Clare. You deserve whatever you get.*

"Wait." She walked halfway to the unit door when she heard him call to her. "Katie," he said. "Katie and Levi."

NOVEMBER 6, 1996

HER Wednesday, 9 a.m. suddenly went silent, the face at the door—now open—demanding her attention with icicle eyes that pinned her to her chair. "I'm in the middle of a session, Mr. Cullen. You can come back in twenty minutes."

He took a step inside. "But it's important."

"Twenty minutes." She ushered him out, hoping Fitzpatrick hadn't seen him. *A clear violation of the therapeutic frame, Dr. Keely.* That's what he would say. And he didn't even know the half of it. The surreptitious touch of her forearm; his scarred, naked mid-section; his blatant admission of attraction. Every time Mr. Taylor moaned at her touch, he'd reminded her who was in charge. *You make me crazy, baby. I can't help what you do to me.* But with Cullen, she couldn't tell.

When the session ended, Cullen waited right outside. Clare felt certain he'd been listening. "How did you get in here?" she asked. He produced a ducat.

"I have my ways. I need to talk to you."

"You interrupted a session. I have other clients too. Their time matters as much as yours does."

He strutted into the office, no apologies. Sure of himself, as if she'd invited him. "I heard about what happened yesterday."

Clare's breath quickened. Her breakfast made its way back up, and she resisted the urge to run to the door and lock it. "I'm not sure what you're talking about." Cullen's mouth hinted at a smile. "What did you hear?"

"I know you didn't mean it. You were just saying it to stick it to Ramirez. But he's not too happy about your calling him out in front of his homeboys." Clare felt caught, the way she did when Lizzie asked about her first time. There was no way to explain. No way to deny. "I think I know how to fix it," Cullen said so softly she could barely hear him. She opened her mouth, but the right words seemed to float away before she could speak them. "You don't even have to say anything," he assured her. "In fact, it's better if you don't. Just listen." Clare could hear Lizzie's voice, as real as Cullen's. Her utter shock. Worse, her pity. *Why didn't you just tell me?*

"I know things about him. About the EME. He has drugs in his cell. Heroin. Coke. They smuggle them in every month. He's got some of the officers on his payroll. I know their names. You have to report that. Right, Clare?"

****

Fitzpatrick drummed the eraser end of his pencil against the desk. *Tap-tap-tap.* Clare despised the way he did that. "He thinks it makes him look smart," she'd told Lizzie. "Like he's pondering the fate of the world instead of wasting his last good years sucking up the benefits of a dead-end government job."

"Geez, Clare-Bear. Tell me how you really feel." She and Lizzie dissolved into an easy laughter. But that was last week. Before the dream. Before the yard. Before Dumas' relapse. Before Cullen barged into her office this morning with something "important" to tell her.

The insufferable tapping ceased, and Fitzpatrick issued his verdict. "I'm glad you came to me, Clare. This is a sensitive situation. I assume you reminded Mr. Cullen of the limitations of confidentiality." Clare almost laughed out loud. Cullen needed no reminding.

"Of course, I did. He understands the rules."

"Then we have no choice but to forward Cullen's accusations to the appropriate authorities."

Clare feigned protest. "Is that really necessary? He could be making the whole thing up. You know how manipulative he can be." The twinge of guilt surprised her even as she replayed Cullen's goodbye, his strong hand cupping her shoulder like a small bird while she stood there, shell-shocked. His thumb grazed her clavicle. *Don't worry*, he'd said, quieting something she couldn't name inside her.

"We can't assume anything," Fitzpatrick told her. "But I'm relieved to hear you say that. For a while, I was beginning to think he was snowing you. All that woe-is-me BS about his childhood. You know, they say he caused those scars himself."

She fought the urge to scoff and put on her sweetest smile, knowing it would seal the deal. "No snow here."

"Only sunshine," Fitzpatrick added, basking in her flirtation. "Let me call the Chief. He'll get someone down here from the SSU to take your statement."

"SSU?"

"Special. Services. Unit. I'm beginning to think you slept through orientation."

She shrugged. "There's a lot of acronyms to remember."

"Maybe you were daydreaming about someone special?" He stared at Neal's ruby. "A boyfriend?" Clare knew what he wanted, and she gave it to him. She needed him on her side for now.

"I don't have a boyfriend."

"Oh. It's not my business anyway, I suppose."

You suppose right, asshole. "I don't mind you asking. It's not a secret."

"Well, in that case, I'm newly divorced." He held out his ringless left hand, wriggling his third finger. "Free at last!"

"Congratulations." Clare wondered how far it would bend before it broke.

NOVEMBER 7, 1996

THE instant the taillights vanished from her rearview mirror, Clare thrust her head back against the seat of her car, then screamed until her throat was raw. It wasn't the first time she'd tried to jar loose the memory, send it skittering through her brain on a collision course with death. She'd done this before, years ago. The day after. Skull to the headboard until she felt dizzy. But memories can't be murdered, can't be beaten out. And some memories are stains. Red wine on her favorite white cotton dress. Blood on her panties.

She'd last laid eyes on Rodney Taylor the day he broke his promise. May 30, 1985. "Who was that guy you were talking to?" he asked as she slid into the passenger seat, his hand already rubbing her bare leg. They were three blocks from the school behind the vacant movie theater, and they had to be careful since Lisa had told her mom she'd seen Clare riding with him. *He was just giving me a lift home*, she'd told Lisa, shrugging it off like it was nothing.

She'd gotten good at that. Acting happy-go-lucky. "Who? Mike? He's nobody. Were you watching me?"

"Is he your boyfriend?"

"No," Clare admitted, wishing he was. Wishing she had the guts to lie and say yes. Wishing she wasn't such a spineless loser.

"Don't lie to me." He squeezed her thigh until it hurt, then laced his hand behind her neck pulling her toward him. "I'm jealous, baby. I'm greedy. I want you all to myself." His breath was hot against her skin. "You didn't let him do this, did you?" His fingers were up her dress, inside her. "Because it would destroy me."

She pushed him off. Her first mistake. "We were just talking. Relax." Her second.

"Relax? What is that supposed to mean?" He grabbed her wrist, cuffing it with his hand.

"You're acting crazy. Are you drunk?" He reeked of wine from a half-empty bottle stashed on the floorboard. "It's not like we're a couple." And that was her third. Her fatal error.

"We're not?" He winced like she'd kicked him in the stomach. Until that moment, she didn't really know there was no end to this. Unless she made one. This *was* all her fault. Her curse was her power. Her power was her curse.

"You're married. And I'm fifteen. What do you think?"

His eyes seemed to darken like rot. "I think you're screwing him." All her words—*No! Please! Stop! I'm sorry!*—dead-ended into his palm that smelled like aftershave. His words came instead. "You ungrateful little slut. I should've done this a long time ago." After that she gave up fighting, and REO Speedwagon took over from the radio. *Cause I can't fight this feeling anymore. I've forgotten what I started fighting for …*

The worst part was later. He poured a splash of wine into two paper cups, putting one in her trembling hand. "I'm sorry I called you a name. I love you, Clarie." It spilled down the front of her dress, and she laughed so she wouldn't cry.

The last time she saw Rodney Taylor, he raped her. The next morning, her mother put her on a bus to Los Angeles to spend the summer with her cousin. For the whole seven-hour ride, Clare feared the worst. Her mother had found the dress, the panties balled in her closet behind a stack of board games. Looking back, wasn't that what she wanted?

Turned out, she'd given her mom too much credit. *I met someone, and we need a little alone time,* she'd told Clare, her voice almost inaudible on the scratchy payphone. Lizzie wrote her. *Lisa's mom finally gave her pervy stepdad the boot. Apparently, he was having an affair.*

And then, today. At the coffee shop, waiting for Lizzie. He saw her first.

"Clare? Clare Keely? Is that you?" Like she was an old friend he hadn't seen in a while. She held on to the counter thinking the ground might crack beneath her. Thinking her heart might stop the way a clock would in an old fable—at the exact moment of its maker's death. "It is you. Wow. What's it been? Ten years?" But the ground didn't crack. And her heart kept beating.

"Hi, Rodney." She didn't want to look at him, but there was nowhere else to put her eyes. He wasn't exactly how she remembered. Smaller now, it seemed. Less capable. Just a middle-aged man with a receding hairline and a potbelly.

"Geez, you look great. You always were stunning." He patted her forearm. And she swore it burned. "How are you?"

She imagined this so many times, it felt like déjà vu. How she'd stand her ground, dry-eyed, and calmly tell him to go fuck himself. But not before he knew the price she paid to keep his secret. The parts of herself she'd excised for him. The parts she put in a hole and covered with dirt. "Fine. I'm fine."

"That's great." He produced a card from his wallet. Rodney M. Taylor, Owner. Green River Trucking. In her palm, it felt like a razor. "Hey, if you ever want to catch up on old times, give me a call. I just landed a big contract with San Quentin. You know, the prison? So I'm around here a lot. And I'm uh … divorced now, but I guess you knew that."

Clare nodded, her head floating like a child's lost balloon. "I'm … " *Angry. Homicidal. Screwed up. Confused. Not a teenager anymore. Not interested, at the very least.* " … running late."

"Sure. Of course." He touched her again, the way Cullen had, hand to the shoulder. Squeezing. "Clarie, what're the odds? Must be my lucky day." She felt her face grimace or smile, she wasn't sure which. Her legs carried her out the door, leaving her steaming coffee behind. Rodney followed, waiting as she fumbled with her keys. "I'd love to see you again, okay?"

She was still fifteen. "Okay."

After the screaming was done, she drove away fast. She couldn't face Lizzie. *If you ever see that prick, punch him in the face for me.* Her exact words when Clare finally admitted it. It only took four years, three shots of tequila, and one game of Never Have I Ever. And even then, she'd only spilled half-truths, the ones she could stomach. She didn't tell Lizzie she'd spent most of that summer missing him, the attention anyway. Who would understand that? And when her period stopped coming, well, she couldn't even tell herself.

Halfway to San Quentin, Clare rolled down her window and let a whipping gust of air carry Rodney Taylor's card far, far away from her.

✸✸✸✸

Clare could've gone home and called in sick. But she needed a distraction. Besides, Dumas was still on suicide watch, and she'd promised to check in on him. She slipped into the bathroom at the prison's entrance to assess the damage. Her face ghost white, but otherwise unscathed. Seeking relief from the dull ache at the base of her skull, she released her ponytail. A splash of cold water, and she felt practically brand new. *It's been twelve years*, she told herself. *Just let it go.* Her therapist always used the words *traumatic bond*, which made her think of Elmer's glue, the kind she used in kindergarten. As in, "It's only natural you cared for Rodney, that you clung to him. He made you feel special, but he hurt you. That's the very paradox of a traumatic bond."

At least Ramirez had been taken care of. He and his cellmate were carted off to Ad Seg yesterday, after the SSU found ten bindles of heroin, a wad of cash, and a shank in their cell. Fitzpatrick told her he'd probably end up in Pelican Bay. *All's well that ends well.* It didn't matter how he got there.

It started to sprinkle a little, but Clare headed straight to the yard. She'd see Dumas, take an early lunch, and spend the afternoon holed up in her office, pretending to catch up on session notes. After flashing her state ID, Robocop stopped her at the control booth.

"Hey there, Dr. Keely. Lose your umbrella?"

"Something like that," she said, trying to muffle her impatience. She couldn't do flirty today, not after this morning.

"Want my jacket?" He tugged at his army-green rain poncho as she shook her head. "I'd hate to see you get wet." His eyes wandered to her chest, her white button-down.

"On second thought, maybe I'll take you up on that, Briggs."

He whipped off the poncho, and she slipped it over her head. "J. D.," he reminded her. "Call me J. D."

"I'll return it on my way back, Briggs."

His shoulders slumped, nearly defeated, but then, "Want to wait until it lets up a little? Keep me company?"

Clare hoped he didn't see the hard roll of her eyes. He seemed more relentless than usual today. "I can't."

"Did you remember to pick up an alarm on your way in?" *Dammit.* Of course, she'd completely spaced. Preoccupied by the man she most wanted to forget. That was the paradox of the traumatic bond. "I know that look," he said, grinning. "I've got an extra here for you." He held it out to her, teasing, then snapped it back. "You'll owe me a drink though."

"Keep it," she said, charging through the door into the rain. It fell steady now, and the yard had nearly emptied, save for a group of shirtless men on the basketball court. Under the hood of Robocop's jacket, she could look without being seen. Clare recognized Cullen standing under the basket, hands raised, demanding the ball. He caught it with authority, though it must've been slick by then. Leveling a defender with his shoulder, he turned and shot. The ball took a bounce against the backboard and fell into the netless hoop. Two points. Clare felt a secret thrill when he pumped his fist in the air. They were teammates now.

When she looked back, Cullen lay on the ground. For a moment, as silly as it was, Clare thought he'd been struck by lightning. He curled in on himself like a snail. All the men scattered. But one.

And time did its trick. The one where seconds unfolded at warp speed like a runaway film projector, yet somehow Clare plodded in slow motion. It was familiar to her, this trick. Mr. Taylor paper-weighted on top of her, pressing her lungs flat like airless balloons. He fumbled with the button of his jeans. His labored breaths ticked by for an eternity. And then, it was over. *Or was it?* Whatever part of her was still blameless, he destroyed in thirty seconds max. She'd crossed over some invisible line, though she didn't know it then.

Clare fumbled for her alarm. The one she forgot. The one she refused. The hood fell back from her face, and she tasted rain and the rusty nail of her own fear. Her hands were wet and useless. When she looked at them, they were red.

NOVEMBER 8, 1996

I told you not to come in today." Fitzpatrick loomed in the doorway, shaking his finger at her. Clare was surprised when he noticed her sitting in her office, staring out the window. She felt like a ghost. Invisible, but tethered. To this place. To her memories. The cord to the past, forged in fire, unseverable.

"It wouldn't do me any good to stay home. I'd just keep thinking about it anyway. How is he?"

"Cutthroat? That guy's got nine lives. Lucky for him, it was raining. The shiv slipped out of Rivas' hand before he could do any real damage. The question is, how are you, Clare? Briggs said you were pretty shaken up."

She hadn't slept. Not even a catnap. She spent the night on a frantic search for the missing five minutes. The time she lost between Cullen's bank shot and a seat in the Lieutenant's office, looking at her hands. Her thin fingers, waterlogged and wrinkled. She even thought of calling Neal, but she knew what he'd say. *You disassociated? I'm coming over.* And then he'd hold her, which would lead to sex. Not because she wanted him, but because Neal was sturdy and reliable. The carnal equivalent of an oak tree. Which would only lead to Neal more in love with her than ever, a punishment he didn't deserve.

"It's not every day you see your client get stabbed." Her canned laughter was unconvincing even to Fitzpatrick, as obtuse as he was.

"Do you mind if I ask a personal question?" *It's never stopped you before.* "Are you in therapy?" Clare blinked back tears. "This job can do a number on you if you let it."

"Are *you* in therapy?" A spark of rage warmed her. She felt only half-dead now.

Fitzpatrick returned her glare with a sympathetic smile. "You sound like my ex-wife."

"I've had therapy, okay. I know my issues. I'm fine." She was desperate for him to leave. Instead, he came toward her, leaning on the desk next to her.

"I'm not the enemy here. Whatever it is, you can tell me. You can trust me. I'm your supervisor, remember?"

"What do you think I'm hiding from you?"

He shrugged. "Do you know where I worked before San Quentin? CCWF. Central California Women's Prison."

"You think I'm a criminal?" She gripped tight to the arms of her chair and waited for him to tell her he knew. It was written all over her. Red hands, as red as any guilty man in this joint.

"Just the opposite, Clare. I think you're a victim. You've been a victim. Of something. Am I right?"

Victim. She despised that word. "You're wrong."

****

It was nearly 5 o'clock. She'd waited all day to take this walk, not wanting to seem too eager. But she was eager. Her skin buzzed with a current of anticipation. Though she knew better, yesterday's events seemed to line up like stars in the night sky. An undeniable constellation of synchronicity. Carl Jung called them *meaningful coincidences.* Drawn to those words, she'd folded down the corner of that page in her *Theory of Psychology* book the first time she read it. Clare felt she was being punished and saved all at once.

The officer pointed her down the infirmary hallway. The last cell on the left. Through the large windows, she saw him first, propped in a nondescript hospital bed, flipping through a travel magazine. Here, Cullen looked less like Cutthroat and more like Clive. Especially when

125

he noticed her, smiled, and gave a boyish wave. She slipped inside and pulled up a chair alongside him.

"Have you ever been to Muir Woods, Dr. Keely?" The world started spinning, and for the second time since they'd met, she felt convinced he knew. Impossible, illogical, and completely insane, but somehow, he knew. Then she saw it—the page in the magazine with the redwoods stretching to the sky. "If I ever get out of here, this is where I'm going. I spent some time up there as a kid. I always wanted a cabin in the woods."

"Sounds lovely," she said, feeling herself smile a little too wide. Relief made her giddy.

"Yeah, it is. Too bad the only way I'll ever see the outside of these walls is in a body bag." He tossed the magazine aside, assessing her instead.

Giddiness made her flirty. And bold. "There's always ... what do they call it? Jackrabbit parole?" She'd learned the term from Dumas, and it stuck with her. *Did you know jackrabbits can run up to thirty miles per hour and jump twenty feet?* he'd asked when she gave him a quizzical look. *I reckon if you're trying to break out of this joint, it'd be good to be a jackrabbit.*

Clare was grateful when Cullen smiled. He knew she was kidding. "How are you?" she asked.

"I've been better." He pointed to his side, where Clare caught the outline of a thick bandage. "Doc said I'm lucky. His best shot went right through the muscle. I'll be good as new in a few weeks. But one of the officers told me you saw the whole thing go down. Is that true?"

Clare nodded, and he sighed. It wasn't a usual sound he made, and it surprised her. "Sergeant Briggs told you?"

"Yeah. I think he's got a little thing for you." Cullen winced as he laughed, clutching at his midsection, and she felt a surge of emotion that nearly bowled her over.

"This is my fault. You did this for me, snitching on Ramirez. And now, you're ... " This time Clare touched him first because she wanted to. Her fingers grazed his just under the stiff white sheet, in case someone was watching, and her body thrummed. His hand closed around hers for the briefest moment—a heartbeat—before he let go.

"It was worth it. And anyway, I can't help but feel like it's karma. Me being on the wrong end of a knife." His mouth turned grim. "I know I didn't say it at our last session—you probably think I'm a monster—but I do have remorse for what happened to Emily." Later on, when she'd come back to her senses, she would analyze that sentence. What *happened* to Emily, not what *I* did to her. The minimization it implied.

But something else consumed her now. Set free from a vile place inside her, it left no room for thought. It demanded a life of its own. A shadow life that could only be understood by an equal darkness. She didn't say it out loud. She didn't need to. His earnest eyes plumbed the deepest parts of her and witnessed her silent confession. *I killed my baby.*

****

Clare sat at the bar, Lizzie twirling on the stool next to her. A stranger winked at her from across the room, and she giggled. She hadn't been this drunk since Neal had proposed on that wine-tasting trip to Napa. *Slow down, Clare. You're a lightweight.* He was right, but every glass of red had made the whole marriage thing easier to stomach, until Dr. Clare Barrington seemed like a person she could be.

But loose-lipped, she got reckless. Secrets fell from their nests and broke open. Luckily, she'd passed out on the sofa before she could confess everything to Neal. Not tonight. She delivered her story to Lizzie effortlessly even after two shots of Patrón: *I ran into Rodney Taylor. Yes, that Mr. Taylor. I told him to go fuck himself. It felt good. Really good. Cullen? He's in the infirmary. He has the flu.*

"TGIF," Lizzie said, clinking shot number three. "You've earned it."

"You have no idea." Pain before pleasure, it burned on the way down.

CHAPTER THIRTEEN

DONE

SNIP positioned himself alongside the window, widening the edge of the mini blinds with his finger. Since I hung up on my mom minutes ago, he stayed stuck in that spot. But he managed plenty of glaring at Levi. "You better hope the cops don't show up here."

"They won't."

"Well, if they do, you better hope they arrest you. Or shoot you. Or something."

"And why is that?" Levi asked, poking his head out from behind the bedroom partition. In one hand, he gripped an open duffel bag.

"Because you're gonna have to deal with me if they don't."

Levi emerged with the duffel, now closed, his eyes hidden beneath the brim of an Oakland A's baseball cap. "You do remember I've got five inches, thirty pounds, and a lot of years on you, right?"

"That don't scare me. I beat up your daddy one time, and he was a giant." Snip winked at me, and I tried to smile, but I couldn't. Levi waved me toward the door, half-amused, half-hurried.

"I highly doubt that," he said.

"Alright, you got me. But I was faster than him. God rest his soul." My gaze darted from Levi to Snip and back again.

"Your dad is … dead?" That word made my chest ache. On top of feeling like an absolute jerk for how snotty I'd been earlier about my own father. Levi knew what it was like to lose someone. Still, his withholding was deliberate. Deliberate and infuriating.

"That's why he's here. Right, Levi?" Snip indicted with his scathing tone, but there was pity in his eyes. "Even the Lord can't help a man with a vendetta. He's got two one-way tickets to hell."

"C'mon, Sam. We have to go." With a quick wave to Snip over my shoulder, I pushed past Levi without a word. I was so over being lied to.

****

Levi followed me out the door and down the stairs. His silence tromped the whole way too, wedged between us like a stranger in a crowd. At the entrance to the street, he stopped. "This is where I leave you."

"What? You're not going with me?" The duffel bag made sense now. I felt stupid. Levi had been wrong. I *was* naïve.

"I can't. They'll arrest me."

"No, they won't. We'll tell them what happened. You didn't hurt anybody." That was debatable. Skinny was probably still wriggling out of those zip ties. I hoped so anyway. But I couldn't face my mother alone. And even though I felt tempted to pummel him, the thought of walking away from Levi made my stomach knot. "Well, you didn't hurt anybody who didn't deserve it. Whatever you did was for a good reason."

"It doesn't work like that, Sam. I left with my service weapon without telling anybody. And we both know the cops aren't going to trust me to bring you in. They'll probably be here any minute."

"Then what?" I pointed at the bag slung over his shoulder. "Where are you going? To settle your vendetta? Whatever that means."

"It's better if you don't know."

"Better for who?" I didn't even bother to wait for him to dodge the question. "You came looking for me, remember? I didn't ask for your help."

He nodded. "That was a mistake. Like Snip said, I shouldn't have involved you in my … " I raised my eyebrows, anticipating another vague explanation. " … mess." *Bingo.* He turned away and took one step up the stairs before I pulled him back, my hand cuffed around his wrist. He didn't resist, and I didn't want to let go because the parts of me touching him felt strangely alive.

"Yesterday, I was just a normal girl on a normal trip with her normal best friend. Ever since I met you on that plane, my life has been completely abnormal. Coincidence?"

"You weren't a normal girl. You just didn't know it. I'm not the only one who lied to you. You should ask your mom why your life flipped upside down."

"Clare Keely?"

"Yes, Clare *effing* Keely. At least you believe me now." He peeled my fingers back from his wrist one by one and dropped my hand by my side.

"Maybe if you started with the truth, people would believe you more. Didn't you take an oath or something?"

"Or something." His sheepish grin charmed a smile from me. "I like you, Sam."

"I like you too." And then his brow furrowed. Grim Levi returned.

"That's why the best thing for you is to forget you ever met me."

The sting of those words and his indifferent delivery forced me toward the door. Through it, I saw Chinatown the way Ginny intended. Teeming with tourists, red lanterns, and dim sum. Eyes trained on the street, like a steely defender, I entered the dead zone. That's what Coach Crowley called the place where you stopped being a girl and started being a baller. I answered Levi from there.

"Forget you? Done."

✳✳✳✳

I pushed to the edge of the crowd and headed for Dragon Gate. There was no sign of the cops, and I was grateful Snip insisted I take some money from his cookie jar. Even he knew Levi wasn't coming—of course he did—and I would need cab fare. Yep, I was the only sucker here. But in the dead zone, there's no whining. And certainly no wallowing.

"Excuse me." A small voice beckoned from a nearby doorway. A boy with short black hair was calling to me, pointing at me. An older version, matching black hair, summoned me with his finger. I spun around, taking inventory. No EME. No badges. No Levi. Just four chestnut-colored eyes watching as I approached. They seemed harmless.

"Are you Samantha?" the older boy asked. My skin went cold, a clammy reminder. Even in the dead zone, I was very much alive. I managed a soft *mmhmm*. He extended his hand to pass me a folding fan like the ones on the rack in the China Bazaar.

"What is this?"

"For you."

"For me?"

"For you, Samantha." I studied the fan for a moment. It was the color of paper left too long in the sun. "Open," the small boy instructed. The fan unfurled in my fingers, revealing its design. Two white birds walking in the water. And a message, scrawled in crude handwriting.

Careful, Clare. I know where all your secrets are buried.

"Put your hands up! Get down on the ground!" The fan fell to the sidewalk, trampled by running feet, but I hardly noticed in the commotion. The two boys were pinned like beetles beneath the thick knees of men in FBI vests.

"Samantha, are you okay? Have you been hurt?" A woman I'd never met comforted me. Or tried to. The badge affixed to her lapel read *Gretchen McKinnon*. I wasn't sure how to answer so I shook my head. "Where is Officer Beckett?" she asked me.

"I don't know." But that was a lie. Because over her shoulder, striding long and tall and away from me, was an Oakland A's baseball cap.

CHAPTER FOURTEEN
THE COLOR OF INNOCENCE

TELL me again what happened yesterday at the airport. Start at the beginning, when you and Ginny got off the plane." Though she looked nothing like him, of course, with her delicate nose and cinnamon hair sprinkled with gray, Special Agent McKinnon reminded me of Mr. Willett in Calculus. I always knew when I had the wrong answer because he kept asking the same flipping question. Just like her. This was round three of the what-happened-yesterday game.

I groaned.

"I think Samantha needs a break." I was grateful for my mother's suggestion, even though the only fate worse than Agent McKinnon's relentless inquisition was facing Clare Keely alone.

"Five minutes. And stay close. Time is of the essence here. We've got a girl missing and a predator roaming our streets, as you well know, Ms. Bronwyn. Any small detail could be critical to determining Cutthroat's whereabouts."

I guess she's still going by Bronwyn. I side-eyed my mother looking for a sign, but she kept her face of stone. "Let's go for a walk."

"Fine. But I wouldn't recommend—" My mother's chair scraped the floor as she stood interrupting Agent McKinnon mid-sentence, the *screeee* an intentional affront. I'd never seen her like this. Brazen.

"Five minutes. No longer." McKinnon barked her conditions without lifting her eyes. They were buried in the thick file on her lap. The one I wanted to snatch from her hands. In it, I imagined were all the things I didn't know but desperately wanted to—about my mother, Levi. And the way she guarded it, probably even myself.

I followed my mother to the elevator, an army of questions in position for a full assault. But she shushed me. "Not here." We rode in silence to the first floor, fast walked through the tomb-like lobby, and pushed through the glass doors into the white-hot pavement of summer.

"Samantha! Can you tell us anything about Clive Cullen? Did you see him? Did he speak to you?"

"Ms. Bronwyn, what does it feel like to have your little girl safe?"

"Have you had any communication from Ginny Dalton?"

"Samantha, did Levi Beckett kidnap you? Is he working with Cullen? Has he been arrested?"

Dodging the barrage of questions—sharp and pointed as spears—I backpedaled right into Agent McKinnon, nearly knocking us both to the ground. Stronger than she looked, she steadied me with her hands and glared at my mother with something worse than disapproval. "As I was saying, I wouldn't recommend leaving the building, Ms. Bronwyn. It doesn't appear your listening skills have improved in the last twenty years." She straightened her jacket, then addressed the hungry cavemen outfitted with their words as weapons. "No questions at this time." She opened the door for us, a gesture more demanding than polite. "You can take your break right here in the lobby. I'll come and get you and your daughter when it's time."

Agent McKinnon retreated to the corner and took out her cell phone, pretending not to watch us. A well-worn valley of worry marked the space between her eyebrows. I didn't have a grandmother—she died before I was born—but I imagined she would've been something like that. Crotchety, but concerned.

"Does she know you?" I asked my mother, though the answer seemed obvious.

"She thinks she does, but that's not important right now. There are things I need to tell you." I wondered how long she'd been thinking of this speech. Hours? Days? "You must be confused and upset with me, and you have every right to feel that way. The name Bronwyn is the one I chose when I moved to Texas. The one I chose for me and you. It means white, fair, the color of innocence." Her speech—hollow and rehearsed—told me she'd been practicing for years.

"So it's true then. You're Clare Keely? A psychologist? Seriously, Mom."

She blinked, blinked, and blinked again, as if her old self was too much to bear. "How did you find out?"

"That's where you want to start? How about, *I'm sorry I lied to you.*" My jaw set, I shook my head at her. "Levi told me. I didn't believe him at first. But clearly, I was wrong."

"I am sorry, Samantha. Of course, I am."

"Why did you change your name? And you never told me you lived in California."

"I couldn't. I didn't want to take the chance of him finding us … you. This is exactly what I feared would happen."

"Cullen? Cutthroat Cullen? That's who you mean by *him*?"

She swallowed hard. "He was a therapy patient of mine. I worked at San Quentin, the prison near here. It was my first real job as a psychologist."

"And what happened?"

"Cullen was obsessed with me. He became obsessed with me the more we worked together. He thought I had feelings for him. It was so bad, I had to quit my job and move away. He made up lies about me, lies that made it so I couldn't be a psychologist anymore." I let out a long, rattled breath, and my mother rubbed my back. "It's a lot to take in, I'm sure. But I lied to you to protect you." Funny how the words Levi used to reassure me were completely insufficient coming from my mother.

134

"Five minutes are up." Agent McKinnon signaled to us with a tap of her watch.

"Coming," my mother said, wrapping her arm around me. But my questions kept marching. They would not be denied. I wriggled away.

"Did Dad know about all this?"

"Of course he knew. It still stings, you know, how right he was. He never wanted me to work at San Quentin in the first place." She seemed lost somewhere far away, somewhere I'd never been and couldn't go.

"The notes Cullen left … that last one about knowing your secrets. What did it mean?"

My mother shrugged. "He's crazy, honey. Delusional. You can't make sense of somebody like that."

****

"So let's talk about him." Agent McKinnon pointed to the center of the desk, where she laid a photograph of Levi in his police uniform. "Levi Beckett." She had a way of making him sound guilty without saying anything at all.

"He's not involved in this." *Not true, though I still wasn't sure how.* "I mean, he didn't break the law." Another swing and a miss, but only if you were being by the book about it, which McKinnon definitely was. "He didn't touch me." *Nope.* I suppressed a smile. "And he certainly didn't hurt me. He saved my life."

"Did he tell you to say that, Samantha?"

"No. It's the truth."

"I see." Agent McKinnon made a note in the file. "Did he say where he was going?"

"He told me it was better I didn't know."

My mother patted my arm. "You don't have to protect him."

"I'm not protecting—"

"He's obviously very good-looking. Probably charming too." She fingered the corner of the picture, smudging it a little. "It's okay if you fell for that. I won't be mad."

Agent McKinnon gave a sage nod that seemed meant for my mother. "It happens to the best of us."

I shook my head, all the while contemplating a secret of my own. If they knew about the kiss, they'd probably assume I was completely brainwashed. A full-fledged member of the Cult of Levi. "Yes, he's handsome and semi-charming, but I'm not boy crazy like Ginny, Mom. He told me he was on administrative leave. He told me everything."

"And what exactly did he say about that?"

I replied with a casual hunch of my shoulders, a no-big-deal shrug. "Something about bribing an officer to get his sister out of trouble. A burglary, I think. Or drugs, maybe. It didn't seem so bad."

My mother's sigh implied it was the most ridiculous statement I'd ever made. Then Agent McKinnon joined in. Coach Crowley would've been quite impressed by their double-team. "Did he tell you it was his fault she got in trouble in the first place? He put her up to it. Might've even been there when she broke into the place, but the cops couldn't prove it. And she wasn't about to give up her brother. Not to mention the fact he used his position to acquire information he wasn't entitled to, falsified airline procedure documents, and flew with his service weapon outside of an official capacity."

I deflected my own frustration with my loyalty to Levi by fueling a vigorous defense. "I'm sure there's an explanation. He's not a bad guy."

"Do you have one?" Agent McKinnon couldn't hide her Cheshire cat grin. "An explanation?"

"I assume it has something to do with his dad and Cullen. That's what his friend, Snip, implied. Maybe you should ask my mother."

"Believe me, Samantha, I already have. But your mother has a history of being a bit ... shall we say ... evasive when it comes to Mr. Cutthroat." Her sarcasm was palpable.

Turning to my mother, I held out my hands, empty and ready for an answer. "Well?"

"I—I don't know. I provided therapy to both of them ... Levi's father and Clive Cullen, but—"

"What about the EME?" I ignored my mother's gasp. "Why aren't you trying to find them?"

"How did you know they were Mexican Mafia?"

"Uh, Levi. The horrible snake-in-the-grass con man who has me completely snowed. He seems to know a lot more about you than I do."

My mother shook her head at Agent McKinnon. "I'm sorry. Eighteen going on nineteen, but still very much a teenager. Thanks for reminding me of your immaturity, Samantha."

"Why is the EME after me? Why did they call me the whore's daughter? Is that one of the secrets you buried?"

Nonplussed, Agent McKinnon spoke while my mother stared straight ahead, her face flushed. "It seems the Mexican Mafia has a bit of a grudge against your mother. In fact, we found a photograph of you in Marcus Guzman's pocket. Apparently, he's the nephew of a high-ranking member … " She paused, locking eyes with my mother. " … Arturo Ramirez."

"Another friend of yours, Mom?" I knew I was out of line, but I didn't care. Not one bit. *Maybe I was immature after all.*

A flinch was my mother's only reply, and McKinnon continued. "He's a shot caller for the EME. Guzman may have kidnapped Ginny thinking she was you."

I scrunched my face in confusion. "But he's dead."

"Yes. Very. His throat was cut."

"By Cullen?"

"We're looking into that. There's a possibility they were working together. Or more likely, Cullen was using Guzman. He's good at that … using people. After he killed Guzman, the EME went looking for you. They have associates all over the city. And when they want revenge, they get it. You're lucky to be alive, Samantha."

Screee. Holding a trembling hand over her mouth, my mother fled the room, and guilt set in, heavy as a stone on my chest. I stood, ready to chase her, but Agent McKinnon stopped me.

"Let me talk to her. Woman to woman." I nodded as she hurried out the door, resigned to the fact that a complete stranger had a better chance at an honest conversation with my mother. From the desktop, Levi still smiled at me. *I like you, Sam.* So I reached to flip the photo over. That's when I realized the file sat on the chair, open. Practically begging to be read.

I only saw one page. One part of one page. Sometimes knowing a little is worse than knowing nothing at all. Agent McKinnon didn't even scold me when she caught me looking. She must've known what I read was punishment enough.

CONFIDENTIAL: PROPERTY OF FEDERAL BUREAU OF INVESTIGATION

Name:	Levi James Beckett (see photo above)
DOB:	7/1/94
Height:	6'2"
Weight:	195 pounds
Education:	Berkshire High School, high school diploma, awarded 2013
	St. Edwards University, Bachelor of Arts in Criminal Justice, awarded 2016
Occupation:	Police Officer, Austin Police Department, Academy graduate, 2015
Known Relatives:	James Dumas, father. Deceased (November 25, 1996). CDC# B66882 Manner of death, suicide.
	Eliza Dumas, mother. Deceased (August 14, 1997). Manner of death, suicide.
	Kate Dumas (Beckett), sister
	David and Sandy Beckett, adoptive parents. 383 Willow Court, Austin, TX
Notes:	Administrative leave to begin June 20, 2016, pending investigation into allegations of bribery and misuse of confidential data.

****

A ghost of my mother returned. A pale shell discarded on the beach. Hollow inside, so all you hear is air rushing through. She looked past me and folded into her seat. The only sign of life was in her hands, shaking a little, but she slipped them under her thighs to quiet them. "I'm okay," she told me before I could ask.

"You've both had a long day. It's probably a good idea to get a hotel room and get some rest. We can help you with that. It goes without saying we recommend you stay close by." She waited for my mother to acknowledge her. In the awkward silence, I nodded instead. "We will be sending a couple of officers with you. Standard procedure for your safety. When we have some information—"

A stern voice interrupted her from the doorway. "Excuse me, Agent McKinnon, there's something you need to see." He extended a hand inside, passing her a cell phone with a sturdy black cover that looked a lot like my mother's. "This just arrived."

Agent McKinnon studied the screen as I studied her. My mother addressed the wall with a vacant stare.

"What is it?" I asked. "Another message?"

Ignoring my question, Agent McKinnon tapped my mother's arm. "What do you make of this?"

I peered over her shoulder. One new text message, a picture attached.

We both know this is between you and me. It always has been. You know where to find me. And you know what I'm capable of. Come alone unless you want her blood on your hands. They're already as red as mine.

I felt still, unnaturally calm, as if I stood smack-dab in the eye of a tornado, watching the entire world spin into chaos around me. Only Ginny's face was visible in the photo. Unlike in my dream, she wasn't peaceful. Not at all. Her skin unmarked, the terror was in her eyes. Still morning-glory blue at their centers, but milky red everywhere else. And wide. So wide. I couldn't look away.

"Any idea where he might be?" The ghost next to me said nothing. "I know it was ages ago … "

"A lifetime." Finally, she spoke.

"Right. I know you've been through a lot, Ms. Bronwyn. It must be difficult to remember." McKinnon's sympathy seemed practiced. I supposed it was.

"Impossible. I've told you everything I know."

"Maybe he hinted at something."

"Like what?"

"A place. A person. Somebody who might be helping him." McKinnon paused. "Rodney Taylor, for example. Has he been in touch? Do you think Cullen would know how to reach him?"

My mother snapped back in her chair, sudden and sharp. Her cheeks aflame, her mouth a small cave, she blinked back tears. Rodney Taylor—whoever he was—knocked her back like a sucker punch to the gut.

"Think hard," McKinnon encouraged, seemingly oblivious. "You know what's at stake."

"I am. And yes, I know." Agent McKinnon relented with a nod, and my mother's silence grew deep and wide like a river too treacherous to cross. I wanted to yell at her. To tell her Ginny's life depended on her. But I stopped myself. The way she wrung her hands, she seemed broken. Finally, three soft words, "There is something."

Agent McKinnon reached for her pen. "I'm listening."

"He always talked about an old friend who had a cabin somewhere in Vermont, I think."

"Can you give me anything more specific? You never mentioned this before."

Before. There it was again. Evidence of some other life. Pre-Samantha. "Umm … I don't have a name or anything if that's what you mean. I'd actually forgotten all about it. But one time he told me if he ever got out, that's where he'd be headed."

"Excuse me, ladies." Agent McKinnon left me with the ghost.

"Mom, are you okay? You seem—" She was already up and dragging me toward the door.

"We need to leave now."

"Are you crazy?" She certainly looked it. Alien. Unhinged. "Why?"

"I'll explain everything in the car." I raised my eyebrows in disbelief. "Now, Sam."

"Okay, okay. What about the cops? Did you just lie to them?" It occurred to me I didn't know my mother at all. Not really. Not as a person.

"By the time they figure it out, we'll be long gone."

NOVEMBER 12, 1996

CLARE plodded up the hill toward the prison gate, a poisonous mix of dread and anticipation sloshing in her stomach. Usually a three-day weekend did the trick, restored her sanity. Not this time. She'd spent most of Saturday on her knees, staring down the throat of the toilet puking up Friday's regrets. By Sunday, she was empty, save for that awful, familiar feeling she'd done something wrong. And of course, she had. So many things. Starting at the beginning. The slumber party. *Why did you let him touch you?* There was no answer for her own question or the guilt that grew inside her like a seed— slowly, slowly, and then all at once. Until she couldn't stand it. That's when she broke down and called Neal. *I saw Rodney*, she told him. And then he came over.

It felt cold in her office, even with the space heater Fitzpatrick loaned her running at full blast. She left her jacket on and opened Cullen's file to the back. After last week's lunacy, she was grateful for the reprieve of the Veteran's Day holiday. It meant she wouldn't see Cullen for another week. Maybe she could find Doctor Clare Keely by then. The psychologist. The professional. She wasn't sure where she misplaced her, only that she'd been most certainly lost, leaving a nutcase, a complete screwball to substitute. A screwball who had sex with the reliable, sturdy, boring oak tree. Because after Neal sat up with her and listened to all her half-truths, she owed it to him. It was the least she could do. And just as she feared, he stuck around all morning, all afternoon, all evening. *I miss this, Clare. I miss us.* Until she finally insisted he leave.

She found what she looked for wedged between an old time card and Cullen's rap sheet—an informational chrono from his first therapist at Wasco. She'd remembered it yesterday morning when Neal was moaning into her neck. *I love you.* One sentence at the end she'd glossed over. She fought the urge to push Neal off her and make a note to herself, even though she knew she wouldn't forget.

> **Clive Cullen participated in individual therapy with the undersigned clinician from March 1991 to January 1992. Mr. Cullen attended sessions regularly and was actively involved in identifying therapeutic goals, including gaining insight into his history of violence with women and learning to better manage his interpersonal relationships. Diagnostic impressions: Personality Disorder Not Otherwise Specified with Antisocial, Borderline, and Narcissistic traits …**

She traced the text with her finger, skimming through until it landed. Bull's-eye.

> **Juvenile court documents indicate no history of early maladjustment or parental abuse or neglect.**

Maybe Fitzpatrick had been right about Cullen snowing her with his Dickensian tales of a wretched childhood. She marked the page with a pink Post-it and pushed it to the corner of her desk, angry with herself. It wouldn't be the first time a man had duped her. Rodney always played the sympathy card. *My wife is screwing her boss behind my back. She won't even look at me anymore. I don't know what I'd do without you, Clarie. Probably just off myself. End it all.*

Come to think of it, he wasn't really that good at it. But she'd been the ultimate sucker, which made Neal's offer all the more tempting. *Do you want me to hurt him? I can't believe he had the nerve to talk to you. I'll do it. You know I will. For you.* Clare couldn't imagine Neal hurting anyone. Still, that wasn't why she told him no. If Rodney Taylor suffered, she wanted to be the one to do it.

"Knock, knock." Startled, Clare spun in her chair, her heart flitting as fast as a hummingbird's wings. Cullen was grinning from the doorway. In his hand, another ducat she hadn't approved.

And there it was again. Dread. Anticipation. "We weren't scheduled for a session this week."

"I know." He came inside without being invited. "I figured you wouldn't mind if I stopped by to say hello. They discharged me from the infirmary over the weekend." Clare watched him walk toward her. She forced a tight smile.

"I'm glad you're feeling better." *I should tell him to leave.*

"Me too. It was really nice of you to visit me." He stood next to her and set his hand on the desk. She stared at it. The way he caressed the surface seemed a signal meant for her. *He remembers,* she thought, as if he wouldn't. "Is that my file?"

She nodded, relieved for a place to put her own hands. She turned to the page she'd marked. "I was planning on asking you about it at our session on Monday."

"Ask me now." Clare followed his fingers as they disappeared into the pockets of his prison blues.

"Did you lie to me about your mother?"

"I've never lied to you. Why would you ask me that?" She turned the file and pointed to the sentence. Cullen threw his head back, revealing the softness of his throat, and laughed.

"Dr. Perlmutter? That guy didn't have a clue. He never asked me about my mother. He wasn't half the therapist you are." *Don't be a sucker.* Clare goaded her pride until it subsided. "Anyway, just because something isn't documented doesn't mean it didn't happen. It's real even if nobody knows, right?"

Clare saw herself, sixteen, sidelong in the mirror. Mostly, she avoided looking, but that day she'd caught her reflection. Whatever was inside her, it wasn't growing. It was as lifeless as a peach pit. She wondered if it wasn't a baby at all but a demon sent to destroy her, devour her from the inside out. *I'm sorry*, she told it, not knowing why, since it was dead anyway. Or hell bent on killing her. "Right," she agreed. "Of course it's real."

"Dr. Keely? Is everything okay in here?" She heard Fitzpatrick before she saw him. And when she saw him, her mind went blank. Like a hard return on her computer screen. "I didn't think you had a session with Mr. Cullen this week."

"Here's my ducat," Cullen said, producing the small yellow slip.

Fitzpatrick's unruly caterpillar brows drew closer together as he scrutinized the paper. "Is this legit?" he asked Clare.

Sometimes you have to tell a lie. To your best friend. To your ex-boyfriend. To your supervisor. "Yes. We rescheduled last minute." Even to yourself.

NOVEMBER 15, 1996

SOMETHING was off. Clare could feel it the instant her heels clicked against the cement inside the control booth. All eyes on her. All but Robocop. He busied himself at the desk, acting as if she was invisible. Since Cullen had been stabbed, Fitzpatrick had visited Dumas, giving Clare a bare-bones status report that morning. *He's doing alright. Didn't say much, but I think he's okay to come off suicide watch. Are you sure you're ready to get back out there? I can handle the case if you'd like.*

Of course, she refused. She liked Dumas and worried about him—especially with Thanksgiving right around the corner. But now, standing here, she questioned herself. Yesterday's unease clung to her like a wet towel.

"Hey, Briggs. How are you?" It rang false. Mainly because she never spoke first. Half the time, she prayed he wouldn't see her. Men always saw her.

No answer from Briggs, and the guard buzzed her through. She held the door and tried once more. "Briggs?" Maybe he didn't hear her the first time.

"How can I help you?" Sans dark glasses, but more Robocop than ever, his voice confirmed her worst fear. She *had* done something wrong.

"Just wanted to say hello." The other officers watched in amusement, and Clare felt a warm rash crawl up her neck.

"Hmph."

Her face on fire now, she fled out the door, grateful for the slap of cold air. At least she could pretend it was the wind making her eyes tear. *Do not cry. Not here.* Clare pinched the skin between her thumb and forefinger. Lizzie taught her that trick the first week of junior year, even though she never knew the truth of why Clare couldn't stop crying. *My grandpa died.* That was all Clare said. It wasn't really a lie. Her grandpa was dead after all. Had been for years. She couldn't tell Lizzie about those two pink lines, the pregnancy test she stole from Walgreens, confirming what she'd known for months. If nobody knew, it wasn't real. And nobody would ever know.

"You should've talked to me first, Clare." Robocop was suddenly right behind her. "When there's an issue with my officers, you come to me—understand?" He lowered his shades in the glare of the sun, and she saw her surprise in her reflection.

"What are you talking about?"

"I'm talking about Sampson, Martinez, and Bennett. They were walked off the job yesterday."

Clare swallowed the lump that was growing in her throat. It barely went down. "Why?" She knew why.

"Please don't give me that little-miss-innocent act. It doesn't work anymore."

"I had a legal obligation to report what Cullen told me. What was I supposed to do?"

Robocop's laughter, shrill as the scream of a bird, frightened her more than his gruff voice. "I protected you that day Ramirez sucker punched Cutthroat. I tried to stop you from going on the yard Thursday. But you wouldn't give me the time of day. And this is how you repay me—you get my officers fired. Now Bonner's on my ass wondering what did I know and when did I know it."

Halfway through his diatribe, Clare went numb. All she could see was the door to West Block. She would say whatever she had to, whatever was necessary to get there. "I didn't know those were your men, J. D. Really." She reached for his arm, and he let her touch him. "I should've come to you first. You're absolutely right." Beneath her hand, his bicep tightened. To Clare, it felt like a writhing snake. "Let me take you out tonight. Drinks on me."

"Well, I appreciate the apology." Clare couldn't see his eyes, but she felt them undressing her. "As for those drinks, I knew you'd come around. I'll meet you at 7 at that little dive bar off Third Street, where all the officers hang out. Now be safe out there." After his back was all she could see of him, she pinched herself off and on all the way to West Block. At the door, she used her sleeve to wipe a runaway tear from her cheek and marveled at the irony of its wet, mascara-colored existence. She'd stopped herself from crying about being sixteen and knocked up by Rodney Taylor, so how the hell did J. D. Briggs rattle her?

****

Dumas wasn't alone. "Meet my cellie. Eddie Bailey."

A lanky arm waved to Clare from the top bunk. "Call me Snip. Everybody does."

"Snap?" Her imagination took her to the darkest place it could find. Eddie Bailey snapped necks. Pale, delicate necks, not unlike her own.

"No. Snip."

"Oh." *Job hazard*, she thought. Always assuming the worst. Still, she put an absent-minded hand to her collarbone.

"He's a barber. A damn good one. I finally let him give me a little trim." Clare grinned and nodded her approval. Dumas appeared clean-shaven and bright-eyed. Better than he'd looked since she met him.

"You seem good today."

"Yep. I'm glad to see you. Your replacement, Doctor Fitzawhozit, was a real downer. One more meeting with him, and I would've been forced to do the dutch, as they say."

Fitzawhozit. She had to remember that one. "I don't think I can take all the credit for that smile. Did you see your family?"

"Sure did. Had a real long talk with the missus. She said that even if they take away our conjugal visits, she and the kids will be up here every week for regular visiting. And they just assigned me to the kitchen. Me. A cook? We had a good laugh about that one, seeing as how I can hardly boil water."

"Ain't that the truth," Snip said, snickering. "Good thing there's no chance of the food getting any worse." Dumas smacked the bunk above him, casting a conspiratorial side eye at Clare.

"The best part … I'm gonna see an attorney about appealing my case."

"Sounds like you found a little bit of hope. Do you think you're ready to start meeting in my office again?" Clare opened her pocket calendar before he could refuse. "How about Monday, 10:30 a.m.?"

"I'll be there."

The lilt in Dumas' voice was magic, like one of his coin illusions. If only for a moment, Robocop disappeared. "Nice to meet you, Snip. Take care of Mr. Dumas for me."

"Will do, Doc."

Clare left them chuckling behind her.

****

"Sorry, I'm late. I—uh—spilled something on my blouse. I had to change." *C'mon, Clare. You can do better than that.* But Robocop seemed to buy it. In truth, she'd sat in her car—parked a safe distance from his empty Jeep—until 7:15 p.m., watching the neon OPEN sign flicker off and on and off again. At 7:20 p.m., he'd pushed through the bar door, scanning the lot. His face told her what she would've guessed. He wasn't the kind of man who liked to wait. As penance, she offered the sweetest smile she could muster.

"You're forgiven. In fact, I'd like to personally thank whatever it is you spilled, because you look incredible in that dress." *Jesus.* He didn't waste any time.

"Thank you," she said as he ushered her inside, his hand barely resting on the small of her back. "It's nice to have an occasion to dress up. I can't exactly wear this to work."

His mouth opened wide—so wide—when he laughed that Clare turned away. That thick, salmon-pink tongue lolling in the

148

center of perfect white teeth revolted her. She knew its intentions. The things it wanted from her. "If you wore that dress to work …" Mercifully, he left the rest unspoken, shaking his head in amusement instead.

"I see you started without me," she said, motioning to the half-downed beer in front of him. "Drinks on me, remember?" She hated herself for offering almost as much as she hated the inflection in her voice. It was necessary though. There were things she wanted too.

"Don't worry. I started a tab." He ran his hand through his honey-colored hair, mussing it. "Honestly, I was nervous."

"Why?"

He gestured to her with an open hand. "Isn't it obvious? I didn't think I'd ever score a date with Clare Keely."

"Oh, is this a date?" She watched his teasing eyes twinkle at her. He leaned in. She backed away. This sport, the push and pull, felt effortless. And Clare didn't let herself feel guilty. Robocop brought this on himself.

Three-and-a-half beers later—three for Robocop, a half for Clare—Cullen's name came up. "So tell me about this nut-job client of yours." *Finally.* But she feigned ignorance. "The ratfink. You know, Cutthroat the canary."

"J. D., I can't talk about my patients. Especially not here."

"Oh, c'mon. Gimme a little somethin' I can rub in his face. That guy is the luckiest SOB in Quentin. I'd like to take him down a notch."

She produced a laugh. "Hey," she said. "Did you know … "

Robocop's loose expression sobered with her question, and she cursed herself for being too eager. "Know what?"

"I shouldn't ask. I know you don't trust me anymore." Her lower lip pouted a little. Just enough.

"Of course I trust you. Are you kidding?" His hand found her knee and rested there, waiting for permission. She scooted closer, granting. "Ask me anything," he said.

"Did you know Cullen was greenlighted?" She'd learned that word from Dumas too. "That Rivas was going to stab him that day on the yard?"

Robocop polished off beer number four with one long swig and slid his hand a little further up her leg. "Whaddya say we finish this conversation in my Jeep? Maybe take a little drive?"

His touch made Clare tingle, and she felt dizzy. Sick. "Okay, but—" Before she could set the rules of the game, he hopped off his stool and swaggered to the exit. She tossed a wad of cash on the bar and followed him.

Across the parking lot, the black Jeep loomed like a hearse. Clare grabbed his hand before he reached it. "On second thought, I have to get up early tomorrow. I think I'd better go."

He stopped cold, and Clare saw how it would go. He would drag her, rubbing her arm raw with the effort. Call her every vile name in the book. Then toss her in the backseat like a rag doll and take what he'd always wanted from her—from the first day she walked onto the yard. "Alright, party pooper. But let me walk you to your car."

Clare fumbled with her keys, anxious to make a clean getaway, disappointed in herself. "So this means we're friends, right?" he asked, helping her with the door.

"Friends." She repeated it back to him, uncertain. It felt like a promise she didn't want to make.

"I tell all my officers you can be my friend or my enemy. There's no middle ground. Once you pick a side, there's no going back."

She twittered. "Friends it is, then."

"With possibilities, I hope." The kiss felt inevitable. His lips pushed themselves onto hers. And the tongue she reviled, now pickled with alcohol, thrust itself into her mouth. But it was the smell—the heavy musk of Aqua Velva—that nearly buckled her knees. That smell didn't belong to him. That smell was Rodney Taylor's.

NOVEMBER 18, 1996

CLARE plucked a single, dying chrysanthemum from the vase on her desk—*he loves me, he loves me not, he loves me*—discarding each butterscotch petal into the trash at her feet. After that kiss, Clare expected Briggs to give chase—she let the answering machine take his call the next day—but she never figured him for the flower type. The vase had been waiting on her desk since last Thursday morning. No note.

"He loves me," she said aloud, snickering to herself.

"Lucky fellow."

"Clive, you're early." Clare hid behind her hair, letting it fall like a golden curtain around her face as she glanced at her watch. "I was just about to toss these flowers."

"Yellow chrysanthemums." He waited for her attention. "Looks like you've got a secret admirer." Baiting her, as usual.

"What do you mean?"

"Well, when she wasn't tagging behind some deadbeat like a stray puppy, Mommie Dearest worked in a flower shop. Yellow mums mean somebody likes you." He settled into the chair opposite her, stretching his legs under the desk dangerously close to hers.

"Good to know." She dumped the contents of the vase, feeling a little guilty as the yellow petals met an unceremonious end in her trash can. "You know, you can't keep showing up here early and unannounced."

He flinched. "I didn't think you'd mind. Not after last week. You stood up for me with your boss."

I lied for you, he might as well have said. She wasn't ready for this. Not on a Monday morning sans coffee. "Is this about your feelings for me? Should we revisit that subject?"

"Yes, let's." He leaned forward, his stare so intense, Clare had to look away. "Mine haven't changed." There was a question there, implied. A gaping hole of a question, a hole with no bottom, a hole Clare feared falling into.

"Maybe I've given you the wrong idea by letting you stay last week ... agreeing to your plan with Ramirez ... "

"Holding my hand?" he whispered.

She teetered on the edge, the soil slipping beneath her feet. "I didn't hold your hand, Clive. I was comforting you. That's what therapists do."

"You're right. Of course. Wishful thinking, perhaps?"

"I'd call it projection. Or Freud would anyway. You were projecting your own desires on me. Thinking I felt the same as you." She sounded like an actress playing a therapist on TV—a bad actress.

"So you don't? You're not attracted to me?" His eyes played with hers, daring her.

"We were talking about you, remember?"

"And this is me asking you. Just between us. Not as a therapist. As a woman." And there he was again. Rodney Taylor. He was never far away. *You're more woman than my wife ever was. Look at your tight little body.* Clare had looked at it. Her barely-there breasts tucked away inside a white *Hanes* bra. Her flat stomach, tan from laying poolside with Lizzie. Even two years later, when it was swollen so that she had to cover it with sweatshirts a size too big, his baby floating inside, her body seemed—*to her, anyway*—light years away from womanhood.

"Why is my answer so important to you?"

"Because I've never wanted someone who didn't want me back."

"What would that be like for you—if I didn't?" *Do I?* That same bottomless pit of a question, Cullen's laugh beckoning to her from its depths.

"Different."

"Different good or different bad?"

"Just different."

"And if I *was* attracted to you? What then?" Clare skin's prickled at her own audacity. But she didn't take it back. Cullen returned her challenge with a slippery smile. Smug. She remembered that fevered dream weeks ago, how she wanted his lips pressed to hers. He smiled like he knew.

"You've been hurt, Clare. Some bastard hurt you." Her throat made the noise of a small animal, a whimper. "I don't know how I know, but I do. I've always known things like that. Like with Emily. And Gina."

She didn't deny it. "You didn't answer my question."

"If you wanted me, I'd take care of you. I'd never … " Clare filled in the rest of that sentence with the autopsy report she read in the file on her desk. "I'm different now. Like I shed my skin, you know?"

"It's essential to you that I believe you've changed." She kept a tight grip on Doctor Keely so Clare couldn't slip through.

"Well, do you?"

"Sometimes. Then you say things to make me wonder. Like the other day in the infirmary, you told me you have remorse for what happened to Emily. What *happened* to her. You minimized your responsibility. And you still haven't told me exactly what you did to her."

Clare let out a long breath. Maybe she'd been too harsh. But then, "I know what I did to her. So do you. You've read the file. But if you need me to say it, I will. I had sex with her. Poured her a glass of wine or three. I pretended everything was fine, business as usual. That I didn't know she was screwing around on me. And she never saw it coming. She fell asleep like it was the best sex she'd ever had." Clare suddenly wanted to stop him before he got to the end. "I waited until I couldn't wait anymore, and then I slit her throat." She nodded fast, so she wouldn't gasp.

"Did you take her earring?"

"No one ever asked me that before. *God, you're good.* But, no, I didn't take it. I put one in her ear after. The cheapest hearts I could find. It was my gift to her." Clare hadn't expected that. "My goodbye gift."

"Why?"

"One fake heart. That's exactly what she deserved."

****

"Remorse is a funny thing," Cullen said. He had Clare pinned to her seat, laser-focused on his storm-cloud eyes, lost in the thick of their best session yet. "It's there inside me—guilt, regret—but I put it in a box. A box I don't open unless I have to. How else could I survive?" Clare had never heard anything more true. She'd buried more than the baby, the tiny thing, the intruder that came out of her. She entombed the guilt there too. *How else could she survive?*

A knock at her office door, and Clare was Doctor Keely again. Her stomach nose-dived when she found the clock. She'd lost track of time. Fifteen minutes over. *Please don't let it be Fitzawhozit.* Anyone but him.

"Mr. Dumas, I'm so sorry." Clare opened the door just wide enough to offer a contrite smile. "We went over time. It'll just be a minute."

"I'm not goin' anywhere," he told her, and they both chuckled. "Obviously."

Cullen brushed past her—*was he angry?*—so that his shoulder barely grazed her chest. "It was my fault. I got here late."

154

NOVEMBER 24, 1996

AH, Sunday. Clare loved Sundays. A long run, then coffee with Lizzie. That was the plan. Since she'd mentioned her run-in with Mr. Taylor, Lizzie insisted on a new coffee shop. *It's time to try something different anyway,* Lizzie assured her. *C'mon, Clare-Bear. Men, coffee— variety is the spice of life.*

Clare was grateful. Sort of. She didn't tell Lizzie about the circuitous path she took to Joe's Coffeehouse, the one that took her right by the parking lot of their old haunt. And she certainly didn't mention scouring the cars for his silver Bimmer. *Learn to say it right, Clarie,* Rodney had corrected, the first time he'd picked her up in his red one. *If you're going to ride shotgun with me, then you have to talk the talk, okay? It's Bimmer, not Beamer.*

Her stalking was irrational, completely absurd, but she couldn't stop. Every morning she told herself *not today,* and yet there she was again, idling past, slow and wide-eyed like a gawker at the scene of a head-on collision. She wanted to see him. The way he looked at her—like she was the sun—drew her back like a boomerang. Nobody else worshipped her that way. She hated that she loved it.

Fifteen mornings, she'd come up empty. Until today. She circled around the block to be sure. There were thousands of BMWs in Marin. But she'd committed his license plate to memory since it disappeared from her rearview weeks ago. Like so many things about him, that plate had been burned into her brain. And there it was, double-parked. She willed herself to drive past. A losing battle that ended with her surrender. A last-minute turn into the lot. She shut off the engine, cracked the window, and hunkered down in her seat.

Clare drummed her fingers against the steering wheel, while the anticipation curdled in her stomach. She'd been here before. Waiting for Rodney Taylor. The day she'd returned from her cousin's house in L.A., three months pregnant, she saw that Bimmer parked at the brand-new Blockbuster. He'd had a red one then. Candy apple red. And she watched until he drove it away, following it on her bike. Riding behind him, just out of sight, she felt desperate. Her feverish pedaling straight out of the *Wizard of Oz*. The Wicked Witch of the West chasing Dorothy, smack-dab in the middle of a tornado. That made her the witch. The witch with a secret incubating inside her. But Mr. Taylor channeled Oz himself. Great and powerful—that's how she saw him then. She would tell him everything, and he would make it go away. That much she knew.

He had parked at the football field in the spot where they made out sometimes. *I wish you were a cheerleader*, he'd told her once, fumbling with the buttons on her shirt, oblivious to the cold sting of his words. She'd tossed her bike to the ground nearby, stalking toward his car like a strange creature. He wanted to see her—of course he did—but she didn't feel like herself anymore. What if he didn't like her? *What if he did?* She pressed her hands to her belly, wondering if it knew she'd begun plotting its demise. And then, cruel trick, a girl appeared. A girl she recognized. A freshman. Blonde and long-legged, just like her. The girl opened the door to *her* passenger seat, and Clare could only watch. That was the *real* last time she'd seen Rodney Taylor, his head leaning in toward the cherry-stained lips of a San Marin High cheerleader.

But now, she didn't have to watch anymore. She didn't have to wait. She plumbed the depths of her glove box until she found it. Put there just for this. Fifteen days of planning. She had to move fast, but not too fast. *Cat-like*, she thought. *Like Cullen sneaking up on me.* There were easier ways. Removing the caps, for one. It had to be this way so she could feel it, so she had to work for it. She crouched down alongside the car wishing she could take her time, savor it. Just a steak knife from her kitchen—but clutched in her hand, it looked as fierce as if it was meant to cut flesh. That thought brought an unexpected excitement. It sliced through the shell of her and awakened the numb parts. It felt good to be bad. So good. Too good. *Like I could throw off sparks*, she thought. When she plunged the knife through the black rubber, her body shuddered with the release. It wasn't Mr. Taylor's face she pictured, but the girl in the red Bimmer.

****

"You little hussy," Lizzie teased between sips of coffee. "A hook-up with Neal and a make-out sesh with a cop. Who's next, Cutthroat?"

"Okay, first off, that's not funny. Second, J. D. is not a cop." Clare wrapped her hands around the hot mug to quiet their shaking. She tried not to look at them so Lizzie wouldn't notice. *Relax, Clare. You stabbed a tire, not a person.*

"Correctional officer. Same difference. A sergeant no less. And third?"

"Third, we didn't make out. It was just a kiss. And fourth, he was drunk."

"It must've been some kiss." Clare laughed and shook her head, going along with Lizzie's banter. "I mean, he called the next day, and he sent flowers. I've had boyfriends who didn't do either, much less both in the same week."

"Actually, I'm not sure he sent the flowers." Clare put her palms against the cold countertop. *Was that blood under her fingernails?* She curled her fingers in and out again, and it was gone. "Clive told me yellow chrysanthemums mean you have a secret admirer." Fitzpatrick was her prime suspect, the flowers a sick little experiment he devised to suss out her boundaries.

"Oh, it's Clive now, is it? Why is he giving you relationship advice?"

"It was just a comment. An innocent observation." The voice in her head cackled at her own idiocy.

"Right, because he's so innocent. Pure as the driven snow, that guy."

Clare rolled her eyes. "At least he didn't act jealous. He's weirdly possessive of me as his therapist." *Not as a therapist.* She heard him correct her. *As a woman.* "I'm surprised he didn't throw the flowers out himself."

"Unless … " Lizzie grinned mischievously. "He's your secret admirer."

NOVEMBER 25, 1996

LIKE any other Monday at 9:15 a.m., Clare's body sat at her desk. But today, it felt empty, an unmanned craft sitting idle, patiently waiting for its driver to return. Her mind remained on the early morning phone call that had jolted her from sleep. It played on an endless loop.

"Hello?" She was already asking a question, her voice groggy and uncertain.

"Is this Clare Keely? Marybeth Keely's daughter?" It'd been so long since she'd heard her mother's name. And when was the last time she'd talked to her? 1993 maybe. Right after husband number four. Or was it five? "Are you there, ma'am?"

"Yes. Yes, I'm sorry. I'm here. I'm Clare Keely."

"Ms. Keely, this is Officer Hutchins of the Los Angeles Police Department. I'm calling to inform you that your mother was in a car accident early this morning."

"Is she okay?"

"I'm sorry, but no. She passed away in the O.R. The driver, Frank De Marco, was pronounced dead at the scene."

Clare waited to feel something, but nothing came. Only the tinny sound of her mother's voice, twittering about her quickie Vegas marriage to someone she called Frank the Tank. "Oh."

"The vehicle struck a telephone pole. Alcohol may have been a factor. We don't know too much yet."

"How did you find me? My mother and I … well, we weren't exactly close."

"She had a picture of you inside her wallet with an old address. You were the only next of kin we could locate. Is there someone else we should call?"

"No. It's just me." After she laid the receiver to rest, she padded back down the hallway to her bed and buried herself beneath the covers. The ceiling, blank like her, stared back. But she was good at this. She knew what to do. Alanis Morissette, until sleep crept in.

Anybody else would've called in sick. Not Clare. She showed up early as penance for what she'd done. What she'd brought on herself. She was a bad girl, always had been. That's what Rodney Taylor knew about her. That's why he liked her. He saw she would go along with him, that she might even enjoy it. That she was the kind of girl who would stick a knife into a man's tire and get off. And now, someone, somewhere was punishing her for her badness. But it wasn't God because He didn't exist. There was a devil though. Of that, she was certain.

A soft knocking at the door brought her back. "Dr. Keely? Clare?" Cullen and his quicksilver-blue eyes were on the other side. Early again, but she didn't mind. Not today. Today, she was desperate for a compelling distraction, one strong enough to anchor her to reality. "I know, I know. I'm early, but I couldn't help it. I had a revelation."

"It's okay," she said, stepping aside to allow him entry. "I'll let it slide this time." Whatever the price, she would pay it later. "Let's hear this revelation."

"I was thinking a little—okay, a lot—about our session last week. And it hit me. The brutality of what I did."

Mind and body, Clare hummed again. She moved to the edge of her seat. "Tell me more."

"Of course, I knew it was a horrible crime. I intended that. A knife is so intimate and so devastating. Exactly what I wanted. I needed to feel her pain. I needed her to feel mine. But seeing you, the way you looked at me, when I said what I'd done … how I'd done it … I could hardly bear it."

160

"How did I look at you?"

"Like I was Cutthroat. The monster everyone thinks I am."

"And that disturbed you?"

"Very much."

"Why, do you think?"

His soft laughter went straight to her spine. In a good way that felt bad. Or a bad way that felt good. Either way, it felt familiar. "Your opinion matters to me. No—more than that. You captivate me."

It was Clare's turn to laugh, and all the things balled tight inside loosened a little. "Captivate. Wow."

"I'm not supposed to say that, am I?"

"Well, let's see … " She reached for the dictionary on her desk, letting the razor-thin pages slip like silk beneath her eager fingers until she found it. "Captivate. To attract and hold the interest of. I suppose, by this definition, you captivate me as well."

Clare had lost the wheel again. She veered toward that same edge, daring herself to fall. Cullen was her own personal telephone pole. And she was about to smash into him. Instead, she swerved. "My mother died." Saying it out loud made it real. And when it was real, it hurt. She blinked back tears.

Cullen said nothing. She was grateful for that, because she couldn't take it back. "Were you close?" he asked, finally.

"I'm sorry. It was inappropriate for me to share that. I just found out this morning, and I probably should've stayed home. Let's get back to you and your revelation." *Get your head together, Keely. You didn't even like your mother.*

He frowned at her, but nodded, compliant. "It's simple really. I understand now that no woman could ever love me. Not after I tell them the truth. I saw that in your eyes when you looked at me."

"So you feel unlovable?"

"Could you love someone like me? Could anyone?" Cullen's eyes watered and spilled over. She never expected this. Not from him. "I'm going to hell, you know," he told her. *So am I*, she thought. "Actually, I'm already there," he said, gesturing to the walls around him.

"You feel doomed."

"Wouldn't you? Seriously, tell me. If you met me under different circumstances, would you be my girlfriend? Would you write me letters? Come and visit me in this shithole?"

"If you weren't in here, and we found ourselves face-to-face, who knows?" Clare flipped up her palms. "There are good things about you, Clive. Things someone might find attractive. Things someone could love. After all, finding a woman has never been your problem. Some might even say women can't resist you."

"So you're telling me I could seduce you if I wanted to." *Probably.* Clare ignored the voice in her head. The bad girl who had already done enough.

"I'm saying your problem is not in the finding. It's in the letting go."

He cocked his head to the side, thinking. "Attachment is the root of suffering, right? Isn't that what they say? Heck, I even got a little jealous last week seeing you laughing with … what's his name? That string bean that tried to off himself."

She tapped her watch. "Maybe we can talk more about this next week."

"But we still have thirty minutes."

"Exactly."

Cullen grinned at her. "I get it. It's a test, right? An exercise? To see if I can let go."

"Can you?"

She needed him to leave. He was a kind of fire she wanted to touch, already knowing it would burn. Still, she felt a twinge of regret when he rose and walked toward the door. He leaned up against it— coy and casual—in a way that made her wonder if he was testing her too. "It's not easy. You're my favorite hour of the week. But if you think it will help me … "

"I do. I want you to notice how it feels to surrender control." She stood, ready to dismiss him, but he didn't move. Clare took another step toward the door, toward him. So close now she could smell the soap he'd showered with that morning. She could see the dark stubble peppering his chin, and she wondered how it would feel underneath

162

her fingers. Her hand lifted without her permission and reached for him, brushing the sleeve of his shirt, resting on his bicep. She looked at her thumb, pressed against the edge of a freckle, and concluded she had lost her mind.

"It feels like that." It came out so quiet, she would question whether he'd said it all. Then, he turned the knob and disappeared.

****

"You ended your session early?" Fitzpatrick ushered her into his office with a hurried wave of his hand. Clare kept her eyes off his, staring at the coffee stain on his chest instead. Like a Rorschach inkblot, it took the shape of a fist—a baby's fist—small and brown.

"Yes. I just … my mom died." It wasn't a lie. At least she could hold on to that. "She was killed in a car accident early this morning. I thought it would be good for me to come in to get my mind off it." But instead she'd nearly made good on Lizzie's preposterous suggestion.

"Oh, Clare. I'm so sorry to hear that. Is there anything I can do?" Fitzpatrick's thin lips turned down in pity. "Anything at all." She could imagine the *anything* he had in mind.

"We actually weren't that close. I hadn't spoken to her in years. I really didn't expect it to affect me this way. Maybe it's something to do with Thanksgiving being right around the corner."

"Sometimes it's those sorts of relationships that wound us the most. There's no closure. No chance for resolution." Clare felt the sting of truth. There were so many loose ends unraveling, dangling from her heart, she'd lost count. "Maybe that's why you cut your hour short. It's classic displacement, right?" She fought the urge to roll her eyes. "You redirected those feelings of a premature ending onto a substitute target, Mr. Cullen. Perhaps we could examine that during our supervision tomorrow."

"Okay." Her agreement sounded hollow, but it was the best she could do. "Would it be alright if I went home now? Took a personal day?"

"Of course." Fitzpatrick approached her with his arms out-stretched. "You look like you could use a hug." He didn't wait for her to answer, wrapping his arms around her the way a child might hold a cat. Clare stopped squirming and gave in, quieting her body until he released her. "Has anyone ever told you that you smell like lavender?"

"I don't think so," Clare answered, while the badness inside her drew a picture in her head, painting Fitzpatrick's coffee stain red. It was a bloody fist now, an X-marks-the-spot where she'd sunk a knife.

Dumas waited for her in the hallway. *Dammit.* She'd completely forgotten. At least he was smiling. "Did you forget about me?" he asked.

"Of course not. Unfortunately, I have to reschedule our session. I'm not feeling so great."

His face darkened with concern. "Oh no. Hope it's not the bug that's going around. Snip's been out to the infirmary for the past two days."

"Could you stop by tomorrow instead? How about noon?"

He nodded. "Works for me. I've got nothin' but time."

****

Clare's hand pressed hard between her legs. Later, she'd regret this. She hadn't done it in so long. But now, there were no thoughts of any kind. No room for regret. Everything but her body disappeared. And that's why she liked it. She moaned *Rodney* against her pillow. He was with her in her bed, in every bed, even when he wasn't. It was *his* hand rubbing her there. His hand inside her. And then, it wasn't Rodney at all. She realized it mid-shudder, mid-release, when she saw storm-cloud eyes and stubble, hands stronger than Rodney's, and a taut stomach marked by pain. She laid there afterward bathed in shame, the mid-afternoon sun sneaking past her drawn curtains, until the phone rang.

Five rings, and the machine picked up. "Hello, you've reached Clare Keely. Please leave your name and number, and I'll get back to you as soon as I can." Then, the beep.

"Clare ... uh ... this is Dr. Fitzpatrick. I'm sorry to bother you at home. I know it's a bad time. But I need to talk to you. They ... uh ... they found James Dumas in his cell this afternoon. Hanging. He's dead."

164

CHAPTER FIFTEEN

EYE OF HORUS

CLARE Keely sat behind the wheel of the rental car. She looked like my mother, sounded like her too. The few words she'd said, anyway. But the way she was pushing the 40-miles-per-hour speed limit through Muir Woods, hugging the turns like she knew them, I couldn't be sure. I snuck a glance at the back of her neck, where a few blonde tendrils escaped from her ponytail. It was still there. Her Eye of Horus tattoo—to ward off evil. *When your father died, I felt cursed.* That's what she told me, years ago, rubbing the ink as if it was a talisman. I'd been afraid to ask anything else. It was the most mysterious thing about her, and I didn't trust it. For the first time, I felt relieved to see it there. Definitive evidence this impostor was my mother.

"Are you going to tell me where we're going?" I asked. "How about what we're doing here? Why you lied to the police? Rodney Taylor? Anything?" She gripped the wheel so tightly, her knuckles turned white. Her lips pressed together so no words could escape. "Mom?" I gave up. Wherever she was, whatever wall she'd disappeared behind, I couldn't reach her.

I pressed my face to the window, leaning my cheek against the cool glass, and searched the redwoods for an answer. Bellwether is flat as a sheet in every direction, I'd never seen so many trees. They blocked what remained of the sun, stretching their ancient arms through the fog and toward the sky, in reverie. High, so high I had to crane my neck to find slivers of sunlight peeking through the dense canopy.

"Was Ginny wearing earrings?" When it came—finally—her voice was throaty, raw. So unexpected, I nearly jumped.

"Probably her gold stars, the ones her mom gave her for graduation. But I'm not sure." I shrugged. "Why?"

"She was missing one in that photo he sent." I breathed through a wave of nausea. That photo. Ginny's eyes—red rimmed and desperate—were impossible to unsee. I certainly hadn't noticed her earrings.

Quiet again, my mother offered no explanation. She slowed the car and navigated the road's shoulder, pulling to an abrupt stop. Nothing around us but those thick, grounded sentinels watching, waiting. A silent army, they unnerved me. The things they might have witnessed.

She opened the door. "Stay here," she said, almost as an afterthought.

"Are you kidding?" In the glow of the headlights, the fog was rising up from the ground like steam, but when I stepped into it, it was icy cold. "I'm coming with you."

I expected her to argue, but she only sighed as she trudged—no hesitation—into the forest. I could barely hear her soft counting over the crunch of the underbrush beneath my feet. I knew better than to speak. At three hundred, she paused, and so did I. She swallowed hard, then pressed on into the utter stillness. Deeper and darker, until the road was a warm and distant memory. There were no paths, no markers, but she knew the way. *The way to what?* Three hundred fifty, and she stopped, right at the base of a magnificent redwood. Its trunk had a small hollow, the perfect size for a raccoon or a skunk. My mother crouched low and pawed at the dirt.

"Help me dig." I laughed out loud. It wasn't funny. Not at all. Seeing my mother root her hands into the earth, her face already red with the effort, disturbed a part of me I couldn't name. So many things bubbled up inside me, pushing to the surface, they needed an escape. So, I laughed. The kind of hysterical laughter that leaves you aching and breathless. My mother barely noticed. Even when I doubled over, she didn't look up. And I only laughed harder. And harder still, until the tight cord within me unwound. My stomach loose and exhausted, I took a step forward and spotted it through watery eyes, just beneath my feet. Lucky, because if I hadn't, I would've fallen in. Sprained my ankle. Or worse.

"I think you're digging in the wrong spot," I said, gaping down into the deep hole. At least four feet down. Further than we'd have ever gone with just our hands. Rich, black soil piled on either side. And in it, something indiscernible. "Someone's already been here." In my mind, that someone was a him, but I couldn't say that out loud. Not here. Not in this place. This place that felt enchanted. *Him.* It sounded too much like an invitation, a hex.

Wide-eyed, my mother spun on her heels, brandishing a broken tree branch in her hand like a weapon. She seemed alien in the way she stalked, making a slow circle around us, peering into the woods where it was all tangles and shadows. My heart thwacked against my rib cage, demanding to escape from here, to flee the way I wanted to.

"He's gone," she said finally, confirming my worst fears. "Is it empty?"

I shook my head not knowing if that was good or bad. My mother trudged toward me and joined me at the edge. At her sides, her hands were caked with soil. Her cheeks smudged with it. The freshly dug earth smelled of Bellwether after a heat shower. Those sudden moments of release that pour down in late August, when the air is too hot to breathe. Ginny and I would put on our bathing suits and run through her yard like little girls soaking in the last bit of freedom before school started.

"Three-fifty—to the right of the tree with a mouth. How did I miss it?" she muttered, talking but not to me. A fat drop of sweat rolled down her nose, and she wiped it with the back of her hand, leaving a new dirt smear. Then, without warning, she lowered herself down, legs deep, into the hole and produced a box from its bottom.

"Here," she said, passing it up to me. I didn't want to take it. It didn't belong to me. Or my mother. It belonged to the past. To Clare Keely. I had no choice but to accept it. It wasn't heavy, and I tried to feel reassured. "Don't open it." *As if.* It was secured with a combination lock, and my own dread was enough to keep me out. Instead, I studied its strange markings: 200 cartridges. 7.62 mm. M13. Overhead fire.

"What is it?" I asked.

My mother planted her palms in the dirt and hoisted herself up and out, grunting with the effort. "It's an old military ammo can. Weatherproof. Good for burying things." *Things.* I supposed *things* were better than *people.* I didn't want her answers, so I didn't ask any more questions. I wasn't ready for all of Clare Keely yet. "I stored it here for safekeeping."

The wind picked up a little, slipping its invisible fingers through the trees. Their prehistoric trunks didn't budge, of course. Fire, flood, nothing could move them. But their branches were fickle, stirring and rustling, their soft whirring the soundtrack of a nightmare. My mother heard it too. She took the box from me and started walking, head down, as fast as she could go. I followed her out the way we came. In silence. With a single question turning over and over in my mind like the stones beneath my feet. *Safekeeping from whom?*

****

We drove for a while with the box a stanchion between us. It sat there, a tight-lipped guest, holding its secrets, while my mother piloted us through the forest and the last remnants of daylight. I heard her humming softly—she did that sometimes when she was nervous. After she stopped, she released a long, rattled breath. "I had to get out of there," she said, taking the box onto her lap. "It felt haunted, didn't it?" I nodded and laughed, a little giddy with relief.

In the soft light of the car, her fingers shook as she spun the dial. Three times to the right. Stop. One time to the left. Stop. One time to the right. Stop. Just like my locker at school. The shackle popped open, and she turned to me, almost surprised. "It was so long ago."

"You buried it?" It came out like a question. I hoped it was a safe one, the kind that skirted the boundary of all I didn't want to know.

"In 1997." She cracked the lid, and her face paled a sickly white. I wanted to run away. To never know what was inside. If a ghost roamed those woods, it had hitched a ride with us. It hunkered in there, biding its time, its bones cooling and turning to dust. And we were about to release it.

The box open now, my mother reached inside and removed the items one by one. She placed them on the console.

A massive wad of one-hundred-dollar bills, wrapped tight with a rubber band. *Maybe this won't be so bad.*

A large enveloped, unopened.

A gun. The same kind we had at home. My mother removed the clip to check it was loaded, then released the slide to chamber a round. That unmistakable sound always twisted my stomach. It came with a warning—the first rule of gun safety. Never point your weapon at anything you're not willing to destroy. *What was Clare Keely willing to destroy?*

A note was last, scrawled on a scrap of paper. Transfixed, she held it longer than it took to read. I finally plucked it from her frozen hand like a petal.

> *My dearest Clare,*
> *Three-hundred-fifty paces to the right of the tree that looks like a mouth. It was all there, just the way you said it would be a lifetime ago. But I've left it for you—all of it—because I know where you're going. And it's only fair you have a weapon. As you know, I prefer knives.*
> *Yours always,*
> *Clive*

CHAPTER SIXTEEN

BUZZARDS

WHEN we get there, you have to stay in the car." My mother didn't tell me, but I suspected *there* was Muir Beach. We'd been following the signs for the last few miles—still hurtling faster than the posted speed limits—in what was shaping up to be the blackest night I'd seen since home. She hadn't mentioned the note folded in my palm. The note that addressed her like a lover. The note penned by a murderer. "Promise me you'll stay in the car. No matter what."

"Get where?" I played dumb.

"Samantha! Promise me!" Her voice so last-gasp, so imploring, I couldn't deny it. It sounded like the wail of a trapped animal.

"Okay, okay. I promise." When she looked at me, her eyes were wild, but focused. I only stared ahead, scanning the narrow road. Not another car in sight. I wished for a crash. It wasn't so far-fetched. After all, it had happened to my grandmother. All it took was one hairpin turn a little too fast. My mother would lose control and send us skidding broadside into the trees. They wouldn't mind. They'd seen worse. That was the only way this would stop. My own rancid desperation rose up like acid in my throat. Hot and sour.

"If I don't come back in thirty minutes, drive to the city and find Agent McKinnon. Do not come and look for me." She floored it now like her foot had its own life—a miserable life it wanted to end. I reconsidered my wish and dug my hands into the seat at my sides, holding on as tight as I could. "Slow down, Mom." A bird struck the car with a sudden, sick thud. Its brown wings fluttered against the windshield and went still.

"Oh God," she said. "Oh God." She slammed the brakes, and I jolted forward, bracing myself against the dash. The bird's small body lay on the hood, broken. "Oh God," she repeated again, rocking against the seat. "It's dead, isn't it? I didn't mean to do it." I watched my mother with wariness as she dissolved in tears. Clare Bronwyn didn't cry. Not at movies. Not at funerals. Not at my graduation. Not even when we found buzzards circling her favorite cow, and she had to put her down with the rifle she kept in the shed to scare off coyotes. But this Clare was different. "I'm so sorry." I couldn't tell if the apology was meant for me or the bird. Either way, she kept saying it, soft like a prayer, as she put the car in park and got out. Cupping the bird in her hands, she carried it to the edge of the forest and laid it on the grass. When she returned, her face calmed again.

"We're almost there," she said, driving away as if nothing happened.

My mother's weakness made me bold. It was now or never. "Are you going to see ... *him*?" Of all the questions I could have asked, it was the dumbest, the answer so obvious she didn't need to give it. So obvious it could have been written on the sign in the car's headlights, as clear as the bold white letters: **MUIR BEACH, GOLDEN GATE RECREATIONAL AREA**.

She guided the car into the empty lot and took the gun from under her seat, where she'd placed it. "You remember what I told you, right? Don't look for me." She left the car running and opened the door. The air rushed in, cold and wet.

"You're leaving? Just like that? With no explanation?" I grabbed her arm to stop her, and she made a face like she'd been stung. "Why did you even bring me with you?"

"I meant to tell you everything on the way here. That's why. And I thought I could do it, but I can't. Not yet."

"Everything? You mean there's more?" *More than Clare Keely, the psychologist? More than a box buried in the woods? More than a note from Clive Cullen? More than that?* The swell of anger I'd been stamping down since this morning broke through, and I heard the indignation in my voice. My mother offered only a sheepish shrug in lieu of an admission. "What are you waiting for? Go ahead. Tell me."

"I have to find Ginny first. Cullen's right. If she dies, it's my fault. I've already done enough. There's blood on my hands." She glanced nervously at her fingers, wrapped tight on the gun's grip, as if she expected them to be dripping red.

It was hard to be mad, to stay mad, when she seemed so fragile, as delicate as the bird that met its end against the windshield. "It's not your fault, Mom. How could you stop him? And he came after *me*, remember? How do you know he's not watching us right now, just waiting for you to leave?"

For a moment, my questions silenced us both. Beyond the lights of the parking lot, the night extended on forever. I imagined Clive Cullen beneath that dark veil, marking time, sharpening his knife. But I didn't let myself picture Ginny. "This is about me, Samantha. What I did to him. I'm the only one who can fix this. I'm the one he wants." I nodded because I couldn't speak. "I love you," she said. "Lock the door." She closed it without looking back and headed in the direction of the beach.

****

This is crazy. I sat up tall, flipped up the visor mirror and caught a glimpse of my harried frown. *And this is what crazy looks like.* It seemed like an hour, but only six minutes had passed since my mom abandoned me on her utterly unromantic stroll on the beach, armed and in pursuit of an escaped convict. I almost started the hysterical-laughing thing again, but then I kicked the ammo canister on the floorboard, spilling the contents around my feet.

The unopened envelope presented a welcome distraction, so I retrieved it and examined it more closely. Its edges were tinged with age, but otherwise it was completely nondescript. Inside, I felt something hard and flat. I slid my finger beneath the seal, and the glue gave way, prompting an annoying pinch of guilt at my chest. Surely there were times when snooping was permissible, even appropriate. Surely this was one of them.

I emptied the envelope onto my lap. Two passports tumbled out. Two faces I recognized. Two names I didn't. The first face belonged to my mother. A younger version, anyway. Blonde and shiny. She flirted with the camera without smiling. I'd never seen her do that before. As pretty as she was—and believe me, all the boys at Bellwether High never let me forget it—she detested pictures. Apparently, Clare Keely did not. The other face belonged to Cutthroat Cullen.

If I didn't know the passports were counterfeit, I wouldn't have been able to tell. Not like the obvious fake licenses Ginny scored for us last year, the ones we brought with us for the hot spots. I would've believed those two cunning half-smiles—those four clever eyes—belonged to Kevin and Anna Johnson of Beverly Hills. I held them side by side under the light. They looked good together, a handsome couple. And that disturbed me most of all. Not the secrets she'd unearthed, but the ones that stayed buried, the ones I could only guess at. The skeletal remains of the life before me.

I leaned back in my seat and conjured the only sure-fire thing that helped me relax. I stood at the free-throw line, ball in hand. *Never break routine.* I bounced the ball three times, then spun it between my hands. I took in a quick breath and set my sights on the square above the hoop. The ball left my fingers in a rainbow arch and plummeted downward with enviable rotation. It headed for the net—on its way to *swish*—so I could start again from the beginning. *Never break routine.* But it didn't get there. Mid-flight, a man's face appeared in the window, and I screamed.

CHAPTER SEVENTEEN
LONG AND WEIRD

I registered the baseball cap first—Oakland A's. That looked familiar. Then, the eyes. Bright, green, and unmistakable. Finally, the voice. Smooth and direct, even though it was muffled by the window. A voice that would have the right answers. A voice that would tell me what to do. "Stop screaming." I didn't think I had been, but I clamped my hand over my mouth just in case. "Open the door."

"Did anyone ever tell you that you make a lousy entrance?" I asked Levi, lifting up on the driver's side handle. I tried to stifle my relief. I didn't want him to know I was glad to see him. Not until I knew he was glad to see me.

He shrugged, lowered the duffel bag from his shoulder, and climbed inside. "I tapped first, but you didn't hear me. Did anyone ever tell you," he mimicked, "that you have the scream of that chick from *Psycho*?"

"You mean Janet Leigh? The blonde bombshell? I'll take that as a compliment." I let my grin mirror his, wide and sly. He *was* glad to see me. "Speaking of psycho, it looks like you're following me again. What are you doing here?" It wasn't my real question. I wanted to ask how he knew about this place—*no*—how my mother knew. Someone had to unmask Clare Keely, but I was still too scared to see underneath.

"Same as you."

"What *am* I doing here?" Levi snuck a glance at the passports on my lap, and I covered them with my palm. Administrative leave aside, he was still a police officer, and I was fairly certain my mom had done something—possibly a lot of things—that were not exactly legal. "Maybe you can shed some light."

"Hunting a serial killer, I presume," he said, gesturing to my closed fist. "Where did you get those?"

"Long story," I said. "Long and weird."

"Well, you can tell me on the way then." He turned off the ignition, removed the keys and handed them to me.

"On the way?"

"You weren't just going to let your mom wander off in the woods alone, were you?"

"She told me to stay here. And how did you know—"

He interrupted me with a murmur of disapproval. "If I remember correctly, she also told you not to come on this trip in the first place."

"I should've listened." *If only I could take it back.* Rewind. I desperately needed a do over.

"Then I'd be all alone out here."

"I get the feeling you'd do alright. You probably work better without a partner. Especially a naïve eighteen-year-old from the sticks, right?"

"Usually. But don't sell yourself short. After all, you are a Texas girl. I hear they're pretty scrappy despite their overwhelming lack of experience."

Ignoring my eye roll, Levi slipped a small flashlight from his pocket and exited the car. He motioned for me to follow, then started walking toward the road. The wrong direction. "She didn't go that way," I called to him through my open door, still planted in my seat.

He stopped, but didn't look back. "That's probably what she wanted you to think. I know where she's going. Trust me, it's this way."

"How do you know?"

He groaned and turned to me. I expected exasperated Levi—jaw clenched, brows furrowed—but his face didn't give him away. Or maybe he had more patience than I credited him with. Probably a side effect of dealing with wackos like Skinny. "It's a long story. Long and weird," he parroted. I watched the corner of his mouth turn up, and I made a decision. Maybe I was more Keely than Bronwyn.

"I guess you can tell me on the way then." I put one foot on the ground and waited.

"Partners?" he asked.

"On one condition." Two feet on the ground now, I stood firm. "I need an answer. An honest one."

"What's the question?"

Sometimes, asking is like heaving up a half-court shot to beat the buzzer. Other times, it's drawing back on a bow and setting free a piercing arrow. I knew it would hit its mark, and it would sting. But I did it anyway. Before I took a single step in his direction, I needed to know the score. "What does your dad's death have to do with Cullen? I know he committed suicide."

His reply came with no trace of mystery. For once, no slipperiness. Just a straight arrow shot right back to me with unequivocal pain. "That's the thing, Sam. He didn't."

CLARE skipped her morning run. She couldn't be late. That would look bad. Not that it could look any worse. Her client was dead. And she hadn't reported for work at all yesterday. No call, no show. She spent the day after—after her mother, after Cullen, after Dumas—*making love* to Neal. His words. It didn't erase the *before*, but it dulled her senses enough. Neal thought he'd comforted her, soothed her pain. Really, she was just holding her breath underwater.

Sans her usual three miles, she still lumbered up the stairs to her office like her legs were bags of sand. She wanted to turn around, get back in her car, and drive as fast as she could to anywhere but here. If it had been up to her, she wouldn't even be here at all. She pleaded with Neal. Literally begged him to let her stay in bed. It embarrassed her to think of it now, how she'd latched onto his waist, slipped her hand beneath the waistband of his boxers, and made him think she wanted him. She said things too. Things she didn't mean. Like, *I love you. Let's start over.* But Neal had more willpower than she'd expected. He forced her to go. *They can't blame you, Clare. You did nothing wrong. Show them your notes. Cooperate with the investigation. You're a professional. Act like it.*

She wasn't a professional. That's what she wanted to tell Neal. *I was a heartbeat away from shoving my tongue down Clive Cullen's throat.* What would Dr. Neal Barrington say to that? She laughed out loud, then clamped her hand against her mouth, shutting it tight until the impulse passed. Fitzpatrick had already arrived. So had Bonner. She saw their shadows through the beveled glass. They were probably talking about her right now. Talking about what a professional she was. *Not.*

Straightening her blouse, a demure button-up, she knocked softly. Maybe they wouldn't hear her. "Come in, Dr. Keely."

"Good morning." It wasn't really. In fact, it was downright awful, but the men nodded in unison.

"Have a seat, Clare." Fitzpatrick gestured to the metal folding chair he'd brought in just for her, positioned directly across from them, and she sat.

"I'm sorry I missed worked yesterday. I was—"

Fitzpatrick silenced her with his hand. "I'm sure you were overwhelmed. We completely understand." Clare could tell by their smug faces they didn't. "Lieutenant Bonner and I wanted to review protocol with you so you know what to expect in the coming weeks. We want to be completely transparent. No surprises."

Bonner's cheeks plumped with the kind of backhanded pity that can only come from arrogance. "As you know, Mr. Dumas hung himself on Monday afternoon." *Dumas.* Until then, she hadn't let herself think his name. "He was discovered by one of our officers shortly after he returned to his cell from the chow hall. Now, as I'm sure you know, when an inmate takes his own life, we're obligated to investigate. Between you and me, I'd rather just chalk it up to our good fortune. One less sorry bastard in here getting fat on our taxpayer dollars." Fitzpatrick chuckled, prompting a forced smile from Clare. It seemed essential to agree. That's what a professional would do. "But it's not up to me, of course. His family will have questions, and we have to give them answers."

"Where are your session notes?" Fitzpatrick asked. "We'll need to review them ASAP."

"They're in my office. I can get them now. It'll just take a—" Anything to escape.

"That won't be necessary," Bonner interrupted, offering another smirk. "Dr. Fitzpatrick will retrieve them after we're done here. It's part of the protocol." Clare entertained a fleeting fantasy of balling up her fist and nailing him in his upturned nose. *Just following protocol*, she would say, twisting her heel into the portly cushion of his stomach on her way out the door. "Dr. Fitzpatrick tells me you had a session scheduled for the 25th. Is that correct?"

"Yes, but I—"

"You canceled it last minute."

"Because my mother died." Clare cursed herself. She already sounded defensive.

"I see. So you were distraught?" Bonner exchanged a purposeful glance with Fitzpatrick.

She shrugged. "That's not really the right word."

"What is the right word, Dr. Keely?"

Clare saw storm-cloud eyes and salt-and-pepper stubble. A freckle she'd traced with her thumb. She saw a child's bloody fist where Fitzpatrick had dribbled his coffee. She saw Dumas, grinning. Not even a trace of anger, though she'd forgotten all about him. "Distracted," she said. "I was distracted."

Bonner made a noise, throaty with concern. "Did you speak to Mr. Dumas that morning?"

"He came by for his session, and I told him we could reschedule for the following day."

"And how did he seem to you? In your professional opinion?" Clare bit the side of her cheek to keep another laugh from escaping. Maybe she could be a professional after all. If Bonner said so.

"Happy. Relaxed. Euthymic." Clare added that last word for her own amusement. She knew Bonner would have no clue what it meant, but would be too proud to ask.

"Euthymic," he repeated. "Okay. Did he mention any plans when he left?"

You mean aside from hanging himself with a bedsheet? She desperately wanted to say it, to level him with sarcasm, but she kept it in where it festered like a hot blister. "Nothing specific. I think he said something like *I've got nothing but time*. He was joking around."

Bonner turned to Fitzpatrick. "I'm no expert, but isn't this sort of thing fairly common? When a person finally decides to off himself, he feels better. Like a sense of relief. Is that what happened here?"

"No," Clare answered as a mute Fitzpatrick fumbled with his tie. "He wasn't suicidal. He was hopeful. He didn't kill himself. Is it possible that ... " Until she said it aloud, Clare hadn't known what she thought. But now, she felt convinced. " ... somebody else killed him? Made it look like a suicide?"

Bonner and Fitzpatrick both chuckled at her. "Sounds like you've been watching too much *Law and Order*," Bonner told her. "Or are you a Grisham fan like me? That sounds like his next bestseller."

"So it's never happened?" Clare asked. She knew it had, of course. And she delighted in knowing she'd cornered him in the worst way, stuck between a lie and an admission he might be wrong.

Bonner's jaw tightened. "Remind me, Dr. Keely. How long have you been a licensed psychologist?"

She knew where this was going. She didn't answer—her eyes locked in a stalemate with Bonner's—until Fitzpatrick cajoled her. "Answer the question, Clare."

"Since July."

"Four months," Bonner said. "And how many suicidal patients have you treated?"

"None." Unless you counted Rodney Taylor's half-hearted, pre-coital threats. And you considered him feeling her up in his back-seat a form of treatment.

Bonner could've stopped there. He'd proven his point. But Clare knew men like him. They didn't stop until they stripped you bare. Not even a shred of dignity left to cover yourself. "Do you know how long I've been working at Quentin? Twenty-five years. That's longer than most marriages these days. Hell, it outlasted my marriage." *No surprise there*, Clare thought. "Now you may have book smarts, but you're just a little girl in here. You've got a lot of growing up to do."

Fitzpatrick winced. Humiliated for her, his cheeks flamed. That was worse than anything Bonner could've said. Or so she thought. "All the evidence here points to the suicide of a very depressed man with a lengthy sentence ahead of him. A case like this should have been assigned to a seasoned clinician. Someone with a little more life experience under her belt. I suggest you cooperate fully with this investigation. Do that for me, and I'll do my best to shield you from any outside repercussions."

Bonner shook Fitzpatrick's hand before he departed. Clare was prepared to withhold hers, but he didn't even offer. Just gave a little wave. When he closed the door behind him, she stood and stared at the shadow of her face in the glass. She wanted to run, but there was nowhere to go. She was twenty-seven, but she felt sixteen. She was childless, but she'd held a baby in her arms. A blink, and it was gone. She wondered if murder counted as life experience.

****

"Are you alright, Clare? I'm sorry about Bonner. He can be a real asshole sometimes." Fitzpatrick's arm around her shoulders brought her back.

"What did he mean, *outside repercussions?*" She took a step away from him to free herself. "Could I be fired?"

Fitzpatrick shook his head. "Doubtful. But the family might try to sue you and the prison for negligence, malpractice, or some other BS cooked up by a greedy attorney."

"You saw him that day, right? Dumas? You saw me talking to him?"

"I heard a snippet of conversation through a half-closed door." *Well, that didn't take long.* Fitzpatrick had already begun distancing himself.

"And what did you think? He didn't seem suicidal, did he?" Her voice came out high, screeching. It frightened her a little. "Did he?" she said again. "He didn't. I know he didn't. He had just talked to his wife last week. He was so happy about it."

"Sit down, Clare. Try to breathe." Fitzpatrick pushed the folding chair toward her, and she collapsed into it. "I'm going to tell you something, but it's just between us. It doesn't leave this room. Lieutenant Bonner thought it was best you didn't know. But, I'm fond of you, and I think you deserve the truth." Clare nodded as he sat across from her, their knees close enough to touch. "Dumas had received a telephone call right after he left your office. It was from his wife." Fitzpatrick put his hand on her knee and left it there, but she felt too desperate for the rest of the story to care. "She'd asked for a divorce."

NOVEMBER 28, 1996

CLARE clutched all that was left of her mother—an urn, half-filled with slate-gray ash, on her lap as they drove. Neal wanted to wait, but Clare insisted on going today, even though it was Thanksgiving. She needed to escape, to feel San Quentin shrinking behind her, smaller and smaller until it looked like an ant she could crush between her fingers. She needed the expanse of the road ahead, the radio cranked up until she couldn't hear the obnoxious discord of her own singing voice. *This* was therapy. But Neal—sturdy, reliable Neal—spoiled her oasis. He wouldn't shut up about Dumas. Two hours into the six-hour drive back to San Francisco, mid-Goo Goo Dolls, he started up again.

"I really think you should consult an attorney, Clare-bear." She sighed, hard and heavy, hoping it would deter him. John Rzeznik was about to get to the good part. "This is your career we're talking about. Everything you've worked so hard for."

And scars are souvenirs you never lose. The past is never far. Did you lose yourself somewhere out there? Did you get to be a star? Don't it make you sad to know that life—

"Clare." That tone. The way he scolded her like a child. She hated him.

"Fitzpatrick said even if they sue me, it's the prison they want. The prison has the money. Not me. Besides, last I checked, you didn't even want me to work there. Now you're acting like I did something wrong."

Neal turned down the radio. She felt an argument coming on, stirring up the pit of her stomach like the wind before a storm. "Did you?"

"What's that supposed to mean?" He raised his brows in that know-it-all way. Accusatory. Like Clare masterminded every disaster. Or at least one. The one he would never let her forget. "This is totally different than my postdoc. And I can't believe you're still blaming me for that. How was I supposed to know his wife would find out he'd sent me flowers? It wasn't a big deal."

"Actually, it was a big deal, Clare. They weren't going to sign off on your hours, remember? Without that note from your therapist, you wouldn't be licensed."

"Fine. Whatever. I didn't handle it properly. The way Dr. Neal Barrington would. But I never encouraged that guy. Even he admitted he was obsessed with me."

It bothered Clare when Neal didn't fight back. Like he'd grown tired of her. "Look, let's just focus on the present, okay? You said you were distracted with Dumas. And you cut your session with Cullen short. That's not like you. Maybe you missed something."

"Like what? It was a two-second conversation. There was nothing to miss. How could I have known his wife was going to end it with him? The last he told me they were better than ever."

"It's okay to admit it if you screwed up. You've been under a lot of stress lately, especially running into you-know-who. It wouldn't surprise me if you weren't totally focused."

"Thank you, Lieutenant Bonner. I appreciate your support." Clare turned away toward the window to punish him. But she wasn't satisfied. "You know, I was stupid for thinking we could ever make this work. You don't get me, Neal. You never have."

"What don't I get? What is so mysterious about the great Clare Keely? So you were abused as a kid. I get it. Your mom was a floozy. I get it. Men take advantage of you. I get it. You have flashbacks. Poor boundaries. Hang-ups about sex. You've got issues. I get it, Clare. I get all of it." He steered the car down the nearest exit ramp and turned into a gas station parking lot. Always careful. Safe. That was

184

Neal. "Do *you* get it? We're supposed to help people deal with their problems, but you seem hell-bent on running away from your own."

She opened the door before he could stop her. Twisted the ruby from her finger and threw it at him. It bounced off the seat and landed unceremoniously at his feet, where he regarded it open-mouthed. Like a knife she'd just aimed at his apple-red heart. "The only thing I'm running away from is you," she told him, willing herself not to cry. She tucked the urn under her arm and made her escape. "I'll find my own way back."

"Be reasonable, Clare. Are you really going to hitchhike? At a truck stop? And what am I supposed to do with your car?" He struggled to reach the ring on the floorboard, his mouth twisting awkwardly with the effort. She almost felt sorry for him. "Please, just let me drive you home. I won't say another word." He patted the seat, then dropped the ring in the cup holder. "It's still yours. It always will be." Whoever Neal loved, it wasn't her. It was a pretend Clare. The Clare she might've been. He would figure it out eventually—the repulsive thing she really was. He was halfway there already, analyzing her like one of his patients, cataloguing her scars, the ones she thought she'd hidden so well. The fact that he saw it all anyway, that disgusted her.

"You're spineless, Neal. Boring. Not an ounce of passion. You can't even argue with me. That's exactly why I could never love you. Why I never did." She slammed the door as hard as she could to properly punctuate her lie. And then Neal did something she never expected—he drove away.

****

"Clare, wake up." Lizzie nudged her shoulder. "We're back." Clare wasn't really sleeping. She hadn't slept at all. But it was easier to feign slumber than to face a firing squad of questions. And when you call your best friend from a payphone at a truck stop in Los Banos, begging for a ride on Thanksgiving night, there are bound to be questions. Clare opened her eyes and saw it right there in front of her, parked in her assigned spot in the complex. She walked to it, half-expecting Neal to be waiting in the driver's seat. He would take her inside and make love to her again.

"Are you going to call him?" Lizzie asked, peering in the windows. "It's locked."

She shook her head. "I'm sure he'll bring the key by tomorrow."

"What about the urn? I don't see it in here."

"Knowing Neal, he probably took it with him for safekeeping. Like someone would want to steal a vase of ground-up bones." She forced a light-hearted chuckle to hide the ugliness of the truth. The urn waited in the first stall of the truck stop bathroom where she'd abandoned it. She couldn't tell Lizzie how good it felt to leave her mother behind. Or how bad.

"Oh my God," Lizzie said, pointing inside the car. "That guy has it so bad for you. I feel sorry for him." Clare pressed her face to the glass and followed Lizzie's finger to the cup holder, where the ruby ring glinted in the streetlight. She suppressed a smile and shrugged.

"I should probably try to give it back. Nicely this time. Or sell it or something." After Lizzie left, she'd find the spare car key and come back down. She would slip it back on her finger. That ring was hers. It always would be.

NOVEMBER 29, 1996

THE answering machine picked up the first of Neal's calls at 6 a.m., but Clare was already gone, halfway to San Quentin. She admired her hand on the wheel, relishing the contrast of the blood-red ruby against her skin. Though she would never admit it to Neal—to anyone—it made her proud to be claimed by someone. Someone painfully normal like Neal. It was a statement. Pretend Clare was lovable. If only she could hold on to her.

But already, real Clare was in charge. She'd set her alarm for 5 a.m., gotten dressed in darkness, and floored it to the prison. She usually spent at least ten minutes circling the rows to find a parking spot. Not today. A bare-bones staff handled Black Friday. Even Briggs had the day off. Clare imagined him camping out to be the first in line for a new TV or VCR. Maybe even a Nintendo 64, if he played video games. *Of course he did.*

She took the stairs to her office two at a time. The hallway deserted and pin-drop quiet, Fitzpatrick's office dark. At her door, she paused. Looked right, then left. No one. She had every right to be here, but her flip-flopping stomach told her otherwise. She slipped inside, locking the door behind her. Fitzpatrick had cleaned out her notes folder on Wednesday, leaving it empty. It sent a hot knife of rage through the center of her, but she wouldn't be distracted. *Take that, Neal.* She'd come for one thing.

Dumas' file was stacked with the others at the corner of her desk. She opened it and flipped the pages with urgency. Each turn cranked her nerves, winding them a little tighter. *What if Bonner took it out? Baited her here?* Just when she convinced herself he was waiting outside the door, listening to her breathe, she found it.

In case of death notify: Eliza Dumas

She scrawled the address and phone number on a Post-it she buried in her pants pocket for later. Then she sat back in her chair and closed her eyes, relieved. It only lasted a moment until something else gnawed at her. An urge. An urge with sharp, determined teeth. It sank in and wouldn't let go until she relented.

"Mullins, South Block. What can I do for you?"

"Uh, yes. Hi. This is Dr. Keely. I was wondering if you could send an inmate to my office."

"Today?"

"Yes. Right now."

"Aren't you supposed to be at home eating leftovers, Doc?"

Clare laughed. "Probably. But I need to see Clive Cullen. He's in 128 Low. It's important."

"Alright. I'll send him over. Happy Thanks—"

She dropped the phone in its cradle before he could finish and stood up, her legs shaking a little. *It's fine*, she assured herself. *A legitimate request.* Cullen would know if the inmates were talking. He would tell her if her theory about Dumas made sense. Their cellblocks were close. Maybe they knew each other. Asking an inmate for advice was definitely not on the list of professional behaviors, even ethical ones. But technically, she was on vacation. She didn't have to be a doctor today. *You can be a woman.* The thought came in a man's voice she recognized as Cullen's. It surprised her, but she didn't push it away.

When he knocked ten minutes later, Clare ran a hand through her hair and smoothed her sweater, suddenly self-conscious. She'd never been *this* alone with Cullen. It terrified her in one way, thrilled her in another.

His eyes smiled. It was the first thing she noticed. The way they crinkled at the corners, softening his face. "Well hello, Dr. Keely."

188

"Just Clare today." He stepped inside and pushed the door closed behind him. "Lock it," she said. The words, the authoritative click of the latch, turned her on. Pretend Clare would've been repulsed. "I'm sorry to bother you. I just—"

"I heard what happened with your client. I'm so sorry. He was a good guy."

"So you knew him? James Dumas?"

Cullen stood close to her. Close enough to suck her in. But he smelled clean and strong, and his skin radiated heat. She didn't move away. "A little. I talked to him a few times on the yard—and that one day when you let me monopolize his session."

"Ha, ha. Very funny. If I remember correctly, you didn't seem to mind."

"I didn't. I'll monopolize you as often as I can. Speaking of which, did I pass the test? Letting go? Is this my reward?" His gaze spotlighted her. So intense, she looked away. He stepped back, letting the cold air in between them, and sat down. "Just kidding. What do you need?"

What do I need? Her mind went blank. She couldn't say she didn't know. That she simply wanted to see him, talk to him, be near him. "They're saying it's a suicide, but I'm not sure I believe it. Has anyone said anything?"

"Not to me." He frowned at her. "This isn't your fault. I hope you know that."

"I'm not so sure Bonner would agree with you."

"Are you serious? What a prick. He's probably just mad you won't sleep with him."

Clare stuck out her tongue in distaste. "I'm fairly certain he's not interested in sleeping with me. At least I hope not."

"Trust me, Clare. Every man at Quentin is interested in sleeping with you."

She leaned back against her desk, laughing. Giddy almost. She could've been anywhere. A bar. A park. A prison. Cullen made it easy to forget, easy not to care.

"You've got a great laugh." On his feet again and an arm's length away, that same force field opened up around him. She let it draw her in. Pretend Clare never had any fun. It felt good to let go. It was a holiday, after all. "I'll keep my ears peeled about Dumas and let you know on Monday if I hear anything." He reached for the door. He was leaving.

"Wait."

****

The message light blinked at her. Three missed calls. Two from Neal and one from Lizzie. But there was no hurry. Clare flopped onto her bed and giggled. She would regret it in the morning—all of it— that much she knew. And she hadn't even done anything wrong. Not really. *So I asked a serial killer for a hug. It's not like I kissed him or anything.* That's what she would say to Lizzie … if Lizzie knew, which she didn't. Wouldn't. Ever. *But I wanted to kiss him.*

Clare wrapped her arms around herself, pretending. It wasn't the same. The length of his body—warm and taut—wasn't pressed against hers. His breath wasn't tickling her ear. There was no one whispering, *This feels good, but I don't want you to get in trouble.* No one pulling her in closer when she said it was okay. And it was more than okay. But only once. I won't do it again.

She reached into her pocket, found the number she'd written, and cradled the receiver in her hand. Now was the time to do it, while she was still feeling brave and alive. Before pretend Clare took over and made her loathe herself all over again. She dialed and waited. The rings seemed endless, so many Clare lost count. So many, she almost gave up.

"Hello." The woman's voice was flat and cold. The way Clare imagined it would sound, but worse. Maybe this was a mistake.

"May I speak to Eliza?"

"That's me. Who's this? If you're selling something, it's not a good time."

"My name is Clare Keely. I'm not selling anything. I work as a psychologist at San Quentin. I was your husband's therapist, and I wanted to express my condolences for what happened to him."

190

"What happened to him?" There was anger there beneath the ice. "He offed himself. Suicide didn't happen to him. *He* happened."

"I'm sorry. I can't imagine what you're going through. I shouldn't have called."

Clare expected her to hang up, but she didn't. "Well, why did you, then?" She sounded more exhausted than angry now.

"I'm not sure. I guess I wanted to try to understand a little better. I liked your husband. He had a kind heart. I wish I could've known him longer."

"Did they tell you I talked to him that day?"

"Yes."

"They made it seem like it was my fault. The way they kept asking what we talked about. And I already feel guilty enough. Hell, let's face it, I *am* guilty. James is the one who told me a divorce would be best for the kids. He didn't want me waiting around for him. He'd said it before, and I always talked him out of it. It wasn't what I wanted."

"So you didn't ask for a—" Clare heard a child's soft whimpering. It grew louder, more insistent until it was the only sound in her ears. Like it was coming from inside her own head.

"Do you have children, Ms. Keely?" Eliza shouted over the crying.

But Clare wasn't on the phone anymore. She'd been transported back to that day in her mother's bathroom, her mother gone God-knows-where. Her legs spread. The worst pain she'd ever felt pinning her to the ground. Blood everywhere. More blood than she knew was in her body. And it was all over her hands. Under her fingernails. Sticky and warm. It was dead—it had to be. It came too soon.

And she didn't go to the doctor, didn't take those vitamins Lizzie always said would make her hair shiny. She never felt a kick. She didn't even gain much weight. But still the dead thing inside was strong. Strong enough to kill her, to rip her open from the inside out. She pushed hard one last time to finally be rid of it. To be rid of the thing that tethered her to the foulest parts of herself. It was dead—it had to be. Then, it cried. So loud. Too loud. Loud enough to issue insatiable demands. To twist her soul inside out.

"Ms. Keely? Hello?"

"Yes. Yes, I'm here." Clare doubled over like it was still happening. She focused on the Post-it note clutched in her palm and breathed. In and out. In and out.

"Do you have children?"

I did, but I killed her. I smothered her with my mother's hand towel. The one embroidered with her initials. And then I buried her in the woods in a shoebox. "No. But, Mr. Dumas—James—told me you have a little boy and a girl on the way. Levi and Katie, right?"

Eliza went quiet for a while, not answering, and mercifully, the child did too. "I don't know how to go on without him. Why would he do this to me? Why?"

That was a question for a professional. Pretend Clare would recite a few lines from the chapter on bereavement. Maybe recommend a book or two. But the Clare who sat alone and barelegged on the linoleum with a scrub brush, scouring the floor with bleach until her hands were raw, that Clare couldn't give lip service. The Clare who lugged the heaviest stone she could find to mark a grave she dug herself owed a penance she could never pay. "I'm going to do my best to find out."

DECEMBER 6, 1996

IT wasn't only once like she'd promised herself. Already, it had happened twice more. At the end of Monday's session and again today. Cullen showed up for no reason, fake ducat in hand, just to say hi. To check on her. Clare knew what he wanted because she wanted it too. And she gave it to him. Tingling, she locked the door as quietly as she could. In the stillness of her office, that small sound seemed to expand. To take on a life of its own. To travel down the hallway. She waited for the knock, for Fitzpatrick, for someone, anyone to stop her. She needed to be stopped, but there was no one to do it.

"I heard something on the yard about Dumas," he said. "He owed money to the EME for some legal work. An appeal or something. Do you think it's possible they were involved? Trying to get to you, you know?"

She felt a rush of relief. "I've been thinking the same thing. But I felt crazy. Paranoid. Bonner wants me to let it go. So does Fitzpatrick. I'm meeting with him this afternoon. I don't know what to do." And then, just like that, Cullen's arms were around her, and her body pressed to his. Each time, he took their embrace a little further, upped the ante. But she couldn't blame him, because she didn't mind. *You want this, Clare*, as Rodney always reminded her. Even now. She felt Cullen's expert hand slip under her sweater to the small of her back. It was cool against her flushed skin.

"You'll do the right thing," he told her. "You always do." Clare nearly laughed at that one. *The right thing*. Whatever that was, she was light years from it. And then she said the most pathetic thing. Pathetic because she didn't mean it. But mostly because she'd said it twice already. Twice promised, twice broken.

"We can't do this again." And then, he left, sentencing her to the next three hours of purgatory. Muddling through her Friday afternoon appointments, barely listening.

At five o'clock, she stood outside Fitzpatrick's office summoning her courage. "Come in, Clare."

He seemed already halfway gone for the weekend. His shirt sleeves rolled up, his tie loosened. "I just spoke with the Lieutenant. The official investigation has been concluded. James Dumas died by his own hand."

"But—"

Fitzpatrick sighed as he held up his hand to interrupt her protest. "That's not all we need to discuss." Her insides took a nosedive. He'd heard the click of the lock. He knew what she'd done with Cullen. "Did you contact Eliza Dumas?"

"Yes. I wanted to offer my condolences."

"Did you really think that was appropriate?"

She shrugged. "I'm sorry. I should've consulted with you first. It was an emotional time, as you can imagine." Play the sympathy card. That should do the trick.

"I can imagine. Lieutenant Bonner, not so much. Need I remind you, you've still got four months left in your probationary period. And he's not a guy you want to cross."

"I think it's too late for that," she said, chuckling. "Just for the record, I don't agree with the results of the investigation. Mrs. Dumas said James was the one who brought up the divorce, and today, Cullen told me there's talk on the yard he owed money to the EME."

"You saw Mr. Cullen today?" *Dammit.* She wished she could make a joke about a Freudian slip, but Fitzpatrick wouldn't buy it. He knew how much she detested his constant references to Freud. "You've been talking to him about this?"

"Of course not. He brought it up. He knew Dumas was a client of mine."

"I see." Fitzpatrick's code for bullshit. "Well, it's best you don't speak with anyone about this—especially the inmates. I would think that goes without saying."

"It does," she said, with as much assertiveness as she could muster.

Fitzpatrick loosened his tie the rest of the way and tossed it onto the desk. "Any plans for the weekend? Want to grab that drink?"

****

She never thought she'd be thankful for a date with J. D. Briggs, but she was. So thankful. If the choice came down to him or Fitzpatrick, she'd take Robocop any day of the week. Besides, she planned on going fishing again. Surely, Briggs had heard something about Dumas. So yesterday she suggested the same dive bar because it was a lot easier to catch a drunk fish.

Clare eyed J. D. as soon as she walked in. Her dress—a short, red number—was riding up, but she didn't dare pull it down. She sauntered over to him like he was the only too-big-for-his-britches guy in the place and planted a kiss on his cheek.

"Whoa," he said. "You look way too good for this place. Let me take you somewhere nice."

"Next time." A wide grin parted his lips. "What?"

"Sounds like you just guaranteed date number three." He squeezed her knee and left his hand resting there, taking a swig of his beer with the other.

"Easy there, cowboy. Let's take it one at a time." She winked at him and watched his cheeks turn rosy. This whopper had already swallowed the bait.

"So I hear you're public enemy number one with Bonner … "

"Am I?" She flagged down the bartender and ordered a shot. No harm in loosening herself up a little. "He thinks I watch too much *Law and Order*."

"Well, there's talk going around you told him to kiss your you-know-what."

"Seriously? That never happened. But at least I'm on the right end of the rumor."

"Don't worry. Your secret is safe with me, bad girl."

She clinked the edge of her shot glass against his beer mug. "To being bad then," she said.

****

Robocop was a horrible kisser. Not that she was surprised. Most men kissed the way they acted—and he was no exception. Pushy. Aggressive. And totally unaware. But she couldn't stop now. Inside his Jeep, she'd hooked her fish. Now to reel him in one sloppy kiss at a time. If only she could get Rodney Taylor out of her head. *Put your tongue in my mouth when I kiss you.* She shouldn't have downed that shot. It made the thoughts harder to stop, his voice impossible to silence. And that damned Aqua Velva didn't help.

She pulled away and wiped her mouth discretely with the back of her hand, hoping her disgust didn't show on her face. "So you'll ask around about Dumas? Investigate this thing with the EME?"

"If it's important to you." He nibbled at her neck. "But, in the meantime, promise me you'll let it go. Don't piss off Bonner. Let me handle that jackass. You're no match for him."

"I know. I promise."

He took her hands and wrapped them around the back of his neck. He wanted her to want him so she tried to oblige, tugging him back toward her. "I like kissing you, Clare. You're pretty great at it." He wasn't the first man to say it, and she knew exactly who she had to ~~thank~~ curse for that.

CHAPTER EIGHTEEN
ONE-WAY TICKETS

LEVI walked a step ahead of me, the pinprick beam of his flashlight useless on a night this black. The moon just an opaque sliver. There were no streetlights, and we'd passed the last of the houses at least five minutes ago. Not even the occasional car to make us feel less alone. But there was anonymity in the dark. Maybe that's why Levi kept talking. So I followed and listened. "You really think Clive Cullen murdered your dad and made it look like a suicide?"

"I don't *think*, Sam. I know. Snip told me."

"But he didn't see it, did he?"

Levi sighed, exasperated with me. "Of course not. Nobody *sees* anything in prison, if you catch my drift." I didn't really, but my admission would only confirm that life in Bellwether had made me anything but worldly.

"What did Cullen have against your dad?"

"Don't know. I'm not sure how well they even knew each other. The only common denominator is ... " Another sigh. This one contemplative but resigned.

"Let me guess. Clare Keely."

"Bingo." He flashed the light up ahead where the paved road met gravel. "This way," he said, the pebbles already crunching beneath his boots.

"Doesn't the prison investigate stuff like that?"

"Look, I've seen the report." I wondered if that was part of why he was in trouble. "It was just a formality. It didn't even scratch the surface. They assumed he hung himself because he was depressed, and my mom said something about getting a divorce."

"And your mom?" I asked, gingerly. "Do you think she ... " I couldn't bring myself to say the words, and for a while, we continued in silence. Just the sound of our tracks on the dirt path. The soft *hoo* of an owl now and then. And further away, noises I couldn't name and tried to ignore.

"My mom couldn't live with the guilt. I think she robbed that place with my dad. He had an unidentified female accomplice. That's my theory anyway. I was only two when she ... died. Everything I know about my parents comes from a file."

"At least you have something. My mom doesn't say much about my dad, and she told me it hurt too much to keep his pictures around. He died when I was just a baby."

"Your mom believed it."

"Believed what?"

"That something else happened to my dad. That he didn't choose to die, to leave us to fend for ourselves." Levi stopped, and a part of me half-expected my mother to emerge from the tree line with Ginny, all of them laughing at me for their perfect prank. "It's not in the report though. She wrote an addendum, and they buried it. I pulled a few underhanded strings to dig it up, but I'm guessing McKinnon already told you that." I waited for him to elaborate, but instead he pointed to a dim yellow light in the distance. It could've been a firefly the way it flickered. "That's where we're going."

"And when we get there?"

In the flashlight's glow, I watched his eyes until he looked away. "I don't know."

198

"You're going to kill him?" It's not a question if you already know the answer. But I made it sound like one anyway.

"Don't you want him dead? He took Ginny, remember?" I did remember, of course. And I figured the world was probably better off without Cutthroat Cullen. But the way Levi's eyes shone when he said it—so determined, so decided—it made me think of Snip and those one-way tickets to hell.

"I don't want you to be the one to do it."

****

The gravel road narrowed just wide enough for a single car. From one side, the redwoods bore witness. They saw what we saw and everything we didn't. In the other direction, bare dirt that unnerved me even more. Because in the pitch black, it seemed to promise a fall into oblivion. "Are you absolutely sure we're going in the right direction?"

Levi nodded and shone the light on our path. A set of footprints in the dirt. Most likely my mother's. But in the dark cave of my mind, they belonged to Cutthroat, one of those shadows flitting just beyond my view. Up ahead of us, a mailbox, barely standing on its post, marked the entrance to another road. I imagined someone like my mother taking the curve too fast and dead-ending into it. "How did you find this place?" Even my whisper was too loud.

"My sister." He put a finger to his lips. "We're getting close." And then, he did the unthinkable. The flashlight clicked, and the night swallowed the last pinprick of light. I lost my bearings until Levi's hand closed around my wrist and pulled me closer to him. "Give it a second," he said. "Let your eyes adjust. Then we'll head around the back of the cabin."

I blinked. Then blinked again and waited as the vast nothingness took the form of Levi's shoulder. His arm. The hand not holding mine. His gun. And the vague outline of everything beyond him. "I'm okay," I mouthed. Even though I wasn't.

Stargazing with Ginny was like this. The complete and essential absence of light a necessary evil. Enigmatic even, if we were being brave. But the night always caught up with us after the coyotes started yelping. Their cries built to a feverish din until a single howl sent us scampering inside every time, collapsing in laughter once we knew we were safe. A lone howl. That's how the scream came. The one I recognized as Ginny's. And I wished I had somewhere to run to. Instead, I clung to Levi like a grounding rod, the air around me electric.

"C'mon." He pulled me along behind him to where the road disappeared into tall, weedy grass that concealed a landscape of junk leftover from another lifetime. We skirted a makeshift ravine—the bed of a pickup truck, half-filled with rainwater—and a towering mountain of tires as we ran, nearing the back of the cabin. The porch light flickered last gasp, off and on and off again. That was my firefly. And it was dying. It sputtered once, twice, illuminating the broken front window—I saw!—and then, it went dark.

I opened my mouth to unleash my own howl, but Levi clamped it shut with his hand and snatched me out of view. His heart thudded against my back. Or maybe that was mine. Between ragged breaths, I tried to make sense of what I'd seen. But it was just fragments of red and terror and people I loved. They didn't fit together. Didn't belong together. And yet, I couldn't shake them.

"Was that Ginny?" Levi spoke so softly, the words barely stirred the air by my ear—and until he repeated them, I thought they might've been my own, uttered only inside my head. I started to tell him, to find the voice caught in my throat. But the porch light began to buzz again with a dim glow, giving him the answer before I could say it. *Yes.*

"Please." Ginny squealed like a rabbit clamped between sharp teeth. The broken glass distorted her face, blurring the sharp edges of her panic. But she was bleeding. That much I could see. A thin line of it ran down her neck. So red it looked unreal. Cullen held her effortlessly, pinned in front of him with his forearm. In his other hand, the knife he'd promised my mother.

"Let her go, Clive. She's done nothing to you. *Nothing.*" Her back to the window, I couldn't see my mother's face. But I'd never heard her speak that way. As if she could coax an animal—a wild one she knew by name. "We can talk about this. Just you and me. We can go somewhere."

Cullen's sudden laughter raised the hair on the back of my neck. The laugh of a doomed man. And I thought of Snip's warning. Guilty men can be desperate too, and this one cackled like he had nothing to lose. "Talk? With you? Where did that ever get me?"

Levi positioned us alongside the window, the front door at our backs. His gun raised, he angled for an opening. But it was useless. I could see Ginny's purpose. Both pawn and shield. There was no clear shot from here. "I thought you said she had a gun," Levi murmured as a quick scan of my mother's hands came up empty. I shrugged.

"So you don't want to talk. I understand." My mother beguiled him again, her voice more snake charmer than psychologist. "Why did you go through all this trouble to get me here then? What do you need from me, Clive?"

"It's not what I need. It's what I want." Cullen squeezed Ginny's neck in the crook of his elbow. "What you owe me."

"You're hurt. I know I hurt—" Cullen's bitter guffaw interrupted my mother. Undeterred, she began again, more gently this time. "I hurt you. But you don't have to do this."

"Hurt me? Hurt me? Hurt me?" With every repetition, Cullen's voice raised until it threatened to blow out what was left of the fractured window. His grip tightened, Ginny's face straining with the effort of breathing. "You did the one thing you knew would break me. And it turned me. Back. Into this. Into a monster." He punctuated each phrase with a forceful wring of Ginny's throat. "You betrayed me, Clare. Worse than any of the others." *The others.* I wasn't sure what it meant. Only that my mother's shoulders slumped when he said it. And Ginny gasped for air.

"Do something," I hissed. "She can't breathe."

"Stay put," he said, dropping the duffel bag at my feet. "I'll go in through the back." Levi disappeared around the corner of the house before I could stop him. Now that he was gone, I felt acutely aware of myself. The creak of the wooden slats beneath my sneakers. The

201

rise and fall of my chest. The delicate sound of my swallow. I leaned against the window frame trying to quiet it all.

My mother stepped toward Cullen, her arms outstretched. A gesture that seemed familiar to her. To Cullen. "I had no choice, Clive. Please forgive me. Please." He paused and, for a moment, the lines etched in his forehead softened. His hold on Ginny loosened, and she sucked in a panicked breath. My mother must have noticed too. The spell he was under. She took another step and another. Until her hands were close enough to touch him. "It wasn't only me I had to look out for," she said.

And like the clean snap of a stem, the spell broke in two. On one side, my mother still reaching, plaintive. On the other, Cullen, turned to stone. His face hard and cold as marble, he pressed the knife firm against the wound on Ginny's neck, and the bleeding started up again. "Imagine my surprise when that hoity-toity bitch, McKinnon, dropped your little bomb on me after you vanished. She relished every minute of that. Tells me I have a daughter. That *we* have a daughter."

No. No. No. The crack in the window widened like the gash on Ginny's neck. So wide I could fall in. And my head was spinning, spinning, spinning. I reached for Levi, arms flailing, before I remembered he'd gone. And the porch light's insistent buzz became the swarm of flies from my nightmare. A black cloud, a thousand prickly legs sticky with Ginny's blood, and I floundered in the middle of it.

I stumbled back.

Maybe I was still dreaming. The kind of dream that jerks you awake just before you tumble into the void. Maybe I would wake up too.

If I let myself fall.

CHAPTER NINETEEN

DEAR OLD DAD

NOT asleep. Not a dream. *Real,* I thought. Real, because my palms ached beneath me, sore from where I landed. Real, because the porch light spotlighted me in a ghostly glow that sent me scrambling for the shadows like the mice in my mother's barn. Real, because Cutthroat Cullen heard me scream. "Get up, Samantha." And he knew my name. "Time to meet dear old dad."

I staggered to my feet, afraid to look at him. To see him register my presence, measure me up. To follow the blood trail down Ginny's neck to her shirt where it blossomed like a rose. But worse, to see my mother's eyes, sinking stones of agate, meet mine in seeming confirmation. *Cullen, my father?* Real.

"Come inside." He beckoned to me, blade in hand, as my mother shrieked at the window. So wild, so do-or-die, I could barely make out the one word she repeated again and again. *RUN!*

I listened, but my legs refused to obey. Logs of lead, they fixed me in place as if I'd just run an hour's worth of liners, the way Coach Crowley sometimes got even with us for a disappointing game.

"Don't be like your mother. Don't play games with me." Statue Samantha heard, saw. Did nothing. "If you won't come in, I'm coming out. As soon as I get rid of this baggage." He wound one hand around Ginny's hair and pulled her head back, exposing the smooth valley beneath her trembling chin. Her tears came without sound or effort. She resembled the girl in the field, peaceful at a distance.

"Let Ginny go, and I'll do what you ask." My voice didn't sound like my own. It belonged to Statue Samantha and came from a place inside that was frozen solid. "Take me instead. I'm the one you wanted anyway." I stuttered to a start, my legs barely working again, and turned the doorknob.

A protest wheezed from Ginny's mouth. My mother gasped my name in disbelief. But Cullen only laughed as I came inside. As if we were in the middle of father-daughter day at school and I'd cracked the funniest joke he'd ever heard. I searched his face, trying to find something of myself there. A curve, a line, anything familiar. There were the eyes, of course. Blue like mine. But his sky was different. Too perfect to be believed. Mixed-up somehow. The kind of sky that unsettles people at a funeral. Disrespectful in its utter blueness.

"Ginny, Ginny, Ginny. Everyone is so concerned about you. And to think, you wouldn't even be here if that pendejo Guzman could follow orders."

"You were working with him?" My mother got the words out. Barely. They seemed to scratch in her throat like tumbleweeds.

"I wouldn't say that. He worked for me. He didn't have a choice." Cullen postured with his knife, then threw back his head, cackling. "The EME working for me—ain't that a hoot? And he thought I was going to let him live. Like I said, pendejo. If you want something done right, do it yourself. Isn't that what they say, Dr. Keely?"

I waited for my mother's entreaties. A clever comeback. Words to soothe the savage beast. But she didn't say any of those things. Instead, she raised the gun tucked carefully into the waistband of her jeans and pointed it at him. Half of his mouth curled in a sneer, and I understood why her hands shook. "You're right, Clive. I'll do it myself before you hurt anyone else."

204

"Go ahead. I dare you." Nostrils flaring, he charged toward her, dragging Ginny along for the ride until there was no space between his skull and the muzzle. I heard my mother's breath catch in her throat, and for a moment, I wasn't sure if she was going to kill him or kiss him. Then he spit words from his mouth like something rotten. "Do it. One to the head. Put me out of my misery. You already stuck me in the back, so what does it matter? And to think, I loved you."

"Loved? Is that what you told the woman you just dumped in the Bay? You don't mean loved, Clive. You mean controlled. I was nothing but a puppet to you. Just like her. You pulled the strings, and I danced. So if you want to talk about betrayal—"

Cullen pushed his forehead against the gun, butting it like a bull. "If that's what you think of me, do it now, before I tell our precious daughter all about you. Do it." My mother stopped speaking, the indignation sucked out of her. As she stroked Ginny's face, she looked at me. Ginny's tears were dry now—her eyes vacant. She was the girl in the field, already dead. "I'll tell her how you begged for it. How you wanted me. This is all your fault, Clare."

My mother kept her focus on me—"Close your eyes," she said—and pulled the trigger.

****

Close your eyes. She'd told me that before. Two years ago, summer, when the cow she'd called Boots went off alone in the corner of the pasture, and we'd found her lying on her side, bloated and glassy-eyed. One shot in the air to scatter the buzzards, she raised the rifle then stopped. *Close your eyes, Samantha.* I'd never told her that I'd kept them open, that I'd watched Boots' head open like a flower, that I'd seen her body seize once and go still. Because I didn't know why.

This time, I listened. Squeezed my eyes shut as tight as I could, and I didn't stop squeezing until I heard a dead man speak.

"Do you really think I'd be stupid enough to give you a working gun?" Cullen stepped away from my mother. She pulled the trigger again and again. Nothing. Each empty click broke something inside me. "To leave the firing pin in? Jesus, Clare. I didn't go through hell to let you win."

"It's a good thing I'm here then." Levi. *Finally.* "And my gun actually works. So you may want to rethink your strategy."

"And why would I do that?" He chuckled to himself. "Who's this loser? Another one of your conquests, Dr. Keely?"

Levi fired once, the bullet making a clean hole in the wall over Cullen's shoulder. Ginny let loose a yowl, cut short by Cullen's hand. He clamped down hard on her mouth until she stopped struggling.

"Levi! What are you doing?" I yelled over the ring in my ears. "You'll shoot Ginny."

"He's going to kill her anyway. Aren't you, Cutthroat? This is just a game to you. Pieces you move around on a chessboard."

"Do I know you?" Cullen asked.

Levi fired another shot. "Levi Beckett. Son of James Dumas. The man you hung twenty years ago. Made it look like a suicide. Ring any bells?"

"Seriously? You've been drinking a little too much of the conspiracy Kool-Aid. Next you'll be telling me I shot JFK. Or I'm a member of the Illuminati. I didn't hang your dad. As far as I recall, he offed himself over some broad. Helluva stupid reason if you ask me."

Levi lunged for Cullen, knocked him back. But Ginny was his lifeline, and he wasn't letting go. He fell against the wall, scooting down the length of it with Ginny on his lap like a rag doll. "I'll make you regret that." He poised the steel tip at her cheek and ran it across her skin like the blade of a skate on ice. She didn't cry out. Didn't squirm. I felt sick at the sight of the metal point momentarily disappearing in her flesh, but I couldn't look away. Ginny's eyes met mine.

"I'm sorry, Sam." She didn't have enough breath to finish the sentence, so my name came out more of a soundless squeak. "This was a bad idea."

"It's not your fault. I agreed to go along with your half-baked plan. Since when did they ever end well?" The part of her that was still alive, still Ginny, managed a small smile. It sent the blood in a new direction, marking her face like a twisted clown.

206

"Shut up." Cullen raised the knife again, and I started toward Ginny until my mother stopped me. She snatched me back and pushed me toward Levi.

"I'll do what I should've done in the first place. I'll help you get away," she told him. "Just take me instead."

"Mom, have you lost your mind?" She didn't answer me. Her silence, a resounding *yes*.

"Now you're getting it, Clare. Always as smart as you were beautiful." Cullen sprang up, pulling Ginny to her feet, and pointed outside with the urgency of someone who had a plan. Someone who got exactly what he wanted. And it wasn't me. "Start walking," he told my mother. And she did. Like he was the puppet master after all, holding all the strings.

It happened the way Boots died. The way our point guard broke her jaw. The way Levi kissed me. With no happening at all. It was just done. There wasn't even time to shut my eyes. Levi raised his gun and fired at Ginny. She slumped toward the floor, buoyed by Cullen's arms.

Exposed, Cullen dropped her in the doorway, stepped over her, as he barreled toward my mother. I willed her to run, to fight, to do anything but stand there. A Bellwether deer. That's what she was. The one I'd seen in my rearview mirror after clipping her flank. Soft doe eyes darting, legs wobbly. Resigned to her fate—whatever it might be—she didn't move.

Levi's second shot skittered off the doorframe. His third came too late. Cullen ducked around the door and crashed into my mother, the Bellwether deer frozen in his path. He held her as tight as a lover and dragged her, backpedaling toward the darkest space between the trees where the night had no end. My heart stopped and started with each *pop* of the gun as Levi chased after them. But when the gun fell silent, it was worse. And worse still, when the sound of an engine rumbled across the grassy field louder and louder—high beams casting a blinding light that reached to the road and beyond—then soft again like distant thunder. Levi fired one last-ditch shot at the black truck that most certainly belonged to Cutthroat's last victim, and a wail came to life inside me, pushed its way up my throat. It was ready to be born.

CHAPTER TWENTY
A HUNCH

YOU shot me." Ginny wasn't the girl in my field after all. Not dead. Very much alive. And bleeding profusely from a coin-sized hole in the side seam of her jeans, where Levi had put a bullet.

"He's a cop." Like that explained everything. With a nod of confirmation, Levi leaned down to inspect her leg.

"I *saved* you," he said. "It looks like a flesh wound. No major damage."

"You *shot* me," she repeated. And I wondered if she could say anything else.

"I shot you. A lucky shot. Couldn't have aimed it better if I tried. You're going to be okay."

Ginny watched him with eyes dull as gravel. Then she bolstered herself against the doorframe and tried to stand. Halfway to her feet, she dropped back to the ground with a yelp and scooted inside the cabin instead.

"Easy," I cautioned as Levi unbuckled his belt and stripped it from the loops of his blue jeans. One side of Ginny's mouth turned up, trying to smile.

"Wow. You don't waste any time, Levi Beckett. But you're really not my type." Her mouth laughed, the sound as clunky and hollow as a broken bell.

"Actually from what I've heard, anyone with a Y chromosome and a pulse fits the bill. Now, stay put." I kneeled next to her and held her hand as Levi wrapped the belt around her upper thigh. "Did Cullen tell you where he was going?"

Ginny's lips trembled, the way a breeze flutters the leaves. Slight but persistent. "Once he found out I wasn't Sam, he was pissed. That other guy, Marco … well, I guess you already know about … " Her voice trailed off along with her eyes somewhere far beyond our view. I rubbed her shoulder to bring her back. "After that, he hardly said a word to me. Just your standard scream-and-I'll-slit-your-throat mumbo jumbo."

"Weird," Levi said. "No offense, but I'm surprised he didn't kill you."

I widened my eyes at him. To me, he'd gotten pretty close. Close enough. But Ginny just nodded. "Me too. I know this sounds mental, but I had this feeling he didn't want really want to."

"Was that before or after he practically choked you unconscious?" I muttered, neither of them listening to me.

"How did you get here?" Levi asked.

"That truck he stole, I guess. I was sort of out of it for a while."

"Drugged, probably." Levi cinched the belt as tight as it would go. "This might hurt a little." Ginny nodded through gritted teeth. "But it will stop the bleeding until you get to the hospital." He produced a cell phone from his jacket pocket and flipped it open.

"2004 called. It wants its phone back." Ginny's teasing seemed meant for me, trying to convince me she was still herself. But underneath her joke, her breathing was quick and shallow.

"It's from Snip," Levi said to me. "I guess he slipped it into the duffel when I wasn't looking." He pressed three buttons—9-1-1—and held it out to me. "Stay here with her. I'm going to look for them."

I imagined waiting here, safe, on the floor with Ginny, the night and everything hidden in it locked outside. "I can't."

210

"You can't? What does that mean?"

"It means she can't just sit here while her mom is out there with *him*. Duh. It's all brawn and no brains with this one, huh?"

"Him," I repeated. Stuck on that word. It rattled in my head. "You mean, my dad."

Ginny squeezed my fingers between hers, and her hands stopped shaking. "That psychopath may share your DNA, but that's where it ends. He's not your dad." I shrugged, wishing I could agree. Wishing it could be as simple as the title of my eleventh-grade biology project: *Your DNA Is Not Your Destiny*. Oh, the irony.

"I have to come with you," I told Levi.

"Fine." He redirected the phone to Ginny. "But we have to leave—now. They've got a head start on us. We'll call you in a while to check in, if it's safe."

"Go," Ginny said to me, sensing my hesitation. "I'll be fine." She pressed the call button and brought the phone to her ear, her hand trembling again.

I headed for the door and started jogging toward the road, back the way we came, before Levi could change his mind. When I glanced over my shoulder, mid-stride, Levi had just looped the straps of the duffel bag around his shoulders. He sprinted to catch me.

"You better run a little faster, Officer," Ginny called after us. And I felt the hint of a smile, but it only lasted a few foot strikes.

"Did you know that Cullen … ?" I didn't bother to say the rest. The kicked-up dust in my mouth tasted like hope and sadness. The truck, my mother—still close, still beyond reach.

"I had a hunch."

DECEMBER 9, 1996

THE letter waited for Clare on her desk Monday morning. A crisp, white envelope, sealed. A typed address, official. A single stamp, perfectly aligned. The kind of letter so pristine, so coffin-like, it could only hold bad news.

Dear Dr. Kelly,

This letter is to advise you that the Board of Psychology has received an inquiry regarding your conduct. After reviewing the information received, the Board is requesting a written response from you regarding the allegations. Please be aware that the Board is not currently conducting a formal investigation; rather, we are requesting your response as the first step in our informal review process. The complaint states that you provided substandard clinical treatment to patient James Dumas, an inmate at San Quentin State Prison, which contributed to his death by suicide on November 25, 1996.

Clare folded the letter and returned it to its paper coffin without reading the rest. She tucked it inside her desk drawer, hoping for its magical disappearance. Then she opened her pocket calendar to review her schedule for the day, though she knew it by heart. A single name stared at her. It could've been written in blood. *10:30 a.m. James Dumas.* Last week, she'd considered crossing through it, but with her pen poised to strike, she stopped herself. It felt disrespectful. Callous, even. Too final. So she left it there, marking every Monday for the rest of December.

Now, with that letter boring a hole through her soul, she felt glad. The last thing she needed was some stuffed shirt from the Board who couldn't even bother to spell her name right quizzing her about it, questioning her motives.

Well, Dr. Kelly. Oh, pardon me. Dr. Keely, is it? How do you think your client's family would feel seeing that mark through Mr. Dumas' name?

Did you ask your client if he was suicidal before you rescheduled your session?

No? And why not? You knew he was depressed. It's right here in your notes. Did you even care?

Or were you too busy entertaining sexual fantasies about Clive Cullen?

Guilt, that slimy worm, took a bite of her heart, and it stung. A better therapist, a reasonable one, would've seen this coming. She hadn't even deciphered the *why* of Dumas' crime, much less this. Half of the book of his life—not just the final pages—ripped out by his own hand, leaving it all unfinished. Cursing, she tossed the calendar onto the desk harder than she'd intended, sending a stack of papers flying into the air. Wayward doves, one by one they fluttered down, homing in on the doorway.

"Lose something?" She realized right then—that voice pitching her stomach in the best worst way—she was in big trouble. The kind of trouble that doesn't feel like trouble at all until it runs a blade across your throat.

"Only my mind," she answered, beckoning Cullen inside.

****

"You seem preoccupied," Cullen said, fifteen minutes into their session. She tried to keep up the formalities with the standard psychologist-patient routine. *How have you been feeling? What's on your mind? Tell me more.* But resistance was futile. It was all a cover, a way to fill the time until she broke her promise again. She shifted in her chair, crossed and uncrossed her legs, fidgeted with Neal's ruby. And it hit her. She was Rodney Taylor. *You're bad for business,* he always told her. *How am I supposed to concentrate on anything but this?* This being her. Her lips. Her skin. Her pink panties. It scared her, the power she had without even trying, without even asking for it. *I want you all the time.* And now, here she was, the tables turned.

"They concluded the investigation on Dumas." She had to say something. And not the something she was thinking. "If you can call it that."

"And?"

"Suicide."

"I don't buy it."

"Me neither, but what can I do? Bonner would relish nothing more than serving me a pink slip."

Cullen sat forward in his chair, practically whispering. "You didn't tell him my theory did you? About the EME?" Clare shook her head. She couldn't imagine telling Bonner anything but where to stick it. "Good, because there's a lot of talk about him. I'm not sure I believe it, but … "

"Talk?"

"They say he's a mule."

"Excuse me?"

His laugh warmed her. It was kind, not derisive, the way Fitzpatrick's would've been. "It means he works for somebody. And not the warden. Smuggles in contraband, calls in favors. That sort of thing."

"Well, he's certainly a jackass," she said, laughing along on the outside. Inside, she tucked Cullen's nugget away—a mule?—for safe-keeping. It made sense.

"I got this today." She opened the drawer and reached inside. "I couldn't read it all." She slid it to him across the desk and watched as he fondled the envelope waiting for her permission. "Go ahead."

"Are you sure?"

The question stunned her into self-awareness. Her tongue felt thick and strange, her chest hot. "Uh … yes? No, wait. I'm sorry. I've made this about me again. I'm an awful therapist." Horrified,

214

Clare listened to the methodical drone of the clock's minute hand, strangely loud in the quiet between them.

When she finally summoned the courage to look at him, his eyes were like the sky in springtime. Cloudless and gauzy blue. "Clare, this *is* about you. You and me. I can't stop thinking about you. About us. What should I do?"

She felt compelled to answer. He had that kind of presence, always dropping her to her knees. "What do you want to do?"

He stood, walked to the door, locked it with the care of a cat burglar. "I think you already know."

****

Clare licked her lips. They felt raw. And she hoped they didn't look it. If he'd noticed at all, Fitzpatrick would say nothing. *It was just a kiss.*

"Did you kiss the girl who worked in the library too?" she'd asked Cullen before he left. Before she reapplied her red lipstick and straightened her blouse, not meeting her own eyes in her compact mirror. She remembered the woman's name, of course—Gina—but Cullen didn't need to know that.

"Gina, you mean?" When he shook his head no, she assumed he was lying.

"Have you ever … with a client?"

"Of course not." One lie deserved another. And really, the first time didn't count anyway. That guy *was* obsessed with her. She'd only kissed him that once. On the cheek. Just to thank him for the flowers. Thank goodness nobody believed him. The flowers had gotten her in enough trouble.

Clare tried to still her mind, snuff out Cullen's flame, while Fitzpatrick read the letter. "It doesn't surprise me," he said finally. "In these sorts of cases, the family usually seeks legal action. They need someone to blame."

"But Mrs. Dumas didn't seem upset with me. If anything, she was angry at the prison. With Bonner. He's the one who talked to her, isn't he?"

"You are the prison. In the eyes of the law, you're one and the same. You and Bonner and me. All of us. We're on the same team."

"It doesn't feel that way." He nodded as if he understood, but he couldn't possibly. "That letter is addressed to me."

"Let me help you. That's my job, remember? Use me, Clare." It sounded dirty, the way he said it, the way he punctuated it with a self-conscious chuckle. And just like that, she felt him notice her lips, stare at them. *It was just a kiss.* But that was another lie. Clive Cullen kissed her like he did everything else. Deliberately, intensely, recklessly. As if he'd set a fire. That kind of kiss was bound to leave a mark.

Fitzpatrick grinned wickedly. "You've got lipstick on your teeth."

DECEMBER 10, 1996

JUST do it already," Clare whispered to herself, her hand hovering over the receiver. "Don't be a wuss." She needed to hurry. Lizzie would be here any minute for a resurrection of their long-dead college tradition, Taco Tuesday. Lizzie's idea, of course. Something about Clare needing more fun in her life. "This isn't fun," she murmured, but dialed the number anyway.

Just like the first time, the shrill ringing went on forever. No answering machine. Just the operator's tinny voice. "The person you are trying to reach is unavailable. Please try your call again." Clare hung up, relieved. But her stomach lurched when Lizzie knocked seconds later. *That was close.*

"Coming, Liz." First, a check of herself in the mirror. She hoped two coats of lipstick and a prayer would conceal the blue spot she'd found on her bottom lip his morning. When she touched it, it ached a little, but she knew she would miss it when it healed. Because it would never happen again. *Hear that Clare? You slut. Never.* Those were her words, but the voice sounded deep and shaming like Rodney's.

"I'm growing old out here, Clare-bear." Clare scurried into the kitchen and rummaged through the cabinet until she found her cocktail glasses and shaker. And the tequila, of course.

"Sorry," she said. "Just let yourself in. I'm getting the 'ritas ready."

Lizzie bounded inside with her usual enthusiasm, carrying a bag from their favorite Mexican spot. "Now you're talking. I've been looking forward to … "

The rest was lost, drowned out, by the harassing ring of the telephone. Caught in the middle of her kitchen, Clare darted like a squirrel in one direction, then another. To answer or not to answer. For no reason she could think of, both seemed to promise a swift demise.

"Aren't you gonna get that?" Lizzie asked. "It's probably your hot lover boy calling from prison. He wants to lock you up, girl." Clare's face drained of its color. Lizzie *knew*. Somehow. She knew.

"What?" Her hand, driven by instinct, touched her mouth.

"Uh, J. D. Briggs? Remember him?"

Clare produced a laugh more canned than a television sitcom and made a decision. "Hello," she said into the phone. The only reply came as a rattled breath. "Hello? This is Clare Keely."

"I knew it was you calling. Haven't you put my family through enough already?

"I think you have the wrong number." It was Eliza Dumas, and she definitely had the right number. Clare cursed herself for not thinking of that *69 thing Lizzie always warned her about. *It's so hard to stalk boys nowadays*, she'd teased at the time.

"I don't have the wrong number, Doctor. The guy from the prison, he told me about you. That you didn't take care of James like you should have. You saw how depressed he was. Nobody told me he was on suicide watch. Nobody told me his therapist was fresh out of college. What the hell do you know about—" Clare returned the receiver to the hook, steadied herself, then turned to face Lizzie.

"Wrong number."

✳✳✳✳

Two margaritas in, and Lizzie wouldn't let it go. "You seemed pretty shaken up. Are you sure it was a wrong number?"

Clare downed the rest of her drink. "Positive." She'd been careful to blot, not rub, but the lipstick ring on her glass worried her.

218

"And the person didn't say anything?"

"Nope. It was probably some perv. He was doing the heavy breathing thing."

"He?"

"Fine," she conceded. "He said my name a few times, before I hung up on him."

"That SOB. I can't believe he had the nerve to call you. Especially after you gave him a piece of your mind like you did."

"It wasn't Rodney Taylor."

"The hell it wasn't."

Clare shrugged, too tipsy to argue. "I guess it could've been."

"We should mess with him. Call him back. *69 his ass."

"I'm not calling him back."

"Fine. Then I will." Lizzie headed for the phone with determination. And Clare felt something essential slipping away, just beyond her grasp.

"Wait. Lizzie, wait."

"You want to do it, right? Pretend you're the cops or something."

Clare shook her head. "I lied to you."

"About what?" The list had grown too long to catalog.

"I never told Rodney Taylor off. I wanted to, but when he asked me how I was, I could barely muster the word *fine*."

With a deep sigh, Lizzie flopped back onto the sofa. "I think we need another round," she said.

****

After Lizzie left, insisting she was fine to drive, Clare scarfed the remaining taco and washed it down with tequila straight from the bottle. Vaguely nauseated, mostly anesthetized, she dialed Eliza Dumas once more. She tried counting the rings this time but kept losing her place, as if she was deep underwater, listening to the muted sounds of life up above. When the recorded voice scolded her again—no answer—she set the phone in its cradle and let the weight of exhaustion, heavy and absolute, pin her to the sofa. Her eyes closed.

Ten minutes later, Clare startled awake, her heart rattling around like a pinball in her chest, her guilt awake too. But then, it was always there—amorphous—pulsing under her skin, just a fingernail's scratch away. It took the shape of a wine-stained cotton dress ... a ruby ring ... an abandoned urn ... a shoebox. And now, a carefully knotted prison bedsheet.

Clare took a swig of tequila and dialed another number. The one she'd committed to memory, all the while telling herself she hadn't. The one on the card she'd tossed out the window. It gave her a small bit of satisfaction to think of it discarded on the freeway like an empty potato chip bag or a used condom.

"Hello, you've reached Rodney Taylor with Green River Trucking. I'm not available to take your call right now. Please leave your name and number at the beep, and I'll get back to you soon."

"Go fuck yourself."

DECEMBER 11, 1996

CLARE'S head pounded all day. She damned tequila. Damned Rodney Taylor. But tonight's mission would require more alcohol, so she downed a few cups of coffee in-between sessions and told herself to suck it up. At five o'clock, she called Robocop at the control booth.

"Dinner tonight, Officer Briggs?"

"Of course, Dr. Keely." He mimicked her come-hither tone. "You name the place."

"How about yours?" she cooed, revolted at the sound of her own voice. "You bring the wine. I'll get takeout."

He stammered, tripped over his tongue, before casually accepting. "Works for me."

Clare gathered her things in a hurry, hoping to slip out unnoticed by Fitzpatrick. After pointing out her makeup faux pas on Monday afternoon, he'd propositioned her for drinks again, and she was running out of excuses. Not to mention she'd planned a stop on her way out, a stop Fitzpatrick hadn't signed off on.

Clare didn't knock on Lieutenant Bonner's closed door. Not right away. Instead she pressed her ear to the door and listened, picturing him leaned back in his chair, shoes off, feet on his desk. That's how he would sit, as if he owned all of San Quentin.

"Did you catch that Niners game this weekend? Those refs had their heads up their … " Bonner's voice broke off into laughter so loud Clare jumped. "My ex-wife played better defense in the bedroom."

Can you blame her? Clare thought, rapping three times to end her misery.

"Who is it?" Her silence was the purposeful kind, and she savored it. "Gotta go, man." A moment of nothing and then, "It's open." He couldn't even be bothered to get up, but his eyebrows rose when he saw her. She liked that, catching him off guard.

"Ms. Keely. What a pleasant surprise."

She didn't try to pretend any more than he did. "I've come to talk to you about Mr. Dumas. About the investigation."

"I'm not sure what there is to discuss. Case closed, remember?"

Lips pursed to hold back the river, Clare nodded. "It's just that I haven't seen a copy of the report. The findings. I think I'm entitled—"

"Confidential. Sorry."

"Could you at least tell me if Mr. Dumas' alleged ties to gang activity were explored?" She sounded like a reporter, keeping it vague to protect her source.

Bonner pushed back from his desk and Clare caught him stuffing his stockinged feet into his shiny wing tips. It gave her satisfaction to know she had him figured out. "Ms. Keely—"

"Doctor." She wanted to carve that word on his forehead with the sharpest pencil on his desk.

"Dr. Keely, has someone been feeding you a line of *Law and Order* hogwash again? Or are you … What is it you shrinks call it? Projecting?" He stood up and began packing his briefcase. Clare knew it was all for show. As if he took anything home. "The EME had nothing to do with this."

"You seem pretty certain of that, Lieutenant. And I never named the EME. Maybe I'm not the only one projecting." She hadn't planned to say it. Not that bluntly. But now that she had, she didn't want to take it back.

"What exactly are you insinuating? Are you accusing me of something?"

Clare stared blankly, batting her eyelashes. "Now who's been watching too much *Law and Order*?" As he tried to recover, searched for a comeback, Clare removed the envelope from her jacket and slid

222

it across the desk, where it stopped against his briefcase. "I'd like this added to the report. It's *my* statement, the one no one ever bothered to ask for. I find that strange. Don't you?"

He stared at the envelope, but didn't touch it. Like she was the Unabomber setting a trap. Clare wondered how long it would take him to open it, to discover she'd cc'd the Warden. "I assure you our investigation was thorough and detailed, and I stand behind the conclusion one hundred percent. Can you say the same about your treatment of Mr. Dumas? I hear the Board of Psychology is wondering too. I guess you're no Clarice Starling." He gestured to the newest paperback book on his desk, *Silence of the Lambs.*

Clare found the right smile. It was the one she would've given Rodney Taylor in the coffee shop if she'd had the nerve. "And you're no Lennie Briscoe."

****

Clare perched on the edge of Robocop's pool table as he collected the last of their dinner dishes. He unbuttoned his sleeves and rolled his shirt up to his elbows, revealing the tattoo on his forearm. Semper Fi. *Of course*, she thought. Of course, he had a pool table. And a tattoo. It wouldn't surprise her to find a poster of Cindy Crawford taped to his bedroom wall.

"Do you play?" he asked. Clare shrugged, noncommittal.

"A little. Maybe you could teach me."

"Alright." He busied himself, sponging off a bit of stuck-on red sauce, but he couldn't hide his arousal. Not from Clare. A divining rod, her stomach pitched and dipped at the hint of a man's lust. Lightheaded, she took another sip of wine.

"I paid Bonner a visit today," she announced to distract them both.

Briggs stopped scrubbing and frowned at her. "I told you to let me handle it, Clare. You're kicking up a hornet's nest. What did you say to him?"

"Nothing really. I gave him a memo I wrote about Dumas documenting my treatment and my opinion about his alleged suicide. I have a right to my opinion, you know."

He toweled off his hands and walked to her. "Of course you do." Just like that, he was close to her. Too close, too fast. His thumb making small circles on her goose-fleshed arm. And all she could smell, think, see was Rodney Taylor. The thing she liked best about Neal, he always took it slow. But she couldn't blame Briggs. He was right where she wanted him. "Does it really matter if he killed himself? You saw him, what, five times? I don't want to sound cold-hearted, but—"

She stepped away so she could think straight and breathed in deep. "I'm being investigated by the Board of Psychology. So yes, it matters."

"Investigated? Why?"

"Substandard treatment. That's what they said. But Bonner is the real reason. He doesn't like me." Persistent, Briggs closed the gap between them again. "Is he in cahoots with the EME?" she asked.

"Cahoots? That's cute, Clare. Really cute, but can we not talk about work anymore?"

"I'll take that as a yes then."

Briggs groaned as if the weight of the conversation—the weight of her demand—was too much to bear. But he was in deep, and Clare knew it. Desperate to get lucky, presuming it even, he wouldn't screw it up now. "Bonner is no different than the rest of us. It's just prison politics. Whoever told you otherwise is just blowing smoke."

He grabbed her at the hips and scooted her closer. Taking his forearms in her hands, she meant to move him away. But he didn't get it. Not at all. "Like my tattoo, huh? Did you know I was a leather-neck? United States Marine Corps, baby. Through and through." Her body stiffened, but she smiled to be polite. "Let me put some music on. It'll help you relax."

When she didn't protest, he selected a CD from his collection, and Clare prepared to be amused. She counted on it. If it turned out to be something cheesy—and she knew it would be—maybe she could get through what was coming. Backstreet Boys, Bryan Adams. Whatever he thought would get him laid. "This song is a little old, but it's one of my favorites." He was already partway to her, when the song began.

The first few notes, and her heart iced over, the rest of her fever hot. Briggs hardly noticed, not with his clumsy fingers preoccupied by the buttons on her shirt, his face already buried in her neck. "Do you like it?" he asked, humming along, half-singing the words in her ear. "I can't fight this feeling anymore … forgotten what I started … for … time to bring this ship into … Clare?"

Things were expected of her. An answer, the least of it. "It's a classic," she heard herself say.

WELL, I'm *wait-ing*." Lizzie leaned forward, speaking over the morning din of the coffee shop. "And I want details."

"A lady never kisses and tells." Clare stalled, delaying the inevitable. Lizzie would never let her dodge the question.

"It's a good thing you aren't one then, Doctor."

Clare sipped her coffee and prayed for an earthquake. Any natural disaster would do. "C'mon. It's bad luck."

With a hard roll of her eyes, Lizzie retorted, "You're not seriously trying to convince me you're superstitious, are you? The girl who wanted to play with my mom's Ouija board on Halloween? Puh-lease." Truthfully, five months pregnant at the time, Clare had secretly hoped for black magic, poltergeist style. A curse. A portal to the dark side. Any way to wind time back to the day she met Rodney Taylor. And erase it entirely.

"It's Friday the thirteenth."

"I'm not asking you to adopt a black cat. I just want to know if Officer Briggs lived up to my lofty expectations."

Clare nodded fast. *Just get it over with.* "It was fine."

"Fine?"

"I mean, it wasn't all that memorable." That was the truth. She'd awakened in Briggs' twin bed at 3 a.m., wearing nothing but his shirt. Unequivocal evidence they'd had sex, but beyond him singing *that* song, she couldn't remember a thing. She hoped he used protection at least, but Briggs wasn't reliable like Neal, and she doubted it. When she insisted she'd go home, he seemed worried, but didn't stop her.

"Okay, I get it. You don't want to dish."

Clare smiled at Lizzie, as if she'd gotten it right. "I've got to run anyway. Early session this morning."

When they reached the door, Lizzie grabbed her arm. "Hey, I almost forgot. Have you talked to Neal?" *Define talk*, Clare thought. She'd listened to all his messages. Surely that counted for something. "He called me at work yesterday. I think he's worried about you."

"He just wants me to forget about that fight and get back together with him. But he said some awful things, Liz. He told me I have issues, and he just left me there."

"And he took the urn?" she asked.

Clare's coffee forced its way back up, and she swallowed hard, her throat burning. "What? Of course he did. I told you already. I was so upset I left it in the car. He said I could stop by to pick it up this weekend."

"Oh. Well, he told me he didn't have it. That you took it."

She laughed so she wouldn't have to speak right away, afraid her voice would come out as a croak. "And he thinks I'm the crazy one."

****

Briggs waited outside her office door, his back to the stairs. Clare stopped on the second step, watching. Broad shoulders, strong hands, arms that stretched the fabric of his uniform, yet he seemed small somehow. Vulnerable. *Probably because you've seen him naked.* Or maybe it was the photo of his mother he kept next to the bed. Or that he'd mussed her hair and kissed her before she hightailed it out of there. Or that he was holding a single yellow rose intended for her. Admiring him from afar, she felt herself warm to him, the last thing she needed.

"What are you doing here, asshole?" Clare pressed herself flat against the wall, the wind knocked out of her. His voice—harder than the Robocop she knew—frightened her. Her warm feelings scattered like birds.

"I'm here to see my therapist," Cullen answered back. "Is that a problem?"

"Get of here before I take a closer look at that ducat you forged. You're the last face Dr. Keely wants to see this morning."

"You sure about that?"

Clare understood she should do something. Say something. But she stayed fixed to the wall like a petal pressed between pages. She prayed for invisibility.

"I'm warning you, punk. You've got five seconds to scram. Unless you want to spend the rest of the day in Ad Seg—or the infirmary, if that suits you better." Clare winced.

"Does she know what a bully you are?"

Briggs' laugh came from someplace dark. It made Clare wonder if she knew him at all. "Some women like it rough. But you already know that, don't you, Cutthroat?" In the long silence, Clare imagined them standing chest to chest, breathing wildly through their nostrils. And a possibility she had never considered crept in like moss growing thick, thicker, until she felt suffocated. Briggs had raped her. Threw her against the pool table, forced up her skirt, back-handed her once for good measure. She touched her face, certain her cheek would be tender with a bruise.

But then Cullen snickered, and the vision evaporated. "Yellow roses mean friendship, genius."

Clare counted to one hundred before she continued the walk up to her office, shaky and disoriented as if she'd awakened from a nightmare. Briggs offered her a sheepish smile, but nothing else. "Good morning, beautiful."

"J. D.! What a pleasant surprise." Clare marveled at her capacity for make-believe.

After he left, she found the rose discarded in the trash can at the end of the hall. She felt a little sad for it, a blameless casualty of war.

228

She couldn't help but chuckle now that she was composed. Victory and spoils to Cullen.

***

Clare refused to admit it to herself, but she kept one eye on the door all day and felt disappointed when Cullen didn't return. Not that she blamed him. But inside she bubbled over with the feeling she wanted to tell him something. That she'd seen him with Briggs? That she knew he'd sent those chrysanthemums? That she pegged him as her secret admirer? Not so secret anymore. Whatever it was, she tucked it away and acted like a good therapist. Even when Fitzpatrick poked his head in with his usual song and dance.

"It's been few weeks now since Mr. Dumas … " He leaned in the doorway, hand on one hip, trying to look cool. "How would you feel about taking on a new client? Mondays at 10:30?"

Clare frowned. It was unusual for Fitzpatrick to dictate her schedule. "Uh, okay. Who is it?"

"All I know is he's a self-referral. Voluntary. And he's in for a double murder."

Clare took the hit to the stomach without making a face. "Sounds great." She waited for him to leave, but he lingered.

"Plans for tonight?"

"I'm meeting a friend for dinner." It rolled off her tongue, and she was glad she thought to prepare an excuse in advance.

"Was that Officer Briggs who stopped by this morning?" When she nodded, his face fell, disappointed. Or maybe she just imagined it. She wondered how much he'd heard. "He's a nice guy." Fitzpatrick didn't seem to believe it any more than she did.

DECEMBER 16, 1996

YOU came to see me last Friday." Clare decided it best to be blunt. Address the proverbial elephant before it grew too big to contain, broke out of its cage, and unwittingly crushed everyone in its path. Maybe it already had. She'd kissed him after all. On the mouth. *Christ, she'd kissed a client!* "This has to stop, Clive."

"I completely agree. That's what I came to talk to you about. But then I … " He lowered his eyes.

"Ran into Officer Briggs?"

"Did he tell you that?"

"No. I saw you. I saw both of you."

"I hope you're not dating that clown. He's not right for you." Clare cleared her throat with intention. "Oh, sorry. I guess I'm not allowed to … "

"Have an opinion about my personal life? No, technically not. But I understand why you do. This is my fault. I messed up. Badly. I understand if you want to transfer to another therapist."

"Are you kidding?" He looked pained, as if she'd slapped him. "No way."

"Alright." She agreed too quickly, but her relief felt so complete, her chest ached. "Let's just try to keep it professional." Cullen nodded, giving her an easy smile. It occurred to her, not for the first time, this—*whatever this was*—meant more to her than it ever had to him. "So tell me about Gina."

"Really? Okay. What do you want to know?"

"Did you choose her?" *Did you choose me?*

"Choose is a strong word. I noticed her. She was hard to miss."

"So she was attractive?" *Like me.*

"Not just pretty. There was something delicate about her. Something vulnerable. She needed protecting." *I need protecting.*

"From who?"

"Her ex. He was a CO at Corcoran. I got to know her pretty well when I was working there in the library. We'd talk about books that we liked, art, music. Then she told me about Bruce. How he used to slap her around and threaten to make up lies about her and spread them all over the prison. She didn't deserve that."

"You wanted to take care of her." *Of me. Stop it, Clare.*

Cullen looked her square in the eyes, radiating confidence. And again, she wondered if he had some mind trick. He could read her thoughts. "Not wanted, not tried. I did take care of her."

"What do you mean?"

"I'm not sure I should be telling you this, but—"

"Then don't. I mean, if you don't feel comfortable." Only lip service. Inside, Clare fought a fierce, inexplicable need to know.

"Is it strange you're the only person I trust at Quentin?" Clare shook her head, afraid to open her mouth. She wanted to say, *me too.* "I set him up, Dr. Keely. Nobody knows that. Not even Gina. He got fired, and I watched her blossom without him around. It was nice while it lasted."

"So you felt justified?"

Cullen shrugged. "Sometimes I do the wrong things for the right reasons. Or the right things for the wrong ones. Does that make any sense to you?"

"I slit someone's tires," Clare said, the words out of her mouth before she could stop them. Then she needed to explain. "He hurt me … a long time ago."

"You do understand, then," he said, studying the pain on her face. "Did you ever read Carl Jung?"

She nodded. "He's one of my favorites. Why?"

"Jung said, 'How can I be substantial if I fail to cast a Shadow? I must have a dark side also if I am to be whole.'"

She let herself smile, grateful to him for ignoring her slip-up. But more for seeing her, really seeing her. All of her. As unnerving as it was. Even the fault lines that ran deep under her surface, making her whole world unstable, capable of a seismic shift at any moment. A moment like this one.

"That guy … the one whose tires I cut … he molested me." Clare felt the wetness on her cheeks before she recognized the tears as her own.

"I know."

****

"It's almost 10:30," she mouthed in Cullen's ear, inhaling the crisp, clean scent of his hair. *How did this happen again?* But she knew. She'd made it happen. It was her curse to want something like this. Something rotten, something wrong. She'd become Rodney Taylor, rubbing up against the nearest forbidden thing just because she could. If a line existed—and it always did—she drew another one a little farther. Until she crossed it. *At least we haven't gone all the way,* she thought. And didn't Rodney himself tell her it's not wrong if you don't go all the way? But the thing about lines—eventually they lead you somewhere. Raping your daughter's fifteen-year-old friend in the front seat of your red BMW. Carrying your dead baby into Muir Woods. Staring down the tracks, playing chicken with a train. And that train had a name and piercing blue eyes and lips on fire.

"You can run over, right? Five more minutes." His hands were everywhere. That's the way it felt. That's the way she wanted it.

"I have a new client. I should—" *I should. I should.* But it felt too good to stop. And she couldn't tell where his mouth ended and hers began, so she stayed straddled across his lap, leaving it to him and his lips to sort out.

"Whoa! 'Scuse me. I'll come back." At first, Clare thought the voice came from the hallway. A universe away, a dull, drab universe, walled off from her own by the door she thought she locked herself.

232

It wasn't until Cullen released his hands from her waist, stopped kissing her, and sprang to his feet, virtually dropping her to the floor, that she realized she was wrong. Dead wrong. *How could she have been so careless?* A man stood in the doorway. Of her universe. Theirs.

"Tony Perez. I'm here to see Dr. Keely. Uh, the door was open—but if it's a bad time … "

"No. No, it's fine. Come in." Clare expected to die right there. To literally fall to the ground, struck down by lightning. Or shame. She imagined they felt the same—burning from the inside out, splitting atoms in two, stopping her heart like a clock someone forgot to wind. But her heart kept beating fast and hard. Her hands smoothed her blouse, the silk hot and moist under her armpits. Her fingers buttoned the ones Cullen had undone. Her legs held her up, barely. And her eyes—oh, her eyes—they could see only one thing. Three inked letters on the neck of her new client: EME.

CHAPTER TWENTY-ONE

HEADS OR TAILS

MY chest burned. Partly from the running, partly from the crying that started halfway back to the parking lot, tears that came out of nowhere and wouldn't stop. Statue Samantha unfroze and started melting. Levi didn't ask if I was okay, but he told me we could slow down if I needed. I shook my head, worried speaking would only make it worse.

We'd just reached the rental car when we heard the first wail of a police siren. Still faint, it splintered the quiet with the brutality of an axe. "Maybe we should wait and flag them down," I told Levi, my breath still coming in staccato wet gasps I tried to control.

"Sam." Not the first time he sounded like my mother. But I felt his hand rub the center of my back, and it settled me. "You know we can't. I can't."

"What do you think is going to happen, Levi? At the end of all of this? Do you think you're just going to shoot the bad guy and walk off into the sunset?"

"That sounds like a Western." His laugh smacked of bitterness, and it made me sad all over again. "I guess I didn't think that far ahead."

"You brought zip ties and a stun gun, so I find that hard to believe."

"Yeah, well I *had* a plan. But it got blown to hell by ... "

"By me? You can say it. It's fine. I won't be offended. Just remember who followed who."

"I was going to say the EME. Now that stun gun is gathering dust in an evidence room somewhere. And a skin-and-bones crackhead is wearing my zip ties."

That got a half-smile from me at least. "So what's Plan B?"

"Get in," he said. He opened the car door and tossed the duffel bag in the back. "We're too exposed out here. They might see us." I couldn't be sure if *they* meant the police or Cullen and my mother. Levi didn't trust Clare Keely, but I didn't want to ask because I couldn't admit the truth out loud: I didn't either.

Inside the car, the cold went right through me. My shirt, clammy with sweat, stuck against my skin, and I shivered. As soon as Levi started the engine, I cranked up the heater and rubbed my hands together in the stream of hot air.

"Do you think the police found Ginny yet?"

"Probably." I couldn't tell if he was lying. "She'll be okay. It'll take some time, but wounds heal. All kinds of wounds."

I nodded because I knew the kind he meant. "Now what?"

He rested his head against the seat and sighed. "I'm not exactly sure."

"What? I thought you knew where they were going."

"My sister had found out about the cabin. When he escaped, I figured he'd try to go there. Past that, well ... " He shrugged, and all the hopes I'd pinned on him came undone and fell away. I would've cried if I'd had any tears left.

"How did your sister find that place? It's pretty remote."

"Turns out Cutthroat is a bit of a mama's boy. The phone records from San Quentin showed them talking almost every day. So we tracked her down, and Katie did a little snooping while she slept. Unfortunately, she's a light sleeper."

"What did you find exactly?"

"Not much besides this cabin. Cullen spent time here as a kid."

I tried to imagine it, *him*—those ice-blue eyes—as a child. A boy's small frame, slight and wiry, playing in the woods, but the face had no features. It was blank. I couldn't picture it. "Why?"

"His father lived here in the sixties, apparently. Off and on. Before he ended up in prison for rape. It was a commune back then." A second siren sliced through, closer this time, and I jumped, kicking the ammo can at my feet. "Let's get out of here," Levi said. "I'll head toward the freeway."

"Which direction? Where would you go if you escaped from prison?"

I watched his lips curled into a slow smile as he plucked a penny from his pocket. "Heads, Mexico. Tails, Canada."

****

"Sam, wake up." Levi nudged me with his elbow, and I groaned. The clock on the dashboard told me I'd only been sleeping for minutes. Just a blink that felt like hours. But it was dark. So dark I wondered if my eyes were open at all. Long-fingered branches scratched against the window. Pinecones crunched like bones under the wheels. I recognized this place.

"Where are we?" I asked anyway.

"We're here."

The fine hairs on my neck bristled. "Here?" I pressed my face to the window. A bird lay dead on the ground, its neck twisted at an unnatural angle. Beyond it, another and another. A line of small bodies leading to a mound of fresh dirt and a woman shoveling. I couldn't make her out, but I knew her anyway. As well as I knew myself. She turned as slow as a jewelry box dancer, in her hands a metal box. "What is this place?" I asked.

"Your grave." And that's when I saw the knife in his hand, the blade so new, so shiny, it would mirror his face back to him. Cullen's face. My father.

I jolted awake, my heart battering my chest like a Bellwether hailstorm. "Are you okay?" Levi asked, pulling off to the shoulder.

236

I nodded fast, not entirely sure. "I had a dream, I guess." I wrapped my arms around myself, noticing my goosebumps. "Scratch that. A nightmare."

"We haven't been driving that long. Tails, Canada. Remember?"

"I remember." With newfound purpose, I picked up the ammo can and brought it to my lap. "But first I think we should look inside."

"Didn't you already … "

"Maybe there's something I missed. You're an officer of the law, right?"

"At this point, I think that's debatable."

"Humor me."

He flipped open the lid and examined the passports, holding them up to the interior light. "Kevin and Anna Johnson?" he asked, incredulous, and I shrugged.

"Did your mom tell you what these were for? They're legit looking. Professional."

"I'm no Sherlock Holmes, but I'm pretty sure she'd planned to help him escape."

"I think you're on to something, Detective." Levi smirked, then sobered seeing my face. He set the cash on the console and picked up the scribbled note. "This is pretty twisted. Typical Cutthroat. Is that all?"

"Well, there was the gun, of course. And the cash. That's it."

I reached for the stack of well-worn hundreds and rolled my thumb along the edges, listening to the soft whir of the paper. "Should we count it? It's a lot of money."

I began ticking off each hundred, then thousand—one thousand, two thousand, three thousand—until mid-way through, the rubber band popped, and the bills spread across my lap.

"Hey, what's that?" Levi asked. I followed his eyes to the floorboard, where a business card dropped from the stack. It looked ordinary enough—like any puzzle piece—meaningless on its own. Crisp white with chartreuse lettering, a little bent at the edges, but when I picked it up, examined it more closely, it became essential.

"I know that name," I said. "McKinnon asked my mother about him." I passed the card to Levi, and he read it aloud.

"Green River Trucking. Rodney Taylor, Owner. Serving California since 1983."

Levi tapped the address with his thumb—75th Street, Oakland. He reached across my lap and popped the glove compartment, pointing to the map inside. Then he put the car in drive and pulled back onto the highway. "I say tails, Rodney Taylor."

CHAPTER TWENTY-TWO
OAK TREE

"ARE you sure your mom never mentioned this guy?" Levi asked, eyeing the business card propped in the cup holder.

I tried not to glare at him. "There's a lot she didn't mention. Obviously."

"Sorry." The way he squeezed my knee—gentle but firm—I forgave him. And I wanted to pretend it all made sense. Me and Levi in a rental car, halfway to Oakland. Ginny's blood, drying on my blue jeans. My mother somewhere with my father. My real father. "What did she say about your dad?"

I catalogued what I knew—"Neal Barrington, psychologist, died in a plane crash the year I was born"—which was not much at all. "And he gave her that ruby ring she wears."

"But what did she *say* about him?"

I sighed. "She hardly ever talked about him. Once, she compared him to a tree."

Levi frowned. "A tree?"

"An oak tree to be exact." I'd come in late from stargazing with Tobey. When she saw my face, flushed and giddy, she sat me down.

Find a boy more like your father, she'd said. "Sturdy and reliable like an oak."

"Interesting," he said, side-eyeing me. I couldn't decide if Levi was an oak or not. "He sounds a lot different than Cullen."

"If he's even real. She probably made him up like everything else." I leaned back against the seat so Levi couldn't see my eyes. "My father killed people." I tried out the words in my head, but they sounded worse out loud.

"So did mine," Levi said.

"But do you know why? That's important, right? The why."

"Is it?" he asked, and I knew I wasn't meant to answer. Not that I had an answer anyway. "There's one thing I know for sure about my dad." Levi waited until I looked at him, blinking back tears again, and smiled. "He wasn't an oak tree. And I can't even blame Cullen for that."

"Hey, is that … ?" I pointed out the window to the blaring lights just past the exit sign.

"Yep. San Quentin. The prison by the Bay. The place where all this started." By this, I knew exactly *who* he meant. I tried to picture my mother driving this road, making that turn toward those gates, those high fences. Muted by the darkness, it might've been a luxury hotel. A luxury hotel with a high-priced view. The highest price.

"Did you ever visit your dad there?"

"Once, but I don't remember it. My parents—my adopted parents—showed me a picture of me and my dad in front of this mural. The one in the visiting room. Snip said I was really shy, that I wouldn't even let go of my mom until it was time to leave. I guess I was scared she'd disappear too. I followed her around like a puppy."

"Uh, Levi?" I fixed my stare on the side mirror, my stomach clenched. "There's a cop behind us."

"I know." He didn't gasp or flinch or tighten his grip on the steering wheel. I might as well have told him there was an ironing board in the rearview.

"How long has it been there?" I asked, trying to mimic his even timbre.

240

"A minute or so. Since we got on the San Rafael Bridge." Levi gestured out the window to the Bay. I squinted to make out the water from the sky, searching for the places where the black waves moved slow and fluid like a moccasin in the grass.

"They're probably looking for this car by now, don't you think?" I asked.

"Definitely. But no lights, no problem, right?"

I exhaled. *No lights, no problem.* Still, it was just us and him. Two dots separated by the blank canvas of the early morning highway. Surely no coincidence. And that's when I saw it. A kaleidoscope of blue and red staining the dash. I sucked in a gulp of air. "Lights. Problem."

Levi cursed under his breath, slowing the car to a crawl until we reached the section of bridge with a narrow shoulder. "If we don't get out of this, just say it was my idea. All of it." He lowered the window, and the cold crept inside until I felt it crawl under my skin.

"It *was* your idea." Outside, a door closed with a soft thud. A simple sound—ordinary—but in the absence of any others, it took on its own life, critical and foreboding.

"And I'm sorry. I'm sorry, Sam."

"Wait—what?" Boots struck the ground with the kind of authority no one questioned. And Levi's fingers drummed on the wheel. The air hummed electric between us, fraying my already ragged nerves, and I sat still waiting for the lightning strike.

"Step out of the vehicle. Both of you." It was the sort of voice I expected from a police officer. I didn't turn to see his face, but I imagined it anyway. The hard set of his jaw. The ice in his eyes, a thin layer of cold to cover his fear. He would shoot me—small-town girl—if it came to that.

"Go ahead," Levi urged. "Do what he says."

"What're you going to do?" I asked, knowing he wouldn't answer. Fearing he might. One step, then another, and the pavement, wet with dew, shimmered under my feet.

The officer addressed me, but I couldn't look up. "Put your hands on the side of the vehicle, ma'am, where I can see them. I wished for my letterman jacket to remind me of who I was. I couldn't remember Samantha Bronwyn anymore. I'd left her behind somewhere.

"Sir, step out of the vehicle. Now." Levi's fingers kept drumming. He didn't seem afraid, even when the man raised his gun, but I wondered if his tap-tap-tapping marked the frenetic beat of his heart.

"Levi … please … "

Three things happened then. Not one—two—three—like a line of dominoes cascading. But all at once. Onetwothree. I couldn't say which came first. Levi spinning his tires, wheels shrieking as he put his foot to the gas, leaving burnt rubber marks on the road and me standing alone, exposed. Another engine revving like thunder building over the horizon. Or a spray of bullets … and the one that found a mark.

Next came the scream. Different than Ginny's. Unforgettable. The scream of a grown man who had known ordinary fear, but never this. The kind of animal scream you'd imagine would come if death himself could lock eyes with you before sucking out your soul. The officer's legs folded beneath him as I watched. His mouth contorted in surprise, then pain. It wasn't the face I'd imagined at all—stoic and chiseled in ice. His cheeks were full, doughy, rough with acne scars. And his eyes were fawn brown.

A bullet buzzed in the air in front of me, and I ducked. Sprinted to the police car and took cover alongside it. Another shot pinged off the door, and I winced as if it had gone through my flesh. I stared at the clean wound in the sheet metal no different than the hole in the officer's chest. And I gagged on the warm, bitter bile rising in my throat.

"Sam! Get in!" Until I heard Levi's voice, I'd been convinced he wanted me dead. Those bullets were his. They were meant for me. Meant to end me as he sped down the freeway toward his revenge. And that's why he'd been sorry.

My mother's rental car steamrolled toward me in reverse, Levi yelling out the window. "C'mon!" I willed my legs to run, to dodge bullets. *Where were they coming from?* I willed my hand to open the door and fling myself inside, curling against the seat like a snail in a shell. I willed myself to turn my head over my shoulder, to glimpse through the shattered rear glass. "EME," Levi said, shifting into drive and screeching away. "Are you hit?"

Hit. That word took its time. *Was I? Hit?* My hand bled. I saw that now. Cut by a shard of glass from the exploded windshield. But as far as I could tell, the rest of me remained intact. "No," I answered, flinching with each *pop-pop-pop*.

With no instruction, Levi passed me his gun. Like it was a basketball, and I'd know exactly what to do with it. I'd only ever shot at a paper target. *Never point your weapon at anything you're not willing to destroy.* That's what I remembered as I stuck my arm out the window and pulled the trigger. That's when I knew Samantha Bronwyn was dead. A self, my whole self, shed like an old skin.

CHAPTER TWENTY-THREE
WHAT'S ALREADY GONE

I couldn't stop shaking. Even after Levi pulled the car to the shoulder, took the gun from me, and folded both of his hands over mine. "Is it over?" I asked. Each word took effort.

He nodded. His eyes were right there. Bright and alive. "We've gotta go."

I cracked the car door and got out, testing my legs like a newborn foal. Strange, but I thought of Cullen and his first steps back into the free world. It must have felt like this. A change so complete it can't be quantified or named. Levi followed me, hoisting his duffel bag over his shoulder and jogging toward the intersection of bridge and highway.

"Don't look," he called back to me. I hadn't planned on it, but his warning issued an invitation. I snuck a glance. Then I couldn't look away. Behind us, the EME's sedan had caught fire. Its front end had folded in like a cardboard box. A man's body lay motionless on the hood—half in, half out of the smashed front windshield.

"Did I kill those men?" I asked. There had been two of them. I was sure of it.

"I told you not to look." Levi stopped, turned around, frowned at me. "You really don't remember?"

I shook my head. The flames licked the sky, where the sun had just begun its slow rise. The heat reached me, and I stepped back.

"They were chasing us. You shot out a tire, and they lost control. Smashed right into the guardrail."

I did that? I did that. The car creaked and groaned in response to my admission, the fire spreading. "How did they find us?"

"Hell if I know. But I don't trust McKinnon or the Feds. They've got their own agenda. And I'm sure that cop blasted our location all over the radio. Any yahoo with a police scanner could've tracked us down." Levi grabbed my arm and tugged me toward him. I relented, letting myself be dragged, but my eyes were stuck on that body protruding from the car's mouth. Through the smoke, his arms had life, wriggling like the legs of an upturned insect.

"Should we help him? I think he's still alive."

"He's not. And we can't. Look." I followed Levi's finger past the wreckage to the harsh glare of approaching headlights. I tried to imagine how the scene must look to an outsider. How it would've looked to me two days ago. Unreal. "They'll call for help. But if we stay … "

"Don't you mean if *you* stay? I haven't forgotten you were going to leave me. You did leave me. Again." The screech of those tires had sounded a lot like betrayal. This time even worse than the first because I hadn't expected it.

"For your own good. You're safer with the cops than you are with me. I tried to tell you that back at the cabin."

"But you are a cop."

"Yeah, you keep reminding me."

"Well, somebody has to."

Levi started running again, and I matched his pace. By the time we reached the bottom of the bridge, sirens cut the quiet, and there was no going back. "Over here," he said, ducking into the trees near the tollbooths. "I'm not a cop right now. Right now, I'm no better than Cullen. No better than my dad. I've got nothing to lose." An

18-wheeler barreled through the pay station, briefly spotlighting our hiding place. Levi reached for my hand, then my elbow, until we were nearly pressed together and out of sight.

"You have things to lose." It sounded lame, and it made my chest ache that I needed to say it at all. He was so close, I only breathed the words against him, and I wondered if he heard me.

"Like what?"

I hadn't expected that. I wanted to look at him, but I buried my face in his T-shirt instead. It was damp with sweat. His warm hand closed around my head, cocooning it against him. "Your job. Your sister. The family who adopted you."

"I let all of those people down. You can't lose what's already gone."

Finally, I summoned the courage to meet his eyes. In them, the answer to a question I hadn't been able to ask even to myself. "Those pills in your backpack … your plan … were you going to … ?"

He didn't deny it. "I set my sister up, Sam. I wanted her to get caught. I thought it would kill two birds, you know? She'd get off the streets for a while, get the help she needed in jail, and I'd get the info on Cullen. I swear I didn't know she had drugs on her that night. They charged her with felony possession. That means prison time. I did that. And everybody knows it."

"What I said earlier, the why *is* important, Levi. The why matters."

"Yeah, well my why sucks. I was just being selfish."

"And what exactly would be selfless about suicide?" He shrugged, and I felt the weight of his shoulders, the burden there. "Are you still thinking of doing that? I mean, is that still your plan? I think I deserve to know."

"Well, Plan A got blown to hell, remember? I'm on to Plan B now." He laughed a little, a small, comforting sound like creek water running over a rock bed. And I wondered how something so fragile could stand up to the harshness of the world. How did anything good survive?

"I'm scared too, you know. Even before all this. Sometimes, I don't know if I can make it on my own next year." Baylor seemed to belong to someone else now, a made-up person.

246

"Think about it. If you can survive the EME and Cutthroat Cullen, college will be a major letdown. A real snoozefest. Just promise me you'll invite me to a game—assuming I'm not in jail, of course. I need to see Samantha Bronwyn, basketball phenom, in action."

I don't know what came over me then. Some strange potion of giddiness, relief, and terror. Whatever it was, it must have been potent stuff to make me as bold as Ginny. I tilted my head up to him, slid my hand around his neck, and brought his lips to mine.

****

"That was unexpected." Levi leaned back against the tree trunk and raised his eyebrows. "You surprised me." Good surprise or bad surprise, he didn't specify. And I didn't ask. But his not-quite smile hinted more good than bad. He'd surprised me too in the tentative way he kissed back, not like the other boys who groped me as if their pants were on fire. *Keyword boys*, I thought. Levi was different. He took his time, held something back, like he knew I was breakable.

Taken aback by my own boldness, I felt suddenly exposed. Shivering, I folded both arms across my chest. "Now we're even."

His mouth twisted to one side, considering. "I don't know about that. I think I might owe you one." I turned my face away, hiding it from the soft glow of the dawn, and grinned.

"To be fair I did warn you," I said.

"I know. Texas girls." Levi pointed to the building adjacent to the toll plaza. "Well, Miss Texas, how do you feel about borrowing a car?"

"Borrowing?"

He shrugged. "Okay, stealing."

"Do I have a choice?"

"Not if you're coming with me." He assumed my answer, walking toward the sparse parking lot dotted with a few cars and utility vehicles. "That Honda looks promising."

"Don't you need tools or something?" Levi dropped the duffel at his boots and reached inside, producing a small screwdriver. "You certainly came prepared. Did they teach you that as a junior officer?"

247

"How do you think I got to Muir Woods? The bus? Every police-man worth his salt knows how to steal a car."

"But they don't go around doing it." My stomach flip-flopped at the thought of all the other things he would be willing to do. Had already done. The things I'd done. The things I would do to get my mom back. Maybe Levi was right. It didn't matter why. Lines were lines. And murder was murder. "Is it really worth all this? Killing Cullen? Have you ever murdered somebody, Levi? Are you prepared to live with that?"

Silence. "I guess I wasn't planning on *living* with it." I pretended to ignore his hard swallow, the water in his eyes that seemed to well from nowhere. "I've always had a one-track mind, you know. When I was a kid, all I could dream about was getting my badge. Like it was my talisman, my lucky rabbit's foot. I thought that badge pinned to my chest would solve everything. And I got it, but … I was still me, still Levi with the same old demons. And my sister was still messed up. It didn't change anything. Then Snip got out, and he told me what he suspected about Cullen, all the talk on the yard. Ever since, I've been hell-bent on avenging my dad. The truth is I didn't even know him."

"And now?"

"You want to find your mom, right?" I nodded, holding back the dark fear that Clare Bronwyn was gone for good. Bermuda Triangle unfindable. "So it's not just about Cullen anymore. You were right. It does matter why. And the why is I want to help you. So yes—long answer—it's worth it."

"Okay." I sounded calmer than I felt. "Let's borrow a car then."

****

It took forty-six minutes to drive our stolen Honda to 75th Avenue. And I spent every single one of those forty-six minutes looking behind us. Waiting for the lines we'd crossed to catch up. But they never did. Not even when I convinced—okay, begged—Levi to stop at a gas station and buy a prepaid phone so I could call Ginny. I'd counted the seconds he spent inside, certain each tick was one closer to our reckoning. Slunk down in the passenger seat, two blocks from

Green River Trucking, I began to wonder if that was the very reason for my existence—a string of crossed lines.

"I really don't think that's a good idea," Levi said, side-eyeing the phone in my hand. Ignoring him, I dialed the number for Snip's burner phone. "Just don't tell anybody where we are."

"I may be from the country, but I'm not that much of a novice. I've seen *CSI*, you know."

Levi replied with a hard roll of his eyes. "Well, pardon me, Detective. I clearly underestimated you."

After one ring, Ginny's groggy voice answered, "Hello?"

"Ginny, it's Sam. Are you okay?" Nothing. Then, "Samantha, this is Agent McKinnon. Where are you?"

"Hang up," Levi mouthed.

"Is that Officer Beckett? Is he there with you? Levi, turn yourself in before you get hurt."

"I want to know if Ginny's okay," I told her. "Then, I'll answer your questions."

"Ginny is fine. The wound was minor. She's resting. Now—"

"Let me talk to her," I demanded.

"Samantha, you're way out of your depth here. This is a dangerous game you're playing. And Officer Beckett can't protect you. We need to know where you are. Please don't be like your mother."

That stung. *Like my mother?*

"It's one thing to be a tramp. And another to be a fool. An utter fool." I smashed the red button disconnecting the call and tossed the phone on the floorboard, staring at with contempt. Levi stared out the window.

"Go ahead. Say it." He didn't. "I told you so, Samantha," I parroted, deepening my voice.

"Do I really sound like that? Like a drunk Santa Claus?"

"A little," I said, grateful for the sound of his laughter.

****

Ten minutes later and nothing. The cheap burner phone lay lifeless at my feet. And outside, only the sparse grass lining the sidewalk moved, fluttering like strips of burnt paper in the breeze. "It's still early," Levi said when I groaned. "You can sleep if you want to. I'll wake you at the first sign of life."

"Not tired. Just thinking." In truth, my body was exhausted, but my brain whirled like a hamster on a wheel, and it wouldn't stop spinning. "Have you ever been attracted to a criminal?" Levi burst into short-lived laughter, stopping when he glimpsed my grim expression. He stayed quiet for a moment, and I stared past him to the row of ramshackle buildings lining the street. In the yard closest to us, a half-deflated basketball had cracked in the sun. It served as a dismal reminder of how far I was from who I'd been.

"That has to be one of the weirdest questions anybody has ever asked me."

"Well, have you? To a person you were arresting? Or somebody in jail?"

"There have been a couple of lookers ... " He smirked. "Not my type though. I always fall for the good girls." He nudged me with his elbow, and I almost smiled.

"I'm serious."

He knew I was, and he raised his hands in surrender. "Honestly, no. But if you're asking about your mom and Cullen—which I think you are—it's completely different. A therapist gets close to you. Figures out how you tick. You trust her."

"It sounds like you think my mom's to blame for this." And I didn't entirely disagree.

"Your mom had a professional responsibility to her client. And that didn't include sex."

"Or escape," I added, feeling like a traitor.

"But I know men like Cullen. They have ways of getting what they want from you, but making you feel like you were the one who wanted it all along. Have you ever heard that line ... something like *Blame is for God and small children*? I guess that's what I'm saying. Nobody's innocent here."

"Nobody," I agreed, eyeing my own partial reflection in the window.

DECEMBER 17, 1996

CLARE couldn't stop thinking about Tony Perez. Actually, it wasn't Tony himself. He was nothing special. Compton born and bred. Incarcerated at seventeen. He'd mowed down two bystanders shooting at a rival gang in his neighborhood. A humdrum case by San Quentin standards. But, his tattoo. Those three inked letters—that's what kept her up last night. It covered his whole neck, and she had tried not to stare at it. Thinking about it now, she couldn't remember most of what he'd said. Something about feeling depressed after his last parole hearing ended with another denial. And there was this, Tony muttering with one foot out the door: *I'll be sure to knock next time.*

Clare took her time getting dressed. Outside, it drizzled off and on, and she dreaded even her short commute. She wanted to play hooky, but that would only make it worse. By the time she forced herself out of the house, it was ten past nine o'clock.

"I thought you were avoiding me." Neal leaned up against her car, holding an umbrella in one hand and a coffee in the other. The sky kept spitting, but she stood her ground, letting the drops dot her striped button-down. For a boring old tree, Neal looked handsome, dignified. And being close to him always made her feel safe—but under the umbrella was too close, close enough for him to read her mind.

"I've just been really busy. I was going to call you tonight." She averted her eyes from his obvious disbelief.

"Right. I'm sure." He extended his hand, putting the warm cup into hers. "This is for you. Black. Two sugars. Just the way you like it."

"Thanks, Neal. That's really kind of you. I'm really late, though. I've got to go. Really."

"Wow. That's a lot of reallys." She hated him then for not letting her off easy like he always did. "What's going on, Clare?" She steeled herself. Neal could be mean when he wanted to be. "You don't call me back. You told Lizzie I took your mother's urn. And you've got a hickey on your neck." Of all the things, that one nearly dropped her. *How had she missed it? And when? Who else had seen it?*

She reached into her purse and fished out the scarf she kept for cold days like this one, looping it around herself as Neal frowned. He would never be so careless to leave a mark on her. "I'm seeing someone." Because she knew that would shut him up, make him forget about the urn and all of his unreturned phone calls.

"Who?"

"Nobody you know. It's someone at work." In her mind, she thought Briggs but saw Cullen's face, desperate and burning for her.

"An officer? Or … "

"Yes, an officer. Who else? A patient?" Her laughter sounded more like an escaped scream she'd been holding in for years. "It's not really your business though, is it?"

"I guess not." She'd exhausted him. Hell, she exhausted herself. "Just keep your neck covered. It's not very professional."

"Thank you, Dr. Barrington. I'll be sure to report to the decorum police for my demerits."

Neal opened the door for her. That's how sturdy he was. Even her sharp tongue couldn't budge him. "Goodbye, Clare." And for once, it sounded like he meant it.

****

Fitzpatrick's office was closed—lights off—when Clare arrived. Maybe he'd called in sick. Wherever he was, she felt glad he wasn't there waiting for her. She never came in this late. And she certainly didn't need his beady eyes judging her. The hallway looked empty. It gave Clare the sinking feeling she'd forgotten something. A meeting. A training. Just in case, she kept the scarf around her neck.

She rushed to get inside, dropping her keys twice. And her lungs fluttered like butterfly wings until she felt breathless. *What's the big deal, Clare?* Finally, she managed to open the door, but her key stuck in the lock. It refused to budge no matter how forcefully she jiggled it. "Forget it," she muttered, leaving it there and cracking the door with her hip.

Clare realized something right then as the door swung open. She caught a glimpse of muddy prison boots propped on her desk. She'd only been surprised—really surprised—once in her life. The first time Rodney Taylor touched her under the table. It shattered something precious and fragile inside her, something she'd taken for granted until then, even with all her mother's failures. The deep-down belief in the goodness of the world. Every bad thing after that was sort of expected. But not this one.

"Buenos días, Dr. Keely."

Clare fingered the alarm in her hand. "Mr. Ramirez." The only two words she could think to say. The way she'd said *excuse me* when Mr. Taylor's arm had brushed against her in the swimming pool. She'd actually apologized. But she couldn't wrap her mind around this. Ramirez. Here. She assumed he'd been hauled off to a supermax a month ago.

"Cierra la puerta," he told her, gesturing to the door. "Close it." And she obeyed. Clare studied his arms. The light brown hair on them still wet from the rain. A large drop rolled down the *M* on his bicep, and he wiped it away. That's when she noticed the gloves on his hands. Thick work gloves, gray and stained with dirt.

"Someone told me you'd transferred to Pelican Bay." *Act normal,* she thought. She turned on the lights and set her purse beside her desk.

His lips curled, hinted at a smile. Under the fluorescent glow, she noticed another tattoo on his face she hadn't seen before. A teardrop just under his right eye. Clare remembered that symbol from one of

Fitzpatrick's trainings. *Usually, it means the inmate committed murder,* he'd said, pausing for their shock and awe. "Nah. My old lady can't drive that far. And I don't like the cold."

"Oh. I see." She didn't *see* anything. "Can I help you?"

"Yes, I think you can. And I know you will."

His voice sounded different than she remembered. Steady. In control. Almost business-like. She held up the alarm to him like a talisman, wishing it had the power to strike him dead. "You should leave before I press this."

"I wouldn't do that if I were you, puta. Unless you want every-body in Quentin to know what you've been doing. Or should I say, who?"

"I don't know what you're talking about."

"I betcha that hothead Briggs wouldn't be too keen on you bang-ing a rat."

"I said I don't know what you're—"

"Alright, alright. We'll do it your way. Lieutenant Bonner will hear what Tony has to say. You see, after he walked in on you strad-dling your boyfriend, you offered him some favors for his silence. You started to take off your blouse, but he stopped you. Poor Tony felt muy, muy uncomfortable."

"That's ridiculous. No one will believe him." But Clare believed it, even knowing it hadn't happened.

"Will they believe him when I tell them what you said to me on the yard last month?" Slow and deliberate, he set his boots back onto the floor and stood up, crossing the floor in two steps leaving mud tracks behind him. His spider-leg fingers scrambled up her arm and traced the side of her face. "Maybe you offered me some favors too. I can think of a few things that might shut me up."

"No." Such a small word and smaller still when she squeezed it out of her throat.

"I thought you might say that." He tugged on the edges of his gloves, pulling them tighter. "That's why I came prepared. 'Estar preparado, Arturo.' That's what my mom used to tell me. So you can press your alarm if you'd like, but by the time anybody gets here,

I'll have snapped your neck like a chicken bone. And who do you think will get the blame? Me or your puto boyfriend whose prints are everywhere? He likes to leave his mark, eh?" He tapped the soft spot under his jaw, smirking at her, and she knew her scarf had come undone.

"Please leave." The walls closed in tighter, and Clare fought for air. Her panic went straight to her hands—like it always did. The shaking started, and she dropped the alarm. The clink of it against the tile sounded a million miles away.

"Pobrecita. Relax. I won't touch you. You don't ever have to see me again. If you do this one little thing."

The M on his bicep seemed to writhe. Like his snake heart was right there under it, pulsing. If her hands weren't useless at her sides, the pen on her desk would've done nicely, sliced through his skin as easily as Rodney Taylor's tire. "What do you want me to do?"

DECEMBER 18, 1996

FEELING better, Dr. Keely?" Fitzpatrick poked his head in through the crack in her office door, and she jumped, her heart off to the races before it could register she was safe for now. "I think there's a bug going around."

She kept her head down so he couldn't see the lie cross her face. "Probably the flu or something." That something being Arturo Ramirez. Even with her eyes wide open all night and staring at the television, those muddy boots wouldn't go away. Neither would the gloves with their dark-brown fingertips. It was dirt. Of course it was. He'd probably stolen the gloves when he'd been assigned to landscaping. But, in her mind, those stains were blood. Hers soon enough, if she didn't do what he'd asked.

"I brought you some information from the safety training." He dropped a stapled packet of paper on her chair. "The one you missed yesterday morning," he added when she failed to properly disguise her confusion.

"Oh, right. The training. Was it … interesting?"

"Riveting." Fitzpatrick chuckled at his own joke. "By the way, did you want to make up our supervision session?"

No, no, and no. "Sure."

"Are you busy now?"

Very. Clare gazed at her barren desk. Not a single file folder to speak of. "I guess not."

Fitzpatrick made himself comfortable in the chair opposite her, before she'd even invited him. He unwrapped a peppermint and popped it into his mouth. She watched him shift the candy with his tongue, right then left, until he pocketed it in his cheek and grinned. A squirrel with a nut. "Well, then, how was your new client?"

She wasn't ready to dive into the deep end, but he pushed her. "Actually, I'm hoping he could be reassigned."

"Why?"

"Did you know he was in the Mexican Mafia?"

Fitzpatrick made a noise of understanding. When he spoke, his tongue was Christmas red. "A dropout. He's not an active member anymore. It shouldn't be a problem."

"It makes me uncomfortable. I don't feel safe."

"Perhaps he reminds you of someone from your past? Someone you didn't feel safe with?"

Here we go, Clare thought. Sigmund Fitzpatrick, rearing his pompous head. "It's not that at all. I don't think he's done with the EME, and I don't trust him. "

Fitzpatrick laughed again, that condescending little twitter that made her want to rip his throat out. "You do realize you work in a prison, Dr. Keely. I trust my clients about as far as I could throw them. And even that might be an overstatement."

"I … I ran into Ramirez … on the yard. You told me he'd been transferred."

"I thought he would be, but his cellie confessed to the whole thing. They charged him with drug smuggling and possession of a weapon. Shipped him off to Crescent City. They had to let Ramirez go. Yesterday, I think. I should've told you sooner. Is that what this is about? Ramirez?"

Clare shrugged, but she wanted to throttle him. "Does it really matter?" she asked, trying to control her voice. "You wanted to reassign Cullen, so reassign Tony Perez instead."

"I feel you getting angry with me. I'm not saying no. I'm just asking for a little self-reflection from a psychologist. Don't you think your distaste toward him might be worth exploring further? When

I first started, my supervisor told me something. He said, 'Fitz, to make it in the pen, you have to get comfortable with being uncomfortable.' Can you do that, Clare?"

She felt tears coming—hot and insistent—like water from a hose left in the sun, but she squashed them fast. Didn't he realize she'd been doing that her whole life? "Of course."

****

Briggs worked late that night. Clare didn't know how, but Ramirez made sure of it. "Just this one thing?" she'd asked him, her voice still quivering. He'd held up one gloved finger, pressed it to his lips and nodded.

At seven o'clock she dotted perfume on the back of her neck and left her office. She headed for the control booth, passing through the dark courtyard where the only pool of light came from a tall lamppost. It was so quiet, she swore she could hear the ocean butting up against the rocks. She'd never been here this late, never at night. The place seemed haunted. And why wouldn't it be? *Did you know they used to hang people at Quentin?* Fitzpatrick had asked her once, probably trying to impress her with his historical knowledge. And every chance he got, he couldn't help but mention the execution last May. Like he'd been there when they'd injected Keith Daniel Williams with a lethal dose of bittersweet revenge, the kind that never feels as good as you thought it would, as good as you needed it to. Clare's eyes strained, searching beyond the shadows. But if there were ghosts, they'd long since scattered.

She stopped before she reached the booth and leaned against the wall to get her breath under control. It came in short, forceful bursts like she'd been running. She wound her hair around her hand and lifted it from her neck, somehow moist with perspiration in the frigid December air.

Don't be a baby, Clare. That's what Rodney Taylor told her the first time he made her put her mouth on him. *Don't be a baby.* That was the same day he took her picture with one of those old-fashioned Polaroid cameras. *Something to tide me over for when we can't see each*

258

other, he'd said. *Pose for me*. And he laughed when she stuck out her tongue. *Do something sexy*. Clare had no clue how to be sexy, so she copied the thing she'd seen her mother do in the mirror, pursing her lips together. The way Mr. Taylor stared at her with his mouth open, she knew she'd done something right.

At the edge of the courtyard, something moved, casting a long, wide shadow. The door to the past smacked shut, and there was only the right here, right now. "Y el paquete?" *And the package?*

Then, Clare heard a voice she recognized. "We're on, Torres. Santa's coming a little late this year. December 28. The kitchen. Now get out of here." Lieutenant Bonner stepped into the light, shifty-eyed, and hightailed it back toward the prison exit. A heartbeat later, a man—an inmate—dressed in prison blues headed in the opposite direction. When he passed beneath the lamppost, she noticed his hands, each one tattooed with a different letter: *N* and *F*. That one she remembered. Fitzpatrick would be proud. Nuestra Familia. The EME's mortal enemy.

Clare pressed herself flat to the cold brick like a lizard, a chameleon, and held her breath until her lungs hurt. From here, she could see Briggs through the small window in the control booth, thumbing through a magazine and looking bored. He waved Torres through and she sucked in a gulp of air.

She willed herself to go inside. To do what she came here to do. Her life depended on it, after all. Putting her hand to her neck—brittle as a chicken bone, apparently—she recited Ramirez's warning under her breath and approached the entrance to the control booth, ID in her hand. When Briggs spotted her, his dour frown brightened. This was going to be easier than she thought. And that made it worse.

"Well, aren't you a sight for sore eyes?" He winked at her, and his partner groaned. "Shouldn't you be snuggled up in front of a fire somewhere?"

"I wish," she said, releasing her smile like a fishing line, slowly to tease him a little. "Could I talk to you for a sec? Alone."

"You don't mind, do you, Watkins?" His partner rolled his eyes, as if to say—*yes, I do mind, asshole*—but grabbed his jacket and shrugged it on. "It'll have to be quick though, Clare. There's supposed to be two of us in here at all times or some procedural mumbo jumbo."

"Oh, it'll be quick." She giggled at Briggs' raised eyebrows. With Watkins halfway out the door, Briggs started to exit the booth, but Clare stopped him. "I want to come inside," she said, lingering in the doorway.

"Clare … " She kissed his neck. "God, you're hot. But you know that's not allowed."

"Oh, come on. I thought you liked it when I pretend to be a bad girl." It wasn't pretend, and Clare knew it. She grabbed him by the belt and pulled him to her, before he caught on.

"I do, but … oh, screw it."

"Exactly," she whispered.

"Wait right there. Don't move." Watching him move with purpose—a man on a mission—Clare felt sorry for him. *This is what men do*, she thought. *This is what moves them.* Ramirez had all but told her the same, though he'd put it more crudely. *Briggs will do anything for a piece*, he'd said. She didn't argue with him, but she wondered how he knew. How he seemed to know everything.

Briggs spoke into the phone. "Hey, T-Bone, could you do me a solid?" Laughter, and then, "Can you go dark over here for a sec?" He kept his eyes on Clare the whole time, mentally undressing her no doubt. After hanging up, he beckoned her inside, his face already flushed.

"What was that all about?" she asked. She needed to be sure. Ramirez warned her to be careful. Actually, it was less of a warning and more of a threat. *You get caught, the deal is off,* he'd said, running a hand across his neck.

"Damn cameras everywhere. But I negotiated a little privacy."

He picked her up and sat her on the table just in front of the large metal panel, where the keys dangled like ornaments from a tree. She leaned back and hoisted her skirt around her upper thighs. Briggs wasted no time, stanchioning himself between her legs, his mouth already covering hers.

Two minutes later, three if she was generous, Briggs stuffed his shirt back into his uniform and grinned ear to ear. And she had the keys Ramirez wanted tucked inside her jacket pocket. "When can I see you again?" he asked.

"Friday. Dinner?"

He nodded and cupped her face in his hand. "Hey, what's that?" His thumb traced the bruise on her neck. "Is that my handiwork?" Clare's stomach lurched at his satisfied leer.

"Curling-iron burn," she said, no hesitation.

****

She felt buzzed leaving the control booth. Like she'd just downed a shot of Patrón. It would hit her later what she'd done. She knew that. Another line. A big one. Another step closer to oblivion.

In the shadows of the courtyard, Clare heard a noise. A low whistle. A bird, maybe. An owl. "Clare." A talking owl. When Cullen stepped into the light, she almost laughed.

"What're you doing out here?" He shushed her and pointed to a spot between the buildings so dark a person could disappear completely. She did a slow spin to check for prying eyes and walked to where the night swallowed him. His hand encircled her wrist, drawing her in, then he released her. Just one touch, and her skin felt electric.

"I work building maintenance now. Odd hours," he whispered. "Besides, I could ask you the same, Doc."

She opened her mouth, deception poised on the tip of her tongue. It came so easily now. But she didn't want to lie to him, so she said nothing. "I'm glad it was you out here."

"Who else would it be?" His playfulness gone, he sounded worried. "That guy yesterday with the tat, he didn't say anything to you, did he?"

She shook her head. "Just that he'd knock next time."

"Dammit, Clare. I'm sorry. It's my fault. Did you hear that asshole, Ramirez, weaseled his way out of Ad Seg? I worry about you."

"I'm okay," she said, half-believing it. He started to reach for her, his fingers almost to her hip when he stopped. She looked at his hand, then up to his eyes, and she read his mind. He could kill her. Right there. Right now. If he wanted to. Unafraid, she leaned in, closing the distance between their bodies, and kissed him. They were invisible here—and even if they weren't, she didn't care. Not with Cullen's stubble scratching her cheek, rough and insistent. The needful pressure of his tongue against her own. She buried her face in his shoulder to suppress a moan.

"You make me forget where I am," he said. "It reminds me of something."

"Of what?"

His soft laughter drew her closer. "I don't know. The last day of school. Summers at that cabin in Muir Woods." His lips brushed her ear, and she shivered. "Freedom, I guess."

In daylight, it would've sounded melodramatic, like something from a soap opera. But here, now, it was perfect. And she understood completely. He made her forget too. Not where, but *who* she was. Even the spoiled parts, the unmentionable ones—gone. She guided his arms back around her and drank him in. He nuzzled his face in her hair, and she could feel him breathing. She hoped Briggs' Aqua Velva stench wasn't still all over her.

"Meet me somewhere tomorrow after count," he said.

"My office?"

"No. It's too risky after what happened yesterday."

"But … "

He understood without her telling him. "There are dead spots like this one. Places where the cameras don't see. Will you?"

"Yes," she said, steamrolling toward oblivion.

DECEMBER 19, 1996

CLARE woke with a start five minutes before her alarm, her body stiff as a corpse, her stomach wound tight as a hanging rope. At least she'd slept. Her eyes cut to the dresser. In the television glare, the stolen key ring winked at her, and relief came in like a wave. *Where would it go anyway, silly? It can't walk away on its own.*

She threw back the covers and padded across the floor, taking it in her hand. The keys were like something out of a movie. Large, bronze-colored, affixed to a silver ring. Each with its own number and unique, jagged teeth. These teeth unlocked something essential to Ramirez. Which made them dangerous, that much she knew.

Clare pretended at normalcy. She showered, blow-dried her hair, dressed, and examined her neck in the mirror. The spot had faded overnight to a pink thumbprint. Barely there at all. A part of her wanted it back, wanted Cullen to claim her, to mark her as his own. But the sensible part covered it with a dab of concealer. And she was out the door and into the gloom of a typical Thursday.

Lizzie waited at the coffee shop, twirling on a stool and sipping her peppermint latte. *This is the first test*, Clare thought, trying to smooth the frayed edges of her nerves.

"They say perpetual lateness is a sign of daddy issues, Clare-Bear."

Clare tossed her purse on the counter and laughed. "Do they? And who are *they* exactly?"

"You know, your people. Headshrinkers."

"Well, they are probably right. I wonder if Fitzpatrick would buy that."

"Speaking of Fitzawhozit ... " Lizzie always called him that now since she'd shared Dumas' nickname. But it ached a little every time, reminding her. "Is he going to help you with the Board of Psychology thing?"

"Doubtful. I mean, he said he would, but ... "

"Yeah, I'm sure he wants to *help*." Lizzie made air quotes with fingers. "If it involves you naked in his bed."

"Lizzie!" Clare felt her chest splotching with a hot rash of shame. Like she'd asked for him to hit on her. "He's my boss."

"C'mon. He's a perv."

"I know, but he's my supervisor." *Why am I defending him?* she thought as the words left her mouth.

"Your pervy supervisor. You said it yourself. Are you defending him now?" But Clare knew the one she really was defending was herself. What it said about her that men saw her this way—and only this way. Or the other option. Worse. Unthinkable. This was how she saw herself.

She sighed, back-pedaling. "I need him on my side is all."

"And you don't need Neal on your side? He's majorly pissed at you."

"He told you that? He called you again?" It came out harsher than she'd intended. Rapid-fire and jealous-sounding.

"To ask about *you*. Don't you think you owe him a conversation? He's a good guy, Clare. A really good one."

"Why don't you date him then?" she asked, but Lizzie talked over her.

"And you've been stringing him along for years. Now you've got this other poor sucker, J. D., on the line. And Fitzawhozit. And Cullen. Hell, this guy probably wants to do you too." Lizzie stuck her thumb behind her to the mustached barista. An innocent bystander, he pretended not to hear her. "Save some for the rest of us," she hissed.

Clare felt raw, as if Lizzie had stripped away her skin. "It's not like I enjoy it or anything. I'd give anything not to be noticed for one day. For one flippin' day just to be like ... "

264

"Me? Like me? So dull and ordinary?"

"That's not what I meant. You're twisting it."

"Woe is Clare. Always the victim. You think I don't know you get off on these guys bird-dogging you? Rodney Taylor fucked you up. Royally." And there it was. The hammer intended to shatter. But just when Clare thought it was over, Lizzie added, "You should go make out with Cutthroat. He's on your level."

Clare couldn't remember the last time they fought—college probably—but Lizzie always got the last word. Not this time. She gathered her purse, slung it over her shoulder. It felt heavy and important with the key ring tucked inside the lining. "I already have."

****

Anger made her bold. She charged into the prison entrance, a bull in a china shop, flashed her ID and opened the mouth of her purse for the guard.

"Morning, Dr. Keely," he said. "Anything in here I should know about?" He winked at her, teasing like he always did. And, just for Lizzie, she paused to examine how she felt. Annoyed, a little disgusted. Bored mostly. *There*, she thought. *I don't like being bird-dogged.*

"Just the usual contraband," she joked.

He barely looked inside her bag. She almost felt disappointed, given the time she'd wasted sewing in the lining, stitch by perfect stitch. At the very least, he could've examined it more closely than he did her breasts.

"Alright. Have a nice day, Doc. And happy holidays." That was it. Some lines you blaze through so fast, they don't seem like lines at all.

Clare knew Ramirez wouldn't come for the keys himself. He'd told her that much. *Package it up real good, real legit, in a brown bag. Like your lunch. Third pew in the chapel. Noon. That's where you leave it.*

From her office threshold, she took a quick peek down the hallway. Fitzpatrick's light was on, and she heard the dull drone of his therapist voice. This time she double-checked the lock on her office door before she slit the soft lining of her purse with a letter opener. Inside the paper bag, she'd arranged an apple, a granola bar, and a

PB&J with banana, as legit as it gets. Careful but quick, she stuck the keys under a napkin and maneuvered them to the bottom of the pile. Then she rolled the bag shut and marveled at her work. Her third-grade lunch sack reincarnated. Back when her mother could be bothered with things like packing a lunch for her only child. Back before Clare became—*how did Lizzie put it again?*—royally fucked up.

****

By ten minutes after noon, Clare had made her delivery to a cemetery-quiet chapel and taken the stairs back to her office. She felt so light, she skipped steps, reciting words of relief with every footfall. *I did it. It's over.*

Fitzpatrick waved to her from his desk as she passed, his other hand cradling a bologna sandwich. "You seem happy as a clam today, Dr. Keely. By the way—"

"Must be the holiday spirit," she interrupted, hurrying past before he asked her to join him for lunch. Truthfully, she'd forgotten about Christmas altogether until that morning when a perky new hire had poked her head in, offering a wreath for her office door. She accepted, but only because it covered most of the beveled glass on her window. You could never be too careful. Plus, with sleigh bells affixed to the oversized red bow, her door jingled every time it opened. A small price to pay for an alarm in plain sight.

Clare noticed the blue slip on her desk right away, but she let it linger, let the feeling build from a dull ache to a steady, delicious throb—no less powerful than the beat of her heart. Finally, she flipped it over expecting to see Cullen's block handwriting.

Her balloon deflated as she examined the dry cleaning slip issued from the prison laundry. *Pick-up. Thurs, 12/19 by 7:00 p.m.* Clare heard some of the staff took their clothes there on Mondays—cheap labor—but she'd always found it a little strange. The idea of those men—hulking and clumsy and criminal—touching her things. There must've been a mistake.

The bell on the door sounded, and Clare flinched. "Come in," she said, but Fitzpatrick's scuffed loafers were already halfway inside.

266

He offered her a cookie from a metal tin, leaning so close to her, she noticed the dusting of green sugar on his mouth.

"I guess Cutthroat found you." He eyed the blue slip, and Clare swallowed hard, trying to form words. "That's what I was trying to tell you. He said you had some dry cleaning for pick-up." Fitzpatrick ran his tongue over his lips, smacking them. The sugar disappeared. "I didn't even know he worked there."

****

The dank smell of sweat hit her first. Piles of laundry—most of it sheets and prison blues—reached high on either side of her. Dumpster-sized bins full of it. Clare moved in the dark, past the folding tables to the wall, where a thin stream of light came from underneath a closed door. She looked at her watch. 7 p.m. on the dot.

"Hello?" she whispered, feeling a little light-headed. A little deranged. What was she doing here? *Banging your client. That's what you're doing. Crossing the last line.* But Clare silenced Lizzie's disdainful monologue. She couldn't stop herself. Not now. Sometimes life unfolded at the speed of a locomotive, rolling through the countryside. Other times, it sliced like a bullet train—so fast it threatened to break her in two, to strip the skin from her bones.

Clare watched the light from beneath the closed door. It flickered on and off, and on and off again. A signal. Every part of her awakened. Every part of her felt alive. Not like all the other times—with Briggs, with Mr. Taylor, even with Neal—when she shut herself down, put her body on autopilot, and left someone else in charge.

It felt momentous, opening that door, because it was her decision to make. In the corner of the small closet, black as a cave, Cullen waited. "You came," he said as she shut the world out behind them. He didn't move closer to her, as she expected. His eyes, once she could see them, regarded her like something wild and sacred. Something to be revered. "Are you sure about this?" he asked. "Just say the word and I'll leave. I'll get a new therapist. Even put in for a transfer if that's what you want. I'll do anything for you, Clare."

267

She understood now that this, too, was her decision. To go to him. Or not. His hair felt damp to the touch, and he smelled like soap. His skin hot as a fever. She felt him sigh when her fingers ran down his chest. "Will you tell me the truth?"

"Ask me anything," he said.

"Did you send me those flowers? The yellow mums?"

"Yes," he whispered, and she kissed the corner of his mouth.

"Do you know what happened to Dumas?"

"No. Only what I told you." She slipped her hand under his shirt and tugged it up and off. The knife wound on his side, the EME's handicraft, felt smooth, nearly healed. She traced it with her finger and pulled his body flush with her own.

"How many girls were there?" His breath hitched, and she feared he wouldn't answer. He wasn't ready.

"Three. Only three. Jennifer. Sarah. Emily." She tasted the soft skin of his neck, felt his hips drive against her, and still he didn't touch her.

"Did you know this would happen?"

"Yes." She took his hands in her own and put them where she wanted them.

****

Afterward, he didn't leave right away. He held her close to him on the hard floor, wrapped in a scratchy gray blanket that felt like heaven, and the tips of her fingers found the scars on his stomach. *You know, they say he caused those scars himself.* She numbered them in her head— *one, two, three … eight, nine, ten … twelve*—until her counting drowned out Fitzpatrick's nasally voice, his preposterous explanation. Cullen kissed the side of her head and brushed her hair back. "My turn," he whispered. "Tell me one thing about you nobody else knows."

DECEMBER 20, 1996

CLARE couldn't stop moving. Her hands. Fidgeting. Her foot. Tapping. Her mind. Racing. She kept watching the door. Listening for those jingling bells. No one came, of course. She'd canceled her morning clients with some lame excuse about catching up on paperwork. But really, she needed time. Time to sort out what she'd done. And why—now that she'd done it—she didn't feel guilty at all. In fact, she hadn't slept so soundly in years. She'd turned the ringer off because Lizzie wouldn't stop calling, and snoozed right through her alarm.

She closed her eyes, trying to conjure Cullen's face. She wished she had sat up and turned to look at him when she'd told him. Instead, she buried her face in the crook of his arm as she talked. Told him the whole story while he stroked her back. He only stopped once—for a second—right when she said it. "I smothered her." Then he started up again, his fingertips soft as a feather.

Clare reached for a tissue from her desk and dabbed her watery eyes, smudging her mascara no doubt. But at least it gave her something to do. She snagged her purse and beelined for the single-stall bathroom at the end of the hall to freshen up her makeup.

It's okay. It's okay. She didn't imagine it. He'd actually said that. Over and over until she started to believe it. She repeated it now, out loud to herself, not caring if anyone noticed. She needed to see him. To listen to him say it again. He'd told her something else too. Words so powerful, she tried to unthink them. *If I ever get out of here, I'll kill him. I swear I will.* They frightened her. In part, because she knew it would never happen. In part, because she wished it would.

Clare didn't hear the boots that slipped in behind her as she rummaged in her bag for the tube of mascara. Or the fingers that locked the door. Then there were two faces in the mirror and a hand over her mouth.

"Shh. Silencio." She bit Ramirez's finger. "Pinche puta." Those were swear words. She didn't need Señora Costilla to tell her that, but the way he said them close up against her ear, he might've been whispering sweet nothings. She pitched and squirmed in his arms. A desperate fly in a web, her struggles only pinned her tighter. "Stop fighting, and I'll let you go."

She nodded, and he released her. But her knees gave way, and she collapsed to the floor. "What do you want? I did what you asked."

"Cállate. Keep your voice down."

"Or what?" she shouted in vain, most of her co-workers vanished to lunch.

"You know what. We own you now, puta." Clare pushed herself into the corner by the sink, as far away as she could manage. "You work for me."

"You said *one* thing. One."

"Did I? Uno?" He scrunched his forehead in feigned confusion. "Solo soy muy estúpido. What do I know?" He held up two fingers. "Dos, por favor. I need you to set a trap for a rat." His smile wasn't a smile at all. He bared his teeth. "You, cariña, are the cheese."

"A rat," she heard herself repeat. Clare pressed her hands against the cool tile. It looked familiar somehow. The pattern—tiny flowers. The color—sickly green. Her mother's bathroom. And blood ran everywhere. More blood than she knew her body could hold. And her hands were red.

CHAPTER TWENTY-FOUR

POLAROIDS

ASIDE from a skin-and-bones dog rummaging through a discarded trash bag, there were no signs of life to speak of at Green River Trucking. Levi had spent the past hour on essentials—reloading his gun, wolfing down three granola bars, and perusing radio stations for any mention of Cullen or himself. And there were plenty.

> The FBI is searching for Samantha Bronwyn and her mother, Clare, who were not heard from after leaving the San Francisco station yesterday afternoon. Agent Katherine McKinnon described the situation as dire and reported fearing for the women's safety. McKinnon confirmed earlier reports that Virginia Dalton has been found alive and transported to UCSF Medical Center for treatment of a gunshot wound. No other information about her condition was released. Still at large is convicted murderer Clive Cullen, who is now suspected in the deaths of two civilians, including San Quentin employee Rosemary Trotter, who supervised him in a vocational computer

class. Levi Beckett, a police officer in Austin, Texas, has also been identified as a person of interest …

"So is this your first stakeout?" I asked him, desperate to talk about something else. Anything else.

"I had to go along on one in field training. It's not as glamorous as it sounds."

"I'm getting that," I said, giving an obvious nod to the food wrappers at our feet.

His wry smile warmed me a little, and I imagined Ginny elbowing me in the ribs. *At least you've got a hot guy on said stakeout.* "Well, just wait until you have to go to the bathroom. I hope you can scrounge up a bottle from the dumpster over there."

"Are you serious?" That's—"

Levi turned up the radio at the sound of a name. *James Dumas.* "Hold on, I want to hear this."

Mr. Beckett's father, James Dumas, served time in prison with Cullen in the 1990s before he committed suicide. Beckett's mother took her own life a short time later, leaving him and his sister in the care of the state. Sources from within the FBI have been tight-lipped about a possible connection between Beckett and Cullen. In other news …

"How long were you in foster care?" I asked.

He sighed, and I wished for a take-back. "Long enough to know it's not a place a kid should ever be. My sister and I got separated for a while. She had it a lot worse. Girls usually do."

I left that one alone, filling in the blanks for myself. Somewhere close by, church bells rang low and mournful, matching Levi's grim expression. I silenced the radio. "Uh, is it Sunday?"

"I sort of lost track of the days," he said.

"Me too, but that would explain why the place is so deserted. It's probably closed today." The burner phone buzzed on the floorboard, sending a jolt up my spine. I picked it up cautiously, like it might explode in my hand. "It's a text from Ginny."

I'm okay. McKinnon just left. Was asking lots of weird questions about your mom and some guy named Rodney Taylor. Told me not to contact you without her permission. As if. She tried to take the phone, but the doctor wouldn't let her. I think he might have a thing for me. Where r u?

"Well, by the sound of that, we're in the right place," Levi said. "But if we wait, McKinnon will have her people crawling all over this place and all over me."

"Only one way to find out. I'm not sure I can sit here much longer anyway."

Levi took my words as a call to action. He secured his gun inside his waistband, along with a pair of Snip's work gloves, and opened the door. "Wait—"

"Don't even think about telling me to wait here. This place is creepy."

He chuckled at me. "I thought I was creepy."

"You are," I teased. "But there are varying degrees."

"So you must like creepy guys, huh?"

Laughing, I shook my head at him, but a part of that stuck like a prickly burr in my heart, the kind that latches onto a cow's tail or a shoelace. The kind you can't pull out without sticking your fingers. My mom had a thing for creeps. Obviously. And my dad was one. *What did that say about me?*

"Just you," I bantered back, before he read my mind. "And barely." As we walked, I kept my eyes on Levi's back, trying not to gawk at the buildings as we passed. Most of them were run down, boarded up. Some were marked with graffiti. The worst one had a shadowy space underneath where critters lived, plastic-covered windows that looked more like black-cauldron eyes, and a rusted shell of a truck out front.

The entrance to Green River Trucking lay beyond a tall fence, the padlock removed and discarded on the ground. I left the sidewalk and stood in the grass—knee-high—peering over to a row of 18-wheelers. Only one of the stalls was vacant. Past them, gravel and more weeds nearly obscuring the sign out front. The door stood open like someone waited for us just on the other side. "Maybe it's permanently closed," I whispered.

"Those tracks look fresh." Levi pointed to the tire-sized marks in the grass. "Stay right behind me." As if I had the intention of going anywhere else.

We slipped inside the fence and made our way around the perimeter. The sun had already begun its lazy crawl into the sky, and I shaded my eyes from the glare off the white gravel. That sinking feeling started in my stomach, beads of sweat pooling beneath my hair as we neared the door. Levi stopped moving, and I heard it too. A low buzz. The sound from my dream. A single fly—fat and black as coal—perched on the handle. It flitted away the moment Levi nudged the door with his boot.

Sunlight spread across bare cement, and the buzzing turned to a steady drone. The room was sparsely furnished with a dilapidated desk, a metal folding chair, and a file cabinet. A rotary phone hung from the wall next to an open key box, one set missing. Where the light didn't touch, the floor seemed to move, to pulse, to writhe with life. "Sam." The way Levi said my name—the deep hollow of that one syllable—meant something unspeakable just beyond my view. "I think we found Rodney Taylor."

****

The last time I threw up I'd just run liners in Bellwether's gymnasium in the dead heat of August. Cheerios and scrambled eggs all over my brand new Nikes. After that, I stopped eating before practice.

Damn granola bar. It was the only thing in my stomach. Well, not anymore. I drew in a shaky breath and wiped my mouth with the back of my hand. "It's okay," Levi told me, rubbing my back. "You don't have to look." But it felt impossible not to.

The swarm of flies directed me to a puddle of orangey liquid, spilled in haste from a plastic bottle. Past that, the body. It slumped against the wall, the head tilted to one side, as if he'd fallen asleep. His mouth slackened. His eyes closed, thank God. Thin gray hair

274

matted against his forehead. Blood pooled on either side of him from a gaping wound at his neck. One hand stayed clutched toward his throat, frozen in a futile effort to defend himself. Neither Levi nor I said it aloud, but I figured we were both thinking it. Cutthroat. Cut. Throat.

Levi approached the body, and the flies scattered in all directions. I imagined their sticky little legs landing on my arm, skittering across my forehead, leaving tiny prints of orange juice mixed with a dead man's blood. I fought the urge to vomit again.

He covered his hands with Snip's work gloves and reached inside the man's pockets until he produced a wallet and a cell phone. "It's him," he said, returning the wallet to rest inside the blood-soaked khakis. He scrolled through the phone, the furrow in his brows deepening.

"What is it?" I asked.

"A text. Unknown number at 4 a.m. *Has she been in touch with you?*"

"That's it?"

"Not exactly." He flashed the screen toward me. "Another one at 5:30." *You don't want to know what happens to people who don't answer me.*

"I suppose you think the *she* is my mother? That somebody knew she would come here?"

Levi busied himself with the file cabinet—*meaning yes*—searching drawer by empty drawer until he arrived at the last one. Locked.

"Can you pick it?" I asked.

"No need." Levi jingled Rodney's belt, a set of keys affixed to it. "It's probably right here."

I walked to the spot where Levi crouched, trying the keys until he found the one that fit. I felt numb, like a pretend person, but the locked drawer drew me like a magnet, a vortex that sucked me right in.

"Unbelievable," Levi announced with an ironic laugh. He tossed a batch of magazines on the desk.

"*Barely Legal?*" I read the first title aloud.

"Porn."

"Really? What gave it away?" I averted my eyes from a bare-chested girl my own age, a cheerleading skirt on her bottom half.

Levi rifled through a stack of them to the bottom. "There's something else." A large business envelope. He undid the metal tabs and let the contents slide onto the desk. He'd already made sense of it, cursing under his breath, before I stopped gaping.

Rodney Taylor collected photographs. Polaroids. In the ones I could see, the girls were clothed, some of them barely. All blonde, all young. Teenage-ish. Their bodies posed, pursing their lips like Ginny did in her selfies. But the eyes bothered me most. Desperate, confused, haunted. "He's definitely got a type," Levi muttered as he flipped through the pictures, revealing names on the back he read out loud, drawing a breath after each one.

"Margot."

"Suzie."

"Madison."

"Amber."

"Beth."

The rhythm broke, and his face looked pained.

"What is it?" I asked.

Levi held the last photo out to me, but kept his fingers latched tight to the corners. Like he hadn't made his mind up yet. "Is this … ?" And then he let go.

CHAPTER TWENTY-FIVE
ON THE PREMISES

LEVI inspected the key box while I studied the photograph, unable to take my eyes from it. At home, my mother had no pictures of herself. She'd told me a house fire had destroyed them when she turned sixteen. So I couldn't be sure that girl was her—blonde wispy hair, freckles, eyes blue as the crayon—but it seemed likely. The photo looked to be the oldest of the bunch—I could tell by the faded color, the filmy coating—and his favorite. It had the worn edges of an object well-loved. The name on the back left even less room for doubt. *Clare.*

"What do you think?" Levi asked. "Is it her?"

I nodded. "Do you think … I mean … why did he have it?" I already figured, of course. I wasn't that naïve. But I needed Levi to say it, because I couldn't.

He looked away. And I wondered if he would say it after all. "Victims, I'm guessing. Sexual abuse." I felt grateful when he kept talking. It meant I could hide my face a little longer. "But that's not the question. The question is, why would your mom have his card?"

Of course, I couldn't answer, and the silence stretched like a rubber band. So tense it threatened to snap. That's how I felt inside.

Pulled taut between the two Clares. Still, I felt sorry for both of them. Clare Keely for having to abandon her entire self, leaving her like an unwanted puppy on the side of the road. And Clare Bronwyn for going along with it. An accessory after the fact. "Did you figure out which truck is missing?" I asked finally.

"Yep. 009." He pointed to the number above the empty key ring. "Easiest mystery yet. Even for a delinquent cop." I knew he wanted me to laugh, but I could only manage a sad smile. "But that's not the best part. I think we can figure out where they are." I saw what he had in mind. A sticker affixed inside the key box that read *Truck Tracker: Never lose sleep over your fleet! Track 'em with Truck Tracker. 1-800-A-TRUCK.*

"It's worth a shot."

Levi dialed the number on Rodney Taylor's rotary phone. "Uh, yes. This is Rodney Taylor. Green River Trucking. I need to track one of my trucks." I'll admit Levi saying that with a straight face got me feeling a little lighter. "The password? Just give me a sec. I know I wrote it down here somewhere." He looked at me expectantly. Like I would know it. "Is it, *password?* How about, *Green River?* I'm sorry. I seem to have misplaced ... "

"Probably Clare," I muttered.

"Is it, *Clare?*"

"Okay, yes. Truck 009. I'll hold." Levi avoided my eyes again, and I didn't blame him. Odds were he'd never met anybody whose family was more screwed up than his. And to think, a few days ago, I thought my mom and I were mind-numbingly normal. "Are you sure? Because it's not ... I don't see ... Alright. Yes, ma'am. Thank you for your help."

Before he returned the receiver to its cradle, Levi put his finger on his lips and reached for his gun in a way—fast and deliberate—that made me shudder. "She said 009 is still on the premises," he whispered.

DECEMBER 21, 1996

CLARE had considered ending it all before. Doing the dutch like James Dumas. But it had been a while. Over a decade. So long, she'd forgotten that feeling. The complete abhorrence of being in her own skin. The paralyzing disgust. She lay in the half-filled bathtub, motionless and heavy, a beached whale waiting in vain for the sea to draw her back home.

The last time she did this—bathtub, razor—she'd returned from Muir Woods, dirt and blood under her fingernails, intent on her own annihilation. But her mom had come stumbling in through the door, half-drunk, half broken-hearted. *I'm back, baby. He dumped me. Where are you?* By that time, Clare had already made a small incision, a barely there slice in the milky-white skin on her wrist. She hated her own cowardice. Hated that *this* was harder somehow, harder than murder. *Clare? Honey?*

Dripping wet, Clare slid the blade to the back of the medicine chest, on the shelf with the things her mother never used. Rubbing alcohol. Cold medicine. A dusty thermometer. And away from the other things. Valium. Nail polish. Condoms. She stuck an adhesive bandage on the cut and promised herself she wouldn't try again. If for no other reason than to deny her mother the satisfaction of calling herself a victim for the rest of her life.

But now, her mom was gone. And she'd come this far. Softening a store-bought razor with a lighter. Plucking out the blade with surgical precision. She held it between her fingers and marveled at its sharp edge. Sharp enough to cut through all her self-hatred.

Clare wasn't sure how she'd made it through the rest of yesterday. The long, shaky walk back to her office. *I need you to set a trap for a rat.* The afternoon spent dodging Fitzpatrick, inventing an excuse to get out of dinner with Briggs. *I need to set a trap for a rat.* She collapsed on the sofa, sat there staring at the wall until the room got dark. *I have to set a trap for a rat.*

It came to her suddenly—a burst of light and energy—and she'd driven at 1 a.m. to the all-night drugstore for a new package of razor blades and a Bic lighter. Because she couldn't set a trap for someone she … loved. She tried out the word, and it fit in a strange, uncomfortable way like playing dress-up in her mother's clothes. Of all the things Mr. Taylor took from her, she couldn't forgive him for that one. Love got all mixed up, a grimy stew of shame and lust and loathing she wanted to gorge herself on.

Clare ran her finger across the underside of her wrist, feeling the sinewy rope of her radial artery pulsing with life. She knew enough to know she'd done it wrong before. Lengthwise, not across. That was the trick. She held the blade and counted the reasons to die. A long list that started on the day she let Mr. Taylor touch her—no, scratch that, on the first day she *liked* it—and ended with her letting Dumas down.

Mid-list of miseries, the telephone rang. Clare had no intention of answering, which made its blaring more obnoxious than usual. A 2 a.m. call could never be good. But she had no family left, meaning no possibility of an untimely death notification. She figured it was Briggs, hard up for what Lizzie would refer to as a booty call. Or it was Lizzie, herself, with another fake apology. Maybe even Neal, though she doubted it. She'd burned that bridge one too many times. Regardless, she sank further into the tub, letting the water pool around her jaw as the machine picked up.

"Um, hello. This is Eliza. Eliza Dumas. Are you there? I know it's late, and I haven't exactly been … friendly." Clare popped out of the water so fast a small wave gushed over the side of the tub, taking

280

the razor blade with it. She didn't even bother with a towel. "I need to talk to you. Just please call—"

"Hello? Eliza? Don't hang up."

"Oh."

"It's me. It's Clare. I'm so glad you called."

Eliza laughed softly. *She had a nice laugh*, Clare thought. Disarming. "I should apologize for ignoring your calls. I've just been out of sorts, you know? And they told me you were negligent."

"Who told you that?"

"The Lieutenant that came to see me right after James died. Brunner? Banner?"

"Bonner."

"Yes, that was it. Bonner. Anyway, after you called last time, I got a letter in the mail. From James. Apparently, the prison kept it back for the investigation."

Water puddling beneath her, Clare fought back tears. "What did it say?"

"Not much of anything really. It wasn't so much *what* it said, just the way he said it. Like he was okay again. Looking forward to things. To the baby." A sob caught in Clare's throat. It felt immense, like all the pain in the world pressing up against a dam inside her. "I remembered what you said about trying to find out what happened to him. That Lieutenant doesn't care. To him, it's ancient history. Case closed. That's what he told me this morning."

"You talked to him?"

"I had to after what I'd read. You met Snip, right?"

Clare remembered, of course. Dumas' wiry roommate with the charming smile and silly nickname. "Yes, Eddie Bailey. He was in the infirmary when James … " It still hurt to say it, but Eliza sounded too preoccupied to notice her discomfort.

"That's him. He put me on his visiting list on account of him being real close with James. Or at least that's what I thought. Then he tells me he'd heard some talk on the yard about some funny business that day."

"What did he hear exactly?"

281

"Can I call you Clare?" She didn't wait for an answer. "Clare, can I trust you? Can I trust you to help me get some answers?"

Clare didn't hesitate. "Of course." She thought of the razor blade. The one she would find on the bathroom floor later and hide in the medicine chest near the things she never used. "I'll help you however I can."

In the long pause that followed, Clare imagined Eliza curled on the sofa, her son sleeping in a crib nearby, a photo of James on her lap. "Snip told me the guards switched duty that afternoon. There was a new guy in charge of West Block. Never been there before. Hasn't been there since. Some puffed up Sergeant with a Semper Fi tattoo. That can't be a coincidence, right?"

DECEMBER 22, 1996

CLARE slid into the booth at the back of the diner and pretended to study the Sunday brunch menu. She kept one eye on the door, waiting for Briggs. She certainly wasn't hungry, her stomach filled to the brim with butterflies. The poisonous kind. In fact, she couldn't remember when she'd eaten last. Toast yesterday morning? Maybe. It tasted like cardboard, so thick and bland in her mouth, she'd chased it down with a shot of whiskey. Because that's what you do when you decide *not* to take a razor blade to your wrists.

She'd taken extra care getting ready this morning. Dressed like she'd come from church in a pale-blue shift dress that matched her eyes. She let her hair down and kept the makeup simple, understated. The good little Catholic girl. Briggs would gobble that right up. When he sauntered in, she flagged him down with an eager wave.

"Hey, good-looking," she teased.

His smile seemed stiff, a little nervous. "This is for you," he said. "Merry Christmas."

Clare looked at the thing on the table. An army-green metal box wrapped with a clumsy red bow of yarn she could tell Briggs tied himself. She'd never seen anything like it before. "What is it?"

He chuckled as he squeezed his hulking frame into the booth next to her. Clare would've preferred he sit across from her, where she could keep her eyes on his. "I messed up. I forgot to ask for a box." His whisper close to her ear, conspiratorial. "So I used this old thing.

It's an ammo can. Indestructible like me." He pushed it toward her, still laughing. "Open it."

"I didn't know we were doing presents," Clare said, almost feeling sorry for him. She hadn't even considered it.

"It's okay. I already got what I wanted." Clare wondered if he meant her or the sex or both, but it wasn't the sort of question you could ask. She fiddled with the bow, hoping whatever was inside was returnable. Cracking the lid of the canister, she saw something red and silky. She reached in past the lingerie to the bottom and withdrew a wooden nameplate for her desk engraved *Dr. Clare Keely.*

"One for work. One for play," Briggs explained, blushing more than she would've expected. She kissed his cheek, sucking in a gulp of Aqua Velva.

"Thank you, J. D. It's incredibly thoughtful of you."

Beaming, he opened a menu. "So shall we eat?"

****

"I've been meaning to ask you something," Briggs said, between heaping bites of a maple-syrup-drowned short stack. "The other day … when we … uh … you know … "

She nodded, grateful he hadn't tried to articulate the exact nature of the *you know* that went down in the control booth.

"Did you happen to see a set of keys laying around? Or could they have fallen in your purse maybe by accident?"

Don't oversell it, Clare. "No. Why?" The most believable denial is a straightforward one.

"Some keys turned up missing. And Bonner's got his panties in a wad."

"Which keys?"

"Kitchen and pantry. Probably one of those dump trucks who can't get enough mystery meat in the chow hall."

"Dump truck?" she asked.

He put his arm around her and squeezed her too tight. "I keep forgetting how green you are, Clarie. Dump truck is prison speak for a slob. Fat. Lazy. Good for nothing." Clare plastered a smile, stuck on

284

that nickname. No one had called her Clarie since Rodney. She sipped her orange juice, buying time to compose herself.

"Speaking of work, did you ever hear anything more about Dumas?"

Briggs groaned from deep in his belly. "Geez. Not that again."

"It's just that I heard you were assigned to West Block that afternoon. You hadn't mentioned it."

"What—are you checking up on me?" He loosened his suffocating embrace, and she wriggled free, but his words clamped down just as hard.

"No, of course not, I just—"

"Because I don't appreciate that. You hear a lot of things going around the yard. Doesn't mean they're true. Does it?"

Clare knew a loaded gun when she saw one. And she wasn't about to touch it. "I didn't mean to offend you. Really. I'm just so worried about this board investigation. It's my job, J. D." She pointed to the nameplate he'd positioned opposite her on the table. "My job's on the line."

His face softened like she'd hoped it would, and he leaned in toward her. "I'll talk to Bonner. Maybe he can get this whole thing cleared up for you." She felt his hand slide up her leg, and she fought the urge to grimace. "I can't wait to see you in that little red number."

Instead, she went with it. Upped the ante. "Don't you mean you can't wait to see me out of it?"

"Touché."

DECEMBER 23, 1996

THE day after Clare laid Rodney Taylor's baby in the ground—it helped to think of it as *his*, not hers, certainly not theirs—she went to school. She clung to routine, to putting one foot in front of the other for as long as she could, until the distance between herself and that unspeakable day was long and wide. Now was no different. She did her usual run in the biting cold, forced down a bowl of oatmeal for breakfast, and drove five miles out of the way for coffee. Best to avoid Lizzie if she could.

She planned to spend the rest of the morning in a deliberate countdown to 9:30 a.m., Cullen's session time. Door locked, lights off, because the last thing she needed was another surprise visit from Ramirez. And she didn't have the stomach to handle Fitzpatrick today. But, as usual, he didn't get the memo.

"Morning, Clare." Fitzpatrick leaned against the wall by her office. He'd been waiting for her. "I need to talk to you." Her heart took off fast as a fox, the dogs behind her, trailing her scent. Part dullard, part bloodhound, Fitzpatrick seemed to have half a nose for trouble. "I was hoping I'd catch you before my nine o'clock meeting."

"You caught me."

"Indeed." He twittered like a schoolboy. "I signed you up for a staff presentation in the new year. I hope you don't mind."

She relaxed a little. "The topic?"

"Whatever you'd like. Your dissertation, perhaps? I seem to remember it had forensic relevance."

He knows. He knows. *He knows!* "Neonaticide." The word rolled off her tongue, detached, as if it wasn't an essential part of her, as connected as the very umbilical cord she severed. As if she hadn't handpicked the topic, desperate to fix herself somehow, to unearth the *why* that had always eluded her. Her own. "Baby killing," she clarified. "Usually shortly after birth."

Fitzpatrick's eyes widened a little, but he hid it well. "Intense, but important work. I imagine those poor girls are often misunderstood."

Poor girl. Clare saw herself bloodied and alone in the bathroom and nodded. "The typical perpetrator is relatively isolated. Or at least that's how she perceives her situation. Often, she won't admit she's pregnant. Not even to herself. Sometimes, she may believe she'll miscarry or the baby will be born dead. Magical thinking, you know? Usually, she's surprised when it comes. Shocked, even. And then she panics. She acts impulsively. Can you imagine?"

After a long pause, Fitzpatrick replied. "Remarkable. That level of denial."

You have no idea. "Remarkable," Clare repeated.

****

Clare sat still as a spider. Breathing in. Breathing out. With each inhale, her paranoia loosened its grip on her neck. With each exhale, she was a little more sure Fitzpatrick had no idea what she'd done. *How could he?* At 9:20, she answered a soft knock with a tentative, "Who is it?"

"It's me. Clive. Are you ... " She opened the door just wide enough to see his face, then yanked him inside, turning the lock and checking it twice. " ... okay?"

Clare had planned on easing into it, breaking the news gently. But now that he'd arrived, now that Fitzpatrick had her on edge, the words tumbled out without her permission. "Ramirez is blackmailing me. I—I did something ... for him. I shouldn't have. It was so stupid. Now he wants me to set you up." It felt so good to release it—like coming up for air after holding your breath underwater—that she almost laughed.

"What did you do?" He didn't say it, but his tone suggested it. Clare shrank away from him, wondering why all men saw her that way. Even Cullen. Even Neal.

"Not *that*. If that's what you're thinking."

He took her by the arms and turned her to face him. "God, no. I would never think that." A smoky fire burned in the blue-gray of his wide eyes, and she felt foolish for doubting him.

"I took some keys from the control room. Briggs said they unlock the kitchen."

"Briggs knows?"

She shook her head. "He knows the keys are missing. Not that I took them."

Cullen stayed quiet for a while, but his body talked to her. A whole conversation. He dragged the chair into the corner—as far from the door as it could get—sat down, and pulled her onto his lap. With both hands, he smoothed her hair from her face, holding it in a loose ponytail as he put his mouth on hers. The way he kissed her, it was as if their lives depended on it. Hers anyway. After he'd pulled away, breathless, she wished they were back in the laundry closet last Thursday when she didn't have to stop herself from wanting him.

"Tell me everything Ramirez told you."

"I'm supposed to meet you somewhere … the laundry closet. For a rendezvous. Only I wouldn't be there. It would be him or his goons instead. The EME. To kill you."

"Did he say when?"

"He'll let me know." Clare shuddered at the idea of it. Alone again with Ramirez and his twisted smirk and devil eyes.

Riled, Cullen paced the length of the office like a caged beast. His jaw tensed just before he smacked his fist on the table, sending her brand-new nameplate tumbling. "I can't believe I let you get mixed up in this." With a long drawn breath, he retrieved the nameplate, taking a closer look. "Is this new?"

288

She ignored the question. Briggs meant nothing, and she'd only put the damn thing on her desk in case he popped in to look for it. But Cullen wouldn't see it that way. "You? I'm the one responsible."

"Fine," he agreed. "We'll split the blame. Eighty, twenty."

"Me, eighty. You—" A shadow at the door, obscured behind the wreath and beveled glass, froze her in place.

"Everything okay in there?"

"It's fine, Dr. Fitzpatrick. We're just finishing up our session."

"Alright. Just checking. Looks like your 10:30's out here waiting."

Cullen touched her hand, gave it a quick squeeze. "Just be yourself," he said. "Act normal."

She didn't want him to leave. Without him, she felt exposed. A turtle without a shell. "I'm not sure I know how to be normal."

"Welcome to the club," he said with a wink that could melt ice.

****

Tony Perez acted normal too. An entire session went by, and he hadn't so much as looked at her cockeyed. Still, it lingered there in the room. The feeling both of them were pretending at something, playing roles worthy of an Academy Award. For the rest of the afternoon and the whole drive home, she analyzed that hour for signs of a crack in his façade and came up empty-handed. He told her about his childhood in Compton. Single mother. Father in prison. Siblings to feed. He joined the Compton Varrio Tokers at fourteen in search of a family. He seemed nice enough for a murderer.

Clare navigated the turn into her apartment complex, feeling relieved to see her cramped parking space, her green door, her cheesy welcome mat. Sometimes your body knows before the rest of you. And Clare's body was a finely tuned antenna, humming at any sign of danger. She felt the prickles on her neck, tingling fingers up her spine. Then, she saw it. A small, feathered lump. A canary. Not the kind of bird that just happens to drop dead on your doorstep. She knelt down to inspect it, smoothing its bright yellow feathers with her finger. The bird's neck twisted, the angle severe, the head nearly broken off.

She found the note underneath the broken body.

>*Dear Dr. Keely,*
>*Keep your mouth shut. Do what you're told. December 28. 7 p.m. Remember, we can find you anywhere, and this is what happens to canaries.*
>*Sincerely,*
>*Your friends*

Clare read the note again. December 28, the arrival date of *el paquete*—the package Torres and Bonner discussed. It couldn't be coincidence.

"What the hell is that?"

Clare jerked back like she'd been shot. She tried to figure out which was worse. The menacing note folded in her hand or Neal, open-mouthed in front of her, eyeing the dead bird as if she'd killed it herself. "A canary."

"I'm not asking what kind of bird it is. I'm asking what it's doing at your front door."

Clare shrugged unapologetically. Like that was a reasonable response. "What are *you* doing at my front door?"

"Seriously?"

"Well, how do I know you didn't put it here?" It was cruel, but desperate times …

Neal just shook his head. She could see now why it never would've worked between them. Darkness can only be understood by darkness, and Neal didn't have a dark bone in his body. "Yep, you got me. And there's a bunny boiling on the stove inside. Go on in. Check it out." He didn't intend it to be funny, but she smiled anyway. "Do you want to tell me what's going on here? What's going on with you? Lizzie called me last week. She's sick about you, Clare."

"And you?" *Lizzie told him,* she thought, utter terror coursing like a drug in her veins. *She told him what I said about Cullen.* "Are you sick about me?"

"No." His roots firmly anchored to the ground, Neal didn't look away from her. "I feel sorry for you. Whatever you're doing, whoever you're doing it with, you're in way over your head."

"So you don't care?" Her heart cracked down the middle. She wanted him to care. She wanted him not to.

"Did you have sex with him?"

"Who?" she asked, clinging to innocence as long as she could.

"You know who."

"Is that how you decide if you care?"

"That's how I decide if there's any of *my* Clare left for me to care about."

She couldn't say it out loud, but Neal read her silence. He spun around without another word, and Clare watched him walk away. In her mind, she raged at him. Screamed so loud, her throat was raw. In her mind, she yelled, *Your Clare never existed anyway.*

CHAPTER TWENTY-SIX

I stayed close to Levi as he prowled toward the back entrance of Green River Trucking, my eyes focused on the freckle on the back of his neck—at the intersection of chestnut hair and tan skin. It seemed the safest place to look. The room had begun to warm in the midmorning sunlight, cooking the smell of death and fear until it felt hard to breathe. One glance in the wrong direction, and I'd be hunched over again, empty-stomach heaving.

Levi peered through the small window at the back, then turned the handle and nudged the door ajar. Like a springtime field in Bellwether, the weeds grew knee-high here and thick. So thick, Levi gave the door an extra shove to force it open. So thick, I felt the grass pull against my jeans. Like it wanted me to stay put. Around the perimeter the same tall fence boxed us in. Chain link and razor wire.

"Geez, it looks like a prison," I muttered, gazing up at those menacing teeth meant for intruders like me. Even from down below, they threatened. They promised a cut to the bone.

We started with the first of three unmarked metal buildings, the first two smaller than the last. Levi tried the handle—unlocked—before he cracked the door and let the sunlight in. It reminded me of the time Ginny and I broke into the old Miller house on Halloween afternoon, the one everybody said was haunted by the ghost of Mrs. Miller. *Bad things can't live in the daytime*, Ginny had said, her voice steady, and I believed her. But these demons didn't scatter in the soft, pale light. And I braced myself against the wall, dizzy.

A few cots, strewn with blankets, dotted one corner. Whoever slept there had just awakened. A brimming pot of black coffee waited on the warmer plate. Two cups, still empty. A loaf of bread, unopened. A hulking, muted beast of a television broadcasted a soccer game, business as usual. In the center of the room, a fan undulated, blowing its cool breeze as gentle as a whisper. To me. To Levi. To the man with half a head lying still on the floor behind the row of cots, the fabric of his loose-fitting T-shirt billowing in the manufactured wind.

"Holy shit." Fumbling with his gun, Levi pulled the door shut behind us. In that airless tomb, the only sounds came from the fan and our own lungs desperate to keep up with the sucker punch of our surroundings. I didn't look at the man again. Instead, my eyes watched the soccer game, the ball passed between feet, skillfully up the field toward the goal.

"What did that?" I asked finally. Hearing the panic in my voice made me more afraid. *What*. Not who. I knew better, but I half-expected something inhuman to creep out from its cave, its mouth wet with blood and skull bits. Something wild and ferocious and inevitable. That would make sense.

"Probably an assault rifle. It's a high-muzzle velocity weapon." When I stood there, open-mouthed, he added. "It causes major damage. Obviously."

The soccer ball bounced off a knee and skittered out of bounds as Levi moved past me toward the man, his footsteps weighted with dread. Back in play, the ball propelled toward the net, only to be swallowed and spit out by the goalie's frantic hands.

"There are two," Levi said.

"Two guns?"

"No." The ball rested on the turf, waiting, accepting its fate like me. "Two men." Surprise compelled me to look, but Levi's back shielded me from the worst of it. Only the man's splayed legs, his feet bare. The blood spatter that could've been paint if I didn't know it wasn't. I noticed it now in the television's glow—a fine spray, up the drywall like mice footprints. "And Sam ... " He paused for a heartbeat, and I prepared myself. "They both have tattoos. They're EME. It looks like somebody surprised them."

While Levi busied his hands, rifling through a backpack propped in the corner, I sank against the drab wall behind me, wishing I could blend into it. Disappear. "What does Rodney Taylor have to do with the EME?"

Levi turned around, his face drained to a sickly color, the hue of chalk and revulsion. "One guess," he answered, presenting me with a brick-shaped package covered in brown paper and plastic. "There's more where this came from. At least five kilos."

"Drugs?"

"That's their thing. The Mexican Mafia controls most of the drug trade in and out of prison."

I took the package in my hand, felt the weight of it. It seemed innocent enough. But I imagined a dark heart pulsing underneath the ordinary wrapping, and I couldn't wait to be rid of it. Like it might bite if I held it long enough. I tossed it onto a small wooden table in front of the nearest cot. "It smells like ... "

"Coffee." Levi finished my thought. "They package it that way for transport. In coffee grinds, detergent, cheese. Anything to throw the dogs off the scent." Before he stood up, he swiped a blanket from the floor and covered the dead men. *For me*, I thought. Then he motioned me to fall behind him as we headed back toward the door.

"Are you ready?" he asked. I wasn't. Not at all. But I nodded. *Two more buildings*, I told myself, and inside one of them, my mother. She had to be. And that comforted and terrified me all at once.

"What about the gun?" I asked.

"Not here." *Out there, then.* Levi turned the handle. His boots crunched the grass. I found his freckle and followed.

294

DECEMBER 24, 1996

BRIGGS pointed across the yard, puffing his chest the way he always did when he thought he was being helpful. "That's him. Raul Torres. They call him *el Oso—the Bear*. Want me to wave him over for you?"

Torres moved like a bear on the handball court, slow but fierce, his paw strikes packing a wallop on the small blue ball. He carried all his weight in his stomach. It extended past his shoes and shifted when he moved. The rest of him was dense, muscles wound tight as rope. *Winnie the Pooh on steroids*, Clare thought. "No, I'll catch him later."

"Are you sure he requested a psych? Doesn't seem like the chatty type."

"Fitzpatrick told me he put in a request. But I'll double-check before I call him in." She marveled at the ease of her deception. Clare could be a good liar when her life was at stake. "Does he speak English?"

"As well as you and me when it suits him." Stern-faced, Briggs guided her off the yard onto the dirt path at its perimeter. "Be careful, Clare. He's hardcore NF. They've never been able to prove it, but he's probably a shot caller. You know what that is, right?"

She rolled her eyes and laid on the sarcasm. "Yes, Sergeant Briggs. I'm familiar with the term."

He scanned the yard for onlookers. Finding no one of importance, he tapped her butt with a flick of his wrist. "Careful, Doctor. Insubordination will get you called into my office."

"I hope so." She elbowed him playfully in the side, seeing the panic in his eyes one second too late. Bonner greeted them both with a gotcha smirk.

"Good morning, Dr. Keely, Sergeant Briggs. You two sure have gotten friendly."

"Yes, sir." Briggs fell right in line like a good soldier. "Sorry, sir."

"J. D. is awfully fond of you, Doc. In fact, he made a special appointment with me just to talk about you and your little problem with the Board of Psychology. Seems you've made quite an impression on a lot of menfolk around here."

Clare fought the urge to slap him senseless. She bit the side of her tongue to distract herself. Now was not the time to be blunt. "Not intentionally."

"Of course." He patted Briggs on the shoulder, making him look about five years old. "J. D.'s always been a sucker for a pretty face."

"And a sharp mind," Briggs added, with a little too much enthusiasm. "Clare … uh, Dr. Keely, is the whole package." *El paquete.* Only this package—her—was full-on Unabomber. And she delighted in the knowing, even more in their not knowing, that she was rigging an explosion.

****

Clare studied Raul Torres' face with the dispassionate calm of a practiced surgeon preparing for the one-thousandth incision. The fear in her belly simmered at a low burn.

She felt it.

Acknowledged it.

Ignored it.

She could do that now. *Because fear is like pain*, she thought. The scars build up thick like calluses, until a cut that would bring anybody else to their knees ached like nothing more than a sore tooth.

"We both know you're not here for therapy." She spoke first. That seemed important with a guy like this.

296

The Bear shifted forward in his chair, leaning toward her desk, one elbow on each knee, his tattooed hands nearly resting on his oversized stomach. "No sé ingles, Doctor."

"That's not what I heard. You speak English just fine." Torres shrugged one shoulder, almost bored. But his eyes followed her with purpose. And he'd come here voluntarily when she summoned him from South Block. A curious bear, that's what he was. Sniffing the air, trying to decide whether the sweet taste of honey justified the long climb up the tree. "Mr. Torres, I have a proposition for you." A slight raise of the eyebrows confirmed her suspicion.

"Proposición?" He sat back and stretched his legs, leering at her. The tip of his tongue lingered on his lips, then circled his mouth, wetting them. A sound came from the back of his throat—thick and guttural—halfway between hunger and desire.

"Not that kind of proposition." Clare listened to her voice. Steady. Sure. Convincing, even to herself. "I have something you want more than that." She paused to meet his eyes, round and cold as marbles, and didn't look away. "El paquete."

The Bear didn't startle easily. He didn't jump to his feet or cry out or shake her until her spine cracked—the way she imagined Rodney Taylor would've reacted to the word *pregnant* had she ever dared to speak it. Not that Raul Torres wasn't capable of violence. Those hands were most certainly as red as Cullen's. As red as her own. But he took a measured approach. And even so, that word leveled him. Clare knew it. His deception wasn't as necessary as hers, and his face gave it all away. The muscles in his jaw, buried somewhere under those thick jowls, tensed. His forehead creased ever so slightly. And for an instant, just that one, he stopped breathing.

"If you don't want to lose it—whatever *it* is—to the EME, I suggest you hear me out. You can have your cake plus the icing on top. And it tastes a lot like revenge. Sweet revenge." However bittersweet, however poisonous, there were few things so irresistible. Clare knew that firsthand.

Silence squatted in the space between them, tricky and tense. A staring contest, and Clare wouldn't lose. Finally, the Bear stood up and considered the door, then her. "No sé ingles," he repeated with less conviction.

"Mierda," she snapped back. *Bullshit.* The rowdy boys in the back of Señora Costilla's class had taught her that one. "This is a one-time offer. Are you interested or not?"

His hand swallowed the doorknob and started to turn. Clare's skin prickled with panic. She had figured him wrong. All wrong. *I blew it*, she thought. Not even beginning to contemplate what that meant. For her. For Cullen. For her plan to save them both.

"Posiblemente." From where she sat, *possibly* sounded a lot like *yes.*

****

The first week of grad school Clare's clinical psych professor had passed out sheets of paper and asked them to draw a house. Clare practically groaned out loud at exactly the kind of mumbo jumbo she'd promised herself she'd never do. While everyone else including the boy-next-door-type to her right—Neal, she found out later—pored over their work, she'd sketched hers as quickly as possible.

"Lots of openings," Neal had whispered across the aisle as she ran her finger over the spacious picture window she'd drawn, the oversized door left ajar, the paned opening in the attic. "Interesting." In that pointed way that really meant *weird.* Later, back in her apartment, she'd thumbed through her textbook searching for the interpretation. The deep significance of her scribbled pencil strokes. *Strong desire to engage others. Neediness. Possible boundary issues.*

Clare laid her cheek against Cullen's bare chest and thought of that house. The wind would whip through it from end to end, the rain coming as it pleased. Strangers would too. The sort of people no one else would invite in. Vagrants. They'd sit at her table, put their grimy hands all over her things. Clare's house had so many openings, there was no room left for her.

"You're being quiet." Cullen's breath tickled her hair, stirring up a heady mix of leftover lust and unease.

"Just thinking." Of course she was. How could she not be? Though neither of them had mentioned it yet. Too busy undoing buttons, pressing mouth to skin, body to body. Every time with Cullen it felt hurried, like making up for something. "Ruminating, I guess."

"Uh-oh."

"Am I crazy?" she asked him. "Do you think this is crazy? Us?"

When Cullen laughed, sea-blue eyes crinkling, everything else about him faded to wallpaper. And the laundry closet felt more like home than any place she'd ever been. He gestured to himself. "Crazy patient, remember? Are you sure I'm the right one to answer those questions?"

"No, but I want you to anyway."

He sat up against the wall, leaving her cold beneath the thin blanket. "Sometimes people are drawn to each other, Clare. Like you and me. It's not crazy. It just is. You can fight it … and lose. Or you can ride the wave."

"I think I might love you." It had been so long since she'd said it to Neal, it sounded strange. Her voice a child's, she couched the words in uncertainty just in case.

"Don't say that. Don't say that unless you mean it."

"I do mean it." Whatever it meant.

She heard his breath catch the way she gasped when Neal gave her that ruby. Face-to-face with something she wanted and didn't want all at the same time. Cullen didn't say it back, but he touched her cheek with tenderness. "What're we going to do?"

A loaded question. Clare chose the simplest answer. "Ramirez wants you here on Saturday at 7 p.m."

Cullen gave a solemn nod. "It must be a cover for something. A distraction, you know? If all the guards come running, they won't be there. Wherever *there* is."

"The kitchen," she said, certain now. "El paquete. I overheard Bonner telling Torres about a package, a delivery on Saturday."

"Why didn't you tell me?" He sounded more hurt than angry, and Clare winced at the thought of disappointing him.

"I guess I didn't think it was important."

He frowned as if he didn't believe her, but he didn't say so. "That's why Ramirez wanted those keys. That SOB. is planning to steal it right out from under them while I'm bleeding to death on this floor."

"Steal what?"

"Drugs. A shitload of drugs. There's nothing else it could be. Un-fucking-believable."

Clare felt Cullen warming beside her, as if his belly had filled with glowing coals. Each word spit from a fire of rage. She turned his face toward her and kissed him, half-surprised when his lips didn't sear her own. "I have a plan," she said, but it didn't soothe him the way she expected. Flames—sudden and intense—lit behind his eyes like they'd been there all along, simmering.

She held herself as still as she could against him, trying not to be afraid. Why should she be? He wasn't upset with her. But she saw Rodney Taylor. She heard him too. *You ungrateful little slut. I should've done this a long time ago.*

Clare did the only thing she could do. Play offense. She slipped her hand beneath the blanket and pulled his mouth onto hers.

"Stop. Clare, stop." Cullen held her by the wrists, then moved away from her, releasing. The empty space between them felt brutal. He reached his hand across it and brushed her hair back from her face. "I'm sorry. You just seemed … out of it." She wanted to explain, but it seemed impossible. Impossible to say out loud. Impossible that he already knew. So she turned away. "So what's your plan, Doc?" he asked finally.

He wanted her to smile. And she wanted to feel relieved, but she didn't. She kept her gaze on the door, not because she worried about being discovered. She'd left that line in her rearview mirror. She just couldn't look at him and tell him. It felt too raw, too desperate. Like he'd blown all the walls of her house down, obliterating all the intruders with one gust. And it was just her at the table now. All that was left was to wait for him to come inside.

"I want to help you escape."

"Why?"

She hadn't expected that. The how, she knew. The when, the where to. But the why stretched out as blank as that sheet of paper before she gave herself up on it without meaning to. Neal had seen right through her and her house drawing, before she'd even gotten his name. "I don't know, but I'm going with you."

CHAPTER TWENTY-SEVEN

GAME SHOW

I felt like a game-show contestant, sidling up next to Levi as he unlocked the second metal building with the key he'd pilfered from the lockbox. *What's behind door number two?*

Biting cold air. That's the first thing I noticed after he cracked the door. "It's freezing," I whispered, following Levi's finger to a portable air-conditioning unit, humming just inside the threshold. The dark was the second. It cloaked the whole room. Even with the sunlight streaming in, the color stayed a muted shade of gray. Like the sky in winter.

The best part about door number two—no dead bodies. Only wooden crates. Rows of them and a rusted file cabinet at the back.

"I have a feeling I know what's in here." Levi slid the top off the closest crate, the potent smell reaching me before he could say it. "Coffee. Lots and lots of coffee."

"Does that mean ... ?"

"Only one way to find out." He plunged his hand elbow-deep inside the grounds and fished out another brick-shaped package like the one we'd found.

"If this guy, Rodney, was a drug kingpin, why is this place such a dump?"

Levi didn't answer right away. He split the rows of crates, heading toward the file cabinet with intention. He pulled on the first drawer. It didn't budge. "I think it's intentional," he answered. "He didn't want to attract too much attention." He yanked again to no avail. "Come help me turn this thing over."

The file cabinet reminded me of one I'd seen in Bellwether High's administrative office. The paint was chipped and faded, its brass handles dulled, the corners corroded with age and neglect. Heavy, but frail somehow. Like a tired old cow put out to pasture. We flipped it over and Levi examined the bottom. "Can you open it?" I asked.

He nodded. "See that hole. Once I push on it … " He slid his finger inside. " … and raise the catch … " I heard a promising click. " … the drawers should open."

"Is there anything you don't know how to break into?" He smirked as he fumbled through the file folders. "It's a little unnerving, Officer."

"Unnerving or indispensable?"

I shook my head at him. "Both, I suppose."

Levi plucked a paper from the innards of the cabinet. "Take a look at this. Rodney Taylor was no struggling businessman." The sheet had a bank logo at the top and a list of deposits and withdrawals. Mostly deposits. Mostly cash. And a lot of it. Roughly a hundred thousand dollars a week.

"Holy cow. Do you think my mom … was she in on it?" I waited for Levi to say *yes*. Nothing surprised me anymore.

"I doubt it. But who knows?" At least he was honest.

"What's that?" I asked, peering over his shoulder into the open mouth of the drawer. The tab read *Classified*.

"We've gotta go, Sam." He shut it, expecting me to follow.

"I know, but … " He made it halfway to the door when I'd opened the folder, spreading its contents on top of the crate. I'd been wrong. *This surprised me.* Shocked me, even. "Levi? You might want to take a look."

"Sam, seriously."

"Fine. But don't you think it's a little strange for a trucking company to have classified FBI documents laying around?"

I held the cover page up to him, watching his eyes scan it and get wide.

Operation Candy Man: FBI Multijurisdictional Task Force

Mission: To stop the illegal transport of narcotics from Mexico to California

Special Agent in Charge: Katherine McKinnon, San Francisco

DECEMBER 25, 1996

AT 6 a.m., Clare made the drive across the San Rafael Bridge into Oakland to the address she'd scrawled on a scrap of paper. A cold rain slicked the roads and spotted her windshield. On any other day, traffic would've backed up for miles—all those careful drivers—but today, there was no one. *Merry Christmas, Clare.*

She put the radio on full blast to drown out the voice in her head. But it felt useless. Rodney Taylor had set up permanent shop there. And today, he was relentless. Fresh from their call last night.

"Rodney Taylor, Green River Trucking. How can I help?" He'd answered on the first ring. An eager beaver.

"Hel—lo." The word got stuck halfway up and Clare had to force it out, will it from her throat.

"Clare? Clare Keely?" His excitement sickened her.

"Hi, Mr. Taylor—uh, Rodney." Almost as much as her deference. Her submission.

"To what do I owe this pleasure?"

"I need to see you. Tomorrow. It's … it's urgent."

The catch in his breath told her what she needed to know. He would be there. Anywhere she asked. "On Christmas Day?"

"Yes. I wouldn't ask if it wasn't important."

"Are you in trouble, Clarie?"

She forced a little sob into the receiver. Fake, but it came from someplace real. "I can't talk about it on the phone."

"Is this why you called here a few weeks ago? You were upset. You—"

"I miss you," she said. "I think about you all the time." That would get him back on track. She could picture him sitting on the edge of his recliner, practically salivating. Already aroused with anticipation. "Just like way back when, you know?"

"I do know. More than you can imagine. Where should we meet?"

Clare pulled up to the gate. The freshly painted sign marked Green River Trucking assured her she had the right place. But she already knew. Rodney's silver BMW took up the space in front of her. New tire, of course. She undid the top two buttons of her silk blouse, hiked up her skirt, and shook out her hair ready for Plan A. Seduction. Then she reached across the seat and popped the glove box taking her backup plan firmly in her hand.

Years ago, Neal had laughed at her, then hugged her too tight when she'd told him she'd bought a gun. *What for?* he'd asked her, not even trying to hide his melancholy. *Just in case.* Because she couldn't admit she'd lost time imagining it pressed to Rodney's skull. That she'd pulled the trigger a thousand times in her mind. The real reason she kept to herself. She had a gun because someday she intended to use it.

****

On the phone, Rodney told her he'd relocated to Oakland to cut costs, but from the looks of it, he was doing just fine. Better than fine actually, silver Bimmer notwithstanding. Clare hunkered under her umbrella, passing a fleet of shiny big rigs on her way to the door. She took one last glance at the sky, wishing for thunder and lightning bolts. Weather fit for her plan. But it rarely stormed that way in California. She'd have to settle for fat, relentless raindrops and puddles of mud.

Rodney waited for her inside, swiveling on his leather office chair like a nervous teenager. Decked out in an awful oatmeal sweater and khakis he'd outgrown years ago. She could tell he'd tried. He looked her up and down, grinning wide, clownish. "You look like an angel—a Christmas angel."

"I'm not an angel," she said, swaying her hips as she moved toward him.

He didn't get up. He just stared at her standing over him like maybe she really was an angel. Or the ghost of Christmas past, dragging the heavy chain of his sins behind her. Finally, he put his hands on her hips—she let him this one last time—and closed his eyes. He moaned to himself, as if she wasn't there at all. "You're a fallen angel, Clare. Sent to drag me back down to hell."

"I'm a person, Rodney. A fucked-up person. But, when you met me, I was a little girl."

His hand dropped, and he pushed away from her, wheels rolling back toward the wall. "You were thirteen. And you didn't act like a little girl. I mean, look at you. I didn't do anything you didn't want me to, Clarie."

She froze for a moment. Her heart went still. She'd forgotten how expertly he leveled her with one measly sentence. Sentences she'd been hearing on repeat for what felt like her whole life. "What about when you raped me? When you broke your promise? What about that?"

He lowered his head like a scolded puppy. "I loved you. I just couldn't wait anymore. Not when you were about to give it up anyway to some horny teenybopper. I'm sorry I hurt you, but you can't still be mad about that. It happened years ago."

Clare reached behind her back and showed him the gun. Pointed it right at his balding head and watched his bottom lip start to quiver. It was the best thing she'd ever seen. "I got pregnant, Rodney. *You* got me pregnant. I was sixteen years old when I had your baby on the floor in a bathroom. It was a girl. And I killed her and buried her and never told anybody while you forgot all about me and started screwing some cheerleader in the back of your fancy car. So yeah, I'm still mad about that."

"Jesus Christ, Clare. You should've told me. I would've helped you ... take care of it."

"I'm telling you now. And you're going to help me. You're going to give me whatever I ask. Understand?" She pushed the gun flush with his skin, making a round, red indentation in the flesh. His face crumpled and he started to cry. "Answer me."

"Okay, okay." His tears were hot and ugly and mixed with snot and sweat. Clare felt proud she'd never let him see her this way. "Whatever you want. Anything."

"I need fifty thousand dollars in cash by Saturday and a truck to take me across the Mexican border."

She thought he might laugh. It sounded made-up. Like a scene from a cheesy Bruce Willis movie, the kind that would've been his favorite. At the very least, she expected some questions. But he just nodded. "Please put the gun down. Please."

"I'm not done yet."

"Please, Clarie. I love you." And she knew he did in the sick, twisted way he taught her.

"Me. The cheerleader. Those are the two I know about. Have there been any others since then? Were you doing this to Lisa too?" His pathetic crying slowed like a dripping faucet, and he looked everywhere but at her.

"Not to Lisa. No."

"But to someone else?"

His shoulders shrugged almost indiscernibly. "It was always you, Clare. You were the first. The one I really wanted. I never got over you."

"How many?" she asked.

"I don't know. Honestly, I don't. One or two, I guess. A man has needs, you know?" *Did she ever.* "But I stopped. I stopped. I stopped!"

She didn't take her eyes off him—not for one second—because she needed to remember this moment. Every quivering, sniveling detail. It had to sustain her. "Goodbye, Rodney." And then, she pulled the trigger.

****

Clare sat in her car letting the rain fall in sheets around her. She felt sheltered there. No one could see her cry. The tears were not for herself. *Well, maybe a little.* But mostly for the girls who came after.

My fault. She couldn't help but think it. When she'd exhausted herself, she opened the ashtray, picked out the bullets she put there for safekeeping, and reloaded the clip.

Slow and careful, she unwrapped the memory savoring that empty click of the trigger. The way Rodney shuddered before he realized he wasn't dead at all. *It's not gonna be that easy, asshole. You owe me.* But mostly, the way he looked at her, revered her. Like she was God. Or the devil. Or something in between. And he knew she had the power now. Power to give life, power to take it away. And someday, she intended to use it.

DECEMBER 26, 1996

THE day after Christmas. *Ugh.* It always irked Clare with its way-too-jolly, overstuffed, post-holiday hangover vibe. On December 25, people went underground, leaving the streets as bare as the end of the world. She could pretend the world belonged to her alone, her own private snow globe minus the snow. Even when Neal had invited her home with him last year and the year before that, she'd politely declined. It crushed him every time, but it was better that way. The last thing she needed was Neal picturing family ski trips with hot cocoa and fireplace chats and matching parkas for their 2.5 children. She'd learned to stomach the 25th. But the 26th, it was entirely villainous in the way it slapped Clare in the face with her utter aloneness.

But today, *this* December 26, Clare felt like she could fly. Five-mile run on an empty stomach—effortless. She imagined wings stretching out behind her, one gust away from liftoff. She even called Lizzie at home because she knew she wouldn't be there. Lizzie did the holidays big like everybody else. *Merry Christmas, Liz,* she said at the beep. *Talk soon.* A big, fat lie, but that twinge of guilt couldn't slow her down. Lizzie would be just fine without her.

Clare had the day off, of course, but she made the drive to San Quentin anyway, speeding down the blank slate of highway, humming "Jingle Bells" to herself. She cleared the gate with a smile, rattling off an excuse about loads of paperwork to catch up on. As soon as she arrived at her office, she dialed South Block and summoned the Bear. Then, she waited.

The hours dragged at her wings, weighing her down. She read client files and polished up her notes. Not that it really mattered anyway. Not anymore. But it meant something to Clare. She didn't want anyone thinking she'd done a lousy job, shirked her responsibilities. She thought of Fitzpatrick, what he might say to the authorities afterward. *Did she screw her client? Sure. Help him break out of prison? Yep. But at least she kept good notes.*

Her high-pitched giggle—the first sound of life she'd heard all afternoon—startled her. Like it came from someone else. But then again, she felt like someone else.

"Clare? Are you in there?" Her heart leapt, and her eyes darted. Nowhere to hide.

"Dr. Fitzpatrick? Yes, it's me." His shadow loomed behind the beveled glass. She would've rather it'd been Ramirez or one of his cronies with a strangled bird in hand.

"Why are you sitting in the dark?"

She raced to the door, eager to be rid of him. "I just popped in. I forgot my ... " She scanned the room. " ... scarf."

"I see." He stared at the stack of files on her desk.

"What are you doing here?" she asked him.

"I was just asking myself the same question. I suppose I didn't feel up to being alone. It's my first Christmas since the divorce, you know. And I'm not much for shopping. So ... " He shrugged. "Here I am. Pathetic, huh?"

She patted his arm, giving a smile. Underneath the fine, dark hair, his skin had the color of alabaster, and the effort required to touch him—the mental teeth gritting—clipped her wings completely. Clare was earthbound again. "I know what you mean. It can get lonely this time of year."

He looked at her hand when it rested briefly on his forearm. Instead of the lurid grin she expected, he eyed it like an alien claw sent to gut him. "I've been meaning to ask you something."

"Okay." She heard heavy footsteps clunking in the hall behind him. The way a bear would sound if it found its way to her office in San Quentin.

"The other day when you got that dry cleaning slip, you said Cullen worked in the laundry, right?" She made a noncommittal sound and strained to hear past him. There was nothing. "But I checked, and he's been assigned to building maintenance."

"Oh."

Fitzpatrick came inside and pulled the door shut behind him. He hadn't even accused her yet, and her face already flushed. "Remember how I told you I worked at a women's prison?" Clare nodded. "Well, I was young back then, and believe it or not, I was a bit of a scoundrel. There was this inmate. Teresa Moretti. A real looker. She was in on a murder charge. Bashed in her boyfriend's head, when she got tired of being his punching bag. I took a liking to her, Clare. And she knew it. I almost crossed the line."

She waited for him to say the thing he was thinking, but he didn't. "I'm not sure what you're getting at."

"It's not unusual to be attracted to a client. Or a supervisee, for that matter. That story is as old as dirt. It's what you do with it that counts. You know what my supervisor told me when he caught on to my little crush? 'Fitz,' he'd said, 'I'd hate to see you be one of those losers they have to walk off prison grounds because you couldn't keep it in your pants.'"

"What did you do?"

"Between you and me?" He stepped closer to her, and leaned in until she could smell the faint odor of tobacco on him. She'd never seen him smoke before, and it made her wonder if she'd figured him all wrong. Just as suddenly, he pulled away. "Nothing. My supervisor transferred her to another therapist. A newbie. That poor sucker never stood a chance. He got walked off three months later."

"So him and her?"

"Yep. Turns out it wasn't me she had a thing for. She just liked to play the game. And they always win, Clare. No matter how good it feels in the moment, they always win."

Clare felt her wings flutter with new life, brought back from the dead with a jolt and a spark of indignation. Fitzpatrick thought he knew her. Worse, he thought her no different than him. "Thank you for telling me. Come Monday, you can reassign Cullen. I think it's for the best." The beginnings of a smug smile tugged at his lips, so she went all in. "And how about next week we finally grab that drink?"

****

With Fitzpatrick tucked away inside his office, visions of next week's cocktails dancing in his head, Clare peeked down the hallway. No one. She inched the length of it, as quiet as she could until she reached the stairwell. At the bottom, the Bear leaned against the wall like he belonged there. Like the pillar of his broad back held up the entire building. She cleared her throat to get his attention and gestured wordlessly to the bathroom. Then she slipped inside.

She stared at the white throat of the toilet as she waited for her breathing to quicken, her heartbeat to race. She'd avoided this place, walking the extra floor up to the larger bathroom since Ramirez cornered her here—since she'd cowered on the cold tile in the throes of another flashback. *Flashback.* Another pointless term her therapist couldn't get enough of. *I don't like that word,* she told him once. It wasn't so much a flash as an unraveling. One solid tug on the perpetual thread of an ancient memory, and she came apart at all her seams.

But her heartbeat stayed steady, the push and pull of her breath calm, even when Raul Torres slipped a hand inside the door and lumbered into the space that was much too small for the two of them.

"Qué pasa?"

"Have you made up your mind?" she asked him.

His eyes were dark slits, impossible to read. "I'm interested."

"So you do speak English then?" Clare felt a need to poke him just a little.

"You're so smart, Doctor. Muy inteligente."

"I am smart," she said, an uncontrollable grin taking over her face. "That's why you're going to owe me one when I tell you my plan. Agreed?"

"Tell me the plan, then we talk terms."

Clare shook her head. "That's not how it works. I have some-thing you need. But you have something I need."

He ran his hand across his monstrous belly and down his crotch, rubbing himself. "Do I?"

"Keep that up, and I'll press this." She drew an alarm from her pocket, and his hand stilled. "Unless you want to explain how you ended up in the women's bathroom, fondling yourself in front of a staff member."

He mulled it over, muttering under his breath. "Puta."

She shrugged. "You don't have to like me. As long as you play by the rules, I'll help you keep your precious paquete from Ramirez and maybe even get rid of a few EME. Do we understand each other?"

"Yes. Entiendo. So what is it that you need, puta? A bullet in somebody's head?"

"Two passports—legitimate looking. You have people on the outside who can do that, right?"

"My people can do anything if the price is right."

"I was hoping you'd say that."

****

Clare didn't want the day to end. As long as she didn't sleep, the spell would never break. And she would be strong and fierce and on the verge of another life. One where Rodney Taylor didn't exist, had never existed. She fished the envelope Cullen gave her out of her purse and opened it, taking the picture in her hand. In it, he'd stood alone, against the mural in the Corcoran visiting room. "A buddy of mine took it a few years ago," he'd told her. "It's the only picture I've got."

"It will work," she told him, her voice already thick with longing for the weight of him pressed on top of her. But they had to be careful—even more careful—now. And she'd walked away burning. Before she drove home, she sat in her car and watched the waves come in and out until she worried someone might see her and wonder.

She set the picture on her pillow. Cullen's eyes looked back until hers were too heavy to keep open. Eyes so blue it seemed the entire sky lived inside of him.

CHAPTER TWENTY-EIGHT

GRAVEYARD

LEVI ripped the first few pages out of the folder marked *Classified* and stuffed them inside his jacket. Together, we headed for the door. "I don't think we can trust McKinnon." He paused and answered the question I didn't ask. "And no, I'm not just saying that because she wants to arrest me."

"We don't know how that file got here."

"Maybe you don't. But I'm pretty sure Rodney Taylor didn't steal it himself."

"You're saying she gave it to him?"

Levi exaggerated a sigh. "Exactly. Now you're thinking, Detective."

"Because she's … in on it?" When I conjured McKinnon's face, the cinnamon freckles splashed on either side of her elegant nose, I just couldn't imagine it. But it seemed no more unlikely than my mother, the psychologist. Or my father, the murderer. "There's no evidence of that."

"Cop's instinct," he said.

I rolled my eyes. "Or paranoia."

He laughed. "Same difference."

"I'm not saying you're wrong." *Or right*, I added silently as I followed him outside.

The last building at Green River Trucking—door number three—loomed across the field of weeds. It was long enough to hold an entire semi and equipped with a garage door. Levi thought it served as a maintenance shed. Outside, the discarded innards of an 18-wheeler: a few gutted bucket seats, four rusty hubcaps, and a weathered steering wheel. "It's like a truck graveyard," I said.

I waited for Levi to respond with a smart remark—*let's hope it's not our graveyard*—or at the very least, shush me, but he didn't. He beckoned me over to the wall by the entrance, where he pressed himself still and flat as a lizard. Then he touched his ear. *Listen.*

Faint at first, muffled by a rumbling engine, the sounds became voices when I leaned closer. Voices I recognized. Kidnapper and victim. Psychologist and patient. Mother and father.

" … don't understand why you lied about *that*. Of all things."

"You didn't even give me a chance to explain, Clare. You just sent me out there to the wolves."

"What was I supposed to do? And Dumas, was that a lie too?" Next to me, Levi tensed, waiting for the answer.

"No, I swear I didn't do it. Briggs made it all up. Big surprise. That guy would've said anything to get in your pants. And he did, didn't he?" A long time passed with nothing but the low growl of the truck and the whir of the bugs in the tall grass. "Is that why you didn't tell me about our daughter? You didn't know for sure if she was mine?"

"She's yours."

"Yeah, well that's obvious. She looks just like me." *Did I?* I turned to Levi, stricken. *Did I?* He shrugged back. Meaning *yes*.

Another long silence, and my legs started to shake like the last forty-eight hours had finally caught up. I put my hands on my knees to steady them, dug my heels into the ground. Then, "Where the hell are they, Clare? They should've been here by now."

"They'll be here. They owe me. Just calm—"

317

I couldn't hear them anymore. I went down hard behind the battered backside of a bucket seat, shoulder to the dirt and a mouthful of weeds. Until I saw Levi next to me, raising his gun at something unseen, I'd assumed I fainted. I would've preferred it actually. I waited for gunfire. For bodies to hit the ground. But the breeze rustled the air like any other summer day. Two men. They knew where they were going. They were expected, it seemed. One pounded on the door twice with his tattooed fist—a design that looked like a fancy letter N—while the other stood guard, their guns visible, but not drawn.

The man spoke into the closed door. "The Bear sent us to drive you to Mexico."

My mother let them in. I saw her hand on the door, her ruby sparkling in the sunlight. Behind her, a shadow—so close, so dark—it could only belong to Cullen. "It's about time," she said.

DECEMBER 27, 1996

SOMETHING felt off. Before Clare phoned in sick, not even bothering to fake a sniffle or a cough. Before she drove into the bowels of the Fruitvale neighborhood in Oakland where a weaselly, mustached man called Pepe forged two passports while she waited on his doorstep. Before she packed it all into Briggs' ammo can and drove to Muir Woods. Before she counted 350 paces and dug a hole to the right of a tree that looked like a mouth waiting to swallow her. Before all of that, she awakened to the sound of her doorbell and a feeling. The slippery kind she couldn't put a name to, the kind shrinks don't stick on a feelings chart.

Cullen's photo had slipped from the pillow, one edge bent as if she'd been holding it all night. Still grasping it in her hand, unable to part with it, she padded to the door.

Rodney had left the money on her mat like he promised, bundled inside an oversized envelope decorated for Christmas. But he hadn't followed her instructions. Not that it surprised her. He'd always done what he wanted, to whom he wanted, and when. *Leave the money outside my door at 6 a.m. on Friday. Come alone and don't ring the bell. Drive away right after.* Yet, he stood there in the parking lot, gaping at her in her T-shirt that barely covered her underwear.

He opened his mouth to speak, but she slammed the door shut and locked it. And that seed of a feeling grew. She'd felt it before, the morning after Rodney first touched her. Knowing the world had changed completely before she could remember how. Knowing her old life had been broken and could never be put right again. Knowing in her bones she'd set it all in motion.

That night, Clare floored it back from Muir Woods—her hands caked with dirt that would take effort to wash off and that feeling still sitting on her chest. She'd already pulled into the lot when she saw Briggs' jeep, parked and running. Too late to turn around. A glance in the mirror told her she looked inexplicably ridiculous. Her face smudged with mud and sweat, stray needles in her hair, and eyes red-rimmed from her near all-nighter.

"Clare? What the hell happened to you?"

She squinted in the headlights of his jeep as he rolled up the window and climbed out. "Did you come from Quentin?" she asked, though she knew the answer already. He still was wearing his army-green uniform pants with a thin white T-shirt. "Do you want to come inside?" Clare heard herself talking too much, but she couldn't stop. Maybe if she kept it up, she wouldn't have to explain.

"Not until you tell me why you look like … that."

"I fell. I went for a run in the woods—just needed a change of scenery, I guess—and I slipped and took a tumble."

"Seriously?" A meek shrug and a woe-is-me smile. That's all it took. "What are you doing running in the woods alone anyway? It's dangerous, Clare."

"You've been working too hard, Sergeant. It's starting to get in your head. I think you need a little R&R."

He chuckled, sidling up to her and kissing her disheveled face. "If by R&R, you mean this, then absolutely. And, I need to talk to you." She'd never heard Briggs say that before, and it confirmed her unease.

Upstairs, she sat at the kitchen table, twisting the ruby on her finger, while he poured them each a glass of red from the last bottle left over from her Napa trip with Neal. "So, what's up?" she asked, averting her eyes from her fingernails. Dirt that wouldn't wash off in the sink. Dirt as thick and black as dried blood.

"Did you enjoy your little Christmas for one?" *Was he stalling?* "I still can't believe you wouldn't come home with me. My mom would

320

love you, Ms. Fancy Pants Doctor … heck, my whole family would love you."

Usually, this kind of talk would make her claustrophobic, send her darting in search of an excuse that would carry her through as long as she needed it to. "Next time," she said. "I promise."

"I'm going to hold you to that." She hoped her smile, more for herself than for him, didn't give her away. "Hey, remember how you asked me to check into the Dumas thing?"

Her heart lurched. "Did you find something?"

"I did." He placed his hand over hers, comforting her for something that hadn't happened yet. "But it might not be what you were expecting. I don't want to upset—"

"Just tell me, please."

"Bonner got some intel from a confidential informant."

"Bonner? You told him about this?"

"Relax. I didn't tell him anything. I heard it through the grapevine, but I checked it out myself, and it's legit."

"What is? What's legit?"

"Cullen."

She stared at her stomach, expecting to see a knife handle jutting out from her rib cage. The blade stuck deep inside, twisting. That's what it felt like. "What about him?"

"The informant implicated him in Dumas' death. Said he saw him strangle the guy with a bedsheet to make it look like a suicide."

She wasn't sure words would come out, but she tried anyway. "Uh … I … why … "

"Who knows why, Clare? That guy is a psychopath through and through. I know you find him fascinating as a patient, but you can't really be surprised. Anyway, they don't have enough evidence to reopen the investigation, but I thought you should know. For closure."

"Closure," she repeated. Her voice sounded tinny and far away.

Briggs stood up and pulled her with him. She felt light as a feather, following behind him as he led her to the bathroom and turned on the shower. In the mirror, her face looked the same. Just dirty. But her eyes were hollow and sunken, and she couldn't turn away. Even when Briggs pulled her grimy T-shirt over her head, unclasped her bra, tugged her sweats down. Even when he undressed himself, and the glass got steamy. Finally, he swiveled her head with his hand, and it moved slow and mechanical toward him—like a robot someone forgot to wind.

"Let's wash this day off, shall we?"

December 28, 1996

CLARE focused on slowing her walk by staring at the concrete track beneath her feet. The ground glistened with morning dew, little drops that caught the first sunlight and sparkled. It could've been beautiful if her brain had room to consider such things. She wanted to sprint to West Block, bust into Dumas' old cell, and shake Snip awake, demanding answers. Though he'd been in the infirmary when it'd happened, he was the only person she could halfway trust, the only person she could think to ask. Aside from Cullen. It ached to say his name even in her head.

She would've never been able to explain going to work on a Saturday. Or why she couldn't do brunch with his friends, like Briggs suggested. Or why she'd stopped him last night, pushed him off her, and feigned a headache. Instead, she left Briggs asleep in her bed, his mouth slack and drooling on her pillow. *Stick to the plan*, she told herself, loading a small suitcase of essentials into her trunk. She marveled at how light it felt, how little of this life she wanted to take with her.

The officer buzzed her into West Block, and Clare waved to him as casual as she could. "Dr. Keely here to check on Eddie Bailey. He said he felt pretty depressed this morning."

"Snip doesn't need checking on, does he?" The officer turned to his counterpart for back up, but the other man just shrugged.

"My supervisor called me at home and woke me up. So, if I could just do my job and get back to my Saturday, I'd really appreciate it." *Geez, Clare. You are a bitch. And a lying one at that.*

With a raise of his eyebrows and an exasperated exhale, he allowed her in. She bolted down the cement corridor to cell 215L while the officer waited, open-mouthed, for his thank you. "Mr. Bailey? Snip?"

The sheets on the upper bunk rustled, and a shock of brown hair emerged from beneath them. "Huh? Who's there?"

"Clare Keely. I met you a while back."

"Dumas' headshrinker?"

To her own surprise, Clare chuckled. "Yep, that's me." Snip hopped down, spry as a fox, and walked to the cell front. "Are you alone?" she asked as he rubbed his eyes awake.

He gestured to the bottom bunk. Nothing but a bare mattress and a meager pillow. "Is that a trick question? I'm not seeing things, Doc. Are you?"

Clare took a deep breath and lowered her voice. "Just checking. I need to talk to you about Dumas."

"I already told them everything I know. I wasn't even here that day. Wish I had been, I'll tell ya that."

"This is *off* the record, Mr. Bailey."

"Ain't no such thing in prison."

"Please. You can trust me." She wasn't above begging. Not anymore. "What do you think happened to James?"

"Like I told the Lieutenant, I don't know." He watched her face for a moment, the hard lines in his forehead softening. "But he didn't seem like somebody about to end it all. Just my opinion though. I ain't no doctor."

"Did he have any enemies?"

Snip laughed. "We all got enemies in here. But James didn't have no more than anybody else. Are you in some kinda trouble about this? Bonner told me you might come asking questions. Said I wasn't supposed to say nothing. They're not trying to blame you, are they?"

Clare shrugged, far too desperate, far too gone, to waste her time on Bonner. "Sort of. But that's not really why I'm here."

"So why are you here then? Why don't you just go on and spit it out?"

So she did. "Clive Cullen. Did James know him?"

"Everybody knows that guy. A real arrogant SOB, if you ask me. I never saw James talk to him, but then again, we weren't attached at the hip, you know. Do you think he had something to do with it?" Snip asked, and she fought the urge to leave as quickly as she came.

"I hope not." It was the most honest answer she could give.

Snip looked past her, down the empty concrete hallway, and lowered his voice. "Well, I for one wouldn't be surprised," he said. "But I'm sure you've heard the rumors on the yard." Clare let out a shaky breath that said she hadn't. "Let's just say ain't nobody wanted you as a therapist, Doc. Cullen don't like to share. But you probably know that better than anybody."

She caught another breath and held it in until her chest hurt. "Know what?" she asked.

"His m.o.—when he has to share, somebody usually winds up dead."

Clare bit the inside of her lip to keep her panic at bay. "Is there anything else you didn't tell Bonner? Anything at all? Even if it might not seem that important."

"There's plenty I didn't tell Bonner. That guy's crooked as a dog's hind leg."

"Like what?"

"Well, for one thing, I'd heard that shifty-eyed CO Briggs was down here in charge. This ain't his post, so I figure that don't smell right. He'd lick Bonner's boots if somebody asked him to." Clare nearly cackled at the thought. "And the real kicker, James told me himself he'd seen something. Before you ask, he didn't say what. Only that he saw something he wasn't supposed to see. He seemed real worried about it."

"When did he tell you that?"

"Best I can recall, it would've been that morning before I got sick. Probably about the time he got back from your office." Snip gave her a sly grin. "Were you doing something you weren't supposed to, Doc?" Clare froze, caught in his brown eyes. She'd done so many things she wasn't supposed to, she couldn't really remember which wrong things she'd done when. "I'm just messin' with ya."

Clare nodded and slogged away without bothering to say good-bye. White noise whooshed and whirred in her ears. Above it all, a refrain so steady and familiar—*it's all your fault, Clare, all your fault*—she didn't even turn around when Snip called her back.

****

Clare barreled back to her office like a runaway train. Her hands trembled as she paged through Cullen's file, twice slicing her finger on the paper's edge, leaving half of a bright red print as a mark of her carelessness. Her thoughts jumbled, bled together, made no sense.

Cullen and Dumas and
Briggs and Cullen and
Bonner and Ramirez and Torres and
Cullen and Cullen and Cullen and—

"He lied to me." She said it out loud to silence the rest. But it didn't feel right. She couldn't believe it. Didn't want to. Still, she knew her own game, the tricks she'd played on herself, the blinders she wore that made her capable of anything. *Remarkable—that level of denial.* That's what Fitzpatrick would say, dressing her down with her own words. *The most primitive defense mechanism? Really? I expected more from you, Dr. Keely.*

She cradled the phone in the crook of her neck and dialed the number on Cullen's *In Case of Death Notify* form. She'd done it before—once—in September, but hung up after one ring. This time she held the line for what seemed an eternity.

"Hello?" A woman's voice, but not what she'd expected. Timid, mousy. The sort of woman who scared easily.

"Is this Vanessa Cullen?"

"Yes, it is. Who's calling?"

"This is Lizzie Conway at San Quentin State Prison. Do you have a few minutes?" *Sorry, Lizzie.*

326

The woman's breath hitched, then started up again, shallow and ragged. "Is Clive okay? Is my boy okay?"

"Yes. Yes, he's fine. No need to worry. I've been working with him on—"

"His appeal? Are you an attorney?" Clare made a noise of surprise, mistaken as agreement. "Oh, thank God. It's about time somebody believed him. *Us.* You do believe him, right? You're the fourth attorney we've tried."

Clare pressed the soles of her feet into the ground as hard as she could, fighting the sudden sensation it had given way beneath her. "Believe he's innocent? Uh … do you?"

"Of course." It came out short and firm like the strike of a knife. "Clive could never hurt a fly, much less a woman. A woman he loved. Though I never did understand what he saw in her. That Emily, she had issues. Like my Clive always says, 'It's no wonder she got herself killed.'"

In the vacuous silence, Clare heard Cullen's echo. *Emily. You remind me of her.* She spoke because she had to. "What was Clive like as a boy, Ms. Cullen?"

When Vanessa laughed, Clare pictured her. The same blue-gray eyes as Cullen's, crinkling in the corners. "Spoiled."

"Oh?" The word barely made it up and out of the back of her throat.

"Well, I had a good excuse. Making up for lost time. He lived with his dad until he was thirteen. But we don't like to talk about that."

"Why?"

"His father was a sick man, Ms. Conway. Ask Clive. He'll show you the scars. That man tried to poison my son against me—I know he did. Clive would never admit it, but Lord knows what he told him. I think that's why Clive turned out the way he did, with a savior complex. Always wanting to rescue these poor little girls from their poor little lives. It sounds horrible, but I actually felt relieved when his father died in prison a few years ago."

"What was his name?"

"Barrett. But I'm not sure how that's relevant? What law firm are you—"

Clare hung up fast, as if the phone had smacked her across the face. Then she typed the name into the inmate database on her computer and waited for an answer.

Barrett Cullen (deceased). Twenty-five years to life for first-degree murder and rape.

****

Clare had never really prayed for anything in her life. Sure, her mother had dragged her to church whenever *she* started feeling guilty. *Lord, please make me a better mother*, Clare had heard her whisper once. But Clare would just sit there, admiring the stained-glass windows— certain if God existed, He would've answered her mother by now. Certain He would've struck down Rodney Taylor with a vicious bolt of lightning the moment his hand grazed her thirteen-year-old knee. Certain He didn't let girls like her get pregnant, not *that* way, not at sixteen, not by the devil himself. But, huddled in the corner of her office, Clare prayed. Mostly, for the end of the world. An earthquake—*the big one*. An atomic bomb. Something so devastating no one she knew could survive.

And then, she called Neal.

He answered—*of course he did*—like he'd been waiting for her to need him, to require rescue, and she started talking—spilling over, more like it—with no explanation.

"Slow down, Clare. Where are you?" It wasn't even a speed bump. She blew right past it.

"He lied to me, and I don't know what to do. God, I'm so stupid. I'm going to lose my license. I—"

"Clare, stop talking."

"I'm so sorry. I've been awful to you, and you were just trying to help. And Neal, oh God, I did something really bad. A lot of things. Not just one."

"Shut up!" Neal never yelled. Not like that. Not with rage. "Goddamn it. I can't hear myself think. Where are you?"

"I'm at San Quentin."

"Meet me outside the gate. I'll pick you up. Twenty minutes." He hung up, and Clare felt emptied, exhausted. She laid her head against her desk, the wood cooling her cheek. This time she prayed for something else. Something impossible. She prayed to go back, back to the beginning. The beginning of September. The beginning of grad school. The beginning of those nine months, before a baby grew inside her. The beginning of Lisa Taylor's slumber party. The beginning of anything. Just not today. Not the end.

****

The room felt cold. The stares, glacial. The only warmth, Neal's hand around hers, and she clung to it, knowing even that was temporary. He'd made that clear. *This is it, Clare. I'll do this with you because I love—I loved you. But, when we leave here, don't ever call me again.* He must have known how impossible that sounded, especially now, because he added, *Pretend I'm dead if you have to. Whatever it takes. You need help, and I need to move on.*

The redhead Clare didn't know yet spoke first.

"Dr. Keely, my name is Gretchen McKinnon. I'm a Special Agent with the FBI We talked on the telephone earlier. I understand you already know Lieutenant Bonner. I agreed to let him sit in today since he's kindly allowed us to conduct this interview here at San Quentin. It's only fair he knows what's going on in his house."

McKinnon smiled at Bonner the same way Clare might have, trying to placate his ego, already aware of what an ass he was, that kindness had nothing to do with it. She reminded Clare of herself. Young. Perceptive. Far too pretty to fit in a man's world. And for no other reason than that, Clare liked her. "If it's okay with you, Clare— may I call you Clare?—I'll be recording this interview."

Clare nodded, as if she had a choice. The click of the tape recorder sounded like the first shot across the bow. A warning. And then, the questions fired like arrows. Each one pointed. Each one poison-tipped and aimed at her soft places.

Who suggested the escape? "He did, of course."

When did the inmate first suggest the escape? "I don't remember."

What did he say exactly? "If you don't help me, I'll tell them we had sex."

How many times did you engage in sexual intercourse with the inmate? "Just once."

Is anyone else involved in the escape? "Rodney Taylor. Green River Trucking."

Did you take any steps to plan the escape? "I contacted Rodney and asked him for money and a truck just like Cullen told me to. But that's it."

Where was he going? "Mexico, I think."

Clare didn't look at Neal. Not once. But he squeezed her hand hard every time Bonner guffawed with disbelief, every time McKinnon pressed her for more. A signal to remind her of the stakes, to cue the story they'd practiced. Neal knew the truth, most of it anyway. He knew the real and ugly and unspeakable answers—*I suggested the escape. I had sex with him on the floor in the laundry room. Two times. I thought he loved me*—the answers he'd told her to bury some place safe, not realizing the irony there. Those answers shot bullets to his heart, Clare knew that much, but he took them the same way he'd taken last year's revelation about the married guy with the flowers. The way any self-respecting oak tree would. Without flinching.

Bonner reached a hand across the table and shut off the recorder. It was the saddest sound Clare had ever heard. "I'm sorry, Agent McKinnon, but I can't listen to any more of this. You may be fooled by Dr. Keely—you won't be a doctor much longer, my dear—but I don't believe one word of this. She's been carrying on with that criminal for months now, jeopardizing the safety of everyone who works at this institution." He looked at a spot on the wall above Clare's head, apparently too disgusted to meet her eyes. "Are you aware of the penalties for aiding an escape from a correctional facility?"

Clare kept her lips pressed tight together so nothing could slip out. But in her mind, she thrust a knife right to the center of his throat.

McKinnon offered another sympathetic smile. "I understand your frustration, Lieutenant. It must be difficult to accept that this happened here, right under your nose. But, I assure you, I am more than capable of getting to the truth." She didn't wait for a reply. The recorder whirred back to life. And Clare squashed the urge to hug her.

"There are serious penalties for the sorts of things you've described, Clare. However, I think I speak for everyone here when I say no one wants to see you behind bars." For once, Bonner bit his tongue, and Clare relished knowing how hard it must have been for him, how that would keep him up at night. "You're not the one to blame. This is Cullen's m.o. He manipulates women better than the best of them. Doesn't he?" Clare couldn't make herself agree, so she said nothing. "Would you be willing to help us catch our man?"

"Will I be charged with anything?"

"Not if you assist in his successful apprehension. It's likely you'll face other consequences though. The revocation of your license, for example. Unfortunately, there's nothing we can do about that."

"I understand."

"Is that a yes?"

"Yes."

"Is there anything else we should know? Anyone else we should investigate?" Neal warned her this would come. *Be smart, Clare*, he'd said, and her heart swelled. After every foolish mistake she'd made, he still thought she was capable of being smart. *The EME, the NF, these gangs are powerful. Ruthless. They know where you live. Just keep your mouth shut.* When she opened her mouth to argue, he silenced her with three words. *Remember that canary.*

Clare turned her head slowly, deliberately toward Bonner, letting her silence speak for her. She watched his face until the ghost of fear passed across it and a little longer still, until Neal nudged her. "I don't want this on tape." McKinnon clicked the recorder off again and nodded at Clare. "Arturo Ramirez. He runs drugs for the EME."

****

Cullen arrived outside Clare's office at fifteen till seven just like they'd planned. By the time Ramirez's men went looking for him in the laundry closet, he'd be clear of San Quentin, beelining for her car in the lot, keys in hand. Ready to drive to Muir Woods and unearth their future. Taking his place and ready for battle, Torres and the NF. McKinnon didn't know about that. The gang fight Clare had set in motion. McKinnon didn't know about a lot of things.

Cullen's shadow appeared in the beveled glass, and Clare caught her breath. He stood there a moment before he knocked, and she wished she could read his thoughts. Not that it mattered. It was too late now anyway.

"Hi," he said, peeking in as she cracked the door. His boyish grin nearly broke her heart in two.

Say something, Clare. But she feared *something* would give her away, so she pulled him inside, backing up until she felt the edge of the desk behind her thighs. Then she kissed him like it was the last time. And Cullen kissed her back like the first. The gentle, reserved way he touched her face, chock-full of promise and possibility. She tugged and grabbed and held on like there was nothing beyond this and it needed to count for something. He separated first, taking a full step away from her. Her face flushed. She could feel it burning.

"What are you doing?" he asked. "The officer will be here any minute. We have to stop."

"I didn't call the officer." Clare paid close attention to his eyes. Part hurt, part hope, part confusion. That's what she found there. The look he'd give later—the one she wouldn't see—when he'd realize she had sent him to his doom. "It's okay," she said, and the dull blue brightened again. "I've got something better, easier. And we don't have to hurt anybody." She pointed to the bag in the corner, where she'd stashed the uniform and ID badge Bonner gave her. They belonged to Officer Swanson, a rookie. "I swiped it," she lied.

"From where?"

"This bar in town. All the officers go there after work. They'll be drinking all night. He won't miss it until the morning. And we'll be halfway to Mexico by then."

Cullen didn't say anything, and Clare felt certain she'd been caught. The most important lie, and she managed to mess it up.

332

Maybe she didn't want to get it right after all. "I wasn't going to hurt anybody, Clare. I told you. I could've just tied him up."

"I know, but I—"

"I just don't want you taking risks like that. If you get caught … "

"But I didn't." He dropped it with a single nod that implied they'd talk about it later, that there would be a lifetime to talk about it. Or maybe that's only what he wanted her to believe. She'd come to accept she couldn't tell the difference. Then he stripped out of his prison blues and tossed them aside, with a smile as wide as she'd ever seen. She wanted that feeling. Coveted it. The release of leaving an entire self behind and starting again. Even if it was only make-believe.

From the office next door, a muffled sound harder than a footstep startled them both, and Clare fought to control the jolt of adrenaline that told her to run. "What was that?" Cullen asked, edgy. He slid into the officer's jumpsuit in a hurry and shoved his feet into black boots.

"I didn't hear anything. Fitzpatrick's not working today. Maybe it's the janitor."

"Should you check?" She nodded and opened the door to the hallway, walking out halfway, pretending to be wary. McKinnon insisted they be close by in case anything went wrong. That was FBI speak for *in case he tries to kill you.*

"No one," she said. "We're clear."

He chuckled softly. "I'm getting jumpy, aren't I? It's just, we're so close. I don't want to blow it now."

"You won't." *I already did.* "You remember how to get there?"

"Of course."

"I drew you a map in case you forget. It's hidden under the mat." Another thing McKinnon didn't know. Clare wasn't about to give up Muir Woods. She'd buried too much of herself there. It belonged to her and nobody else. "There's a change of clothes too."

He nodded. "When will you be there?" *Never.*

"As soon as I can. I'll wait for a while. When I'm sure you're clear, I'll call a taxi to take me to Rodney's. Then we'll pick you up at the cabin." *You'll be in cuffs before you reach the parking lot.*

"Clare … " His voice lowered, dark and serious, and Clare knew he was about to make this harder. "If I don't make it out of here, if they catch me—"

Oh God. "Don't say that."

"I want you to know I'll never give you up. Not any of it. I'll take it all to my grave."

She couldn't stand to be in her own skin. She wanted to shed it and slither away. But Cullen seemed to expect nothing in return. He didn't even look at her. He'd already buttoned the jumpsuit and clipped the ID to his pocket. "How do I look?"

She tried to choose words she wouldn't regret. Words that wouldn't haunt her. When that proved impossible, she picked the words he wanted to hear instead. "Like a free man."

CHAPTER TWENTY-NINE
DRAGON

LEVI crouched next to me, eyeing the door.

"Were those guys EME too?" I asked.

"I don't think so. The EME don't like your mom."

I started to agree, to ask him *what next*, to brush at the grass stuck in my hair, but I never got the chance.

The sky erupted. A few days ago, I would've expected to see an explosion worthy of the random bursts of color that lit the Bellwether football field every Fourth of July. Now, I knew better. I hit the ground again and huddled like an animal in the weeds. Bullets pinged the buildings, tore through metal. Somewhere glass exploded. The EME! It had to be. They'd come for my mother, guns blazing. Two of them, but in the haze of gunfire, I couldn't tell them apart. They moved together—one sinewy dragon, spitting fire from its mouth, shouting its battle cry.

"Stay down," Levi told me. "We've got to get better cover. We won't last here." I hugged tight to my knees, making myself as small as I could behind the row of discarded seat backs. A gash already ripped through the top of one, the foam falling like snow around me.

Levi shot as he ran, taking cover alongside the building. The men fired back at him, and the shot glanced off the sheet metal.

"Sam!" I peered up out of my cocoon, and Levi motioned to me with his hand. "C'mon. I'll shoot. You run." Another round of gunfire sent Levi darting backward.

Uh, no. I shook my head. "I can't," I yelled.

Levi stuck his hand around the corner and fired again. One half of the dragon went down, stunned. Somehow still alive, even with a bullet-sized hole torn in the front of his T-shirt. His face, familiar to me like a demon from a nightmare I couldn't shake.

"Yes, you can. You have to. Just like in the hotel. Remember?"

And I did. I remembered. The big bad wolf of a man with oil-slick hair who pounded his way in, the tattoo like a garrote around his neck. He'd returned to finish the job. "Quién es ese?" he asked, struggling to his feet.

His partner shrugged, keeping the eye of his gun trained on Levi's spot. "No es Cullen. Leave it for now."

"Go, Sam!" Levi shouted, and my feet took off, sprinting through the weeds toward him. A bullet sliced the air just behind me, and I dove the rest of the way, landing with a thud in the dirt.

I forced the words out, my lungs burning. "It's the guy from the Westin."

Levi nodded. "EME. They're wearing vests."

"As in?" The sun shining right at me, I felt cold.

"Yep. Bulletproof."

A vicious chop of a boot pounded against the door, and I jumped. Levi leaned around the corner, fired, and snapped back, dodging another *pop-pop-pop* of bullets.

"Doc-tora Clare? Doc-tora Puta? We know you're in there with your boyfriend." The man's voice singsong, his accent heavy, the intent clear. Abject terror. "Don't make us come inside." He kicked again, just rattling her cage. The door nothing but a formality. With a gun that merciless, he could go in anytime he wanted. Take anything. Do whatever. I tried to imagine my mother on the other side, but I couldn't. The mother I knew had no place here. She stayed behind in Bellwether, sipping iced tea on our front porch and counting fireflies.

I'm trembling again, I thought as the side of the building shook beneath my hand.

A soft rumble built to a steady roar, and I thought, *thunderstorm*. Then, *earthquake*, when all I could see opened up around me. The garage door crumpled in on itself like paper, and the head of a beast—an 18-wheeler—pushed its way through, blasting back at the EME with a hail of gunfire from the cab.

I covered my ears as the EME shot back. Levi too. Until thin white smoke rose up like fog. The truck kept moving, slow and labored in its death march, even after the windshield bloodied and shattered. The man with the *N* tattooed on his hand took a last gasp, dropped toward the steering wheel, and tumbled out the door. His partner jumped from the passenger seat, fired one last round, and collapsed a few feet from us. One of the EME lay crushed beneath the truck. My mother and Cullen nowhere. The only sign of life, *el lobo feroz*. Not so big and bad anymore—a wound in his leg left a red trail behind him—but still a wolf. A wolf with a weapon.

"NF," Levi whispered, eyeing the dead man's tattoos from our hiding place behind a hunk of twisted metal. "Nuestra Familia. It's another gang. A rival." A gang on my mother's side apparently.

As the wolf stalked around, dazed, the door of the main building opened, and Agent McKinnon strutted out, gun drawn. "What's going on here?" Her bark demanded answers.

I let out a breath of relief and started to call her, but Levi's hand held me like an anchor to the earth. Then, she fired. A shot to the flank and the wolf went down. My own legs went numb and folded beneath me. No chance of getting up now. I stopped breathing, stopped looking, when McKinnon aimed again. This time, after, he made no sound.

"Clare! Clare Bronwyn! It's Agent McKinnon." Just like that, her tone became concerned and imploring. "Are you in there?"

"Clare can't come out right now," Cullen announced, stepping from the truck's backside, an assault rifle in his hand. He pointed it at

McKinnon. She pointed hers back. "She's a little tied up, as they say. But what do you care? Clare didn't want to believe it when I told her, but I know what you've been up to." He waved his free hand wildly, gesturing to the chaos around him. "The game you've been running. And now, you're here to kill us both, aren't you?"

McKinnon didn't answer him. "Clare, it's going to be okay. I've got backup on the way."

"I'll bet you do. More of Ramirez's scraps sent here to do your dirty work."

When McKinnon spoke again, her bark had bite. "Here's the problem with being a criminal, Cutthroat. When you finally decide to speak the truth, nobody believes you. And before you can convince them, you're already dead."

"I believe him." Levi advanced toward them, his own gun aimed at McKinnon. In the other hand, he waved the top-secret pages like a flag of surrender. "I believe you shared classified information with the EME to help them smuggle cocaine across the Mexican border. I believe you used Rodney Taylor's business as a front for illegal activity. And I'm guessing you might have known about his penchant for little girls. Is that what you held over him? Is that how you convinced him to sell his soul?"

"Officer Beckett—can I still call you that? You're one to talk, dragging your sister into your pathetic little daddy detective story. Here's a hint: It wasn't Colonel Mustard in the ballroom with a candlestick. And as much as I'd like to pin it on Cutthroat, he didn't have the cojones to fight back in prison. Not like that. Clare had him all soft and googly-eyed. But later on, he took the credit for it. Just like I knew he would. And who could blame him after the good doctor left him high and dry?"

My mother emerged then, and I gasped. Not tied, not gagged, not handcuffed. Free to do whatever she pleased. And her hands, bright red with somebody's blood. On the ground at her feet, the dead NF's rifle. I willed her to look at it. "Snip told me," she said instead. "Twenty years ago, he'd told me Dumas saw something that spooked him. I thought he meant me and Cullen. I thought Cullen got jealous and … " She hung her head, and I wanted to run to her. But I didn't dare move.

"It's always about you, isn't it, Clare?" McKinnon chuckled to herself, but her grip stayed taut, finger poised on the trigger. "Dumas saw a drop go down in the kitchen. The EME don't leave loose ends like that dangling for long. Bonner knew. That double-dealing low life had been running drugs with the NF and the EME for years. He sent his little kiss-ass, Briggs, to make sure it all went down without a hitch. I'd figured it out before the ink dried on your letter of resignation. You can't blame me for taking advantage of his stupidity. And you, so predictable running away like that. Then. Now. But you couldn't leave it alone, could you? You had to come here and muck it all up for me. You know, Cullen cried like a baby when we arrested him that day, halfway to your car. This time you and your daughter— *his* daughter—get to watch him die."

Until then, I'd been convinced of my own invisibility. But now, exposed, I felt like a pawn on a chessboard. I wobbled to my feet to claim my place, to show I wouldn't be sacrificed. Not for her.

In a slow-motion second, the whole game changed. Pieces shifted. The chessboard tumbled and cracked in two. McKinnon fired first, dropping Levi with a shot to his arm. He cried out and rolled onto his side. I lunged toward him, but he waved me back. Already dashing for the cab of the truck, Cullen shot back at McKinnon, narrowly missing. He shouted at my mother as he ran.

"Let's go, Clare!" It sounded like an order, but my mother just stood there, her face indecipherable. "Get in."

Cullen clung to the side mirror, ready to hoist himself into the driver's seat. Ready to drive straight through the fence to freedom. But something pinned him, tethered him to my mother, and wouldn't let him go. Time stilled, and I wondered if he would dissolve to sand like the old parable, unable to pry his eyes from the past.

From behind him, McKinnon lined up her shot. "Watch out!" I yelled, the words expelling themselves from a place I couldn't name. And then, in the instant it took for a firefly to flicker and go out, my mother—Clare Keely—picked up the rifle and fired. And McKinnon fell.

The truck started to move, to pick up steam again, with Cullen imploring my mother. Practically begging. She watched him go, the same way she'd watch me leave her in the fall. Partly unwilling, partly unable to stop the inevitable.

Next to her, Levi propped himself onto his elbow and clutched his wound. His eyes narrowed with focus, Cullen fading from his sights. Not exactly the way he must've imagined it ending, but his forearm twitched with life, with a motive, of its own—to settle the score or to uphold the law, even now, I can't be sure which—and he aimed for the tires.

Gently, my mother took his arm in her hands and lowered it, speaking a word so hushed I couldn't quite make it out. Still, that word—whatever it was—broke him a little. And saved him. His face crumpled. "Don't." If I had to guess, that's what she said.

JANUARY 17, 1997

TWO pink lines. Two. Pink. Lines. Clare crouched over the toilet, dry heaving. She'd already thrown up breakfast. Four days in a row. Still, her stomach clenched and contracted with a life of its own, and she imagined an alien creature fighting its way out. Taking parts of her with it.

"Are you alright in there, Clare-Bear?" Lizzie's voice came from right outside the door, sending Clare into a panic. She wrapped the white stick in tissue paper and shoved it to the bottom of the trash can. For a split second, she was sixteen again until she literally slapped herself out of it.

"Fine. It must've been that sushi I ate last night." At least she sounded normal. Or close enough.

"I told you." Lizzie chuckled. "Raw fish is for sea lions. You are *not* a sea lion. Remember that time you had sushi before mid-terms?" Clare couldn't hear Lizzie anymore. Through the thick stench of nausea, her brain rattled with dates. Thanksgiving, Christmas, and all the weeks in between. The encyclopedia told her morning sickness was common around week six. *I had sex with Neal at Thanksgiving. That's almost eight weeks. And Briggs? Decemberish.* The other possibility—she didn't let herself think it. But it squatted in the back of her mind like an unwelcome visitor.

She stared at herself in the mirror. Her right cheek flaming from her own vicious strike, she pinched the other to bring it back to life.

This is what you deserve. She grabbed the packet of pills she'd been popping since Neal took her to Planned Parenthood in grad school—*someday you won't need those,* he'd always said—and chucked it across the room. It landed in the shower, skittering across the tub's bottom. *How could you be so stupid?* Those little white pills, smaller than a penny. *That's what you counted on?*

"Are you sure you're okay?" Not for the first time since Cullen had been arrested, Lizzie sounded a little afraid of her. Having sex with a serial killer does that to people, she'd realized. And Lizzie still hadn't asked. Not one question. She'd taken the scraps Clare fed her and been satisfied.

"Remind me to never eat raw fish again." Forcing a laugh, Clare opened the door. "Unless I come back as a sea lion."

"Noted." Lizzie flopped onto the sofa and sighed. "So I guess you're officially unemployed now." She gestured to the letter on the countertop. The envelope freshly stamped and addressed to the Board of Psychology.

Clare tried to hide her surprise at seeing a glimpse of the old, joking Lizzie. "Defrocked is more like it. It turns out crazy people shouldn't be shrinks."

"I guess so." And just like that, the old Lizzie vanished. Clare wanted her back, needed her back. Something in her empty stomach moved, twisted. Like tiny fingers squeezing the very last drop, and she thought about bolting for the bathroom. But she inhaled slowly, and it passed.

"The FBI wants me to testify against Clive." She called him that on purpose, trying to get a rise. "Fitzawhozit does too." Or at least he'd said so in the message he'd left on her machine. Clare had been too afraid to pick up. Too afraid to face him now that he knew he'd been right about her.

"Hmph."

"What do you think I should do?"

Clare watched Lizzie trying to decide what to say, how to say it. The same way Clare had measured her goodbye with Cullen.

Eventually, Lizzie decided on saying nothing at all. Just a shrug of her shoulders.

"C'mon, Lizzie. I need your advice."

"You'll do whatever you want to anyway. So why don't you just tell me? Save me the breath. What do *you* want to do?"

Her mouth gave the expected answer. Something about being wracked with confusion, not knowing which way to turn. But after Lizzie drove away, Clare pulled the atlas from her bookshelf and flipped it open. Texas. Then she closed her eyes and laid her finger on the map. Houston. *Too big.* She tried again. Bellwether. A small dot where nobody could find her. It would do. She laid her hand on her stomach, where the alien creature had quieted.

"It's just you and me now."

****

"It's gonna hurt," the man said, tentative, like she couldn't handle it.

Clare nodded. *Didn't it always?* She looked away from him and his Semper Fi tattoo, nearly hidden among all the others. It reminded her of Robocop. And that made her blood boil. McKinnon told her he'd been suspended for their control booth tryst, pending an investigation after those missing keys were recovered in Ramirez's footlocker. But she hadn't laid eyes on him since December. Since the morning after that shower when she'd left him clueless, asleep in her bed. Not that she cared one way or the other really—but *him* being ashamed of her, that rankled her like a pebble in her shoe. As if all of it came down to her. Her and her curse. Her and her demons. And maybe it did. Maybe Briggs was right to stay away from her.

That's why she had to do this. To put the universe on notice. To remind herself. Clare was done with being a siren. Done with men altogether.

Leaning forward, she rested against the padded seat. The man shifted behind her, readying himself. Then, she felt his warm hand brush the hair from her neck, and she stifled a gasp. "The skin back here is real thin," he said. "Sensitive. I just want you to be prepared for—"

"Just do it already."

She closed her eyes and concentrated on the sound of the needle, but he kept talking. "Eye of Horus, huh?"

SEPTEMBER 9, 1997

CLARE felt bone tired, but she couldn't sleep. Not yet. She was someone's mother now. *Again.* The last nine months, she'd dreaded this day for more reasons than she could count. But it came down to one: She didn't trust herself.

After the pain ripped her in two, and the baby cried for the first time—so loudly—Clare unraveled. She'd heard that sound before. Had silenced it with her own hands. A coldness spread through her, wilting her heart like the first frost. And when the nurse toweled the baby off and nestled her against Clare's body, she'd thought, *There's been a mistake. This doesn't belong to me. I don't deserve her.* But the nurse insisted, so Clare complied.

The baby squirmed against her, and Clare worried. *She knows. She knows what I've done. I'm nobody's mother.* But the nurse told her the baby was just rooting for a warm place, so Clare held her tight, as snug as a thimble. She reminded herself she'd prepared for this. She'd done it right this time. Mostly.

It's brave what you're doing, Agent McKinnon had told Clare, when she'd called from a payphone at a roadside motel halfway to Texas. *It doesn't mean I agree, but our case is rock solid with or without you. And you've been punished enough.* Clare hadn't asked what she'd meant. There was plenty to choose from—the revoked license, the job termination, the personal humiliation, and the revelation McKinnon had uncovered, the link between Clare and Rodney. A few months after she'd left, Clare drove to Oklahoma just to mail McKinnon a sonogram photo, ignoring her warning to stay gone. *No offense, Clare, but I don't want to see your face again. Ever.* She wouldn't admit it to herself then, and even now she didn't understand why, but she wanted Cullen to know.

"Samantha." She tried out the name she'd picked. *God heard.* That's what it meant. "Samantha Bronwyn." They both had new names. The baby cried against her swollen breasts, and she soothed her with a soft pat, rocking her a little. "It's okay."

The nurse smiled at her, approving. And the edges of her heart began to thaw.

"Does she get those eyes from her father?"

Clare looked down at the baby's face—so small and precious it made her worry. *How could she ever keep her safe?* "Her father died."

As she expected, the nurse's face crumpled, but Clare wondered if she saw right through her. "Oh, I'm so sorry."

"In a plane crash." So awful, no one could question it.

"What was his name?"

Samantha gazed up at her, eyes as blue as the sky after a Bellwether thunderstorm, and she couldn't deny it. Not to herself. And, for now, that had to be enough. "Neal Barrington."

CHAPTER

THIRTY

CLEAN UP

SOME trip, Bronwyn." Ginny laughed as she leaned against me, the buzz of the hospital droning just outside her room. "I guess we hit all the hot spots, huh?"

"That's an understatement." I hugged Levi's jacket tight to me, the sterile cold seeping into my bones, my letterman probably well on its way to taking up space in some FBI evidence locker.

"Is your mom … okay?" she asked. I shrugged, not sure how to answer.

"They took her to the station for questioning, after she got checked out. Physically, she's fine, but she barely said two words in the ambulance ride over here. And she's been acting like nothing has happened ever since."

Ginny nodded, looking wiser than I'd ever seen her. Maybe it was the nineteen stitches in her cheek, five in her neck. "Go easy on her," she said. "I can't imagine what she went through with Cutthroat. That guy … what a sicko. You know, he told me how he knew about our trip."

My stomach dropped, and I raised my eyebrows at her. "Apparently, his mother's been keeping tabs on her granddaughter for years. And her granddaughter's best friend. She saw my Facebook post." Levi had been right. *A serial killer and a mama's boy.* "Yep, the rotten apple doesn't fall from the tree." I knew Ginny didn't mean it *that* way. Still, I flinched, and she deflected. I let her. "You know, I really hope some clueless professor asks me what I did this summer. Because, I'm gonna—"

"Didn't I warn you about getting yourself in trouble?" Levi interrupted from the doorway. His face half-smiling, half-pained, he moved slower than usual, his body draped in a hospital gown, his arm wrapped and secured in a sling.

"I thought you were speaking abstractly. You should've told me to watch out for kidnappers in airport bathrooms."

"Clearly. I'll try to be more specific next time."

Ginny nudged me with her elbow, her cheeks puffed with pride, and I blushed in anticipation. "But, you really should be thanking me."

"Oh yeah?"

"I am the queen of the elaborate setup, am I not?"

Levi winked at me. "You mean Detective Bronwyn, here? I guess she's not that bad for a civilian." His good arm slipped around my shoulders, and I leaned in to his warmth. He turned his head toward me, eyes twinkling. "As long as you remember which one of us was spot-on about McKinnon."

"Oh, I remember," I teased. "That was right after I found the folder that blew the case wide open. The one you were going to leave behind."

"Alright, alright. It was a team effort. Bronwyn and Beckett," Levi said. "See? I even put your name first." Ginny awwed.

"So what's next, Officer Beckett?" I asked.

"Just Levi," he said. "A civilian like you. I think it's time to surrender the badge."

"You're not going to fight it? After everything you did, I'm sure they'd reconsider. You brought down a major drug operation."

"Accidentally." Levi shrugged. "Besides, I've been thinking a lot about Plan B." The corner of his mouth hinted at a smile. "The police force may be a little too by-the-book for James Dumas' son. How does Private Detective Beckett sound?"

"Hot," Ginny blurted, before I could answer.

I nodded. "Perfect. It's perfect."

****

I sat up straight, eye to eye with Agent Brennan. He'd been sent to clean up this mess—*his words*. "As you know, we've already talked with your mother and Officer Beckett about what happened at Green River Trucking. It's quite a story, and we'd like to hear your version."

I offered him an obligatory nod and started at the beginning. He hardly looked up from his notes, his hand working furiously until the end. Setting his pad of paper aside, he produced his best intimidating stare. "What happened to Agent McKinnon, Samantha?"

I relived it in my head. My mother's face as she pulled the trigger, the determination there. The blood already on her hands—Rodney Taylor's probably—staining them with guilt. But I knew what had to be done, even with my fury at her tightening my chest. I'd practiced in my head just like Levi told me to, just like a free throw, so it came out effortless, smooth as butter. "Cullen shot Agent McKinnon right before he drove away."

Brennan nodded. "I thought you might say that."

Swish.

CHAPTER THIRTY-ONE

RUNNING

EIGHTY-EIGHT miles to Austin. Eighty-eight miles to Levi. Eighty-eight miles between me and my mother.

"I'm not running away." That's what I'd told Levi on the phone last night, listening to my mother humming in the kitchen like nothing had changed. And it hadn't. Not really. That was the unnerving part. Clare Bronwyn acted as if she hadn't unzipped her small-town mom costume and emerged as someone entirely new—Clare Keely. Someone a little whacked and very broken. That much I knew.

"Are you sure about that?" he'd asked. "I want to see you, Sam—you know I do—but don't you think you should work things out with your mom before you leave for college in September? You've only got a couple weeks left." Less, really, since I had to report early for fall practice, but I kept that to myself.

"It's gonna take more than a week, Levi. Or two. Or three. It's a long-term project." I joked, but it hurt. "And she's sort of in denial about it all. I guess she always was. She wouldn't let me watch the news—not even when they interviewed Ginny." Of course Ginny emailed me a link to the video, evidence of her newfound stardom.

With my mom asleep in the next room, I'd watched under the covers as Ginny fielded questions about her brush with death that started in an airport bathroom, when Marco rendered her unconscious with a mouthful of ether and wheeled her out with the trash to Cullen's waiting arms. The camera loved Ginny, even with the scar on her cheek. And she loved it back.

Levi chuckled. "Leave it to Ginny to make kidnapping sound glamorous."

But I didn't laugh. "Cullen's still out there, you know." They'd found the big rig abandoned a few miles from Green River Trucking. Empty, of course.

"I know. But you can't live your life looking over your shoulder. I learned that the hard way. It almost cost me my freedom ... my sister's freedom ... everything." With all his inadvertent heroics, Levi had gotten off with a slap on the wrist—community service, and his sister exchanged jail time for a drug diversion program.

"Exactly. It's all about the windshield. No rearview." I'd stolen the line from one of my graduation cards, and my delivery sounded pretty convincing. But Cutthroat knew how to tug at me, how to whisper in my ear. *Time to meet dear old dad.*

"Alright," Levi relented. "Get your cute butt down here then."

As I drove, I peeked at my reflection, reassuring myself. Still Samantha. I'd been doing that lately. Studying the blue in my eyes, the way it changed sometimes. From blue to gray, depending on the light. Those eyes were his. But what else?

Up ahead of me, the road laid out like a blank canvas, stretched to the horizon. Past it, turns and hills and dead ends I couldn't see. Not from here. But I didn't stop. Didn't slow down. I drove toward it.

AUGUST 24, 2016

CLARE ran fast, kicking up dust behind her, relishing the breathlessness that came with the hard push up the hill just past their house. Her lungs burned, but she liked it. She felt alive. Strong. Maybe even fierce. Not bad for her mid-forties. She stopped at the top to watch the sun dip just below the horizon, the Texas summer dying its usual prolonged death. On the way back down, she let her tired mind wander. Like an old dog, it always stopped at the same places—Samantha, Rodney, Cullen—and sniffed around a little before coming back home.

Just after dawn that morning, Sam had hustled out the door, a backpack slung over her shoulder. A quick rendezvous with Levi before her big first day at Baylor. But Sam scoffed at that word. *It's not a rendezvous, Mom. Rendezvous happen in Paris, not Austin. And we're not even officially dating.* "Yet," Clare added, and Sam laughed, overwhelming her with relief—her daughter still loved her in spite of all her colossal screw-ups—marveling as she watched her go. Of all the things she'd gotten wrong, this one thing, the most important one, she'd done right.

Then she thought of the last day at San Quentin. A well-worn memory from a lifetime ago. Outfitted in that army-green officer's jumpsuit, his hand on the door, Cullen had turned to her with urgency. "There's something I have to tell you," he'd said. "It's important." Even now, her panic felt fresh, as if it only just happened. Like seeing him tied to the tracks while they shook with the weight of an oncoming train.

"I haven't been totally honest with you about my family." She could see the train now, hear it too. "And whatever comes after this, I don't want to start it with a lie."

She'd silenced him then with a finger to his lips. "Tell me after. Later." Because it wouldn't change anything. That train would come whether she liked it or not, severing him in two, and knowing would only make it harder to let him go.

Shaking off her regret, Clare slowed her stride, the house in view. Lit from within, the windows winked at her, inviting her back to the life she'd created from scratch. A good life. *Hers.* But another memory, a new memory flooded in. One she turned and turned like a stone in the garden. Underneath it, worms and rot and reckoning. But good things too. Signs of life.

Before Torres' men had arrived, before the EME had unleashed the wrath of hell, before she'd fired the shot that ended McKinnon, Cullen had smirked at her. *Yeah, well that's obvious. She looks just like me*, he'd said. Pushing the hair back from her face, he'd stopped being angry, twirling one tendril and setting her heart spinning like a child's top. Lacing his fingers with hers. Red on red with the blood they'd spilled together. The cord to the past severed by her own hand, setting her loose in a world without Rodney Taylor.

She recounted the way Cullen leaned toward her and she to him, until the space between them had felt combustible. Until he'd threatened to reignite that ancient part of herself that went cold when she'd sworn off men, sworn off this feeling. So close she'd seen her own reflection in those gray-blue pools. And somewhere in the eyes that claimed her, she'd found a revelation to rival any of Doctor Keely's mediocre insights. Love and murder. Two sides of the same bent penny, both a kind of possession. But Clare couldn't let herself be possessed. Not anymore.

She picked out fireflies in the semi-darkness, as she headed up the gravel driveway, punch-drunk with a newfound freedom. The same kind of freedom Cullen had now. Wherever he was. She'd given him that much at least. No more, no less than what she'd taken for herself. The delicate kind of freedom that's as easily snapped as a wishbone. As false as that old dog collared to a long chain. No matter how fast it ran, it would always end up the same, throttled by the neck. A sad and sudden ache bloomed in her chest, slowing her steps until she realized and stopped cold.

The front door was cracked open—not the way she'd left it—just the screen rattling in the breeze. On the step, a yellow chrysanthemum and a note. She picked up the flower and brought it to her face, inhaling the crisp scent of it. A shiver, delicious and terrifying, slithered down her back. Her hands trembled. Blood rushed to her head like the swell of the ocean, and she held on for fear she might fall. With no one to hear her, she read the note in a hushed whisper anyway.

Clare, come find me.

Now that you've finished Daddy Darkest, please consider leaving a review. Reviews and star-ratings may not seem that important, but to an up-and-coming author, they are essential. They help readers like you discover my books! And they give an author a little "street cred" for those browsing for their next read. So what's the best way to feed an author? Leave a review, of course. You can find all the links to review Daddy Darkest on my website ellerykane.com.

ACKNOWLEDGEMENTS

DADDY Darkest would not be so deliciously dark without the talents of the amazing AnnCastro Studio team—Ann Castro and Emily Dings—who provided all editing services for the book, including developmental editing, manuscript evaluation, line editing, copyediting, and proofing, and Giovanni Auriemma—who gave life to my imaginings and created a cover that nightmares are made of.

We all have a space inside us that we keep hidden from the world, a space we protect at all costs. So many people have allowed me a glimpse inside theirs—dark deeds, memories best unrecalled, pain that cracks from the inside out—without expectation of anything in return. I couldn't have written this book without them.

And to all the shrewd, empathic, and insightful psychologists I know, the redeeming parts of Dr. Keely come from you.

COMING SOON

DADDY Darkest is the first in the *Doctors of Darkness* series of psychological thrillers by forensic psychologist and author, Ellery Kane. Look for the next book, The Hanging Tree, coming soon. If you want to be the first to know when new books are released, sign up for Ellery's newsletter at ellerykane.com.

ABOUT THE AUTHOR

FORENSIC psychologist by day, novelist by night, Ellery Kane has been writing--professionally and creatively--for as long as she can remember. Just like many of her main characters, Ellery loves to ask why, which is the reason she became a psychologist in the first place. Real life really is stranger than fiction, and Ellery's writing is often inspired by her day job. Evaluating violent criminals and treating trauma victims, she has gained a unique perspective on the past and its indelible influence on the individual. And she's heard her fair share of real life thrillers. An avid short story writer as a teenager, Ellery recently began writing for enjoyment again, and she hasn't stopped since.

Ellery's debut novel, Legacy, has received several awards, including winning the Gold Medal in the Independent Publisher Book Awards, young adult, e-book category, and the Gold Medal in the Wishing Shelf Independent Book Awards, teenage category. In 2016, Ellery was selected as one of ten semifinalists in the MasterClass James Patterson Co-Author Competition. Daddy Darkest is her first novel for adults.

85953799R00214

Made in the USA
Lexington, KY
06 April 2018